KYN

KYN

LAURENCE RAMSAY

Sobr Gnome Press

CONTENTS

FOR ALL THE LOST QUEERS WHO CHOSE HOPE

The Boy in the Room

A lone boy sat on the floor of a stark and sterile white room. Waiting.

Gossamer-thin holographic screens, each ethereally translucent, floated in the air around him, encircling the boy in a constantly flowing ring of disparate images that shifted and changed with chaotic discord. Nameless faces, eclectic live-vids, and boxes of rapidly scrolling code flowed around him in the dizzying jumble.

The boy's large gray eyes - the colour of unpolished silver - flitted from screen to screen, studying one intently for a still moment, laser intent, before jumping to the next. The glow of the projections glinted and glittered off his keen gaze, as if dancing across two pools of quicksilver.

The boy sat cross-legged in the middle of the circle, spine straight. A glowing interface hovered above the white tile, and his dexterous hands fluttered back and forth in a semi-circle around himself; flicking and twirling rapidly to smoothly manipulate the flow of the circling holos.

The boy turned to a floating screen of hand-to-hand combat tutorial videos. Neatly ordered lines of soldiers grappled each other into submission, lashing out viciously to disable their opponents with agility and overwhelming force.

He squinted, eyebrows knitting themselves together in concentration as he tracked the movements, the expression bunching up the dramatic slash of dark freckles that cut across his angular face and over his sharp nose. A swirling galaxy of black stars spattered across sandy brown skin.

His attention jumped to another gossamer holo. A shaky handheld vid of a ballet class. Young adults in uniformly black leotards glided fluidly back and forth across the frame.

He studied the neat lines of dancers, each lightly gripping the barre, their lithe forms moving in unison through a series of complex and improbable shapes. Leaping and twirling with seemingly impossible grace. The vid ended after catching a bright faced young woman wiping sweat from her brow as she smiled for the cam, before looping back on itself to start again.

Another screen was nothing but scrolling green lines of self-replicating computer code. Below that, a scrolling text of complicated mathematical equations whipped by at dizzying speed. To the left, a brilliant green flash of a forest grove choked with moss.

The boy shifted his gaze to a slideshow of human anatomy in hyper-realistic pictographs. He briefly studied each, before swiping them away again. The rejected holo flew back into one blank white wall to be replaced with an intranet article dedicated to a detailed regional chronological history. Skimming the article, he swiped it away.

The gray eyed boy manipulated the circular wall of projections with ease, bouncing with a new manic energy while humming tunelessly to himself. Gesturing at a glowing icon by his right hand, he swiped upwards, pulling out a cluster of new files and expanded them.

He studied this new material, intent as he scratched distractedly at his left forearm, picking at the fresh layer of black scabs that had formed over a pattern of interlocking triangles tattooed along his inner forearm. His mind began to wander with the uncomfortable itch of the healing skin and his eyes darted shy, distracted, glances towards one curved corner of the hovering feeds, flicking to a Unity issued ident of another boy his own age. The other child's face was stern and unreadable, his dark hair buzzed short.

He pulled his gaze back to the other circling holos, narrowing down his image catalogue by smoothly swiping away unneeded feeds, trying to eliminate distractions.

Unbidden, like an unconscious tick, his gaze flicked back to the ident. A strange heat rose in his cheeks, and his mind drifted trying to read that stern face despite determined attempts to focus.

He'd gotten to see the other children that morning.

A low mist had hung over the meticulous green of the compound grounds as the children greeted each other with shy waves before digging small hands back into the pockets of their outdoor uniforms, huddled close to the adults for reassurance.

All except the boy with the shaved head.

The shaved headed boy stood with his shoulders back, silently staring at a far-off point somewhere in front of himself, oblivious to the other child and the adults around him.

Memory made the gray eyed boy feel strange. Conflicting emotions tugged at him, and his hands felt uncomfortably clammy as a tingling warmth rushed him and his eyes welled with moisture, threatening to spill over.

His hand hesitated from swiping away the holo.

The Handlers had chosen him to be the first.

The children had been arranged in a loose formation around a large circle drawn in chalk white powder in the compound's expansive green pitch.

The children loved their outdoor time. Each young face was bright and smiling in the fresh air despite the early hour. They stood patiently, too well trained to let their enthusiasm get the better of them and beamed joyfully as they waited obediently for further instructions. Their Handlers stood beside them, staring silently into the center of the chalk circle, not acknowledging one another, arms hung casually at their sides, each loosely gripping a disciplinary rod between both hands.

A stout woman with thick limbs and a drawn, pinched face stood next to the shaved headed boy. His Handler. She placed a hand on the boy's shoulder and shoved him decisively towards the center of the ring.

The shaved headed boy stumbled, momentarily off balance, before catching himself, his face refusing to lose its strange expression.

The gray eyed boy was pushed in next.

His stomach dropped as he felt the strong hand on his shoulder and he looked back at the kindly bearded face of his Handler as he stumbled forward, suddenly unsure of himself. But, seeing nothing but blankness in the adult's face, he reluctantly set one foot in front of the other, moving to stand facing the other boy.

He was confused. Usually, he liked this part. Was good at it too. His skill in the circle a source of pride. Except now there was something he found odd about the shaved headed boy, something that made him feel uneasy. There was a new and confusing feeling spreading through him.

New and confusing but not entirely unpleasant, warming the pit of his stomach, just below the navel.

The pinched faced woman raised her fingers to her mouth and blew a long-drawn-out note that pierced the crisp morning air.

The gray eyed boy pushed memory away, regaining his focus. His fingers slid over the controls, summoning images of his three patron Sentry to the forefront of the circling holos. All other screens shrunk away, peeling outwards to disappear into the walls.

Clean station and bed slab folded into seamless walls, the room was a blank white cube. The three occupied the whole space.

The gray eyed boy shifted, folding his legs under himself to sit back on his heels. Fluttering hands stopped their endless motion to rest, unmoving, on his knees.

"I am a proud tool of The Unity." He recited. "All I need and all I shall want will be supplied by my devotion."

He bowed his head but kept his eyes on the three adults.

Each was stunningly beautiful, two women and one man; other worldly in their unblemished perfection and similar enough in age and appearance that, despite being unbalanced in genders, it was obvious they were triplets.

The gray eyed boy knew from looking at the other children, his Handler, and the floating holos that educated him, that the trio's appearance was a rarity in the walled city. Their skin was like the synthetic milk he drank for midday meal, and their hair flowed in hues of glowing yellow and pale gold. Three sets of eyes stared back at him, each pair a different variant of frozen, brilliant blue.

"You are my Sentry, for whom I reach into the world." He continued through the lines, his voice practiced and precise over each word. "May my actions bring praise to my SPIRE."

He bowed lower, folding at the waist, the fringe of his wavy auburn hair scraping the flawless white floor.

"My blood for my SPIRE. My body for my Sentry." He flowed through the chant. "My devotion to The Unity."

Straightening, he waved a hand in a sweeping semi-circle and the screens folded out, disappearing into the walls. He re-positioned himself back into a more relaxed cross-legged position. Waiting.

Restless fingers drummed against his knees, and he closed his eyes, allowing himself to be pulled back into memory.

The shaved headed boy was a hand span taller than the gray eyed boy, with a solid, husky frame, and he loomed over his slighter peer.

The high pitch whistle cut through the crisp dawn air and the shaved headed boy launched himself at the gray eyed boy, his stoic and impassive face suddenly twisted with a brutish sneer. Advancing in a blur of child's clenched fists and swinging legs, he aimed each reaching blow at the smaller boy's face.

The gray eyed boy threw his arms up, using forearms and hands to ward off the oncoming barrage. Deflecting the force of the blows, he matched the other boy's rhythm, pushing the momentum of each attack away with practiced fluidity. He ducked nimbly under one of the larger boy's swinging arms and shifted back in close behind again to swiftly lash out with a snapping kick that connected with the back of the shaved headed boy's knee, sending the charging attacker sprawling face first into the grass.

The other children whooped and cheered, delighted, as the larger boy slid through the damp grass.

The shaved headed boy pushed himself back onto his hands and knees, attempting to stand. The front of his uniform was stained brilliant green, and he was unaware as the smaller boy moved in smoothly from behind.

Gray eyes flashed dangerously, and the slighter boy snaked a thin arm around the larger boy's neck at the same time that he drove a knee into the hollow of his back, leveraging them both backwards. He dropped his other elbow over the larger boy's shoulder and wrapped his opposite hand over his own small bicep, expertly locking out a control grip across the shaved headed boy's throat, restraining the larger boy to his kneeling position. He finished the grapple by gently placing his free hand in a ready grip on the back of the boy's bristly scalp. The shorn hair was soft under his fingers.

The gray eyed boy beamed up at the bearded face of his Handler. Waiting for further instruction.

The stocky woman was yelling and waving her arms as the shaved headed boy struggled in his grasp. The gray eyed boy tightened his cinch around the other boy's neck, steadily placing pressure on the arteries that ran down either side of the larger child's throat.

The shaved headed boy's breath was coming in rapid gasps.

The two were so close that the gray eyed boy could smell the other's skin. The clean smell of standard issue soap mixed with the fresh, salty tang of sweat.

His heart pounded wildly in his chest.

The larger boy struggled, thrusting elbows back, trying to strike the smaller boy unsuccessfully, their positioning not allowing his jutting limbs to make contact. Reflexively, the gray eyed boy squeezed his own body even closer, the proximity causing more of the strange warmth to spread through him. He felt, then quickly repressed, a desire to run his hand around the other boy's prickly scalp as the warmth in his abdomen grew, not unpleasantly.

His Handler's hand swiped the air, catching his attention and pulling him back from his momentary lapse in focus. The meaning of the gesture was clear. He was to finish up.

The gray eyed boy hesitated.

The shaved headed boy's gasps for air were starting to pain his ears as waves of unfamiliar emotions and sensations swept his body. Desperately ragged breathes became wilder as fingers clawed at his forearm. Wild beats of the boy's heart joined with his own, a reverberating, pounding in his chest. A blinding pain stabbed behind his eyes.

Releasing the other boy, he stumbled back, falling to his hands and knees. He retched, vomiting the contents of his stomach violently onto the grass.

The shaved headed boy scrambled to his feet, hands to his throat, wide purple bruise already spreading, eyes wide with astonishment.

The Handlers quickly hustled the other children back to their rooms.

The solid clunk of an electronic lock disengaging woke the boy from his reverie. The gentle, sliding swoosh of a door opening behind him was followed by rubber soled footsteps on smooth tile.

"Stand and turn Envoy. It's time."

The gray eyed boy obeyed the voice, silently unfolding himself from the floor as he turned to face the speaker. Mentally brushing away the confusing memories, he arranged his features into a carefully practiced expression of blank expectance.

Awaiting further instructions.

The voice had belonged to his Handler, a normally kindly looking bearded man in what the boy had begun to assume was his fourth or fifth ten-cycle. He had a broad smile, and gentle, dark brown eyes.

Now, his Handler's eyes lacked their usual warmth, and he regarded the boy with a subdued professionalism. The doorway stood open behind and was flanked by two Dags, smokey visors pulled down from domed helmets, obscuring the upper half of their faces. All three adults snapped to attention as a final figure entered the square white cell.

The boy's gray eyes widened in awe, the pure white space seeming to expand as the woman entered. He'd seen her face every day of his short life yet had never met one of the Sentry in person. Until now.

The Sentry was smaller in physical stature then both the Handler and Dags, but loomed over them, shrinking them with her presence, the white cell's harsh lighting incapable of dulling her warm brilliance.

The Sentry crossed to the gray eyed boy with gliding steps, hard tips of her boot heels clicking rhythmically.

"Hello Envoy. I am Alexi." The Sentry announced curtly, stopping in front of him. Jewel-speckled waves of white-gold hair cascaded around a pale, heart-shaped face. "Congratulations, today is your day."

Her gaze bore into him, eyes a deep azure blue, steady and unblinking.

A deeply primal fear gripped the gray eyed boy, freezing him in place. He felt as if her eyes were seeking out, then tearing into, the very being of his private self. Hunting for the soft, dark, hidden places that he kept buried inside, seldom visiting. Her lips parted in a dazzling smile as if she were devouring that deep part of him, her teeth tearing at the deep wet meat of him. She wanted to root around and steal his secrets.

A sharp, angry whistle brought him back.

His Handler was glaring at him, fingers to lips, eyes narrowed. The gray eyed boy's hand shot to his chest in a closed fist salute, snapping to attention with drilled precision. Tearing his eyes from the terrifyingly beautiful woman in front of him, he fixed his focus forward, trying to subdue the shaking in his limbs.

"Hold out your arm." The Sentry ordered, her tone soft but commanding, accustomed to being obeyed.

He complied with his free arm, offering the thin limb.

The Sentry grasped the proffered limb and rolled back the sleeve of his uniform. She rubbed at the tawny skin of his inner arm with her fingers. Stark white in contrast to his darker tone.

From the inner pocket of a luxurious floor-length coat, the Sentry produced a palm-length metal cylinder inset with an inject-unit and a delicate tube of clear glass that trapped a black, viscous liquid. An oily sheen that repelled light, the contents of the glass hurt the boy's eyes to look at, the black liquid appearing to swirl and move on its own accord in a way that made his back teeth ache.

The Sentry gripped the gray eyed boy's arm tighter, drawing him closer even as she placed one end of the cylinder against the soft crook of his elbow.

"Recite." She commanded.

"I am a proud tool of The Unity." He obeyed. "All I need and all I shall want will be supplied by my devotion."

This was it. His Ascension.

"You are my Sentry, for whom I reach into the world," he continued, beaming. Pride swelled in his voice. "May my actions bring praise to my SPIRE." Every moment in the first ten-cycle of his life had been preparing his body and mind for this moment. "My blood for my SPIRE. My body for my Sentry. My devotion to The Unity."

The cylinder clicked, and the boy drew in a quick breath as sharp metal pierced his skin. There was a faint sensation of warmth spreading through his arm as the oily black liquid pumped into his veins.

None of the children knew what their Ascension would involve. All they had ever been told was that they needed to devote themselves to their training and studies, so that one day, when they were deemed ready, they would undertake the ritual, proving they were worthy of being fully brought into the service of their Sentry.

The gray eyed boy fidgeted anxiously. Waiting.

He could feel his heart pumping the liquid through his veins, his blood warming as it circulated through his body. Turning, he looked expectantly from the face of the Sentry to his Handler, wondering if he had passed.

They stared back at him, silent. Waiting.

Then his blood was aflame, burning white-hot in his veins.

He screamed. And screamed again.

He screamed until his throat bled. Every muscle in his body had seized up at once, and he crashed to the floor with violent convulsions. He could feel the inky blackness moving through him, like nuclear plasma raging through his veins, burning him from the inside, immobilizing him in pain.

The boy's fingers curled towards his own throat, clawing as he desperately tried to draw in air. His rib cage refused to contract and expand, his diaphragm frozen in agonizing spasm.

The Sentry stood over him, watching dispassionately. Wild eyes looked desperately for his Handler, but the man's face was a stoic mask, seemingly carved in stone. He understood then he'd find no help. He was alone with his pain.

The white room began to dim, void black pressing in at the edges.

The other boy's hair tickled his hand, soft against his fingers.

Strong fingers clawed at his arm, trying for freedom.
Breathing in his scent.

Oxygen! The gray eyed boy's pain-wracked mind screamed at him. He needed to breathe. With every passing moment his agony stretched the world became farther away, his vision ringed by that endless darkness. The face of his Sentry blurred above him. Living darkness enveloped him, screaming his agony back on him. Through the darkness, he understood, in a deep and primal way, was an end to his pain.

There was no oxygen reaching his brain now, he knew this. The holos had taught him every part of the body, how it worked, and how it stopped working.

The shaved headed boy stood with his shoulders back, silently staring at a far-off place. The look on his face, foreign and intoxicating. The gray eyed boy searched his mind desperately for a word to describe it.

Blood vessels had begun to burst in his eyes and tears of crimson streamed down his contorted face. The world had narrowed to a single pin prick of light. He screamed into the void of darkness, but every sound was a toneless buzz. Fire raged in his veins, trying to burn its way out, desperate to reach the pinprick of light.

Defiance

"NO!"

The scream ripped its way out of his pain-wracked delirium. Sheer determination forcing his body to respond. His diaphragm dropped, and his ribs expanded, and he sucked in desperate, greedy breaths. Shaking, he lay, sweat soaked and gasping in ragged, thankful gulps of air on the white tile.

Alive.

The burning in his veins had eased, but not abated. The burning still consuming his body, but it no longer suffocated him in his own pain. He lay, silently weeping and convulsing with waves of agony, a puddle of wetness spreading on the smooth tile beneath him. The rank smell of urine and shame filled the air.

Faintly, he was aware of the Sentry's boots turning on their jagged heels, the clicking vibration through the white tile. He tried to look up to watch her go, but everything in his damaged sight was a crimson blur. To him she was a blood-soaked angel, striding away. The gentle pad of his Handler's soft soled shoes and the thud of Dag boots followed close behind.

The door slid shut. He was alone.

The fire had dulled to a smoldering ache, leaving a deep exhaustion in its wake he was unable to fight, and he gratefully slipped into a blissful unconsciousness. Hopeful he'd awaken. Eventually.

His breathing slowed, his chest rose and fell.

Unaware of time's passage, the gray eyed boy slipped in and out of consciousness. Eyelids fluttering, he occasionally let out a low moan, a guttural and primal sound that seemed to rise out of the pit of him, clawing itself from his curled and shaking body.

The world was made of pain. He could reach out and touch it like glimmering pieces of shattered glass, his touch leaving cracks.

He knew, with each spider webbing crack on the skin of reality, that if he listened closely, really listened as hard as he could, he'd hear the voice. A wet, rasping voice that whispered to him through the shimmering cracks that his pain had left in the universe.

He reached out and tried to grasp at a shard of shattered reality, trying to press it back together with his hands. The glass cut deep into his fingers; his blood dripped into the cracks of reality.

After what could have been hours or even days drifting in and out of a hollow, pain laced haze, the door slid open again and the thud of Dag boots reverbed through the tile. The doors whooshed shut and the locking mechanism engaged with a definitive clunk. Dag boots moved to the wall, and the gray eyed boy was hit with a blast of water that threw his small body across the floor, slamming him into the adjacent wall.

Shocked to full consciousness, the gray eyed boy struggled against the freezing torrent of water, sputtering, and coughing. The blast of water relented as the Dag muzzled the valve they'd opened in the wall, and the boy scrambled to his feet, soaked, but alert. Indoctrinated training snapped to the forefront of his mind, and he rapidly took stock of his situation. Two Dags stood in the room; femur length discipline rods of mirrored chrome gripped in their meaty hands. A mental sweep of his body made him realize, with a wave of relief, that he was free of the burning pain.

Every iota of him ached from its absence.

Dripping wet, the gray eyed boy stared at the Dags, uneasy, his small hands balled into fists at his sides.

"Calm yourself Envoy." A cool masculine voice stated, filling the white cell. "Congratulations are in order young one. You have completed your Ascension, and we are joyful for you to join in full service of the Unity. We know you will make your Sentry proud."

A section of the blank wall to the boy's left slid open, revealing a pane of clear polyplex. His Handler watched from the other side of the clear plastic next to another man the boy knew on sight.

Ethereally beautiful and commanding, the man's resemblance to his sister was both uncanny, and somehow unsettling. Where her glowing radiance had filled the space, his pulled everything from it, dimming the room around him.

"Few survive to the other side of the Ascension, and we regret their loss." The Sentry continued. "But for those strong enough, the Ascension bares miraculous gifts."

The boy stood wide eyed, frozen in place and shivering uncontrollably from an unseen terror divorced from his wet and soaking form.

Instinct, training, and indoctrination, clashed violent in his mind, frantically trying to make sense of what the Sentry was saying, rapidly piecing the implications together.

He had just passed his Ascension.

All the children in his group had just reached the end of their first ten-cycle. The age at which they were to undertake the test. They had never been told in detail what the Ascension was, or what it entailed, to them it was just a milestone expected of them. One of the many that would be demanded in their service to their Sentry and the Unity.

'Few survive.' He knew in that moment, the shattered glass of reality reforming around him. 'We regret their loss.' An atonal ringing filled his head.

The other children were dead.

"Such gifts are unique to each Envoy." The Sentry stated, voice cool and even. "A true blessing that we have bestowed upon you for use in our service."

The gray eyed boy was confused. He felt unchanged. Achy, and exhausted, but like himself. He spared a glance at his Handler. The once kindly man was motionless beside his superior, his face an impassive mask.

"Not all gifts are immediately apparent," the Sentry pressed on, seeming to read the boy's mind. A glimmer of excitement danced in the man's ice blue eyes. "Sometimes they require assistance in revealing themselves."

Uneasy, the gray eyed boy stepped away from the wall. The air was very still.

Responding to some unspoken command, both Dags stalked toward the gray eyed boy, helmet visors drawn low, discipline rods easy in their hands.

The boy shifted his weight, eyeing the Dags.

"Begin." the Sentry ordered. His face split into a wide and perfect grin behind the polyplex barrier.

The Dags were on the gray eyed boy in an instant, raining blows down on him with their discipline rods. Each blow connected with a dull crack.

The boy tried desperately to block the onslaught, but the larger Dags had the advantage of power and size. He raised an arm to block the downward swing of a metal rod and felt the impact shatter the bones of his forearm with a sickening crack. Skin broke and split as bone and tendon exploded outward.

He screamed in pain and terror, even as another blow connected with his shoulder, shattering his collar bone. Both arms hung useless at his side. He collapsed to the floor as more blows rained down, gasping, and crying in desperation, trying to make himself as small as possible.

'Few survive.' His head filled with atonal ringing. 'We regret their loss.'

The stubble of the boy's shorn hair was soft beneath his fingers.

The other children were dead.

The ringing in his ears grew to a crescendo and his voice tore from his throat to meet it as he released a vicious scream and kicked out blindly with his legs. Lashing legs connected, collapsing the back of a Dag's knee, and knocking one of his attackers to the ground with a dull thud.

The world had slowed to a red tinged crawl and the gray eyed boy's blood pounded, deafening, in his ears. The Dags seemed to move around him laboriously, as if against a powerful current. Everything itched.

The gray eyed boy arched to spring from the tile and launched himself on top of his fallen attacker. With lightning speed, he ripped the rod from their grip with one hand before raising it above his head and bringing it back down on their faceplate with a sickening wet crunch. The chrome rod came down again and again, shattering the Dag's helmet and reducing the skull beneath to a pulpy pink smear on the white floor.

The boy raised his arm again, preparing to bring the rod down for one final, definitive blow, when a sudden tearing pain seared through his back and the other guard's discipline rod exploded outward from his chest in a shower of blood and tissue. His own weapon clattered to the blood-soaked tile.

The remaining guard had taken advantage of his companion's macabre execution and used the distraction to impale his own discipline rod through the gray eyed boy's chest from behind.

The boy growled, a rumble deep within his throat, low and frustrated. His opposite hand found the blood slick protrusion, and, with one smooth motion and an echoing scream, he yanked it clear of his chest in a shower of gore.

The remaining Dag froze in shock.

The gray eyed boy threw the gore-soaked rod to the crimson smeared floor with a resounding metal clatter and launched himself at the Dag. Blood-drenched, he leapt onto his assailant, thin legs wrapped around the uniformed adult's torso, grappling them. A small hand snaked around and grasped the back of the Dags helmeted head even as the other firmly gripped their chin. The Dag's neck snapped with a single, violent motion.

The Sentry and Handler watched from behind the polyplex; eyes widened in delight and fear at the ferocious display. The child had been a flurry of primeval violence.

The gray eyed boy rode the collapsing Dag's dead weight to the ground, panting heavily. Bare feet left bloody prints as he approached the protective barrier with slow and deliberate steps. He stared at the two men coldly through the clear plastic, his angular face unrecognizable beneath the blood that smeared him head to toe. Rage churned in the large steel-gray orbs of his eyes, the only discernible feature in the slick crimson mess. Lightning roiling through storm clouds.

The gray eyed boy slammed clenched fists against the barrier with a dull thud, small hands leaving smears of crimson against the clear plastic.

The Approach

"Hello, Benn," Kyn chirped, addressing the occupant of the shiny black transpo that had slid up next him. He tabbed down the volume of his audio feed, dulling the pre-fall electro classic 'Sexy Boy' that throbbed in his ear. Heavy sheets of rain and ward runoff thundered down beyond the angular boundary of the grimy underpass. "Been a while."

Slight and athletically wiry, Kyn bent at the waist and leaned his elbows against the open viewport. Peering into the vehicle's darkened interior, his glossed lips parted in a predatorily sly grin, and he played the tip of his tongue over his teeth.

"Wanna show a boy a good time?" He propositioned, voice dropping to a husky whisper. He raised a loose fist next to his mouth and slid the coiled hand back and forth, tongue pushing out opposite cheek in suggestive pantomime.

Benn, the blandly handsome occupant of the vehicle, stared back impassively, his expression blank and unreadable. The yellow light of the underpass cut jagged blocks of shadow across dark skin. No anger, no frustration, no exasperation at the juvenile display, just blank, waiting.

No fun.

It was the nowhere time before dawn, and the streets were quiet, even in the congested lower wards of the city. A steady trickle of running water snaked down one graffitied wall of the overpass, echoing back towards them.

The tranpso's door folded up and Benn stepped out to the darkened street; the final move in a petty game Kyn forced his counterpart to play, one inspired by boredom and half-hearted rebellion.

"The other two are already on the move." Benn informed him curtly, tapping the back door of the transpo so it too folded upwards. He wore a dark gray suit, retro exec cut, round collar. "Your equipment is in the bag. Objective is in the file. Should be syncing to you now."

The interlocking pattern of triangles tattooed across Kyn's forearm glowed a soft neon blue as his f-Link lit up. The pattern quickly changed shape, shifting across his skin before clumping together to project a small holo that hovered in the air above his arm. A curved edged square, the shimmering projection showed the ident pics of a relatively average looking man and woman, typically bland in a way that easily marked them as mid-wards born. Next to their image a scrolling text listed detailed personal information.

Kyn quickly began to scan the text as he climbed into the back seat of the transpo. The projection was tuned specifically to the lens of his optic so he alone could see it - this told Kyn that Benn didn't know what was in the file, which meant one thing.

Plausible deniability. He was going to make a mess.

"The others?" Kyn asked. Benn was entering their destination into the nav as he set the auto drive on route. "Is it my favorites?"

"If you're talking about Runa and Ashe, then yes." Benn answered shortly. The sleek transpo lurched, pulling out from under the overpass and onto the rain slick streets of the lower wards. "They want this done by morning. If you hadn't made me look for you there would've been time to co-ordinate. As it was, they were prepared to leave without you. Disciplinary action will be taken against you."

Kyn had spent the last few weeks trolling the seediest parts of the lower wards, dodging responsibilities, and dropping his credit the best way he knew how; making himself feel good in as many ways as possible.

Snort it, smoke it, fuck it, suck it. Didn't really matter.

But then the familiar feelings came; the tickling at the back of his neck, the twitch at the nape. Unsettling and making him want to turn his head. A sickness in the pit of his stomach, bile in his throat. His heartbeat would quicken for no reason, pounding in terror against his ribs. A dry, ashy taste in his mouth that no amount of cheap powder or stranger's cock could wash away.

They were looking for him, wanted him to come home.

So, he'd slipped further into the lowers, covering his tracks, making himself harder to find. They'd find him in the end, he knew. No chance of escaping it, he figured he'd at least make them work for it. Good for a laugh that way.

"Ashe hates me you know." Kyn stated lazily, blowing past the chastisement. Neon lit flesh joints flashed by through the tinted windows. A nerve shook tweeker collapsed next to a LED trimmed night cart.

"Yes." Benn paused, a twitch at the corner of his mouth. Amusement crawled past his usually blank demeanor. "I'm aware. The Unity is aware. No one cares."

"They're going to shoot me again."

"Good, I bet two hundred credits on it."

Kyn smirked and raised an eyebrow.

A couple ten-cycles or so older, Benn was taller than the wiry Kyn by at least half a head, with a broadly handsome face, and a balanced muscular physique, straight on brand for every SPIRE employee. His dark skin was well treated and cared for, tight across strong cheek bones, and his hair, naturally wiry, was cropped short, close to the scalp and going to silver around the temples. His look said man of means, approachable, trustworthy, and safe. Pop branded and a million more like him. Forgettable. The most notable thing about him, when Kyn looked for it, was Benn's perfectly manicured hands. Long fingers tipped with well treated and polished nails. Simple, not flashy, but expensive.

Benn had taken over manual control of the transpo, maneuvering them into a turn as they passed through an automated barrier. The transpo's dashboard lit up, ward clearance checked and approved, authorizing the pair for entrance. Benn took the next exit, crossing into the mid-wards and heading for one of the outer industrial edges.

"How's that new lux pad?" Kyn asked, drawling. "With that stunning view of the mountains and the bay! You can barely even see the wall." He stretched nonchalantly, arms raised over his head, and slunk further into the luxurious seat. "Must be nice to wake up looking at that view. Lucky man. So much better than your last place. Congrats, you're obviously moving up in the world. Figuratively and well...physically"

That got the reaction he wanted.

Benn's eyes narrowed, nostrils flaring, and his well-manicured hands griped the transpo controls harder. Kyn could see his knuckles turning white as he tried to suppress a sudden flash of rage.

"Don't play games Kyn." He growled, perfect hands shaking.

"Oh, don't worry sexy. I'm not." Kyn smiled back, white teeth flashing. Predatory. Eyes met through the rear-view glass. Gray the colour of unpolished steel locked with Benn's dark blue. Through the obvious rage, Kyn could see his desired response hidden at the back of the other man's eyes.

Fear.

Kyn allowed the tension to stretch silently, playing with it, before, tilting his head back, he let out a wild, manic, barking laugh.

"Oh, Benn!" He howled. "Benn. Benn. Benn. You are always so much fun. You know that? I really do love getting to see you." He crossed his legs at the knee, distractedly bouncing a booted foot up and down.

"Do you want to grab some food after this?" He asked, turning his attention back out the window. He gave a start, unfurling himself again as he suddenly remembered the unopened duffle beside him.

"Right! Can't forget." He muttered, dangerous smile growing larger across his angular face. He reached out and unzipped the bag. "You didn't just pick me up under that dingy underpass for a nice little chat. Let's go have some fun."

< = >

Kyn stood at the edge of the parkaide looking out across the ward as he softly rocked back and forth, shifting from toes to heels.

He was still wearing what he'd been in when Benn had picked him up. A slim cut, canvas jumpsuit and well scuffed service boots. The jumpsuit was jet black, it's dark colour subtly mixed with an intertwining deep indigo that gave the fabric an oily depth and sheen. A vibrant accent of neon blue piping lined the collar and elastic cinched waist, then again at the ankles, and a heavy silver zipper ran from groin to collar, open to the navel and revealing a snug white slip that hugged his lithe body. The sleeves had been torn off, exposing ropey, athletic arms.

He'd been clubbing and looking to get laid.

Kyn drew the jumpsuit closed, drawing the zipper up under his throat. He gazed out over the congested weave of buildings and mid-ward stacks that stretched out in front of him. An excitement had washed over him, a subtle quickening of his pulse. His nerves tingled like lightening under his skin. Rolling his shoulders, he tilted his head back and forth on his neck, loosening his limbs.

As much as he'd made it difficult for Benn to find him, Kyn enjoyed what was coming.

The black duffel Benn had supplied contained his favored gear and he'd comfortably strapped the various pieces around his person:

iD, a wickedly curved short sword, the single-edged blade night black, beautiful in its utilitarian simplicity, was strapped diagonally across his back, it's draw angle and length allowing him ease of movement within close quarters while still supplying enough reach to keep most on comers out of unwanted proximity. The sleek blade was laser sharpened, and easily capable of slicing cleanly through steel, never dulling.

Across the small of his back, he'd nestled a double-edged dagger dubbed Ego. A forearm-length blade sheathed horizontally, Ego's hilt was smoothly molded with gaps and grooves for Kyn's fingers, ensuring a firm hold while allowing him to flip the dagger through showy and distracting patterns with practiced ease. A thin stiletto dubbed Self was concealed in the top of his boot, its narrow blade finely tuned for the quick and clean execution of a singular task.

Finally, thin leather straps notched with cleverly placed grooves wrapped his lean torso, each groove easily within reach of his nimble fingers and loaded with a disposable throwing blade of clear plastic polymer.

"The others will be in position shortly," Benn instructed, his voice carrying to Kyn on the warm, pre-morning breeze. "One of the Sentry wishes to speak with you before we commence."

Kyn sighed. He hoped it wasn't Alyn.

The f-Link across his forearm started to tingle. Receiving a call. He'd temporarily disabled the tattoo's visual response settings, opting instead for silent mode which alerted him to incoming contacts by stimulating irritation around the dermal implant.

He rubbed his thumb pad over the tips of his index and middle fingers, input sensors installed under the tips of his finger pads acknowledging and accepting the incoming holo-call. A projection appeared in the air above his geometric tattoo. The face of smartly dressed woman stared back at him. Her hair, so blonde it was almost white, was pilled and wrapped in a tight, jewel speckled bun at the back of her head, emphasizing high cheekbones in a diamond-shaped face and a strong, yet feminine, jaw.

Holo held aloft, Kyn snapped to attention - fist pressed against his breastbone, back ramrod straight. When he spoke, he was careful to make sure his inflection showed proper deference. There were few people in the walled city Kyn couldn't fuck with, and this woman was one of them. It was dangerous to not show her respect.

"Good evening, Sentry Alena. It is my pleasure to be your tool this evening."

"Enough Envoy." The Sentry commanded, waving a hand dismissively. She'd used his title, not his given name. Envoy, operative of the Sentry, their tools, their messengers.

Kyn was no one. Born into the service of the Sentry, and by extension the Unity, he did not exist within the system. No records of his birth, genealogy, education, or employment. A ghost within the clustered vertical maze of the walled city.

"Yes, Sentry." Kyn answered obediently, careful not let his gaze drift from her image even as he heard Benn laugh, low and short.

He cracked his face into a practiced, deferential smile. "Pardon Sentry, I thought tonight's matter was strictly need-to-know, above Benn's clearance. Would you like me to send him away?" He asked, faux innocently.

"Correct Envoy," Alena acknowledged, handsomely beautiful face blank. "But this is about you in general, not your task this evening."

Kyn steeled himself at her words, his deferential grin unwavering.

"We grow tired of your games," The Sentry stated simply, voice firm and direct. "We have been lenient with you as of late, but we cannot be expected to tolerate your childish antics anymore." The Sentry's eyes bore into him, and he felt, rather than heard, the measured threat in her voice. "I'm sure you can agree with that?" She asked. Her face radiated strength. The message was clear, she would not ask him twice.

Kyn bowed slightly. "Yes, Sentry."

"Good," Alena continued, tone relaxed, releasing him from her admonishing gaze. "Benn is your Handler now. Once you have finished your task tonight, you are to report directly to him. He will then instruct you on further steps. I admit, it was amusing to watch you test the young man, but enough is enough, we want you easy to find. Noav SPIRE has no use for an Envoy we can't find. Understood?"

"Yes Sentry." Kyn repeated obediently. Internally, he laughed, amused by his superior's dismissal of Benn's age. As well as the man maintained himself, the new Handler had to be in his fourth to fifth ten-cycle at least. Whereas the Sentry herself barely looked a day over her third, even though whispered rumors put her in her late fifteenth.

The glory of power.

Kyn had no doubt the terrifyingly beautiful Sentry had extensive genetic work done. The kind only available to the upper elite. Her pale skin and white-blonde hair so rarely occurring naturally any-more, it would be a reach to think she'd ever been born with it. More likely she'd altered herself, mimicking what had been most represented in the pre-world vids found on ancient servers. The look was replicated by her siblings and across the majority of the Unity members, making it a constant de-facto en vogue amongst the upper and mid-wards.

Though he had never heard of any tech or procedure that could slow aging to such an extent as to accommodate the whispered rumors that surrounded the Sentry, Kyn had no doubt, if it existed Alena would have access to it. Tech that advanced would be well beyond anything that was currently available in the walled city's gray markets, even to the most resourceful. Though, even if she didn't, Alena wasn't one to stop such rumors, the idea of ageless immortality just added more power to the legend of her presence.

"Alright then, get to it Kyn." The Sentry ordered using his chosen name. A shiver ran down his spine. He preferred when she kept it impersonal. "Make your Sentry proud."

The holo flickered out and Kyn started for the edge of the rooftop, taking long easy strides.

"Handler, eh Benn?" He tossed back over his shoulder, not bothering to look. "Congrats. I guess you're officially not a Dag anymore. No more of this interim nonsense either. You're off the leash. Explains the new flat." Kyn moved purposefully towards the end of the parking structure's roof. "Don't worry buddy, I won't be too much trouble." He was steps away from the edge. The flat concrete rooftop they were on would be at least three or four stories above the adjoining building. "And, who knows. Maybe you'll last longer than the last one."

Kyn reached the edge and turned on the balls of his feet as he swung his arms wide. A wild grin split his face. Benn, who stood by the building's rooftop access ladder, watched with disinterest, arms crossed in front of his chest. The sun was just rising, it's light seeping over the edges of the mountain ridge to the east, beyond the city's wall.

Face towards the sky, Kyn could feel the first of the rising sun's rays touch his cheeks as he let his weight tip back into the empty expanse, and he let himself fall backwards into the last of the night. The wind whipped past his face, cooler than it had been earlier. It would probably rain later, he guessed.

Benn's voice broke over his comm.

"Asshole."

Arms wide, Kyn arched his body in a long crescent shape as he fell, inverting to face the quickly approaching rooftop of the building below. His pulse quickened as adrenaline crept into his veins. His vision sharpened, and his muscles coiled in expectation.

Continuing his rotation, Kyn directed his feet at the incoming rooftop. The toes of his boots touched first, and his knees softened, absorbing the impact of his landing in one fluid motion as he rolled backwards, riding the excess momentum over the curve of his spine. Both palms planted to either side of his head and he pushed into ancient, poured concrete, fully extending his arms as he shot his feet towards the pre-dawn sky, extending to balance inverted on his hands with a fluid burst of athleticism.

A slow, rhythmic clap floated down from the parkaide above.

Kyn stepped down from his balance and looked back towards the ledge he'd dove from.

Benn was leaned over the edge of the rooftop, having watched from above, and was bringing his perfectly manicured hands together in a slow, sarcastic clap in Kyn direction.

Kyn raised his left hand, index extended, indicating for his new Handler to wait while he rummaged around in the pocket of his jumpsuit with the right.

"Kyn, I know there is nothing in your pocket." Benn's exasperated voice was in Kyn's ear through the subdermal cochlear implant.

He ignored the older man, still continuing to enthusiastically rummage around his pocket, before finally extracting his fist, he raised it in Benn's direction, middle finger aloft.

"I hope Ashe shoots you," Benn returned, shaking his head as he withdrew from the vantage point, gone from view.

Kyn started to run at an easy pace towards the far end of the storage stack he'd landed on. The rooftop was cluttered with trick-rigged salvage, and he leaped over a strip of solar panels graphed haphazardly across the wide stretch of concrete, before vaulting a grouping of generators rigged around a single power block. He slid under a rainwater collection unit.

The sun had just begun to show itself over the mountains, briefly peaking from behind an expanse of rolling gray clouds that was making a quick trip across the sky from the northwest. He was at the far outer edges of the mid-wards, away from the clustered congestion of the inner city, and the air smelt of salt, imminent rain, and the coastal coniferous forest beyond the wall.

Kyn loved it.

Left hand fingers tapped rhythmically as he ran, dialing through his f-Link interface even as he dash vaulted over a rusted exhaust vent. He switched all visual feed to his optic, then pulled up schematics for the building he was heading towards. Selecting a suitable entrance for what he needed, he dropped the location into his line of sight, creating an easily distinguishable augmented reality waypoint; a faint but unmistakable pulsing white light that hovered over where he needed to be. A small distance metric pinged in the corner of his optic, indicating how far he was to the marker.

That done, he quickly scrolled through his music files, loading a playlist.

The deep synthetic beats of neo-punk legends mutantSlutts started to growl and pulse in his ears just as he reached the end of the storage stack, the rolling tempos filling his body with their driving rhythm, dropping deep down into his gut.

He pushed off, leaping into the expanse just as the lead singer's voice burst into the track, her raw, resonant voice piercing the night with a shattering howl of abandon.

Kyn soared across the gap, twice again as far as his previous leap, legs extended in front of him, reaching for the next rooftop, arms pinwheeling to keep control. Feet barely managed the ledge, but he saved the landing, allowing his knees to soften, absorbing the impact as he threw himself forward, head tucked for protection, fluidly rolling to ride the forward momentum with ease. He was back on his feet, boots pounding rhythmically against roofing tiles.

The AR waypoint flashed dully in the distance, marking his target, still easily visible, even as he moved further into the maze of commercial stacks and warehouse blocks. Agilely tumbling and leaping from one rooftop to the next with a combination of controlled grace and suicidal abandon.

He was headed in the direction of Yummy Otter Corp; a citizen-run brand of chem-patches, narc-bumps, and ze-shots, housed in an above-average sized distribution warehouse in the middle of the districts fourth largest industrial sector.

The Yummy Otter brand had rapidly risen to popularity in recent quarters, partially because they offered a high-quality product tied with a well-planned marketing package that allowed it to keep competitive pricing with the SPIRE companies, but mostly because of their adorable mascot, an animated dancing otter named Otto.

Publicly loved, Otto's stylized hologram depicted a round cheeked otter with overly wide brown eyes and flamboyantly curled whiskers that poked from the sides of his squishable pink nose. His image - stamped in hologram on everything the company sold - performed a tiny, animated jig, while patting his paws joyfully on his silver belly. The mascot had an endearingly lighthearted and wholesome quality, especially in contrast to the overtly sexual and brightly coloured adverts used by SPIRE distributors.

Otto had even become an ad-hock mascot for a recent resurgence in the actual coastal sea otter population. The furry mammals had re-emerged near the outer edge of the northern sea wall after decades of assumed extinction and had been finding unknown ways to cross into the city side, readily becoming friendly with local humans. This posed a problem, as the Unity officially maintained that the sea otters were disease carrying undesirables. Seen as a threat to public safety, they had dispatched squads of Dags to contain and exterminate the problem.

Kyn personally loved Yummy Otter Corp. They made a spectacular brand of powder - Blue Eclipse - that he kept stocked for special nights of naked vid binging, and he made a mental note to try and score some on his visit.

He cleared another gap, then vaulted over a waist-high ventilation tube blocking his path, riding his hip across the rounded metal. The moment his feet hit metal grate on the other side, he continued to run, increasing his pace. The distance metric ticked lower in the corner of his optic; he was nearing his destination.

Approaching a narrow gap between a cramped block of servo lodge stacks, Kyn quickly assessed his next path without slowing. Going through the gap to the far end, then down and along the buildings a few stories, gave him the quickest path to his objective. Conveniently, the opposing walls of each lodge stack were built with alternating groupings of ledges and outcroppings that ran along its face; unrailed faux balconies, nothing more than slabs of concrete jutting from the cramped resident blocks. Moving at his current pace and angle, Kyn was confident he'd be able to cat leap with ease from ledge to ledge.

The playlist in his ear switched to an up-beat, staccato tempo. A good rhythm to keep pace to.

Kyn threw himself across the gap, aiming for the first narrow outcrop. Reaching it easily, he quickly altered course, pushing away from the ledge to fall to his next perch. Repeating the maneuver, Kyn zigzagged back and forth from ledge to ledge, smoothly making his descent.

A SPIRE corp. company ad beamed at him from a passing window.

"Competition Strengths Us All!" The sign read.

Yummy Otter Corp. had grown quickly outside of Unity control. Too quickly. Unity regulators had begun questioning available labor force and tech requirements needed to facilitate their growth.

The independent had even started to affect the profit margins of a smaller, fringe, chem production facility in Alena's holdings.

The Unity needed to send a message.

So, they sent an Envoy.

< = >

Tracing across several more blocks, Kyn neared his destination.

A squat prefab factory building in a row of identically squat steel and polycarbonate rectangles, his waypoint hovered over a security door on the open-air observation deck that snaked around the prefab's top floor. Two security guards patrolled the deck at a leisurely pace, appearing to be enjoying the early morning air.

The music in Kyn's ear droned out to a dull background base and his f-Link buzzed as he took another ledge gap. The geometric pattern swirling and re-configuring itself on his forearm in a subtle wave. Caught mid-jump, he smoothly flipped to kill momentum and dropped down silently to a steel rail balcony. He drew himself quickly into the shadows of a jutting outcrop; this near his target he couldn't risk notice, especially standing casually halfway up a building to take a link call. A finger twitch merged the link request into his comm.

"Yo' dicksledge, what's up?" A familiar, throaty voice ragged him over the comm. Runa. He could hear the sharp clicking of a sugrstik knocking against teeth. "Don't bother opening your cock trap. I don't feel like buzzing right now. Your voice annoys me anyway." Kyn blinked in feigned shock but stayed silent, his ear full of the uncomfortably wet sounds of lips and tongue unconsciously working themselves over a synthetic sweet treat. "So, Ashe made contact through the primary entrance. They've currently got most of the attention on them and are currently moving their sweet ass deeper in. You should be getting a closer look at the inside, right, about..."

Now." His f-Link rearranged itself with a soft, crawling tingle as he received more data.

Casually leaning away from the wall to clock the guards still slowly patrolling the observation deck, Kyn flicked the file open and sent it to unfold in the upper right corner of his vision where it unfurled into a steadily growing map in opaque green. Ashe's own f-Link was utilizing infiltration and decryption protocols to map the facility through their internal systems; giving the other Envoys a detailed layout of the Yummy Otter Corp. headquarters.

Kyn left the data packet to grow in the periphery of his vision as he allowed his attention to be caught up by one of the patrolling guards. Strappingly handsome, he let his gaze drift over the man, admiring how the guard's uniform enhanced firm, ample glutes, and impressively defined shoulders.

'So ya, they want a count on how long they need to entertain everyone 'til you join." The slurping and teeth clicking stopped. Silence.

Kyn continued watching the guard. He was waiting for the other man to turn so he could get a good look at their face, his current angle only offering a bit of a strong jaw line. There was a familiarity about the guard that pulled around in the pit of Kyn's gut, making bile rise in the back of his throat. The corner of his eyes stung.

"Yo, fuckQween. Answer me." Runa's gruff voice snapped. The gritty sound of her teeth shattering the sugrstik reverbed in Kyn's ear.

"My voice annoys you?! Mine?! Do you hear yourself?" He admonished her, tearing his eyes away from the guard to glance around, plotting a pathway to the deck. Line decided, he swiped away his old AR waypoint and placed himself a new one farther into the building, fancifully choosing a neon pink hue for the icon. "Besides." He shot back to the gravelly voiced Envoy. "You do not get to get snippy with me. You just told me not to bother opening up my... what was it? Dick holster?"

"Cock trap." Runa corrected around a short, barking laugh.

Kyn peeled fully from the shadows and approached the edge of the narrow balcony. "Either would be correct," he conceded. He eyed the spot where he wanted to land, just behind the comely guard. "Why are you playing go between anyway?" He asked. "Ashe is fully capable of linking me themselves."

"Yah, well..." He could hear the rustle of another sweet wrapper. "I got bored."

Kyn shook his head ruefully and sighed. He crouched, legs coiled beneath him, muscles tensed in preparation. "Alright, three mins, on my mark."

Uncoiling, he pushed off into the air; arms outstretched. The tug of gravity pulled at him, threatening to plummet him towards the tangle of crossways and streets below. His stomach dropped as he desperately considered for a frozen moment that he could have misjudged the distance. Then, at the last moment before gravity won, his fingers grasped desperately onto a jutting pipe and adrenaline surged through him as he used the sudden pendulous swing of momentum to launch himself wildly across the last expanse of open air.

"Mark!" He yelped.

"Fuck. Hurry up already." Runa groaned, exasperated. She cut the link.

mutantSlutts picked back up, the beat pulsing hard and dark in Kyn's ear.

Kyn hit the observation deck harder than planned and tucked into a fluid roll to displace the sound of his impact. He was back on his feet in a flash, Self drawn in his right hand. Dawn's light was peaking over the mountains and glinted wickedly off the stilettos silver blade as he closed the distance between himself and the guard with two rolling steps.

The guard was unaware of the spry interloper until Kyn reached up and wrapped his free hand around the taller man's forehead.

He pulled the guard's head back in one smooth, practiced motion, while simultaneously sliding his knife hand up under their right arm, gripping the other man in a controlled embrace. An upward thrust with Self pierced the soft skin under the guard's jaw, the thin blade pinning the guards mouth shut as it drove back into his skull. The man let out a quick whimper of alarm, before any other noise was silenced, the stiletto expertly severing the brain stem at the cerebral spine.

The guard was dead before he'd understood he'd been in danger.

Kyn eased the now limp body to the deck. Crouched, he pulled Self from his victim. Storm gray eyes roved over the other man's blank and staring face. There was nothing he recognized there, the familiarity he thought he'd sensed earlier a trick of lighting.

Multi-tasking, Kyn keyed his f-Link to run a hack algorithm, decoding and copying the guard's security access codes, while he wiped Self clean on his victim's uniform. He slid the blade back into the top of his boot.

The patterns of his f-Link tattoo swirled and rearranged themselves, indicating the hack was doing its function.

Drawing himself up to full height, Kyn began slinking with predatory purpose in the direction the second guard had gone. The other patrol guard needed to be dealt with; it wouldn't do for them to circle back around and discover their colleague's lifeless body and raise an alarm. Drawing iD and Ego in tandem as he crossed the observation deck with silent grace, Kyn casually twirled the blades, his every movement radiating lethal skill and deadly intent. His blood had cooled to a deadly calm and his mouth was set in a grim line.

His f-Link settled back into a fixed design, buzzing faintly against his skin. Hack complete.

Kyn rounded the corner at the same moment his target did. The patrol guard's eyes widened in shock at the sight of the lithe Envoy, dressed in a sleeveless jumpsuit and brandishing two vicious looking blades in his direction. No time to process this new image, their mouth gaped noiselessly in surprise.

Kyn's own mouth twisted in a fiendish grin. Taking advantage of the guard's surprise, he swiped iD diagonally in front of himself with his right hand, swinging the blade through a series of sweeping motions intended to drive the guard backwards. The shocked guard obliged, surprise turning to alarm as he stumbled over his own feet in a desperate attempt to gain distance between himself and the blade's deadly edge.

Kyn didn't miss a beat. Pivoting on the balls of his feet to bring himself intimately close to the other man, his left-hand extended Ego with lighting speed, driving it smoothly up and under the guard's sternum to pierce their heart. Blood oozed over Kyn's hand, dripping from his wrist and forming a rapidly expanding puddle at his feet. The guard's dull brown eyes widened as Kyn pushed upwards, driving the blade in further, finishing the task quickly.

The guard had not called out, instead, only a strangled, wet, gurgling sound caught in the back of his throat - his life stopped almost instantly.

Kyn pulled Ego from the dead man and turned on his heels, not sparing a glance back as the guard slumped to the ground in the expanding puddle. He strode towards the neon pink waypoint, calmly cleaning Ego's blade against the front of his jumpsuit as he hummed along to the soundtrack still thrumming in his ear.

A panel beside the automated security door blinked in recognition, reading the copied credentials from his f-Link, and the door slid open. Kyn stepped over the threshold without missing a beat and into the darkened, silent offices of Yummy Otter Corp.

Two mins left.

The Factory

Kyn sheathed iD and Ego across his back as he cut through a winding rat maze of hard plastic cubicles, making his way swiftly through the offices towards a bank of lifts. The lights were down, and his surroundings were indistinguishable from any other mid-ward management office. A calendar app had been left open in one of the drones' workstations he passed, the blinking reminder proclaimed that today was 'Lyna's Birthday.'

The secured panel next to the lifts chirped in recognition of his copied guard codes and a door slide up in response with a mechanical hiss. Stepping in, he tabbed the corresponding square for the lab level directly below. His own angular face stared back at him from the polished mirror of the lift doors. He frowned; stray blood splatters dotted his cheeks, glimmering splotches of crimson wetness easily distinguishable from the dark constellation of freckles across his nose and cheeks. He licked the tips of two fingers and scrubbed away the crimson smears. He'd managed to work up a light sweat, and the dots washed away easily.

Satisfied, he clasped his hands in front of himself and took a deep, centering breath.

The lift slid to a stop and the door opened upward to reveal a chem lab of sterile white and stainless steel.

Six guards waited, scattered around the lab, behind the easy cover of the sleek equipment carts, lab tables, and work counters, each with a handheld k-cannon raised and aimed at Kyn center mass.

Kyn clocked them within a single beat of his heart. Each wore a bland blue and white uniform that marked them as freelancers - contract hires from one of the few security firms outside of Dag control. They were more heavily armored then their counterparts on the observation deck. Flexible nano-carbon body armor protected their torsos and valved breather masks hid the lower half of their faces - presumably, protection against unforeseen exposure to the facilities' products.

Hands neatly folded in front of his waist, Kyn stepped out of the lift and was immediately flanked by the two closest freelancers. Chin raised; he flashed the assembled mercs a wide, toothy grin.

Fingers inched towards triggers, waiting for their commander to give a signal.

Kyn raised his hands slowly.

"Hey everyone." He greeted cheerfully, breaking the tense silence. "I'm just here to pick up something for my boss, then I'll be out of your way."

"This area is restricted." A guard at the rear of the lab barked, their voice deep, with a tone that didn't invite argument. Unit commander Kyn guessed. His pink waypoint hovered over an unmarked door directly behind the rent-a-guard. "You will submit to the voluntary search of your person. Kneel on the floor and place your hands behind your head." The guards flanking Kyn moved closer. "Your weapons will be confiscated, and you will provide clearance level identification. Failure to follow any of these instructions will result in immediate and violent subdual."

"Promise?" Kyn teased coyly. His hands moved for the zipper of his jumpsuit as he turned his head to give an exaggerated wink to the guard on his right. The indifferent barrel of a k-cannon stared back.

Lethal projectile weapons redesigned from pre-fall tech once popular in military and policing, the hand-held kinetic cannon fired a blast of pure kinetic energy that was charged into the weapon battery slot by sliding back the pressure measured loading mechanism. The action of cocking the weapon created a charge that was then stored in the clip to be released as a single fire, high-impact projectile.

SPIRE manufactures had since re-engineered the pre-fall design, splintering the storage system to hold the charge over multiple shots with minor sacrifice to force potential. An innovation which led to the creation of the wide variety of capacity vs damage variations models currently on the market.

The six k-cannons leveled at Kyn were all of the same standard issue security firm fare. Eight rounds per charge, and though lacking the superior stopping power of two-handed or pump action models, at the guard's current range, they'd have no problem riddling his torso with tidy burn holes.

"On your knees!" The commander shouted, obviously not keen to repeat himself.

Kyn's pink waypoint still flashed directly behind the speaker. Time was ticking away.

"Fine!" He yelled back. "But if we're gunna do this everyone has to take part. And try not to get it in my eye, that fucking stings." He turned left profile, tilting his chin to the other flanking guard. "This guy knows what I'm talking about."

The guard grunted, low and aggressive in the back of his throat. Lowering his k-cannon he lunged forward, moving to restrain Kyn.

Moment created, Kyn dove forward with lightening quickness, dodging away from the reaching merc to throw himself headfirst into the lab. Dexterous fingers found the harness straps, and he plucked two plastic blades from the grooves. Arms wide mid-dive, he released the clear slivers and the razor-sharp projectiles cut through the air to connect with both flanking guards, severing vital arteries at the neck with a spurt of crimson.

Hitting the ground, Kyn rolled to recover his feet, before immediately launching himself sideways. Kinetic fire roared past as the remaining guards fired as one, narrowly missing, and exploding lab equipment all around in a shower of broken plastic and twisted metal. Scrambling, Kyn slid across smooth linoleum and pulled himself behind the cover of a stainless-steel lab counter. Not wasting a tick, he scurried spider-like on all fours, splayed low and close to the floor, hugging the edge of the long lab counter. The neon pink waypoint flashed in the corner of his vision, directly across the lab. The kinetic blasts had stopped, and he could hear the crunch of boots over the broken lab equipment that now covered the floor. The other guards would be circling outwards, trying to choral him into the center of the room.

Close to the end of his cover, Kyn switched tactics. Reaching up to grasp the lip of the lab counter, he uncoiled from the floor and vaulted over the waist-high cover, knees tucked to his chest to clear the polished top. Landing lightly on the other side, he surprised the guard who'd been cautiously edging along from the other direction. The guard fired wildly, easily missing the Envoy in their surprise.

Kyn's left hand was behind himself as he landed, and he lashed out with Ego, catching the guard across the forearms, and slicing open an angry red gash that forced them to drop their weapon. The guard stumbled, awkwardly grabbing at their bleeding arms. A pivot on his right heel brought one knee up and Kyn snapped out high and across with his foot, shattering the guard's breather mask in one vicious kick. The guards head snapped to the side and Kyn rode the spiral of his movement, deftly flipping Ego from one hand to the other to slash backhanded across the guard's throat with a single clean swipe, finishing them with a spurt of crimson.

Kinetic bolts fired, shattering glass cabinets and blowing chunks of brittle board from the walls. Kyn managed to keep the dying guard between himself and the others, a rapidly bleeding out human shield, their swaying body held standing by the force of the kinetic bolts that surged into their back.

Kyn snatched three clear blades from his harness with preternatural quickness before his macabre shield could fall and threw them blindly in front of himself in a wild, fanning arch as he dove behind another lab bench.

The dead guard teetered before collapsing in a crumpled heap, motionless. Blood pooled on the linoleum around them.

Low behind his new cover, Kyn waited. His hastily thrown blades had failed to hit targets, succeeding only in driving the other guards behind cover again and giving him a momentary reprieve from being shot at. The crunch of the remaining guards' boots were moving away from each other, trying to circle him.

Repeating his previous trick, Kyn vaulted sideways over yet another bank of counters and landed directly in front of the unit commander approaching from the opposite direction. Unsurprised, the freelancer stood firm, k-cannon level, aiming between the interloper's eyes. Kyn dodged low as his boots hit hard rubber linoleum, ducking under the weapon just as the guard fired. The shot discharged directly above his head, making his ears ring painfully. He thrust down hard with Ego as he squatted, driving the dagger's point through the top of the guard's tactical boot. The guard howled.

Kyn stood, open palms thrusting upwards, and grabbed the searing hot barrel of the guard's weapon with one hand, the base of the weapon's cocking mechanism with the other. He yanked down and towards himself at an angle, easily tearing the weapon from the guard's grasp. A deft twirl reversed the barrel, and he fired a single k-bolt into the guard's visor at point-blank range.

The back of the guard's helmet exploded outwards in a spray of blood-drenched brain matter and bone fragments.

Kyn spun, pulling the trigger twice more, aiming for the final two guards moving towards him. The bolts connected, clean and precise through the faceplate. The last guard was dead before their body hit the ground.

Kyn tossed the now empty k-cannon aside unceremoniously and turned his attention to the security door behind the pink waypoint. His internal sense of timing estimated he had forty-five ticks left in the time he had given Runa.

Fiddling with his f-Link he set about bypassing the security lock, first using his copied guard codes, hoping for a fluke. Denied almost instantly by an angry negative beep, he settled on a more advanced and aggressive blunt force hacking module. The tattooed pattern on his forearm shifted rapidly, flowing across his skin like a wall of cascading water.

Kyn glanced around at the mess of the lab.

In his service to the Sentry, he was no stranger to violent encounters with the various local security firms, or even The Unity's own armed forces, the Dags. The outcome of those interactions usually played out in similar fashion; nameless goons dead and Kyn splattered in blood. He knew in no uncertain terms that seeking answers into the nature of his orders was futile and dangerous. He cared little for why he was at Yummy Otter Corp, or why these guards needed to be eliminated. The Envoys existed to be the messengers of the Unity, and the message was always the same.

No one undermined the Unity.

Yet, despite Kyn's trained de-sensitivity and disinterest, the events of the night had started to itch at the back of his mind. Pieces of ill-fitting information rubbing up against each other. He turned what he'd gleaned over in his mind while the hack ran, toying with the information, looking for why the edges of what he knew felt so mismatched when slotted into a predictable narrative in his mind.

He was familiar with all the freelancer security firms that existed within the city and knew exactly which firm the now dead guards had come from. High priced and well trained, which was the exact problem. Too high priced and too well trained to be guarding a mid-wards narcotics factory.

The buzzing crawl of his f-Link woke him from his musings. Locking protocols broken, the unmarked door slid open, revealing a narrow storage room, dimly lit by a strip of low-level white LEDs set in the floor for guidance. Banks of oni – data storage and recovery tech in various shapes and sizes - lined each wall. The white strip of light reflected dimly in the curved aluminum of their cases.

Kyn's neon pink waypoint hovered at the far end of the light up path, right above a single square pedestal.

Destination reached.

Kyn tapped the thumb and middle finger of his left hand together, tweeking his f-Link to open a comm channel to Runa.

"Hey kiddo, I've got what I need." He reported. A curved black band, like a wrist cuff of polished polymer sat on the pedestal. He picked up the curved band. The augmented pink glow faded from his vision the moment his fingers touched the unknown tech. "Moving to intercept Ashe now."

The band was a reflective onyx black, smooth to the touch, the cuff tight enough he could slip it on his wrist where it would stay secure easily. Cords ran from the pedestal and back into the nearest oni, the rest were interconnected with more hardwires.

"Don't call me kiddo." Was Runa's gruff response. "Also, that was the longest three mins of my life." Her exasperated sigh carried through the comm. "Ashe's three floors down, just before the factory floor. Hurry up, they're in a mood."

"Ashe is always in a mood."

"True."

Kyn casually tossed the curved band up and down in one hand, struck by how deceptively light it was. "On my way." He confirmed, catching the band. A quick inspection for possible identifiers revealed nothing and he slid the smooth piece into an inner pocket of his jumpsuit. Backtracking the light strip, he made his way across the gore splattered lab, back towards the lift. The soles of his boots made sticky, sucking sounds as he trod through congealing pools of blood.

Kyn stepped out of the lift into a blank corridor that stretched in either direction. Figures approached from one direction, half a dozen moving in lockstep, double doors beyond them at the far end of the corridor. The other direction ended in a water tank.

The approaching group was led by an imposing figure that stalked towards Kyn with predatory grace. Indigo blue hair, shaved in sleek, asymmetrical punk strips, framed an elegantly handsome, square face. Luxurious fabrics draped broad shoulders and wrapped around statuesque limbs in flowing swaths of flamboyant colour. Midnight satin skin peaked suggestively from beneath the loose wraps, and long, powerfully muscled legs were clad in tall, alarm yellow synth-leather boots that stopped halfway up the figure's strong thighs. Precariously thin heels struck the floor with each rolling step, the crisp *clack* echoing off the prefab walls.

Kyn was reminded of massive felines seen in learning vids on extinct species; the ones that had once prowled the mountains beyond the resource zone. With strong, willowy limbs and seductive curves, the lead figure moved like liquid metal, exuding an aura of deadly coldness that hung around them like a physical force.

The lead was flanked by a blank eyed man and woman that Kyn recognized easily from his earlier briefing data: Vikta Fama and Eva Scavr - the founders of Yummy Otter Corp. Beyond, a small retinue of hired security guards followed in a tight v-formation, moving with eerie synchronicity.

"Well, hello, darling." Kyn drawled in greeting. He smiled broadly.

The striking figure halted several paces from Kyn. Gently slanted violet eyes held him with an intent gaze.

The air around Kyn seemed to solidify with the look, holding him motionless. Pressure thrummed against his temples, squeezing at his skull with a subtle ache.

"All right Ashe that's enough." He rebuked the taller Envoy with exaggerated nonchalance. The growing tension put his teeth on edge.

Ashe raised a hand and brushed a cascading shock of indigo hair behind one ear. A casual click of two fingers and the motionless guards behind them snapped to attention. Moving in unison, the guards crossed seamlessly in front of Ashe and the two dead-eyed company owners to form a human wall. Handheld k-cannons raised in the same perfectly synchronized beat to level threateningly at Kyn's chest.

"What did you retrieve from the lab?" Ashe asked. Their voice was opposing tones that resonated as one with a wavering, flanging effect. Hypnotic and alluring.

Kyn eyed Ashe wearily before answering. "I think you'll like this one." He retrieved the cuff from the front of his jump suit and tossed the device in an arching motion across the wall of guards. "It's sleek and goes with everything"

Deftly catching it, Ashe inspected the device briefly before disappearing it within the folds of their vibrant wraps

"It's some kind of tech. They had it hooked up to a bunch of oni - trying to figure out what was on it, I'm assuming." Kyn continued. The air around him thrummed, the vibration of unseen pressure increasing.

kneel

Kyn turned his attention to Vikta and Eva. Their expressions were flat and blank. "You two were not doing so well, from what I saw." Approaching the wall of security, he reached out past the still guards and playfully squished Eva's cheeks, pursing her lips, fish like, between his slender fingers. "You were having a pretty tough time getting anything out of there." He mocked in a sing-song voice.

The woman didn't react, her glazed eyes fixed blankly ahead, looking through him. Stepping away from the wall of guards Kyn turned his attention back to Ashe. "You look good." He complimented genuinely. "How ya' been?"

"They were having trouble retrieving anything from the device?" Ashe pressed, blowing past his inquiry. "Any indication on what it is?"

kneel

"Well, judging by their current business model. I'm probably gunna say it has something to do with..." Kyn made an exaggerated show of looking around, then raised one flat hand to his mouth "Drugs." He hissed loudly, voice dropped to a low, conspiratorial whisper. He looked again to the silent Eva and Vikta. "Seriously though, good job. Big fan." He complimented. "That Blue Eclipse is fucking amazing, I'm totally going to grab some while I'm here," He flashed raised thumbs at the pair.

kneel. kneel. kneel

"Cut the shit Ashe." Kyn snapped. The pressure against his temples had increased to an obnoxiously level. "You don't get to have a fucking attitude with me. I'm here. I got the fucking job done." Irate, he stepped forward until the barrel of a guard's k-cannon pressed painfully into his chest and glared at Ashe past the unflinching freelancer. "I'm sorry you don't like how I'm doing things lately but that's my problem. Do you hear me? My. Problem." He pounded his chest emphatically with his fist, words pointed, and direct.

Ashe's face was a cool mask of studied indifference.

kneel

"You. DO NOT. Control me!" Kyn hissed viciously, thrusting a finger at Ashe, punctuating his words. The pressure in his head evaporated, blown away, and a manic energy, like lightening through storm clouds, glinted in his gray eyes,

Ashe met his gaze. The moment stretching silently between them. The corners of their mouth twitched upwards.

"Shoot him." They said finally.

The roar a k-cannon discharging filled the corridor.

Point-blank, the kinetic bolt ripped through Kyn's chest, exploding outwards from his back in a spray of red gore and white bone chips. He stumbled backwards, gray eyes wide, fingers searching wildly at the ragged edges of the wet, sucking, hole that had been blown through his chest. Each shuttering breath was a whistling wheeze as he tried to draw air through the ravaged tissue of an exposed and ruined lung.

Then he was falling forward.

Kyn rolled over with a groan; the sound low and rumbling in his chest, a purr of exhausted contentment. His searching hand grasped at rumpled sheets. Early morning light streamed through steel-framed windows, and he squinted against the dawn-sharp brilliance.

Seeking fingers found the soft skin and muscular curve of Yorri's glutes amongst the morning damp sheets and he gently traced over the warmth of the other man's back. Drawing coiled, looping patterns past the ridge of a jutting shoulder blade, he gently caressed the larger man's nape before finally twinning his fingers in ruffled, sandy blonde hair.

Kyn turned his head away from the offending light of the windows and towards Yorri's sleeping form. He was drooling, face pressed against the pillow, snoring softly. Kyn smiled and leaned across the

derrafoam to plant a gentle kiss on the sleeping man's nose. A hollow metal bang came from across the flat, a knock at the heavy loading bay door. He ignored it.

"Morning." He murmured, before rapidly assaulting every exposed area of the still sleeping man's face with pecking kisses. The banging rang again, louder.

"Get off." Yorri groaned, throwing up a hand to swat at the barrage of affection. He pulled himself deeper into the bedroll, attempting to seek refuge under the drool-soaked pillow.

"No chance mister, it's time to get up." Kyn ordered. "I promised Egar we'd take him to the sea wall today." He sat up on the bedroll and swung one leg over Yorri's slim hips, straddling him, palms flat against the other man's warm, muscular chest. "And I'm not the type of man who breaks his promises." His fingers slowly inched upwards, seeking the exposed pits of Yorri's raised arms.

"Oh, I know what type of man you are." Yorri returned, struggling not to laugh as he abandoned the pillow shield and grabbed at his assailants' wrists, wrestling for control. He bucked his hips; attempting to flip their positions.

Kyn pushed back, slipping the larger man's grip with ease, and pinned him back against the derrafoam. He could feel the other man stirring, awakening beneath him, pressed against him under his straddled position. Kyn leaned forward, arching his back teasingly and ground his pelvis over the hardness.

"You have no idea." He returned, voice thick as he dipped to nip playfully at an earlobe.

The pounding at the metal door sounded again, louder.

Yorri looked deep into Kyn eyes, his own still blurry with sleep, and raised a hand to caress the tawny brown skin of the slighter man's cheek. His fingertips gently traced patterns between the smattering of freckles, and a soft, loving smile played at the corner of his lips.

"I know exactly who you are." Yorri whispered back huskily, breath rank from sleep. He pulled himself up to press his lips passionately against Kyn's.

The banging against the door grew louder still. Resounding bangs that rattled the industrial steel.

Kyn reluctantly turned away from the naked, and rapidly hardening man beneath him.

"FUCK! Hold up ya little shit, I'm coming!" He yelled, towards to the heavy door, moving to dismount Yorri. Strong hands around his hips stopped him.

"Who are you talking to?" Yorri quizzed. Stray beams of morning sun caught his eyes, setting them ablaze in prismatic sprays of greens. Swirling seafoam green, speckled with islands of darker, mossy shades, swirling around black pupils. Kyn forgot the banging, momentarily lost.

"Egar." He answered, finally. "The little reject is slamming at the door. He wants me to let him in. Ya' got to hear that banging."

Yorri ran his hands over Kyn's thighs, tracing over hips to grip the top of the slighter man's glutes; fingers explored the contours of firm muscles, digging in pleasurably.

"He never knocks, just barges in here every time, expecting to be fed. And who can blame him, with you promising to take him to the sea wall?"

The banging intensified.

"So?" Kyn pressed back. Neither needed to raise their voice to be heard, even though the banging was deafening. "Like the reject is ever going to be able to get out of the lower wards and go to green areas on his own?"

"So? It's your responsibility? It's not your fault his parents dumped him down here in favor of having another kid. Both of us were just like him, and we survived without the kindness of heroic strangers."

Yorri let his hands drift up Kyn's back. "He has to learn to take care of himself. You're not always going to be here."

"What?!" Kyn looked down at Yorri, suddenly alarmed. His hands had stopped their rhythmic stroking pattern. Wet crimson splotches dotted the prone man's chest. "What are you talking about? Why would you say that?" Kyn's searching fingers smeared the wetness across the other man's firm skin, trying to find its source.

"Don't worry." Yorri's voice was hollow, round, and didn't come from his mouth.

The banging was louder, the space between them shorter, coming in booming, resonate impacts. Kyn's chest reverberated with each impact.

Yorri's voice was still intimately quiet. "I know what type of man you are."

"What?!" Kyn choked. His breath was coming in ragged gasps now. He felt like every bang was tearing his lungs apart. He grabbed at his chest, fighting for air. The crimson wetness was blood, smeared across the man beneath him, soaking the bed, as if blasted from him with a great force. Kyn grasped wildly at the crimson slick skin, looking to stem the source of the bleeding.

Yorri smiled up at him kindly. He was soaked in blood, the slick redness obscuring his features so only his arresting green eyes shone through.

"You're not always going to be there."

"Fucktwatt!" Kyn screamed.

The world came rushing back at him as air, reeking of burnt flesh, slammed into his lungs and he stumbled backwards, struggling to maintain his feet. The gaping wound in his chest sucked grotesquely as he wheezed desperately. The damaged lung was healing. Slick pink organ tissue blossomed from the ragged edges of the scorched wound, closing over. Flesh and organ knitting itself back together with a mindless, white-hot pain. Fresh grown rib snapped back into place as muscle sewed itself to tendon.

"Shathole!" Kyn bellowed. Blood slicked fingers found his chest harness, and he whipped a fist full of throwing blades ahead of himself.

The entire wall of guards collapsed as one, grasping at bleeding serrations in vital points as they writhed on the floor, choking in their own blood.

Kyn brushed his hands over the front of his jumpsuit, plucking with annoyance at the scorched edges of burned through the fabric. Fresh skin, soft and unblemished, was replicating rapidly over the newly formed bones of his rib cage. The regrowth pain had faded to a burning itch.

Within the space of a couple of screams, a few ragged breathes, and an irritated burst of violence, the gaping bolt wound through his chest had closed. Damage reduced to nothing more than an angry red scrape across his sternum, as if, instead of taking a kinetic bolt through the chest at point blank range, he'd done nothing more than fall and scrape himself on the concrete.

He spread his arms wide, palms up, and smiled good naturedly at Ashe.

"Now, why did you have to go and do that?" He asked. "Seriously, I liked this outfit. How would you feel if I went wrecking all your nice clothes?"

"To remind you of who you are." Ashe snapped, their voice tense and brittle. The air thrummed.

Kyn ran his hands through his auburn hair, yanking at tuffs of it, trying to tamp down his frustration. Regeneration always made him edgy, manic. He wasn't in a mood to handle Ashe's hectoring.

"Yah, as I was saying before you had one of your slack jawed thralls shoot me." He shot back, vicious. "That's really none of your business." He withdrew Ego from the small of his back and lazily swung the razor-sharp tip back and forth between the still non-reactive Vikta and Eva.

"Can we get what we need from these two and be done?" He asked, flipping Ego back into its sheath and stepping closer to Ashe. "Then we can go our separate ways."

"Protect me," Ashe snapped, their voice cracking the air. The two Yummy Otter Corp. founders responded instantly, snapping to life with a sudden surge of movement. The pair crouched down in unison, each retrieving a fallen guards' k-cannon, before moving in front of Ashe. They smoothly reloaded the weapons and leveled them at Kyn.

"Oh, come on Ashe." Kyn whined, hands raised in mock surrender. He stamped his booted foot. "You know this is pointless. I can kill these two faster than you can utter another word. Plus, even if they get lucky." He patted the flesh of his ribs. "Not gunna keep me down long. Come on, getting shot like that really fucking hurts. Obvious point. Not keen to do it again."

"They grow tired of your stupidity. The disappearing, acting out like a petulant child." Ashe lectured. Their violet eyes blazed with rage and disapproval. "They know they cannot discipline you conventionally so they will hurt others to teach you a lesson. You know this."

Unwilling to break eye contact, Kyn looked sheepish. He knew they were right.

"They will use Runa." Ashe's flanging voice was thick with accusation.

"Runa will be fine." Kyn reassured weakly, desperate to believe his own words. "Besides, they probably couldn't use her like that if they wanted to, she's a tough kid."

"They would find a way, they always do." Ashe pressed, tone pleading now, a pained expression on their face. "They will make me hold her down to do it. Please Kyn, do not let others suffer for your disobedience."

Kyn shuddered, trying to repress the images his mind conjured. Shame burned in his gut, and he sighed, defeated. "Alright, fine.' He conceded. "I'll be a good little Envoy. No more acting out."

The shadow of a smile played at the corner of Ashe's full lips, and their expression relaxed to something more resembling camaraderie. "Thank you." They returned softly, their voice, losing its discordant flanging, settled into something that was like cool silk sliding across skin. Kyn felt a shutter at the base of his spine.

Tensions eased, he turned his full attention back to Vikta FaMa and Eva Scavr, still standing with weapons aimed, waiting.

"So, what should we do with these two?" He asked, raising an eyebrow. Sweat had begun to bead on the pair's upper lips and their arms were shaking from the strain of holding up the k-cannons. He could hear the trapped fluttering of their frightened breathing, directly in contrast to their glassy stares and blank expressions.

"You didn't glam 'em?"

"Did not feel the need," Ashe answered darkly, tone not inviting further questioning.

Kyn didn't pry, it was just another peculiarly shaped piece of the night, amongst a steadily growing pile of oddities. He studied the two founders.

On the surfaces, there was nothing interesting about either, at least that Kyn could see. Typical cosmetic enhancements were obvious; expensive skin tinting, augments to smooth the skin of their faces. Getting closer, Kyn noticed tell-tale signs in the dark bruising around their eye sockets, in the blood crusting Vikta's nostril, and the burst vessels in Eva's left eye. Signs of chem abuse that strained their expensive cosmetics. The two obviously knew their products, if not safe consumption habits.

"Are you quite finished?" Ashe interjected, breaking Kyn's focus. He'd been pacing the pair. Without waiting for his response, they turned to Vikta and Eva. "Shoot each other." They intoned, with a dismissive wave, voice flanging.

Two shots fired in unison.

Vikta and Eva slumped over the executed freelancers as Ashe turned on a heel and stalked purposefully towards the exit. Kyn followed, jogging lightly to match pace.

"You know we could've asked them where they got the tech." He pointed out. It wasn't one of their objectives, but a small part of himself was curious.

"Enough time wasted." Ashe retorted, throwing open the doors to a spiraling stairwell that would lead them to the factory floor a level below.

"Oh, so now we're in a rush." Kyn shot back, deftly leaping the stairs several levels at a time. "We had all the time in the world when you decided we needed a stand-off so you could chew my ass out. Come on, you could have at least asked what they were doing here so late, or early, whichever. I mean it seemed odd, right? All I know is I planned on being in bed by now. Preferably not sleeping." He was babbling now.

"We were to eliminate them. Nothing more." Ashe admonished. They had reached the door that would lead them to the factory floor, locked by an adjacent security panel. "We are Envoys, not cultists. Secrets are not our business." They laid a large hand delicately on the door, and eyed Kyn expectantly.

"You're kidding right?" He snorted with feigned disbelief. "Secrets are all we do." He twitched his fingertips, keying up the guard codes he'd copied earlier. "You could easily be doing this hack yourself." He added testily.

Ashe held up a long finger. Their own f-Link, an interlocking pattern of circles, glowed indigo along the side of their slender neck.

"Runa, are you ready for extraction?"

"More then." Runa's gruff voice shot back over the trio linked comm. "It's pissin' rain, hurry your asses up already."

Kyn smothered a laugh behind his hand as Ashe killed the link.

The security panel beeped in confirmation and the factory door opened to a wide loading bay crowded with racks of hard-case shipping cubes stacked and prepped for morning delivery. More freelancers clogged the aisles, k-cannons raised, covering the entrance, and blocking the path to the work floor beyond.

Ashe stepped through; the air trilled around them.

"Stand down" Ashe's discordant voice snapped, whip-like across the air. Every guard in the loading bay stopped at once, frozen abruptly. There was a crashing clatter from somewhere in the rows of shelves.

Unaffected, Kyn followed.

The pair had entered from the far side of the factory floor, a cavernous production space crammed with massive mixing tanks, powder silos, and sorting equipment that reached high into the rafters, several stories above them. Linked catwalks crisscrossed above, connecting opposing sides of a hanging observation deck that ran the periphery of the room. Guards patrolling the deck were frozen and motionless at Ashe's command. Assembly lines for filling, stamping, and packaging wound around everything at ground level, staffed by sickly and exhausted looking workers who were watched over by - now frozen and motionless - shock baton armed guards. The sickly staff watched Kyn and Ashe warily, so far omitted from the glamorous Envoy's thrall.

Otto beamed at them from every product, shipping container, and motivational poster. Joyfully performing his belly pat dance and blinking his large, animated eyes.

The Envoys crossed the factory floor.

"Join."

The workers fell under Ashe's influence as they passed. Immediately stopping what they were doing, each turned obediently to line up and follow with the others. Tired faces alight with a gleeful eagerness as they looked to the striking Envoy with a new, doe-eyed rapture.

Kyn clocked two dozen workers and half again as many guards under Ashe's influence. The muscles of their jaw visibly clenched under flawless skin. Ashe crossed to an empty loading bay near the production floor's rear wall, workers in tow. Poured concrete between vertical steel beams turned to sheet metal higher up. Stopped, the bedraggled workers shuffled in closer to Ashe.

A boom shook the rear wall.

Kyn nudged Ashe. "Does something seem odd about this lot to you?" He asked, glancing at their silent and adoring onlookers.

"Yes." Ashe answered.

"They don't look like typical lower ward servos." Kyn pressed, referencing those who'd sold themselves into a contract of voluntary servitude - most usually in exchange for the chance to pay off credit debts, or secure a place in the mid-wards for themselves or a loved one at the end of their contract. He raised a hand to his mouth, distractedly chewing on the knuckles of his index finger as he contemplated the workers who'd now pressed in around them, jostling each other to get closer to Ashe.

Another bang shook the wall. Something was slamming heavily against the other side.

Each enthralled worker had dark or drab coloured hair, too long and wild to be currently fashionable anywhere in the wards, and they were missing the usual assortment of visual tech mods or augment implants common to virtually everybody within the walled city. They even seemed to be missing the most rudimentary wearable f-Link devices that were given to small children and the poorest citizens in lieu of the more expensive and invasive dermal graft.

"I think they are Wasters." Ashe asserted; violet eyes now fixed steadily on the opposite wall. Their discordant voice had begun to quiver.

The concrete wall shook with another resonate impact. Gray dust billowed into the air.

"Seriously?" Kyn pressed, intrigued. He looked at the gathered workers with renewed curiosity.

The wall shook with another powerful impact, cracks spider-webbed across the surface.

"Okay..." He mused. "So, they've got a bunch of Wasters, what does that mean?"

Wasters were a new occurrence, new slang, used to reference the small groups of refugees that had recently appeared, seeking asylum at the borders of the resource zone. Refugees fleeing the unlivable lands beyond the mountains, or seeking sanctuary from the depraved violence of the Dividers who lurked in the dark forest valleys between the surrounding peaks.

"It means we get to be the rescuing heroes." Ashe answered dully. Another loud bang. The concrete wall shook. "And not to ask too many questions."

Another thunderous impact sent large chunks of concrete flying outward from the wall. The blows increased in tempo.

"Piece of fucking, shit!" A familiar, muffled, gravelly voice grumbled between blows. Another impact dislodged a piece of concrete that struck a frozen guard in the head, knocking them to the floor, dead or unconscious.

The pace of the impacts increased, as did the frustrated cursing, until, in one final resounding boom that shook the factory floor, the wall blasted inwards, showering those closest with rocketing debris.

Runa stood silhouetted in the ragged hole.

An adolescent barely out of gawky puberty, her waif like face was framed by a mass of dark hair; wet, lanky curls gone prematurely gray with a dusting of crumbled concrete. Wide set amber eyes squinted in apparent annoyance as she pulled back a clenched fist and slammed it into a section of offending wall, tearing away another chunk of concrete the size of Kyn's head and widening the hole she'd created.

"Hey." Runa acknowledged, raising a gray dusted hand in greeting. She stepped over the jutting base of the ruined wall and picked her way through the loose rubble towards the others. "Let's get this fucking over with." She proclaimed; rough voice heavy with the annoyed exasperation only an adolescent could muster.

Kyn could smell fresh rain beyond the gaping hole.

Runa wiped her hands across ripped, retro-denim leggings, leaving dust prints. She tilted her head, scanning the room. Her tongue clicked hard against the roof of her mouth.

"Nice, Ashe." She complimented. She flipped her thumb back towards the hole. "Ready to go?"

"More than." Ashe answered thinly, the discordant flanging of their voice shivered the air. "Some of them are getting a bit much."

Kyn could feel the air shift, as if thin sheets of frost. Jagged but fragile, breaking around him with every movement, shattering, then reshaping in his wake.

"I'll be happy to let them loose," Ashe continued. Their eyes gleamed dangerously with malevolent intent. Turning, they shifted their focus to address the Wasters grouped around them. The enthralled workers cast adoring eyes at the willowy Envoy.

"We're going to leave here now." Ashe announced, their voice rising in crescendo, arms wide. A beacon of comfort and protection. "Reach out to the person next to you and grasp their hand." The enthralled Wasters obeyed, clapping onto each other like small children.

Runa suppressed a snicker.

Kyn elbowed the younger Envoy, drawing her attention to the blank eyed guards with a nod of his head. He tapped his f-Link.

"Requests?"

Runa shook rain from her mass of curls. Limp bunches hung around her narrow shoulders, making it look to Kyn as if she were equal parts vengeful sprite and junky waif.

"Acid Rock?" She inquired.

Kyn clicked his tongue. "Oooh appropriate choice," he applauded. "Pre- or Post- Fall?"

"Post obviously." Runa snorted dismissively. "And first wave, not that resurgence shit."

"Through the hole calmly now." Ashe was instructing the Wasters, sounding more like an impatient care giver and less like a benevolent deity. "I will be right behind you."

The Wasters did as bid. Innocently clasped onto one another other like children on yard break as they shuffled out through the hole and into the rainy predawn.

Kyn tapped through f-Link commands as they went. The tattoo waved, re-shaping itself across his forearm, scanning the room for other signals. Latching, the shifting triangles settled, and commands flashed across his optic. Fingers tapping, he broke through the encryption to link with the security frequency. He keyed up a track list, and the echoey, trembling tones of well-known post-fall acid rock group Phase/Shitting filled the factory, the psychedelic melodies blasted from each frozen guard's own f-Link.

Runa clapped enthusiastically and squealed in delight, bobbing up and down on the balls of her feet. She unbuttoned a dark plaid over-layer, sliding it off her shoulders to cinch tightly around her waist, sleeves in a knot, and rested both hands on her hips. An over-sized sleeveless shift with a retro band logo invoked an air of bored nihilism.

"Nice choice." She complimented approvingly. "Here." She pulled two folded pieces of nylon from a back pocket and tossed one handily to Kyn. "I thought you might need one." She supplied.

Kyn, caught the bundle one handed and unfolded the square, revealing a strap waist pouch with a surprising amount of capacity.

"Thanks." He returned, securing the pouch in place below Ego's sheath. He figured he'd be able to stash a tidy amount of product into it before Yummy Otter Corp shut down for good.

"If you two are entirely finished." Ashe interrupted testily; expression pinched. The strain of keeping the locals under control was wearing on them.

"Just about." Kyn replied, adjusting the pouch. Ashe pursed their full lips, sucking their teeth in annoyance.

"You're making this extremely easy." They drawled acidly before approaching Runa. The towering Envoy placed their hands gently on her shoulders. They regarded the younger Envoy silently, seemingly wanting to speak, before settling on a simple, affectionate, squeeze of the shoulders. They turned to the motionless crowd of guards still surrounding the room.

"Shall we finish up then?" They asked, arching one sculpted eyebrow. The last of the Wasters were through the improvised exit.

Kyn and Runa's hands shot up, snapping to attention in mock salute, heels clicked together. They both beamed with mischievously toothy grins.

"Aright then, let us send a message." Ashe's voice flanged, snapping the air.

The atmosphere of the room shifted instantly with their words, growing warmer, the air thick, lapping sludge. The guards began to shake, nostrils flaring, breathing rapid, ragged. A haze of roiling anger and aggression filled the room with the palpable tension of violence. Ashe's influence tapping into a primal, irrepressible, rage that simmered just below masks of civility.

Indifferent to the looming threat of mob violence, Runa picked at the ragged hole in the back of Kyn's jumpsuit with a blunt nailed index finger.

"They shot you, eh?" She confirmed with a smirk. "Called it."

"No." Kyn shot back huffily. "They made someone else do it."

"Same dif," Runa retorted, turning her attention back to Ashe.

The androgynous Envoy had raised their hands, claw like towards the sky. Their violet eyes glimmered viciously.

"Kill each other." They intoned darkly, reverbing voice blending seamlessly with the pulsing, hallucinogenic beats of Phase/Shitting.

The factory floor erupted into a churning madhouse of violence as guards flung themselves at each other in a flurry of brutality as if driven by ruthless pit masters. Ashe's command had whipped them into a blood crazed frenzy, eager to tear each other apart. K-cannon blasts mixed with the screams of the dying as those who had once been colleagues, passing associates, or possibly even friends and lovers, mercilessly launched at each other.

To Kyn's right a female guard drove a shock baton into a larger male colleague's gut repeatedly. The male guard jerked, spasming violently with each jab, a dark wetness spreading across the groin of his uniform. The air was acrid. The female let her victim collapse, his skin smoking faintly, and looked around wildly, searching, before launching herself onto the back of another passing guard.

Ashe surveyed the unfolding chaos before, nodding once, they turned on a precariously thin heel. They stopped outside the gaping hole to glance back, expression inscrutable, their flawless features seemingly sculpted out of cold steel and shadow. Silver rain pounded the street beyond. Then Ashe was gone, disappeared into the pre-dawn.

Left to the churning storm of violence, Kyn turned back-to-back with Runa. Eased into a relaxed alley brawler's stance - deceptively loose but coiled to strike - he scanned the room, ignoring the chaos around him, until he noticed a length of chain, like a silver snake coiled under an assembly line. He crouched low, scouring over the labels of dancing otter adorned packing crates, and scooped up the length of steel links. Cold and smooth to the touch, he calmly wrapped one end around the knuckles of his left hand as he ran the silver links across the palm of his right. He twirled the extra length casually at his hip, testing the weight.

A frenzied guard ran past, and Kyn whipped out, ensnaring the freelancer's ankle with a clanging snap. He yanked back decisively, jerking his snared prey's feet out from under them and dropping the guard face first into the industrial floor. An enraged co-worker was on them in a flash, beating the tripped freelancer into a lifeless pulp with a dead shock baton.

Kyn chuckled at the slapstick violence and went back to scanning the products.

"I'm going to take out the main support beams, then find me some stuff that goes boom. See if I can't light this fucker up." Runa called back over her shoulder. "Grab what you can. Make sure we don't lose any of this lot."

"I don't know. Ashe did a good job raging them up, this a brutal bunch."

"This is nothing. Remember that cultist compound? The nuns were tearing each other apart. They didn't even have weapons."

"Oh yah, the Nuns of Zion. Didn't that really big one light herself on fire?"

"Yup, then she just kept grabbing all the other ones, wrapping them up in her arms, like she were huggin 'em. Place was full of flamin' nuns."

They both shuddered involuntarily at the memory. Runa had been much younger then, and acknowledging that she remembered the events so clearly made the pit of Kyn's stomach roil with an unexpected rage. He clenched his fists, the chain cutting painfully into his palms, and took deep calming breathes, struggling to tamp the sudden rage down.

As if on cue, summoned to stem the flow of his traitorous thoughts, a roaring, meatjack of a guard stumbled into view. Kyn gaped, momentarily surprised. The guard was the worst example of off-market 'roid abuse he'd ever seen. Thickly muscled and bellowing with incoherent fury, the freelancer guard was grotesquely proportioned, chem juiced musculature straining the seams of their guard uniform. The meatjack's neck was a block of vein busting flesh, the head diminutive and blocky, and they gripped a powerful pump action k-cannon in their meaty paws.

Kyn stared, fascinated and baffled at how he'd managed to miss clocking the monstrosity earlier. The 'roid jacked freelancer pumped the charging stock of their k-cannon and swung the weapon around. Veiny eyes bulged with enthralled rage as they leveled the wide barrel at Runa's plaid wrapped midriff and pulled the trigger with a thunderous boom.

Runa grunted and staggered back; hands pressed to her stomach. Shocked out of his momentary stupor, Kyn whipped out with the length of chain, striking with lightning speed, and ensnared the long-barreled weapon. He yanked back, snapping it from the behemoth's grasp. The k-cannon clattered to the floor, spun, and slid to a stop at the slumped Runa's booted foot.

Runa unfolded slowly, hands moving from her mid-section as she stood straight. The fabric of her retro shift was shredded, but the flesh beneath was smooth and undamaged.

"Nice try big guy." She growled, glowering at the towering pile of muscle that loomed over her, dwarfing her. The 'roid guard blinked in confusion.

Runa smiled sweetly. Squatting, she scooped up the discarded k-cannon and held the weapon out in front of herself, loosely gripped between both hands, presenting it to the behemoth as if handing back a dropped toy. The 'roid guard stared at the adolescent Envoy dumbly, before reaching tentatively to touch the offered weapon with one meaty paw.

Sweet smile snapped cold as Runa bent the weapon against itself with a screech of tearing metal, folding both ends towards each other with ease. She casually tossed the folded hunk of metal and fiberglass back over her shoulder, the broken weapon clattering loudly to slide away, lost in the chaos of violence.

The 'roid guard's eyes bulged even further, some realization penetrating the rage filled haze that had over-ridden his rationale brain. He stared at the diminutive Envoy with a slack-jawed, disbelief-tinged fear.

Then he was flying backwards.

Runa had lashed out with a deft snapping kick, booted foot connecting with the 'roid guard's groin, the force of the blow lifting them off the ground and propelling them backwards through the air. The slab of muscle flew several paces before slamming into a steel support pillar with enough force to shatter their spine on impact, leaving a significant dent, and slumped to the ground, dead or near enough to it.

Runa reached out casually with one hand and grabbed another guard rushing by in the swirl of violence by the front of their uniform, and hoisted them above her head. Feet dangling like a child's doll, the guard growled, thrashing, and foaming at the mouth before Runa reversed and brought them back down hard onto their back, slamming them onto the concrete factory floor with a bone-shattering crunch and a spray of blood and teeth. The guard lay motionless, dead eyes fixed and glassy.

Releasing the body, Runa broke from Kyn to square off with the now dented metal support beam. Kicking aside the dead 'roid guard she swung with a haymaker and struck the beam with a hollow boom, bending it even more.

One of several support pillars lined down the center of the warehouse, the thick steel beam took two more solid hits from the diminutive adolescent before buckling. The roof above dipped dangerously as dust and debris rained down, adding to the churning chaos. The screams of the dying were fading, and the last few rage-enthralled guards paced the floor, blood soaked and hunting each other.

Satisfied, Runa calmly proceeded to the next nearest beam to repeat the process. Another approaching guard was sent flying across the factory floor with a casual backhanded swat, doing nothing to deter her destructive path.

Left to his own grisly task, Kyn leapt to a waist-high conveyor belt and started sprinting the length to get ahead of falling debris. He flicked a handful of plastic throwing blades as he ran, aiming at a guard uselessly firing on Runa, cutting them down, throat slit tidily.

The remaining guards were attempting to flee now, Ashe's influence finally fading. Having survived the main onslaught by pure luck, or accident of positioning, the traumatized survivors were now charging towards the nearest exits, desperate to escape the carnage.

Kyn twirled the length of chain, eyeing two escaping guards on the upper catwalk. Taking long, measured strides, he reached the end of the conveyor belt and jumped, feet aiming for the rim of the lowest vat in a cluster of multi-leveled chemical silos. Brief contact on the narrow rim and he pushed off again, twisting to change direction mid-air. He lashed out with the length of chain, snapping it around the catwalk handrail with a resounding clang. He swung over the chaos below.

Runa was continuing her steady rampage, calmly moving across the factory floor as she took out more supports and overturned equipment. Bodies were strewn in her wake like discarded and broken toys.

Momentum killed, Kyn spun slowly in place by one hand. The chain's metal links bit into his hand. He giggled as Runa tipped over the vat he'd just leaped from. Viscous green liquid cascaded from the overturned tank, soaking the factory floor. She thrust her hand through the metal casing of a nearby automated packing device, forcing her fist into the inner guts of the machine. A brief rustle around and she triumphantly yanked the equipment's battery system from its casing with a cascading flash of arching electricity and lazily lobbed the sparking battery into the spreading pool of spilled liquid, igniting it instantly into a roaring wall of green flame.

The sudden wave of heat blasted Kyn, and an acrid yellow smoke chocked the air. Climbing hand over hand he scaled the chain to pull himself up over the catwalk safety rail. Somewhere below, something combustible exploded and the walkway tilted, lurching wildly. Sections of fiberglass and steel plummeted to the chaos below, leaving open, yawning gaps. A portion of one outer wall had already collapsed inwards, the roof no longer able to support itself.

Only two guards were left, somehow spared from each other and the chaos below, and were slowly picking their way across the treacherous catwalk. They inched towards the far upper floor exit, focused entirely on their own survival, unaware of Kyn's presence.

Crouched low, he yanked the chain free with one hand and ran at them, agilely keeping his footing even as the grating lurched from another explosion. The section immediately in front of him fell away, crashing to the factory floor and he leapt, clearing it narrowly. Purple and blue clouds of narcotic smoke added to the thickening haze.

Leaping over a twisted railing to run horizontally along the connecting wall, Kyn cleared another sudden gap, closing in on the escaping guards. He whipped out with the chain, snapping it around the closest guard's neck in one motion before, still running forward, he veered to step one foot onto the outer safety rail and threw himself from the catwalk. The ensnared guard gasped once before they were slammed into the railing, neck snapped, and Kyn swung in a wide arch through the smoke clogged air, the dead guard an anchor point. Looping back to the catwalk, he cracked the final guard with the full force of his momentum, tumbling with them to roll in a jumble of limbs across the steel grate. Kyn overpowered the guard easily as they rolled, and he pinned them to the mesh grate with his knees. Self was free of his boot, poised to finish the nights work.

The guard thrashed and fought, bucking wildly in a desperate attempt to dislodge him, eyes wild and desperate behind her HUD visor. She thrashed her head from side to side frantically until her gaze fell upon her companion's body, slumped against the railing, head twisted grotesquely from the chain's whiplash, and she screamed in guttural terror. The enthralled rage had entirely faded and the face behind the visor was a twisted mask of confusion and horror. Her screams quickly faded to a low, animalistic whimper as the realization of what she'd done dawned on her, eclipsing the knife wielding terror above her.

Kyn felt pity tug at him.

The guard coughed. Billowing clouds of multi-hued gases caused by the raging chemical fires had rapidly filled the factory. The gases burned Kyn's eyes, nose, and lungs, but he paid the discomfort no heed as he ripped the guard's helmet and mask from her head. Her struggling grew weaker.

"Why?" She managed to croak. Bloodshot eyes growing hazier with each drug filled inhalation.

Kyn looked down at the guard, silent for a moment. Features that would normally be hawkish and irate had relaxed under the influence of the noxious fumes, her terror slipped away, replaced with a peaceful delirium. He smiled sadly.

"It's nothing personal." He answered, stroking her cheek gently with his free hand. He let the ticks slide by, letting the narcotics hold her, wrapping her in a blissful haze. "Your employer just got noticed by the wrong people, nothing you could do about it."

She looked up at him then, eyes glazed, starring through him, seeing beyond him. Somewhere within her blood-stained and torn uniform, neo-acid rock still played, muffled by the roar of the warehouse burning around them.

"Are you a demon?" The final guard croaked, the question lost in a silencing wet gurgle as Self slashed sideways, and a razor-thin line of crimson blossomed across her throat.

< = >

Kyn landed with feline grace beside Runa. He swayed slightly before clapping her jovially on one thin shoulder, gripping onto her for support. Finished with the guards, he'd taken to scouring the fire-ravaged warehouse, stuffing his waist pack with a choice selection of undestroyed product, all while steadily inhaling the noxious narcotic haze. The burning air roasted his lungs and burned his eyes painfully. His head swam with giddy dizziness, and he giggled childishly, leaning his weight on the diminutive young woman. Runa stood tall and unflinching against his dead weight.

"Having fun?" She asked, her gravel voice muffled behind a gas mask torn from a dead guard.

"We always have fun." Kyn giggled back, poking her in the ribs before linking both arms around her narrow shoulders. He leaned even more of his weight on her, hanging, his legs dragging limp behind them as she stoically continued forward. Confident the rest of the structure would bring itself down on its own accord as it burned; she moved to exit the flaming factory before it collapsed fully on itself with them still inside.

"Carry me," Kyn whined.

"No."

"Please?"

"No."

Runa dragged him across the rubble and into the open air. The cool breeze, moist with rain, eased his burning lungs, and stung at his scorched eyes. Runa grasped one of his clasping fingers in her own and pulled back, breaking the digit with an effortless snap.

"Fuck!" Kyn yelped, releasing her. He stumbled, finding his feet again. "Fine!" He shouted, huffing with flamboyant indignation.

Rain was falling steadily.

Kyn pulled his finger back in place and stood, face tilted towards the sky, eyes closed, reveling in the soothing coolness on his sweltering skin. His head was already clearing and the pain in his hand was gone.

Runa pulled off her mask and tossed it aside, breathing in heavily as she shook out her wild mane of hair.

"Gunna smell like a dead tweeker for a week." She muttered; nose wrinkled in distaste.

The factory gave a sudden crashing roar behind them as the remaining roof collapsed into the center of the raging inferno. Yummy Otter Corp. consuming itself.

There was commotion on the surrounding streets now. Dag troops - athletic young men and women in khaki green uniforms - ran back and forth dragging hoses between them as they jacked into the nearest water main. The rescued Wasters stood huddled to one side, surrounded by a protective ring of Dag troops who stood between them and a clambering throng of media agents. Hovering oni-cams floated above, skimming over rain-soaked heads, lens lights blaring in the dim dawn. An elegant figure stood protectively in front of the scared and shivering Wasters, addressing the collected swarm.

Kyn recognized Alexi's gold-blonde hair. Rain, distance, and the roar of flames drowned out her words.

Ashe watched the assembled crowd from an adjacent door frame. They had donned a matte black overcoat, blending easily with the shadows. Kyn caught their eye and nodded. Dags rushed back and forth, trying to temper the blaze before it could jump to neighboring factories and warehouses.

A ruggedly handsome Dag sprinted by, and Kyn playfully slapped his bouncing glutes as he passed. The man stumbled over his own feet, sandy blonde head whipping around in surprise and confusion. He noticed Kyn and his face blushed with a mix of bemusement and nervous fear before he turned and ran on.

Through the ward stacks the perpetual gray sky was brightening. Kyn's stomach rumbled, he was ravenous.

"You wanna grab food?" Runa asked, echoing his stomach.

Kyn glanced in Ashe's direction, their earlier conversation replaying in his mind. The tension between them had been resolved but he didn't relish the thought of spending any more time around their judgement.

Their accusation still echoed around his mind.

They'd make me hold her down to do it.

Then, the hawkish female guard, her voice wet and gurgling.

Are you a demon?

"No." He replied. "I'm just gunna grab something at Elsynn's and knock out."

His skin ached, suddenly tight; drying blood on his skin. The rain heavy air was clearing his mind with each breath, pushing past the last of its drugged haze. His nerves still felt raw and shaky, the giddy high crashing drastically against the rocks of sobriety. He wanted nothing more than to retreat to his flat alone, wash off the night, and curl around a bowl of spiced breakfast noodles. He could catch the crotchety old soup vendor just as she opened for the morning.

Runa stood silently beside him, arms crossed over her chest, watching the inferno she'd created consume Yummy Otter Corp.

"Kyn? Can I ask you something?" She asked

"Sure kiddo, what's up?" He returned. Alexi was still animatedly holding focus in front of the rapt media agents and their hovering oni.

"Does it ever get easier?" Runa's voice was uncharacteristically small, and her focus didn't shift as she took a sugrstik from her own waist pouch, unwrapped it, and stuck it in her mouth.

Kyn sighed, catching her line of thinking. "I don't know." He answered honestly.

"Is that why you keep disappearing?" She pressed.

"Pretty much, yah." He offered ruefully, knowing it was the closest to the truth he could explain.

Runa was silent again, seeming to mull this over, weighing it against something in her mind before, sighing, she nodded in apparent acceptance.

They parted wordlessly. Runa raising a hand in a half-hearted salute, first two fingertips cocked at the corner of her forehead in farewell, before blending seamlessly into the rushing Dags to join Ashe.

Suddenly heavy, Kyn turned and started a slow jog towards the fire escape of a nearby pre-fab. He tapped through his f-Link, flagging Benn. He'd report in as promised while he made the quick rooftop trip back to his flat in the lower wards. Not like he had much of a choice.

Does it get any easier?

Her voice had betrayed how young she really was. How young he'd been at her age.

Kyn scampered up the squat warehouse prefab as his f-Link swirled and undulated across his arm. Establishing a connection. Mounting the roof, he kept running, picking up the pace, feet pounding slanted roofing slats, the congested stacks of the city's sprawl looming large around him. Gaining the edge, he jumped into empty space, falling through the crisp dawn.

He should have answered her honestly.

No. It never does.

The Loft

Kyn eased open the steel-framed window with his free hand, swinging the industrial pane outward. His other hand gripped the stonework of the rooftop's jutting ledge, feet dangling freely, cracked side street stories below. Window open, he pulled knees to chest, swinging slightly, then unfurled, sliding feet first through the narrow gap with fluid ease.

There were easier ways to enter his loft, but Kyn, striding through the ground entrance, blood strained, clothing torn, and weapons strapped, would raise attention from any of the ragged assortment of tweekers, rejects, knock offs, and glitches that called the run-down pre-fall factory home. Attention Kyn wanted to avoid.

Information was a key commodity in the walled city, easily traded. The right data chunk could be used like credit to those skilled enough to wield it. Secrets - or even half-truths and titillating rumors – were highly valuable resources. Highly valuable and highly dangerous.

In the lowers one was never far from the canny gaze of a charming cultist spy or cutthroat information broker. Someone was always watching, always listening, skulking in the shadows of a ward disk, passing unnoticed on the skytram platform. That's why Kyn liked it. The devils he knew. That stranger smiling seductively across the night market counter? A cultist, faithful to their Sentry cluster, always on the lookout for anti-Unity sentiment, snitching through a convoluted web of fan sites and message boards. The handsome hacker who cuddles up the moment he sees someone new settle in his district? An information broker, buying and selling the types of secrets that kept the inner political machinations of the SPIREs churning. Both highly skilled in their art and keen to pry away the secrets of others by any means necessary.

Trust no one, Kyn knew. Watching eyes were everywhere. Ears at every door. Ghosts in the data.

Guarded was his default. Thus, the unorthodox entrance.

Boots touched poured cement first as he slipped silently through the gap, easing into the dim space. Morning's light had just begun to trickle in through the grimy panes as the sun rose, peeking from behind the low-hanging gray clouds that perpetually hung over the coastal city. Kyn was more fortunate than most in the lower wards; his converted loft caught a precious hour or so of natural light in the early part of the morning, just as the rising sun peaked over the mountains before disappearing behind the city's vertical sprawl. A precious sliver of light that snuck through a gap in the overhead obstruction of revolving ward disks to trickle through the flat's expansive wall of steel-lined windows, holdover from its days as a modular production factory.

Kyn pulled the pane shut behind himself, latching it closed, and padded across the floor. Heavy droplets of water dripped rhythmically from his clothes, forming small puddles in his wake.

The rain had begun to fall even heavier as Kyn had crossed the city, soaking him as he flipped, swung, and leapt his way across the wards; tracing one level to the next. Yet, despite the soaking, he was still in desperate need of a shower. Blood, his and others, still smeared his torn jumpsuit, matted his hair, and caked uncomfortably to his skin.

Overhead runner lights flicked on - internal systems responding to his f-Link's proximity. A dark, pulsing base thrummed through the sound system, bouncing off worn, graffiti covered walls of more poured concrete and reverbing back in echoing waves. He crossed the sparsely furnished space to approach a metal workbench set in one colourfully spray-painted corner, the layers of tags muted and blurred by time. Unstrapping iD from his back, he placed the curved, short sword next to a re-purposed oni. Ego and the full waist pouch followed.

The oni, a patchwork cube of various recycled polymers, chip decks, and patched wires, flickered to life, activating it's holo display. An external street view cycled up, then a perimeter view of the factory as the oni looped through surveillance footage relayed back from thumb-cams Kyn had placed in and around the decommissioned factory when he'd taken up residence. A clear view of the empty corridor on the other side of the loft's heavy steel loading door jumped to a view of the rooftop, then back again to street level.

Kyn tapped the holo, stopping it. Morning activity had begun to ramp up and Elysnn, the old woman who ran the noodle shop across the street, was moving ponderously through the wet morning, heading to open her shop. Stooped against the drizzling rain, she shuffled slowly, leaning heavily on an ornate cane sculpted from of a single length of wrought iron.

Kyn unstrapped his chest harness. In the holo a gangly adolescent male ran blindly from the opposite direction, unaware of the stooped old woman. The youth, obviously a tweeker, his addiction clear in the jerky and twitching way he moved, slammed blindly into the hunched older woman and Kyn groaned in sympathy. The diminutive Elsynn didn't so much as flinch. The gangly youth stumbled backwards, as if bounced off a solid wall, and stared comically before the older woman lashed out with her cane, sweeping the kid's legs out from under him and sending him tumbling to the flooded gutter with a heavy splash.

Kyn lay Self next to the other blades. He kicked off his boots and unzipped his tattered jumpsuit, letting the sopping remains fall to the floor. Stripped to his pink strapped jock, he picked up an oiled rag from the workbench and proceeded to clean each blade, thoroughly polishing away crusted blood as he continued to watch the feed.

Elsynn was whacking the offending tweeker around the ears with her hefty metal cane. The tweeker had thin arms raised in a lame attempt to protect himself. Kyn could hear Elsynn even with the window latched closed, bellowing curses from below. He tossed the rag back down onto the workbench.

Bending at the waist, Kyn peeled away his scant jock. His muscles ached dully, and he groaned softly in protest at the movement. Casually tossing the balled-up undergarment into a clothing strewn corner, he retrieved a thin blue vial from the discarded waist pouch. Naked, he sauntered towards the shower stall, tawny brown skin turning to gooseflesh in the chill air.

Dialing the hydro restriction panel to his daily hygiene limit, he set the blue vial on a buffed stainless-steel counter, and climbed into the steam shower. Warm mist hissed from the nozzle in the ceiling. A button in the tiled wall dispensed a liquid wash that smelt of forest moss and he lathered up the musky scented soap, spreading it over his wet skin.

Are you a demon?

Kyn lathered his hair, working out tangled knots of caked blood, letting the warm mist lull him and soothe his aching muscles. Luxuriating in the feeling of physical exhaustion that hummed through his body.

I know what type of man you are.

Viscerally dark post-fall electro beats thrummed through the sound system, and he tilted his head back, rinsing off the earth scented lather as he willed the pulsing rhythm to fill his mind. Sink into his body and push away the lingering screams that begged at him in voices that clung to the edge of his thoughts like an oily film.

Yorri!

Pleading voices, pained screams, and dying gasps threatened to overwhelm him, vibrating behind closed eyelids, echoing around his skull. He stood motionless under the mist, forehead resting against slate tile as he breathed in a deep, raged breath, focusing on the sensation of water against his skin. He tried to tune out everything except the pulsing of the music, willing the wailing vocals to chase away the reverbing screams. His hands shook uncontrollably, and the nails of his fingers bit painfully into his palms as he balled his hands into fists against the slick stone.

Suddenly, the water flowed shockingly cold, pulling him from echoing memories, and he gasped. The environmental control had dropped the water temperature drastically, signaling he was near the end of his allotted daily reserve.

Kyn dried himself with a ragged towel hung from an exposed pipe. The sink basin was a shallow bowl of black marble set in the stainless-steel counter, and he ran a forearm over the fogged polyplex mounted above. The mirrored surface lit up, reflecting back his wet nakedness. Steel cold gray eyes stared back at him through a slash of freckles.

He poured out an expensive moisturizer into his palm - a gift from Ashe - and worked it into his brown skin. The oil smelt of sea salt and driftwood and left his skin glistening smooth. A styling cream worked his unruly fringe into something presentable. He admired himself briefly, before, satisfied, he cinched the thin towel around his hips and plucked the purple blue vial from the polished counter. He cracked the stopper and poured out a thin, line of sparkling indigo.

"May my actions bring praise to my SPIRE." He recited solemnly, keeping steady eye contact with himself in the reflective polyplex. "My blood for my SPIRE. My body for my Sentry. My devotion to The Unity."

He bent over the burnished metal, hand to nose, and snorted the line in one, sharp inhale.

Kyn sighed as the Blue Eclipse slammed into the back of his nostril, burning with a pleasant sharpness. Waves of ecstasy coursed through him, and his pupils expanded, the dim light brightening as his head swam with giddiness and a buzzing warmth built in his chest. Blue electricity danced playfully under the surface of his skin. He ran his fingers over the tautness of his chest, pads of his fingertips sliding over the smooth musculature. He traced the sharp line of his pectoral, pausing to brush teasingly past a hardened nipple.

Eyes closed with pleasure he tweaked himself; the Blue Eclipse heightened tactile stimulation, flooding his nerves. He purred, deep in the back of his throat. He could feel himself stiffening against the towel.

"Kyn!"

A muffled voice shouted his name, followed by a heavy, metallic bang against the loft's loading bay door.

A rumbling growl of frustration built in the back of Kyn's throat, and he stopped the slow southward drift of his hand even as his fingers brushed coyly at his curling pubes.

More banging.

The Blue Eclipse had a nasty temper and it pulsed in Kyn's veins, alert to any potential threat, urging him to gut anyone rude enough to interrupt him without reason. He slammed aside the shower stall door and stormed over to check the cycling oni feed.

"Kyn!"

More banging. He snatched Ego from the workbench.

Kyn hovered the feed over his front entrance. A hooded figure, tall and thin, was banging rapidly against the other side of the heavy steel door. The figure turned to snatch a furtive glance behind themselves, and Kyn easily recognized them by their stooped shoulders, and the shock of acid-green punk-hawk that poked out from under a hooded cowl.

Deciding against Ego, Kyn dropped the dagger back to the workbench and snatched up Self, smoothly concealing the stiletto as he folded the thin towel even lower on his hips, and stalked barefoot over to the heavy door.

"Kyn! Come on. I know you can see me out here."

Kyn slid the loading door open with an annoyed jerk and reached out into the grimy corridor to grasp the hooded figure by the collar. He swung them inside before forcefully slamming the door shut again with a resounding *clang*.

"Fucking finally!" Alec gasped. His hood fell back, revealing a startled, but handsome face, diamond shaped and fine featured under a spikey plume of acid-green hair.

Alec moved to raise a hand, but Kyn stopped him. Expertly shifting his grip from the taller man's collar to his wrist, he gave the joint a swift twist, folding Alec's arm against himself as he pushed the taller man backwards into a graffiti covered wall, easily restraining the unannounced visitor with one hand.

"Oy!" Alec struggled briefly. The fingers of his free hand twitched, intent to pry himself free.

Kyn struck, pinning the twitching hand flat against the concrete with lightning speed. He sensually leveraged one thigh between the other man's legs, knee within striking distance of tender areas.

"'ey Alec, I don't remember inviting you." Kyn grilled, voice a low, husky growl. He brushed his lips along the line of the other man's sharply defined jaw. The course fabric of the thin towel ground against Alec's the synth-leather clad hips. He nipped play-fully at the jawbone with his teeth.

"Oy!" Alec yelped again. He arched his back against Kyn's restraining grasp, mimicking his pelvic grinding.

"Little early to be tweeking out, eh?" He chided; breath hot in Kyn ear. The tone was playfully teasing, but he could sense the disapproval beneath the forced brightness.

Kyn pulled back, relaxing his grip, and looked Alec full in the face, deadpan.

"I'm not." He answered, serious. His regenerative abilities had already processed the powerful narcotic, rapidly purging the drug from his body, leaving only a cold aching emptiness behind. Within moments he wouldn't even have that.

Alec regarded him, silent for a tick. His eyes, the green of micro-chips, studied him intently, before, seemingly satisfied, he smiled warmly. Reaching up with a freed hand, Alec ran his fingers affec-tionately through Kyn's auburn hair, brushing the fringe away from his forehead.

Kyn squirmed away from the intimate gesture, the unruly fringe falling back into place. Attempting to cover his sudden discomfort, he stepped back and crossed his arms over his naked chest and leveled a no-nonsense glare at the handsome man.

"Speaking of early." He grilled, shifting the dynamic. "Why are you here? What's going on?"

"What? Can't I drop in?" Alec returned, "I figured you'd be up. Thought maybe I'd tempt ya with some breakfast." He shrugged his slouched shoulders, expression open and honest, hands spread wide, appeasing. Alec stood and approached the world in a way that inferred an endearingly naive shyness. "Maybe tempt you with some of those spicy noodles you like so much."

It was an act.

Kyn made a show of slowly looking the other man up and down with sexually teasing appraisal.

Tall, lanky, with long legs and narrow hips, usually clad in worn, retro-tight rocker leggings, the acid-haired hacker struck a rakishly sexy figure. A hooded moss green vest hugged his lean torso, sleeveless, exposing muscular arms adorned with a cluttered assortment of tech augment tattoos; the purpose of which Kyn had narrowed down about half of. Some he theorized were just purely decoration. More tattoos traced a delicate neck. A rose tangled in a circuit board. Fish swimming through repeating geometric patterns.

Kyn settled his gaze pointedly over the substantial bulge of the other man's crotch. Alec's microchip green eyes flashed hungrily.

"Tempt me you say?" He teased slyly, lips twitched in a seductive grin. He slunk in closer, casually dropping his arms from across his chest as he grabbed firmly onto the other man's hips. He breathed deeply. Alec always smelt crisply of electricity; the sharp clean smell of burnt ozone, hovering over his skin. Now the familiar metallic scent was cut with the faint musk of dried sweat. He'd been running. Somewhere or from something. Kyn breathed in deep. The added masculine musk was arousing, contrasting sharply against the crackling scent of ozone. He drew his tongue in a long deliberate line, tracing Alec's slender neck, tasting salt and stopping to nibble suggestively at an earlobe. He could feel Alec stiffening against him.

They were both breathing heavily now.

"I'm gunna blow you now. You okay with that?" Kyn asked, flashing an impish grin. Alec's eyes lit up, and he nodded his enthusiastic consent.

Kyn tugged roughly at the hacker's restrictive breeches, sliding them down muscular legs as he sunk greedily to his knees. He grasped firmly onto the other man's taut glutes.

Alec tensed under his hands, inhaling sharply with a pleasured gasp, and slumped heavily against the graffitied wall, resting his back into the concrete. He let out a moan of pleasure and relaxed one hand absently on Kyn's head, playing languidly with the kneeling man's hair.

< = >

Kyn slurped greedily, head tipped back to suck down the last warm drops of deliciously spicy fluid. His insides warmed pleasantly. Slamming his empty noodle bowl down, he pushed back from the sticky plastic top - stool tipped precariously - and let out a loud, contented burp.

Alec, next to him along the noodle shop's high service counter, covered his own mouth to stifle a laugh, and shook his head.

Kyn yelped, sudden and sharp. Elsynn's wrought metal cane had slammed down, painfully catching him across the hand, crushing his fingers into the counter with a heavy *thud*. Instinctively, he snatched his hand back, hissing in pain as he reeled backwards, off balance. Saving him, Alec reached out protectively and grabbed onto the low back of the stool, stopping Kyn's fall, and pushed the chair back on its legs.

'Ya glitch'd twit should keep some fuckin' manners, we got fucking, kids 'ere." Elysnn barked peevishly across the counter. A glowing menu holo scrawled across the wall behind. The wizened woman took another wide swing at Kyn, wielding the heavy metal cane with a firm two-handed grip, aimed for his head. The joint motors of the black and white polymer bionic prosthetic that served as her left arm whirred softly.

Saved from his near tumble, Kyn nimbly dodged the incoming swing to crouch behind Alec. He sucked at his crushed fingers, other hand cupped protectively to hide the rapidly healing damage.

"My manners? I think you're the sole educator of off colour language for the whole lower ward. Generations of rejects have learned to curse at your knee!" He shot back, gesturing to the collected groups of youths of varying ages crowded into booths around the narrow noodle shop, and loitering outside the shop window. This early in the day, they all should have been attending one of the Unity sponsored vocational education programs, learning how to become productive members of society, indoctrinating in solid social habits. So that one day, their children's, children's children would have a slim chance at a spot in the mid-wards.

If they lived long enough to survive the next culling, and the one after that.

Eschewing the normative system, the groups that hung around places like Elsynn's chose instead to spend their time and efforts focused on honing skills that would benefit their lives more materially in the immediate future. Hacking, hustling, streetcraft. Learning the flow of working under Unity radar. Skills that could secure them comfort and security, gilding to the harsh realities of life in the lower wards. Elsnn's was where the best biohackers, data brokers, sliders, and cryptos of the wards got their start.

Me. M. E.

Of course, it's me, who else would it be?

It's gunna be.

Its gonna, it's gunna, it's gunna be. Me

Sugary pop blasted from a nearby molded plastic booth, crowded with sour faced youth. Kyn groaned inwardly recognizing the hottest new bop trending the link feed.

I promise there's no one better than me. Oh, oh oh

Who could need anyone else but me?

Kyn glanced towards the booth. The f-Link projected figure of Alexi, dressed in varying hues of pastel purples and blues, hung between the huddled group. The Sentry bopped against a backdrop of unicorns, and sparkling waterfalls as she mouthed along with the earworm lyrics, regularly flashing the camera a manufactured coy expression.

Of course, it's me, who else would it be?

It's always me. No. one. But. ME!

Me. me. me. me. me

Kyn rolled his eyes. This group was doomed to be die-hard Alexi cultists.

Absolutely devoted to a single celebrity facet of the Unity, cultists adored the celebrity personas, obsessing over their chosen Sentry like they were the only that gave life meaning. Living and breathing every aspect of their chosen Sentry's lives as if they were divine, the cultist blindly consumed everything their Sentry produced. Emulation as an act of worship. An act for which their gods spoke to them. Through the holos the personae promised rewards for their devotion. Forums were clogged with subs devoted to the fandom. Cultists linked in to share in their devotion, while trading gossip and information pertaining to their Sentry's perceived competitor's and enemies, real or otherwise.

Kyn rubbed the back of his fingers together, lighting up his f-Link. Thumb drumming, he disrupted the wannabe-cultist feed, seamlessly syncing in a pre-fall server vid-loop of a loudly bleating goat that interjected itself at iconic moments of the song.

Baaahhhaaaaa

The gaggle of youth hissed and cursed. One, a shaved headed female clad in a look reminiscent of Alexi's 'wild lowers scumming days,' flipped him a rude hand gesture.

Kyn responded in elaborate pantomime - welcoming the gesture as a precious gift he stored in the pocket of his torn retro-denim. He turned back to Elysnn and Alec, gesturing at the offending youth with mock incredulity.

"See what I mean? Foul, every one of them."

Elysnn glared and turned her attention back to the batch of noodles she'd been hand pulling. She pulled the doughy carb paste fed from the food synthesizer, twisting, stretching, and folding it into long strands, then cutting them definitively with a square blade attachment that unfolded from the matte polymer of her prosthetic. She tossed the thick strands into a wok of bubbling spiced oil. The doughy carb hissed. Kyn used the opportunity to slip back into his seat.

"You're an ass." Elsynn growled at him.

Kyn smiled back sweetly over the greasy counter.

"...We have taken them into our protection. They will be well taken care of. Warm food, shelter, and medical services, will be available within the safe walls of Noav SPIRE. Once recovered from their trying experience we will then supply them with societal re-education, housing placements and vocational training in the resource acquirement camps of the habitable zone's inner ring..."

Alexi's voice was not coming from the booth now. Alec had changed the projection scroll behind Elysnn to a news stream, and the Alexi devotees had fallen silent to stare rapturously at the wrapping feed.

"...so they can join other recent refugees we have welcomed from the Wastes. We are lucky to welcome them into the loving protection of The Unity."

Alexi stood front and center, surrounded by disheveled Wasters. A raging fire consumed a factory in the background.

Kyn could feel Alec's eye on him. The hacker was staring, not even pretending to show interest in the feed. Kyn kept his expression neutrally disinterested, showing no indication that he recognized the scene.

"These brave souls have suffered greatly, not only the cruelty of the Dividers, but then to suffer the further indignity of unsanctioned forced labor at the hands of the Yummy Otter Corp."

Alexi was, as always, polished to a sheen. The picture of selfless altruism. Her cascading gold-blonde hair fell in silken waves around her heart shaped face. Large azure eyes, wet with restrained tears, bored holes into Kyn through the holo. Her voice quivered with emotion.

"But now the luck of these miraculous souls has changed! They are truly blessed that the Unity was here to save them from the horrific accident that occurred here this morning."

The feed snapped, replaced by a re-run of a popular battle-pit competition. The wannabe cultist youths instantly lost interest and returned to gossiping loudly amongst themselves. Kyn watched the combatants wail on each other mercilessly, trying to appear absorbed in the old episode.

The winner of the season had been legendary a few cycles back. Survived twelve straight matches, and racking up a kill count in the low sixties, securing himself legendary status in battle-pit fandom. Kyn remembered the season finale. The victor narrowly survived the final battle-pit to be crowned victor, before finally being awarded the coveted grand prize - residence clearance for the upper wards.

The lower wards had erupted in celebration that night. Honoring the first lowers combatant to win entrance into the uppers in living memory.

Weeks later, rumors had begun to circulate surrounding the nature of the champion's relationship with a popular, buxom pro-prop model who'd gained fame and popularity during her very public affair with Alyn. Cultists had spotted her and the battle pit champ, meeting in secret, assumed romantically. Nothing to it, the rumors soon died out, quickly loosing public interest.

Then Kyn had been sent to send a message.

Alec rhythmically drummed his fingers on the service top, fidgeting as he stared silently at Kyn, eyes wide and expectant. He leaned in conspiratorially, pitching his voice low.

"What are they like?"

Elysnn was ignoring them, the old woman's attention focused on seasoning a vat of broth, simultaneously barking orders at the cluster of youths who washed dishes in the shop's narrow kitchen.

"Who?" Kyn asked innocently, looking sidelong at the hacker.

The battle-pit champ had been found, pitched off his own balcony. Apparent OD dry dive.

"Oh, come on, you know."

"I really don't."

"Come on. You don't have to be coy with me, I know you work with them."

"Who?" Kyn feigned dumb.

Alec rolled his eyes and leaned in even closer to whisper loudly in Kyn's ear.

"The Sentry, duh." His breath was hot and smelled of spiced broth. "The Unity? It's obvious you know Alexi. The way you pretend to act so calm whenever she comes up. I can see right through you."

"Clever." Kyn purred. He slid a hand between Alec's thighs to cup the other man's crotch, and gave the bulge a playful squeeze. "But I don't do females, or did you forget that already?"

"Please, you'd never pass as mate bait, you're the biggest glitch I know."

"Fuckin' right."

"It's probably the brother. Alyn. Hot snack that one."

Kyn suppressed a shiver of disgust. He covered by spinning his stool to look Alec square in the face, a sly smile on his lips.

"I don't kiss and tell." He countered.

After several heated, non-conversational, couplings in the toilet stalls and backrooms of glitch clubs across the lower wards, Kyn had finally fed Alec a story about being a sold sex servo gone freelance after the sudden death of his elderly owner. Dropping hints about easily leveraging old contacts after buying out his contract in order to secure a steady stream of high-end clientele within the secretive, and hypocritical cliques of the upper ward's elite.

It was close enough to the truth. Except the freedom part.

The cover was an easy lie. The story wore like a second skin. An easy way to explain away sudden and lengthy absences, access to the mid and upper wards, and a steady flow of credits.

"Please, I've traded enough favors with you to know, that is a blatant lie." Alec shot back.

"Never names." Kyn conceded. "That would be an act of career suicide and you know it."

Though he'd tell anyone he was just a lowly freelance code-hack, underappreciated for his talent and genius, Alec was in actuality, an agent for the Informant; the most powerful, independent information broker across any of the wards. Oddly, this was no secret to anyone who knew the hacker.

Kyn had clocked the spy easily when they'd first met. Alec attempted leveraging an initial attraction between them by attempting to seduce Kyn. An attempt made out of tradecraft instinct or direct orders, Kyn had never know, but he'd played along, enjoying both the attention and the distraction. The acid-haired punk had proven to be a skilled sexual partner, always up for a good time; he had a knack for making Kyn laugh and genuinely seemed to show an interest in his well-being.

Though, at times the hacker tried to pry a little too hard behind Kyn's wall of defenses. A habit that was extremely dangerous for him. Kyn had been sent to kill Informant agents in the past. Many times. All in the protection of the Sentry's secrets.

He could never let Alec find out about who he really was. It would put the handsome idiot in too much danger. Besides, he'd grown fond of Alec, developing a close friendship based on required lies and half-truths.

This had made his cover doubly useful. Supplying a plausible source from which to subtly feed Alec the steady stream of rumors and gossip that kept him distracted from the truth of Kyn's reality. All under the guise of the inter client intrigues of the upper elites. In turn, Alec supplied Kyn with intel that escaped the net of his SPIRE contacts - thus, the hacker proved useful, yet harmless to anyone who happened to take too keen notice of their relationship. Keeping Alec close, keeping him fed on small lies, kept him alive.

"Fine, play dumb." Alec sighed, abandoning the effort. He pushed his empty noodle bowl aside and rested his forearms on the sticky top. A spiraling tattoo that wound around his left bicep glowed with a dull purple light. At the same moment, a mousey girl with deep brown skin and spikey short-cropped hair came rushing around the counter's corner. Stopping by the pair she stood on tip toes to stretch child thin arms above her head, reaching up to collect the discarded soup bowls from the high top. Large brown eyes threatened to overtake most of her small face.

Alec was staring straight ahead; eyes glazed over, fingers of one hand rhythmically tapping at the air, reading, and responding to something on his optic feed.

Kyn smiled at the girl and gave her a small wave. Her round face split with an excitedly toothy grin. A small scar above her lip, evidence of a cheap or poorly done dermal graft to fix some harmless birth defect, gave her smile an endearingly lopsided goofiness.

Kyn held out his own empty bowl for the girl, and she scrambled over to collect it. The child moved with a knock-kneed gawkiness caused by mismatched shoes. Canvas and soft rubber, in two blazingly opposing colour schemes, the heel of one was slightly higher than the other - probably the best pair she could scavenge. Her clothes were several sizes too big, worn, but clean. The waist band of her threadbare skirt wrapped and tied several times to keep it from slipping off. Too young for dermal implanting, she wore a patched and busted looking f-Link bracelet, a patchwork of refurbished parts that wrapped around her thin wrist. The tech appeared self-made, foraged from other broken down and cast-off pieces of the original cheap tech. Parts easily found in any mass dumping site, probably from the same place she'd found the shoes.

"Did you fix that up yourself?" He asked, drawing her attention to the cuff.

The girl blushed shyly, but nodded her head enthusiastically, beaming with pride.

"Good with tech?"

She nodded again, goofy smile grown even larger, the genuine expression bright and refreshing. The older children that hung around Elysnn's treated the adults that came through with weary distrust. Often for good reason.

"What else do you like?" Kyn asked.

"Tracing!" The girl answered in an excited high-pitched squeak. She immediately threw her hands over her mouth, as if surprised by her own voice.

"Tracing?!? Me too!" Kyn beamed back at her, matching her excited tone.

He thought back to his earlier, rainy trip across the city, how he'd reveled in the deceptive sense of freedom that leaping from building to rooftop, and across wards levels allowed him. Her interest was no surprise, ward tracing - or stack running - was a common physical outlet for the lower wards' gangs of abandoned children. They could be seen scurrying around in packs, leaping between stacks, weaving above the crowded streets. Agile and fearless in the way only children can be, there were few places within the bounds of the lower wards the little urchins couldn't reach if they wanted. It was one of the main reasons Elysnn let them hang about. Eyes and ears everywhere.

"Where do you like to go?" Kyn pressed.

"Well, I can't go very far, or very high yet." She replied, excitement at having a shared interest ramping her energy. "But mostly I just go through the alleys, up the ward exit lookout. I'm real fast though! Faster than all the kids my age! Even some older ones!"

"Good!" Kyn encouraged. He had used the conversation to lead the urchin back to the sanitizer, collecting dishware as they went.

"Make sure it stays that way too." He instructed firmly, depositing the bowls. He crouched down to her eye level, mischievous smile wide. "Don't want them getting comfortable. They gotta know - no matter how good they think they are, there is always a girl who can beat 'em."

"I bet I could run faster than you!" The girl squealed, excitement transforming earlier meek shyness into brash loudness.

"Ya think so?" Kyn returned, egging her on. "Should we race?"

"Yah!" The girl jumped up and down excitedly.

"Okay. But first you gotta do something." He instructed, suddenly serious. The girl stopped her excited jumping and listened, quit and intent. Kyn moved the first two fingers of his right hand across the back of his left, swiping in the direction of her cobbled f-Link. His own flashed neon blue three times before hers responded in kind.

"You gotta get yourself some new shoes first." He instructed, pointing at her mismatched feet. "And you've gotta train really, really hard." He added, mischievous grin growing wider. He winked. "I'm very fast."

The spikey-haired girl's eyes widened in silent disbelief as she scanned the bracelet's small holo, seeing the credit sum he'd encoded into a flash transfer. Kyn pressed a discretionary finger to his lips.

"'oy! Leave the rejects to their work!" Elysnn barked at him. The craggy old woman had been watching the interaction out of the corner of her eye. "They work for their supper."

She glared menacingly, but Kyn knew it was all for show. He could see the ghost of a smile twitch at the edges of her wrinkled mouth.

"You're one of the good one's Elysnn." He chirped back at her, skipping back around the counter. He swiped the payment for their meal in her direction. The f-Link installed in her bionic arm blinked green in response. Kyn sauntered back to Alec. The hacker was giving him an appraising look.

"You made a little friend."

"Brat stole my chit. I had to shake her down to get it back."

"No one's carried a chit since two ten-cycles back."

"I'm retro."

"You're a softie."

"Fuck off I'm not. Maybe it's just my biological clock ticking."

They stepped out of Elysnn's and into crowded pedestrian street traffic. It was creeping towards mid-day and the morning's drizzle had finally stopped. Runoff from the mid and upper wards crashed down from above in unpredictable waves of dirty rainwater. Cascades of gutter trash and sewage that fell from the rotating platforms and connective structures spanning the sky above them, soaking the unlucky below.

Alec skipped around a puddle as he strode to outpace Kyn. Turning, he grabbed the shorter man by the shoulders to stop him in his tracks.

"I hate that I need to ask this, because you can never be sure with you." He pressed, deadpan serious. "But are you aware you are incapable of conceiving a child? You do know that's not how human biology works?"

"What do you mean?" Kyn blinked with wide eyed innocence.

Alec scoffed, an affectionate smile splitting his face.

The street rumbled and bucked beneath them.

Kyn looked around, playfulness gone. The street rumbled again, pitched. Ward platforms groaned alarmingly above.

Something exploded somewhere in the distance with a deafening roar. Then everything broke into chaos.

The street beneath Kyn's feet rolled with another asphalt splitting rumble, like a wave, as the distant explosion sent a concussive sound blast ripping through the air. Alec clapped hands over his ears. Slivers of glass, polyplex, and torn sheet metal flew through the air, ripped from store fronts and residential prefabs. The ward stacks above groaned laboriously.

Then, everything was still. Silent. Nothing moved. Every person on the street stood, frozen. Terrified animals prepared to bolt. The air buzzed with anxious anticipation.

The silence stretched unbearably.

Then, the screaming started.

Kyn spun. Every advo on the street, every holo feed, every pro-prop, was now showing the same image.

RAGE. RAGE. RAGE. RAGE. RAGE. RAGE. RAGE. RAGE. RAGE. RAGE. RAGE. RAGE. RAGE. RAGE. RAGE. RAGE. RAGE. RAGE.

Four block letters, deep crimson red against a flat black title card.

Then, just as suddenly as it had appeared, the image was gone, and the screaming stopped.

In the emptiness, panic erupted.

Source of the tremors and explosion unknown, Kyn could see no visible threat. Just a sudden surge of people fleeing in blind terror. Stampeding throngs ran for safety in every direction. No one knew where the danger was, or even if it was coming, but everyone had the same plan. Run.

Kyn was thrown to one side as a petite woman barreled into him, shoving him aside in her rush to get off the street. He stumbled away from Alec and into a burly man thundering in the opposite direction. Off balance, he stumbled sideways. Electric discharge crackled, followed closely by a howl of pain and the unmistakable *thump* of a body slumping heavily to the street.

Spinning on the ball of one foot, Kyn regained his balance with ease, just in time to watch a fist sized, hovering gold-plated ball - Sophia - launch a short electric pulse at another approaching stampeder. The branching burst of electricity arched through the air, hitting the man directly in the chest, halting his charge instantly. He dropped, convulsing, to the pavement, steps from stampeding into Kyn.

Kyn nodded his thanks to Sophia. The spherical drone blinked an acid-green light at him in recognition – a hovering fist-sized ball of mirror polished golden chrome - before zipping away to join the three other spheres that orbited Alec's body. Sophia slipped into sync with her sisters - Rose, Dorothy, and Blanche - completing the four-point circuit, and a dazzling link of electricity jumped between them, spawning a spinning barrier of crackling blue electricity that encircled Alec. Debilitating sparks leapt at anyone who dared get too close to the hacker, forcing the stampeding crowd to flow around him.

"Thanks girls!" Kyn quipped to the drones, ducking under their protective orbit to stand back-to-back with Alec, knees loose, hands ups, in a light defensive crouch. He warily scanned the charging crowds. Most were running for safety, trampling each other to get scarce first, desperate to get off the streets. Motionless bodies littered the cracked asphalt.

"So, your place or mine?" Alec yelled, trying to be heard over the chaos. The screaming had stopped, only to be replaced by the crashing and banging of desperate people trying to force their way into street-level shops and residences. Owners, forced to defend their property, fought them away. Weapons discharged and security doors crashed, echoing again and again through the stacks.

"Neither." Kyn answered absently, suddenly distracted.

A group of children who'd been hustling the crowded streets around the noodle shop had scrambled to the safety of the neighboring rooftops and supports when the chaos started. But, as the heavily interwoven infrastructure of the city above gave another laborious groan, they'd scrambled back down and were trying to push their way back through the streets towards the safety of Elysnn's. One young boy stumbled, falling. Adult boots trampled him, and the boy let out a pained yelp, curling into himself. He caught the pointed tip of a woman's pump to the gut.

"Make a path!" Kyn ordered Alec.

"You heard him girls!" The hacker whooped to his circling bots. Two fingers pressed to his lip, he blew, letting out a shrill whistle. Four dots tattooed on the back of his hand glowed golden yellow. The dots shifted, flowing smoothly across his skin. The drones mirrored the glowing augment, breaking apart and reforming into two straight lines of crackling energy that spanned the street, fencing a safe corridor for the fleeing children, Alec and Kyn down the middle. Electricity crackled as rioters slammed into this new barrier, incapacitated by the watchful bots.

Fleeing children streamed past, older ones carrying or dragging the younger. The old woman had her door open wide, ushering the children towards the safety of an open hatch in the worn linoleum.

The downed boy was struggling, trying to pull himself up. Kyn rushed to him. The child's face was twisted in a grimace, teeth gritted in desperate determination against pain. One arm was bruised and bloodied, held protectively against his ribs.

Crouching low Kyn hoisted the boy over his shoulder and turned, sprinting back in the direction of Elysnn's. The boy hissed in pain. Kyn ran past Alec, who quickly fell in behind, protective drone entourage snapping into formation at his back, covering their rear with a shield of crackling energy.

Elysnn slammed the street door shut behind them with a solid thud.

Safely in the shop, Kyn unloaded the boy from his shoulder and gently lay him on the sticky rolled tile. An older cultist girl hustled to the boy's side, a concerned panic clear on her face. She jabbed the boy with a inject-unit. Kyn recognized the common knock-off brand of a reparative med and pain killer hybrid. The boy's pinched face relaxed almost instantly, his eyes gone glassy as he slipped into a blissed-out haze.

Outside the shop's polyplex front, the nature of the chaos was shifting. The stampeding mob had cleared, leaving only those keen to turn the chaos to their advantage. The whooping of looters echoed through the streets and crossways above.

Kyn looked down at the boy. The older girl had propped him into a seated position, back against the service counter, his childishly stubby legs stretched out in front. The boy's head nodded towards his chest, a blissful narcotic smile on his dirt-streaked face, peacefully unaware. The bruising on his arm was already fading thanks to the girl's medicine. She sat next to him, gently stroking his hair, and when she caught Kyn watching, she nodded to him in thanks, pulling the boy closer.

"Alright, everyone down the hole!" Elysnn called loudly, motioning for them to join the others down the bunker latch. She'd activated the automated defense system and corrugated blast shielding blanked the windows. She moved to slam the door's mag-lock into place, sealing them in.

"Hold up! I have to get back out there." Kyn interrupted. He motioned for Alec.

"Like fuck you are!" Elysnn shot back. "This is bad, whatevers happened. It ain't gunna be a simple culling. They're gunna want who did this."

"What she said." Alec agreed, joining the protest. The lanky hacker was pacing anxiously. "The Unity will turn the city upside down looking for anyone involved...in whatever happened." He shook his head in disbelief. He tugged at his acid-green punk-hawk as he paced. "These Ragers are fucked, tripped this time. Do we even know what that explosion was? Do those idiots even care that they're bringing the Unity's wrath down on all of us?"

"That's why I've got to go," Kyn countered, interrupting Alec's panicked rambling. His tone didn't invite argument.

A loosely affiliated group of intranet anarchists, the Ragers were strongly anti-Unity. Long considered more incompetent than threat, they'd previously been content with staging inefficient marches and disruptive protests. Occasionally daring members had waged brief bouts of cyber terrorism against the SPIREs, causing minor economic damage to the city, but those incidents were brief and easily crushed. Any serious acts of insurrection where easily spotted by the Unity's intelligence web before they could become reality. Cut down before truly dangerous plots hit beyond the planning stages. The Ragers were so ineffective against the status quo that Alec had once waxed to Kyn his theory that the whole thing might just be a Unity ploy in the first place. Their own designed and controlled boogieman. An elaborate hoax designed to teach the population how futile rebellion against their saviors really was.

Something had changed.

Whatever the Ragers' previous inadequacy, what they had just done was very real. Kyn didn't know what the target had been, but he'd never experienced anything like that explosion in his entire life within the walled city. Not to mention the blanket hack. That alone would've taken some serious skill and power.

The Unity had been caught with their pants down, humiliated in the public sphere. Their illusion of total infallibility shaken. Kyn knew, with a dreadful certainty that crept up his spine, that nothing about this was going to end well.

The Sentry had probably already convened, determining the Unity's next course of action. Dags would be dispatched, descending on the lower wards with brutal efficiency. They'd target anyone even rumored to have affiliation with the Ragers, disappearing anyone who might offer up useful information under interrogation, and killing others as a warning against future insurgency.

"You gunna go shack up with an upper client?" Alec spat, accusingly. "Ride this out in style? Safe with a collar? Watch us from above while the Dags kill us?"

Kyn's fists clenched. Alec had no idea how close to the truth he was. He had to let the taller man think that he was fleeing in fear, had to let him keep his disgusted assumptions. It was better than the truth. Safer.

Kyn shot a look to Elysnn, ignoring Alec. "Get everyone downstairs, lock down." He ordered. "Assume standard culling protocols. Mask signals, and don't let anyone in, have the kids monitor intranet feeds for change."

"'Ay, ain't need to tell me. I've been livin' down here lot longer than you." The old woman griped dryly. "Survived a lot worse than this as well. Hell'va lot worse than you."

"Doubt that." Kyn returned. His gaze didn't waver from the old woman's heavily creased face, inviting her to read the truth in his steel gray eyes. "Though I don't doubt you've been around - met a lot of different types."

The implication hung between them. Lowering her gaze, Elysnn nodded.

"You're right there." She muttered, hustling away the last few children that huddled around the shop, ushering them down the floor hatch to the bunker below. "Lucky for me the worst take a liking to my cooking." She muttered, shuffling after. She disappeared down the hatch, leaving Alec to lock up.

"Weird." Alec observed. "Weird convo. Weird exchange." He bent, scooping up the unconscious boy in his arms, the cultist girl hovered near.

The sight of the handsome hacker, cradling the unconscious form protectively to his chest, triggered an uncomfortable fluttering in Kyn's chest. He wished sharply for a brief moment that he could stay. He bit the inside of his cheek, repressing the emotion efficiently. Alec was looking at him with a mixture of sadness and pity. The hacker shifted uncomfortably, unsure of what to say, his fist sized orbs floated dutifully behind him.

Not giving him a chance to speak, Kyn turned on his heel and threw the shop door open, striding out into the now almost deserted street. Sensing the coming Unity forces, rioters had sought shelter, and the looters had moved on. Kyn crossed the body strewn street, moving briskly towards the run-down modular factory, the clunk of Alec dropping security locks heavy behind him.

Kyn sighed. He knew he shouldn't let Alec get in his head - the two had no obligations to each other - but he still didn't like letting the other man assume the worst of him. That he was like so many others in the lower wards, abandoning his friends the moment danger loomed. It couldn't be helped, Kyn knew, he shouldn't even be getting close to anyone in the first place. He was an Envoy, his first duty would always be to his Sentry and the Unity.

Alec and the others would be safer away from him.

A message from Runa flashed urgently in the corner of Kyn's optic. Tapping his fingers, he opened it.

It's the wall. They hit the fucking wall.

He read the short message twice, absorbing it, letting the implications sink in.

The towering steel wall that encircled the city had stood for longer than anyone living could remember. Built by the founding Unity members, it had stood for centuries as impenetrable protection against the ravaged world beyond. More so then even the soaring SPIREs, the wall was a symbol of the Unity's unshakeable power. An attack on the wall was a serious blow.

Kyn focused a portion of his optic to compartmentalize, running scans on intranet chatter. Patterns quickly emerged in the scrolling green code. Panic was catching. Wild theories and conspiracies already being born, spinning off into the void left by a lack of official information. With a portion of the wall down, fear of an imminent attack by the dreaded Dividers was spreading, quickly becoming the main topic of all news threads. Growing panic propagated. Despite no evidence of activity over the past five ten-cycles, fear of the ancient enemy, the constant shadowy threat beyond the mountains, was spreading like chemical fire.

Kyn turned, suddenly alert to the whirring hum of an approaching transpo. He stopped in the middle of the street as it came into view, taking a sharp corner, then hurtled towards him, taking little care to avoid the scattered casualties. Kyn calmly faced down the oncoming vehicle.

Close to smearing the Envoy across the cracked pavement, the transpo swerved at the last tick, solar engine screeching in protest, and slid to a stop in front of Kyn. The vehicle's door lifted to reveal Benn, his face its usual mask of inscrutable blankness.

"Good timing." Kyn remarked. "I was just coming to find you."

The factory door flew open and Kyn turned. A sharply dressed man, his bald head gleamingly pale, had strode out, and was descending the cement front stairs slowly, Kyn's loaded weapons harness slung casually over one shoulder.

A sudden coldness gripped Kyn's gut. "Why is he here?" He asked Benn calmly.

Benn didn't reply.

A pain that didn't start in any specific place invaded Kyn's every cell, and he stiffened, every nerve suddenly and instantaneously alight with agony. A tortured scream caught in his pain constricted throat. Spasming, he was unable to escape the all-consuming pain. Agony clenched his jaw shut. Teeth bit through his tongue. A drop in the endless sea of screaming torment. Frozen in place, he convulsed.

The bald man filled Kyn's vision. Round face looming large, eyes a blazing crimson, he watched the gray eyed Envoy shake uncontrollably.

Kyn's vision grew hazier. Somewhere, outside the red rimmed corner of his vision, he was faintly aware of Benn swinging open the transpo's rear storage compartment. The bald man's breath was hot against Kyn's ear.

"May my actions bring praise to my SPIRE." The whispered voice was jagged and harsh. "My blood for my SPIRE. My body for my Sentry. My devotion to The Unity."

Pain clenched Kyn's every nerve like razor wire. He was screaming without sound. Blood-tinged darkness pressed in.

All the blood vessels in his eyes had burst.

The last thing Kyn saw, before the darkness and pain finally stretched wide and swallowed him whole, was the crimson glow of the bald man's eyes.

Two Men in a Room

Kyn woke with a jolt, slammed by a torrent of freezing cold water.

Gasping sharply with shock, eyes wide, he sputtered, choking on the icy blast that pummeled him. Then, just as suddenly as it had started, the water stopped, and he shivered violently against the sudden chill.

He was swinging pendulously, his shoulders and wrists aching dully. The pain cut through the foggy haze that clouded his mind. Alert, he looked around wildly, assessing his circumstances. Searching fingers found the rounded links of interlocking metal that dug into his wrists. His hands had been bound together above his head with a length of chain and his bare toes scrapped tentatively at the smooth white tile beneath him, unable to fully touch. The room was blaring white.

Stripped naked, Kyn's shivering flesh turned to gooseflesh as it dried. The air was climate-controlled cool turned to food storage frigid. His shoulders ached painfully, gravity pulling the joints slowly and painfully out of place, straining ligaments. Experimentally engaging the muscles around the joints, Kyn tried to pull himself up by the shoulders, fighting against gravity in an attempt to ease the strain. Pain shot through him like hot lightening, forcing him to abandon his effort, and he hung limp again. The pain level informed him that he'd been in that position for a while already, probably several hours. His tongue was a thick bloated thing in his parched mouth.

"It's awake." A familiar voice stated from behind him.

Kyn licked his parched tongue over chilled lips.

"It's nice to be home." He croaked, throat hoarse. A pause to work his mouth silently, trying to build up saliva to ease his burning throat. "Glad to see you haven't changed my old room around."

Cold steel pressed against his buttocks. He was spun around, arms crossing painfully overhead, and he forced himself to suppress a grimace as he met the smug expression plastered across his torturer's perfectly sculpted face.

"How's it goin' Alyn?" Kyn asked, wryly.

The Sentry didn't acknowledge Kyn, his brilliant blue eyes studying the naked Envoy. A smooth metal spike gripped in one hand halted the Envoy's rotation from unwinding. Waves of fiery agony burned through Kyn's shoulders.

"Crazy day." He babbled, unwilling to give Alyn the satisfaction of seeing him flinch. "Did they really hit the wall? Looks like the Ragers are getting serious, I didn't even think they had that in them. I mean. Who will keep us safe without the wall?"

Alyn's lip curled with a simmering cruelty.

Recruitment propaganda icon, Alyn was everything the Dags optimized. Muscular and handsome, he oozed chest beating masculinity, chiseled face perfectly reminiscent of the godly superheroes once popular in pre-fall vid caches.

Winter blue eyes watched Kyn coldly, before, with viper quickness, the Sentry plunged the sharp metal spike through the place where Kyn's crossed arms met. Flesh split and bone cracked as the smooth metal skewered his forearms together.

Gritting his teeth, Kyn suppressed a groan of rage and pain, whistling long and low before jumping back into the flow of his rambling.

"I mean, who's going to protect us from the Dividers now?"

Alyn twisted the skewer, a cruel smile cracking his perfect face. Warmth oozed down Kyn's arms. He bit back a howl. Then, just as suddenly as he'd driven it in, the Sentry ripped the spike free, sending Kyn spinning away, arms rapidly uncrossing themselves. He screamed, unable to hold it back any longer, the noise echoing madly off the stark white walls.

Spent, he dropped his chin to his chest, panting heavily. The binding chain creaked mockingly.

Alyn paced in a slow circle around Kyn. Ice blue eyes fixated on the jagged wounds he'd created in the Envoy's forearms, watching in rapt awe as the holes rapidly started to heal. Wet, red muscle bloomed over jutting white bone in fibrous knots, fresh and flawless skin knitted over; all itching maddeningly until the Envoy's flesh was smooth and unblemished, the wounds erased. The Sentry traced the freshly healed area lovingly with the pads of his fingers. From his hanging position Kyn could see delighted wonder in the cold blue eyes.

"Beautiful." Alyn whispered.

"Thanks." Kyn interjected in an obnoxiously nasal bray. "I really take pride in my body, you know?"

The Sentry ignored him as if he hadn't spoken. His free hand snaked behind Kyn's head and gripped firmly at the base of his skull. Icy blue eyes gleamed as he drew back his other arm. The room's blaring light glinted off the bloody tip of the raised metal spike.

"Oh, come on!" Kyn protested, even as the spike came down between his eyes, and the white room disappeared in a crack of blackness.

He was running, boots pounding a frenzied war beat against pavement. His chest heaved, and he gasped in air. Legs burning, he pushed himself to move faster as he rounded the corner of a building wildly before turning sharply to angle down another darkened alleyway. K-cannon fire filled the night and screams echoed in the distance. A culling in full swing. Kyn paid no heed. He didn't care what happened anywhere else tonight. One simple goal pounded through his skull.

Find Yorri.

Kyn cursed as he veered around another corner, easily clearing a gated barrier meant to block the narrow alley that ran the length between two, looming, plex paneled corporate towers.

He'd tried to keep the secret for as long as possible, but now they knew.

Kyn spotted the Dags exiting the far end of the alley and pushed harder. The last of the soldiers were lagging, pausing to throw something onto a huddled pile on the concrete.

At first mistaken for a misshapen pile of refuse, Kyn could make out the clump of sandy brown hair, burnt gold in the bounce of streetlights. The dark skin of a hand, fallen limp against the pavement.

Lips pulled back over jagged canines, Kyn let loose a primal scream of rage and death.

Time slowed, everything fell away, and all he could see was the Dag standing frozen in shock before him and the dark hand, reaching futilely for help. He leapt for the Dag.

He was screaming, but he heard nothing, just deafening silence.

Kyn knocked the terrified soldier back, driving them to the ground as they collided, and landed in an easy crouch over them. Ego was in his hand, pulled from its sheath across the small of his back as he leapt, and he stabbed down viciously, plunging the dagger through each of the Dag's shoulder joints in rapid succession, disabling their arms. Flipping the blade, he slashed horizontally behind himself, blindly slicing through the soldier's uniform, and cutting deep across the connective tendons of both quads, crippling them painfully. He grabbed the struggling face of the incapacitated Dag tightly between both hands - fingers dug into the man's scalp so hard he drew blood - and lowered his face to theirs to let loose another shriek of incoherent rage. Tears of pain and fear streamed down the Dag's face.

Then Kyn was hurrying over to the huddled form on the pavement, curled protectively into themselves except for the one, eternally reaching arm.

Crouching, frantic but trying to be as gentle as possible, he gingerly rolled the mass. His breath caught, choking him as he allowed himself a desperate moment of hope.

The huddled figure flopped limply in his arms. Sea green eyes, glassy and unblinking, stared up.

Yorri.

Ribbons of neon pink from the florescent lined city above reflected in his lifeless gaze and dark bruises and deep lacerations covered almost every measure of visible flesh. He had been viciously beaten. Fresh blood, still warmly slick, tangled his hair.

The tight k-bolt wound was clear, a ludicrously small hole the size of Kyn's fingertip burnt through the other man's chest, right through the heart. The final wound.

Yorri was dead.

A wailing sob of anguish tore itself from Kyn and he clutched Yorri's lifeless body to his chest. Sagging, he collapsed to the rough pavement, gripping Yorri and rocking back and forth as he sobbed.

Kyn cried until his throat was hoarse and the tears stopped. The sounds of weapons fire and screaming still echoed in the distance, but Kyn didn't hear it, the silence of his agony drowning out all other noise.

It was a long time still before he stood, numb, and walked back to the injured Dag still laying in the street where he'd left them. Unable to move and slowly bleeding out, the Dag was struggling to stay conscious. Kyn watched, steel gray eyes impassive as the Dag shook uncontrollably, losing the fight against shock.

"Your friends ran away. Left you all alone." Kyn crouched over the soldier. "But don't worry, I'll see them soon." He promised, then, more bluntly. "I'm going to kill you." Voice flat, devoid of anything human.

His fingers around Ego's hilt were turning white at the knuckles. "I want you to know that I won't have mercy on you." The fear in the Dag's eyes was beyond panic. "But I will kill, eventually."

Kyn gently caressed the soldiers jaw with Ego's tip.

"I just have some questions first."

Life rushed back to Kyn in one blinding flash as the spike slid from his skull with a hollow, wet, *schlock* - a sound he felt, more then heard. Life surged through him, and he lurched violently against the suspending chains, the hole in his skull healing over with a crackle of bone.

"Tell me what you saw." Dispassionate winter blue eyes. Blaring white room.

"Fuck you!" Kyn spat, swinging wildly.

Alyn ignored the obvious insubordination. "Tell me what you saw." The Sentry repeated calmly.

"Don't you have better things to do?" Kyn shot back. "Rager attack? Didn't someone blow a hole in the fucking wall?"

"When you died, what did you see?" Alyn pressed.

"I don't die, you twat. You know that. Not really. I just kinda..." Suddenly exhausted beyond measure, Kyn lolled his head between his overstretched shoulders. "I don't know. Stop. There is nothing. I don't go anywhere. I just kinda remember some shit, then I come back." He rolled his eyes, exasperated. "Shit. You know this. It's the same thing. Every. Time."

"What do you see when I remove the spike?"

"Why are you even doing that? Shouldn't I be, I don't know, looking for the people who blew a hole in the giant impenetrable wall?" Kyn thrashed against his chains in frustration. "Or do your sisters already have that taken care of?" He jeered, reveling in the brief flash of rage behind Alyn's ice blue eyes at the mention of his siblings. Pushing the advantage, he fiddled at the crack in the Sentry's facade.

"Did they order you to stay out of their way?" He taunted.

Alyn's beautiful face twisted with a sneer of rage as he drove the metal spike back into Kyn's skull.

Kyn's knuckles were spattered in gore. Raising a fist, he slammed it back down with a bone shattering crack against the Dags face. Teeth fractured, cutting into his knuckles - deep. Unfazed, he pulled his bloody first back.

"Who ordered it?" He demanded.

The Dag coughed, spitting up blood, but stayed otherwise silent. Kyn tightened his grip on their uniform collar and brought his fist back down, slamming it mercilessly into the Dag's already shattered nose.

"I can do this all night."

"Yes, but can he?" Ashe drawled from across the cramped dorm. The elegant Envoy had languished themselves across one of the cold metal benches folded from one wall of the bunk's sparse eating area. Lips pursed and brightly painted; Ashe crossed their muscular legs seductively. They were presenting slick femme chic in a hip hugging skirt and synth leather boots, sculpted torso cinched into a silken cloth sheath, tight against their alluring form. Their skin glistened and their indigo hair was slicked back. Everything about them looked somehow wet. The f-Link tattoo along their neck pulsed with a rhythmic prismatic light show, dancing along the crook of their clavicle, bright in the tight space of the Dag's quarters.

"I can make it last as long as I need," Kyn returned dully. Releasing the Dag's collar, they slumped heavily back onto the floor, the last blow having rendered them unconscious. He stood and calmly produced a cloth from the pocket of his vest and began wiping at the blood that coated his hands. Jagged abrasions from the Dag's shattered teeth were already healed, the torn knuckles smooth.

"You are not going to be able to punch your way past the chem-programing." Ashe scoffed, heavily painted eyes watching Kyn warily. *"They will not turn on their masters. Cannot. Even if they wanted to."*

Replacing the rag, Kyn proceeded to silently pull a series of small vials of clear plastic from another pocket of his vest, each one filled with a different dull coloured liquid. Crossing to Ashe, he lined the vials on the table next to them with a pointed exactness. Two inject-units materialized from the confines of a third pocket, and he placed these next to the line.

"Don't worry. I came prepared." He muttered, voice low and level. An unbending determination flashed like steel in his gray eyes. *"Besides, who do you think Alyn used to test and refine all his cutting-edge drug regiments on?"* He flicked the lid from the first inject-unit, exposing the sharp needle beneath.

"You know what they say," Ashe retorted dryly, eyeing the needle. *"What does not kill you -"*

"Gives you an intimate knowledge of behavior controlling narcotics." Kyn finished sharply. He selected one of the vials filled with a mustard coloured liquid and punctured the lid. *"Something like that?"* He measured the desired dosage with a cold calm.

"This will keep him conscious, then I can administer the others." Kyn narrated, looking to Ashe. *"We'll have a very narrow window, and what I'm going to give him will only relax the loyalty protocols long enough to ident who ordered the hit. But even though the regiment won't stop him from talking to us, I don't expect him to want to. That's why I'll need you to make him a little more compliant. Good?"*

Ashe sighed as they stood, long limbs unraveling gracefully. Gently placing a large hand on Kyn's shoulder, they looked at him with a mix of concern and pity.

"You don't need to do this."

"They killed him." Kyn snapped sharply, shaking off the hand. His expression was hard, even as his voice caught. He pulled the needle

from the stopper and crossed back to the unconscious Dag. Uncere-moniously he hauled their limp form into a seated position, propped against the wall. "So yes, I need to do this."

He found his target, one of two large carotid arteries running along the neck, and plunged the needle home.

Kyn swallowed down the rising lump of emotion that threatened to choke him. Drowning him in a sea of loss. He looked back imploringly at Ashe.

"Will you help me?" He asked simply.

Ashe sighed heavily, resolving themselves. "Yes, I will help you."

"Thank you." Kyn returned, grateful. He hit the release on the inject.

Brilliant white rushed back and Kyn thrashed against his chains once more, growling in frustrated pain. Adrenaline pumped through him, but he managed to choke down the violent rage that gripped him, stopped short of lunging at Alyn, suddenly intent to tear the Sentry's throat out with his teeth.

"What did you see?" Alyn asked again, calmly stepping safely out of Kyn's reach. The Sentry was well experienced with the Envoy's potential for violence.

"Happier times." Kyn spat, a glob of bloody mucus that added to the splattering of crimson already covering the once sterile white floor. A grotesque abstraction. Repressed, the adrenaline faded, leaving behind the warm glow of euphoria. He'd never really under-stood where he went, suspended between life and death, but when the damage to his body started to heal, pulling him back, he never felt more alive. The ultimate high. His body sang with electricity, reveling in its own power.

It was no wonder Alyn was obsessed with him.

Kyn had been held in this same room many times before, in this exact scenario. These special moments with Alyn a regular occur-rence since Kyn's Ascension - a tick over three five-cycles before.

Alyn was enthralled by the gray eyed Envoy's healing capabilities, and regularly subjected him to a seemingly endless barrage of tests as he matured, bent on discovering his abilities source and limits.

Whether Kyn could truly die was still out to debate. He sure as shit didn't know himself, and that wasn't for a lack of Alyn's trying. Catastrophic organ failure. Total cardiac destruction. Limb detachment. Scorched earth neural-fry. Endless tests and trials and the only thing that could reliably stop Kyn from almost immediately getting back up was severe damage to his brain. And, even then, unless there was some impediment, he would eventually heal, coming back from wherever he went.

Thus, his torturer favored metal spikes.

Kyn knew in the way that the Sentry watched him, that Alyn hated him. Hated that what he saw as a lesser creature had something he coveted but was unable to obtain.

Kyn suspected Alena curbed her brother's more extreme obsessive impulses, stopping him from entirely going for broke and catapulting the irreverent Envoy outside the atmosphere or dropping him in a nuclear reactor for the sheer morbid curiosity. Probably even kept Alyn from injecting himself with the HIR-C9 nanite virus – the inject subjected on Envoy trainees at Ascension. Which was too bad as then that would mean Kyn also had Alena to blame for her brother not falling victim to the virus' 98.7% fatality rate. Shit luck.

Kyn had the triplets to blame for a lot. So much so that, no matter how powerful he felt in those surging moments when he literally rose from the dead; he knew it didn't matter. No matter what he survived, he was still powerless. Still the one strung from the ceiling. No matter what new death he shook off, no matter what small way he tried to fight back, whatever stupid rebellion, nothing changed. They always won.

"They would find a way, they always do, and they'd make me hold her down to do it."

There were so many things worse than physical pain.

Kyn knew it was best to just let them hurt him, he would heal from whatever they threw at him. Flayed skin grew back. His shattered bones reformed. Others didn't get the same luck.

They were his Sentry. They were the power.

That still didn't stop Kyn from being an insolent pain in the ass every chance he got.

"We gunna go again?" He taunted the silent Sentry through bloody teeth. "I was just getting to the good part."

"What did you see?"

"Breaking toy soldiers." Kyn cackled, a wolfish grin splitting his face. His eyes glittered with a predatory glee. "Hunting down those juiced up meat heads of yours. Happier times."

Alyn stiffened at the reminder of the Envoy's most successful burst of violent rebellion, when Kyn had gone rogue, hunting down, and butchering a group of Dags under the Sentry's command. It was still a recent point of contention between the two men and, Kyn guessed, it was, at least in part, one of the reasons for his current situation.

"Yes, that." Alyn drawled, pressing on. "How did you counter their loyalty regiment?"

Kyn let his head lull back against his arms. "That's what this is about? Why didn't you just ask? Or wait, am I a suspect? You think I was involved with the wall?"

"You have successfully broken through the regiment protocols in the past. You have a history of Unity resentment." Alyn swiped at the air, the twisting interlocking square pattern of his own f-Link, visible under the buttoned cuff of his sleeve, undulated white-gold. A holo appeared in the air in front of Kyn, footage from his own security feed, specifically the cam mounted in the hall outside his flat, clear in the floating square. He watched in replay as a hooded figure rushed down his corridor. Alec. The hacker's hood hid his features, and Kyn watched himself open the door, pulling the figure inside, before slamming the door shut again. The towel he'd worn barely counted as more then he was currently wearing.

The footage replayed, looping back on itself.

"You fraternize with known Rager associates." Alyn stated triumphantly.

"He's an agent for the Informant, not the Ragers." Kyn corrected, spitting more blood.

"Any who oppose the Unity are agents of the Ragers."

"The Informant doesn't oppose you; they just know all your dirty secrets."

"Which you feed them."

Kyn laughed.

"Please, I won't even pretend to know the worst of your secrets."

He was puzzled on what the Sentry was looking for, what answer he hoped to find. Alyn wasn't really accusing Kyn, he'd have been dragged in front of the whole Unity if that were the case.

"You have no idea what's going on." Kyn gleaned.

The Sentry was deadly silent in response, then his f-Link flashed beneath his cuff.

Alyn's eyes flicked back and forth, reading the incoming message on optic. His jaw clenched visibly.

The outline of a door appeared in the room's blank wall unannounced, sliding open with a swoosh and Runa strode through. Clad in a sleek black Envoy Ops uniform, her mass of curly hair hung wildly around her face, half masked by a thin sheath of more black stretch fabric that emerged from the uniform's high neck to cover her mouth and nose, molding snugly in place. Brisk and direct, she carried a bundle of more black fabric under one arm, which she tossed to the floor beneath Kyn's dangling feet. Then, unperturbed by his nudity, she hoisted him by the hips, freeing his chains from the hook in the ceiling, and dropped him unceremoniously next to the pile.

"Get dressed. Dividers infiltrated the SPIRE." She ordered, breezing through the shocking information. She saluted respectfully to Alyn. "Sentry, Malvyc will accompany you to join your sisters. He's waiting in the hall." She turned back to Kyn, laser focused. "Alena ordered catch and kill. They can't leave the SPIRE alive." Reaching down, she snapped the chains binding his wrists easily with one hand. The mangled links fell away.

Kyn sighed, thankful, and rolled his aching shoulder back into their rightful place. The pain eased almost instantly, the restriction bruising at his wrists already completely faded away. He could feel Alyn's eyes on him.

Dressing quickly, Kyn found his harness in the pile and buckled each piece in place with drilled efficiency.

"Where are they now?" He asked. The bundle had supplied an identical uniform, and he pulled his own mask up, hiding his lower face.

"Walk and talk." Was Runa's clipped response, making for the door.

Kyn followed, leaving the white room miraculously unscathed, as always.

They passed Malvyc in the outer hall and Kyn nodded curtly in the bald Envoy's direction, careful to keep his expression locked in a determined neutral.

Kyn rarely dreamed, but when he did, one of the things he dreamed about was getting to kill Malvyc.

A smile slit the bald Envoy's oval face as Kyn passed. Dull brown eyes flashed a threatening crimson.

The attack seized on Kyn's nervous system, lighting him up with sudden inescapable pain. Agony burned through him, halting all movement, causing him to twitch involuntarily. He choked, sputtering on the pain.

Then the pain was gone, just as rapidly as it came, and Kyn had control of himself again.

"Fuckwit." He muttered darkly under his breath, falling back in lockstep with Runa. He could taste copper and spit out a spongy hunk of mangled flesh onto the corridor's polished concrete. He'd bitten through his tongue.

"You're not wrong," Runa returned.

The SPIRE

They traversed the curving sub-level corridors of Noav SPIRE side by side.

Away from the stark simplicity and blankness of Kyn's childhood cell, the architecture changed, morphing back to an aesthetic more reflective of the rest of the complex. Steel and stone walls bent outwards at improbable angles, creating a sense of cavernous space. The effect would become even more striking as they moved above ground, the outer walls of the upper levels an opaque and durable polyplex, transparent from the inside, allowing for uninterrupted views of the congested city around the structure. Viewed from the outside, the SPIREs were like improbably massive crystalline stalagmite, grown cancerous from the heart of the city itself.

Runa filled Kyn in as they approached a bank of hyperLifts.

"We have no idea how they got in." She conceded swiping fingers across the back of one hand. Kyn's f-Link buzzed, and a file transfer notification popped up in his optic. Drumming his third and fourth digits, he expanded the file to stream in his optic. More security footage.

"Honestly, we got lucky." Runa admitted briskly. "The systems caught them moving through a bio-scan."

Kyn watched the scene unfolding intently. Caught from a high angle, two figures, wrapped in strange, flowing outfits, rushed down a corridor. The diamond skyline of the upper wards flashed beyond opaque walls, so Kyn recognized the SPIREs' highest levels. The fabric wrapped duo seemed to have triggered a bio-scan - cleverly patched sections of wall, concealed to scan unsuspecting passersby. The system had marked them as intruders once their bio-data didn't sync with floor clearance.

"That was on priority storage." Runa answered, predicting his question, she continued in rapid-fire assault. "We also have no idea how they got that far without triggering any other scans. They're moving erratically - the system only managed to get a brief grab at their bio-data, but most of it's encrypted beyond anything. We've got nothing on heat scans either, they're cloaking somehow. Maybe the outfits? We're following what we can, picking up where they've been, trying to predict where they might be going. It's hard to follow." A bemused shrug.

The Envoys stepped into an open lift.

The only efficient mode of transit within the vertically sprawling megastructure, the hyperLifts were clear tubes clustered around the structures massive central pillar; fast enough to allow a handful of passengers' rapid travel between the SPIRE's hundreds of levels in mins. The pair flashed wrists in front of a square panel and an internal light flashed an accepting green, recognizing their bio-scans and clearing them for the requested level. Reflective silver doors whooshed closed, and the tube rocketed skywards.

Kyn watched the security feed on looped replay, analyzing it. The clip was short, just a few ticks, the two unknown figures shot from a high angle rushing down an empty SPIRE corridor, then out of sight again. The intruders wore wrapped strips of flowing fabric that twisted around their limbs and torsos in intricate patterns, looped from head to toe, flowing around them like smoke. Wide hoods were drawn over their heads, obscuring their faces in shadowed cowls. Both figures radiated the fluid grace and easy athleticism of experienced infiltrators, and, by build and gait, Kyn guessed that they were dealing with one male and one female. As the pair whisked past the bio-scan feed on loop, the one he assumed male turned briefly, checking their rear. Twitching fingers, Kyn scrolled back, pausing again when he found what had caught his eye. A brief flash view under the cowl, blink and it's gone. He crept the footage forward.

The face under the cowl wasn't human. A blank-eyed and glittering skull, painted in a vibrant array of brightly contrasting colours, flashed a skeletally toothy grin from the depths of the hood. As Kyn crept the footage the skull snap changed into the blank face of a retro yellow emoticon with red x's where round black eyes should've been.

Kyn was intrigued.

It was a mask, seeming to utilize a light-based holographic projection tech Kyn didn't know. He liked the effect, and gave the Divider a begrudging internal nod of respect. The images were deeply unsettling, inspiring a creeping fear while serving the dual purpose of hiding the agents' identities.

War masks.

He replayed the footage a handful more times as the lift shot upwards, finally noticing a key detail, almost written off as upperwards glare. It was slight, a narrow film of distortion immediately around the pair, an oily rainbow haze, like looking through the skin of a soap bubble.

Kyn could easily see how the Dividers had earned their legendarily feared status, their seeming other-worldliness sparked a faint tremor in his chest.

"They're fucking awesome!" He exclaimed in awe as the lift finally eased to a halt and the pod door slid up. They stepped out into the sprawling re-engineering department's main lobby. Well above ground now, the jumbled mass of the mid- wards' skyline clearly visible beyond the encompassing outer barriers of semi-clear plastic. Pre-fall skyscrapers glinted with reflected neon, jutting obelisks caught in the claustrophobic tangle of crossways, skywalks, and residential blocks, that linked the tightly packed ward, stretched like steel webbing between the oppressive shadows of the other crystalline SPIREs. Kyn could make out the orange haze of the setting sun, briefly visible through gaps in the twisted urban throng.

"Right?" Runa affirmed, previously serious demeanor edged with childish glee. She produced a bright red sugrsphere from her mass of curls and swiftly unwrapped it. Maneuvering under the seam of her mask, she popped the treat into her mouth.

"What do you think is up with that pink haze?" She quizzed around the synthetic sweet.

"Teleportation." Ashe's informed them, matter of fact.

Outfitted in their own form fitting Envoy uniform, silken indigo hair twisted high on the top of their head in a loose topknot, they approached from across the cavernous lobby like a waft of dark smoke, the translucent marble floor beneath their square heeled boots lit from below by a low, white glow. A unit of Dags moved with them in unnatural lockstep.

"No fuckin way." Runa gasped. Kyn's eyes widened.

Available data showed teleportation had merely been a vague rumor before the fall. A scientific fever dream purely in the theoretical stages. If the Dividers had access to something out of reach before the entire collapse of the most widespread and advanced civilization the planet had yet known, then they far outpaced any tech-heads the Unity had now.

The thought of facing off against these mysterious intruders thrilled him.

Kyn's childhood training had been sparse on details about the Dividers. None had been seen in living memory. All he and the other Envoys had ever been told was merely that they were a highly dangerous threat and must be guarded against at all costs.

"Yes." Ashe continued, reaching the pair. The Dags froze at ready attention. "It's what we suspect the female capable of at least, explaining their erratic movement." They gestured for their enthralled entourage to fan out. "Search the area, make a tight net." They commanded, then turned attention back to Kyn and Runa. "It also explains how they got this far without triggering other sensors."

Leading, Ashe angled the trio towards one of two sweeping staircases of polished black marble that flanked the department lobby. Branching, plex lined corridors led off the main floor, leading into the maze of specialized departments that made up re-engineering. Kyn could hear Dag units sweeping labs and offices, trying to box in their prey. More lined the perimeter of the atrium-like lobby

"They're looking for something, I don't know what, but we need to stop them finding it." Ashe stated, climbing the sheen polished stairs, four new Dags peeled off silently from stone and plex walls to follow. Outfitted in combat hard suits, each gripped a standard issue assault model k-cannon at easy ready as they flowed into protective formation around Ashe, guarding the indigo haired Envoy's flank.

A pre-battle calm had settled over Kyn, his muscles and breathing relaxed even as he became acutely aware of his surroundings. His fingers itched towards the plastic blades in his harness, ready to throw.

Runa crunched serenely on her sugrsphere, mane of curls whipping as she craned her neck back and forth, eagerly looking for the Dividers.

Ashe led them up another staircase and out onto a wide mezzanine that overlooked the sprawling department. Off one side they had a clear line of sight to the labs and offices below, the sweeping Dags covering all possible escape points. On the other, looming beyond the opaque polyplex, was the twisting mass of the city's neon trimmed skyline, its heart gone to fire with the setting sun. Ashe's entourage of enthralled Dags set about silently prowling the mezzanine's unguarded edge. Runa raised her fists.

Kyn wondered if the Dags had any idea what they were looking for.

Ticks wound by in silent tension, the Envoys at ready. It was who Runa finally broke the waiting silence.

"Where, the fuck, are they?" She sighed heavily, fists dropped casually to her sides.

"Hush." Ashe admonished, still alert. Their violet eyes scanned the department.

Runa started to shoot back a profanity laden retort but was cut off by surprised shouts, just as k-cannon fire lit up the labs below. Kyn spun towards the sounds, eyes following the Dags' line of fire and seeing nothing even as the Dags reloaded and continued to fire, seemingly hitting nothing but air, interior plex walls, and lab equipment. He squinted, searching the crowd intently until sudden realization smacked him hard across the brainpan.

Teleportation.

Kyn snatched six razor-sharp plastic blades from his chest harness and threw to his right, aiming at the top of the staircase, directly opposite from where the Dags were aiming. He threw the blades all at once so they fanned out as they cut through the air.

His keen eyes had caught a brief flicker of gossamer pink at the top of the staircase, a neon shimmer that was a rainbow-sheened snap across the air.

Five of the blades buried themselves harmlessly into faux walls or bounced impotently off marble supports, flying beyond the edges of the mezzanine.

The sixth blade found its target, cutting across the gossamer flicker in a crimson slash.

"Gotcha!" Kyn cried triumphantly, drawing iD and Ego in one smooth motion.

Then, the Dividers were on them in a twisting flurry of twirling fabrics and glowing skulls. The intruders seeming to tumble out of thin air, poured from a fist-sized hole of void-black emptiness that had suddenly appeared, hanging in the air. The hole was a yawning blackness rimmed by swirling whorls of neon pink energy that wafted and rippled, pulsing outwards, as if punched through the skin of reality itself. The Dividers slid from this hole with a mind-bending twist of perception, the colourful skulls of their projected masks leering menacingly. The one Kyn gleaned female slid out first. She had her compatriot's arm grasped with one hand and was pulling him along behind, her other hand was clasped to her side, covering the shallow but obviously painful cut Kyn's thrown blade had drawn across her ribs. Blood flowed easily, soaking the wrappings of her torso. The dark and empty eye sockets of her mask seemed to scream at him in defiance.

"Surrender!" Ashe demanded. Their voice reverbed, rattling the air. Their emanating power hit the male Divider as the swirling void of energy snapped shut with his exit and he stopped abruptly, the desire to comply overwhelming him.

Runa moved to subdue.

Surprisingly, the female had somehow resisted Ashe's command. She yanked on the male, suddenly frantic as she tried to keep him moving, her outline wreathed in that strange swirling pink energy. The male stood firm, enthralled. The female's brightly painted skull snapped back and forth between Ashe and the swiftly approaching Runa, understanding dawning.

They weren't the only ones with unusual abilities.

The female grabbed onto the frozen male with both hands, and the wafting energy spread with her touch, wreathing him as well, dancing like an aurora over his wraps and the exposed skin of his hands with an unearthly radiance.

Runa lunged, fist pulled back to strike the female with a powerful punch just as the male shook his head, casting off Ashe's control and stepped away from his counterpart with a swooping underhanded gesture in the adolescent's direction. His projected mask snapped to the bleached white skull of a small mammal, decorated with painted lines of swooping crimson. As if following the gesture, the air around Runa rippled with the strange soap bubble sheen, and the young Envoy rose weightlessly into the air. Thick ropes of hair floated wildly around her face as she rose into the air, her amber eyes wide with reckless delight.

"What the fuck? This is awesome." She crowed, unafraid. The male drew his arm back, as if to throw something.

"Stop!" Ashe screamed, the air crackling brittlely.

Ignoring Ashe's command the male whipped his arm forward, and Runa hurtled backwards, thrown through the air with whiplash force to slam forcefully into the polyplex guarded skyline. Cracks splintered the supposedly indestructible surface. Waif-like frame gone limp, she slid heavily to the glowing marble, slumped, her mass of hair hiding her face.

Kyn watched with blades poised, awe stunned by the flashy show of power. The male Divider had forcefully thrown Runa without physically touching her at all. He threw a quick, unconcerned glance at her crumpled figure, determinedly unworried. On top of being incredibly strong, the adolescent was practically indestructible, her skin unbreakable, muscle and bone unnaturally dense. The young woman could take hits that would break most heavy machinery, and she could bend steel between her hands as if paper. She was probably just stunned. Shaking off his awed distraction, Kyn launched himself at the enemy. iD and Ego swung through sweeping arches as he moved to box in the female Divider even as she grabbed at the male again, assumingly trying to teleport away.

Ashe moved with Kyn.

Abandoning attempts to enthrall the enemy, the indigo haired Envoy had drawn a benign looking baton from the harness strapped across their back. A twist between large hands and the wand unfolded like steel origami, petal curved pieces blossoming into a massive, square-headed, maul. Cleverly designed from a thin, yet incredibly dense, polymer, the bludgeoning weapon expanded outwards in two directions, shaft rapidly lengthening out and down, extending the weapon to longer than Ashe was tall, even as the maul's powerful bludgeoning head unfurled like a deadly square-faced flower. The will-bending Envoy twirled the weapon over their head with easy grace as they rushed forward, aiming to smash the male Divider in the face.

The Dividers dodged the synchronized attack. The female lunging low and to the side, letting go of the male just as Kyn sliced downward with iD, the keen blade sweeping harmlessly past. Altering his swing, Kyn followed through with a windmilling swipe, flipping Ego in his grasp, then stabbing down with the dagger, aiming for her outstretched leg.

Grasping laterally, the female clawed at the empty air and a swirling pink-on-black portal tore open at her touch. The teleporter made a pulling motion, and with a twisting distortion of perception, slid through the portal. Gone. The swirling tear snapped shut behind her.

Ego missed its mark, the dagger's blade bouncing harmlessly off the smooth mezzanine.

Left alone, the male Divider twisted agilely away from Ashe's swinging hammer, narrowly avoiding a devastating blow to the face as he danced away. The Dags, finally reacting to the sudden burst of violence in their midst, were in action now. The air sizzled with k-cannon fire as the soldiers fired on the dodging Divider, who danced away, skillfully misdirecting the Dags' aim with whips and flourishes of his flowing layers of fabric.

Ashe spun on a square heel, following the momentum of their missed swing, and twirled the maul back overhead, swinging to attack again.

Kyn tucked into a roll, diving forward over his own missed swing, and was on his feet instantly, legs coiled before launching sideways at the male, twisting his body in the air to aim a scissoring snap kick to the Divider's chest.

The male dodged both Kyn and Ashe narrowly, throwing the Envoys off balance even as the remaining Dags mounted the mezzanine. Closing in, the soldiers raised their weapons and laid down heavy suppressing fire.

Kinetic bolts rippled across the writhing pink barrier that still wafted over the male, undulating in bursts across the effervescent surface, harmlessly dissipated as they struck the flowing energy field. Unfazed the soldiers reloaded and continued to fire, knowing nothing but progression through overwhelming force.

The Divider coiled into himself, just as Kyn and Ashe both spun back, blades and maul raised to attack again. They swung as one, lethally sure of their target, and then he uncoiled, arms thrust outward, the nexus point of a wave of iridescent pink energy that burst from him in a corona of force.

Kyn was thrown backwards, hit full force by the blast, the glimmering soap bubble sheen of energy rippling in the air around him. Dags slammed into walls and windows, limp bodies hanging suspended against gravity momentarily before sinking, unconscious or dead, to the floor. Others were thrown from the mezzanine, screaming as they plummeted to the lower lobby. Kyn slammed into a support pillar, ribs cracking in his chest on impact. Ashe was slumped to the floor at the base of another support, unconscious; their maul clattered loudly on the black marble as it fell from their grasp.

The male moved to flee, but Runa blocked him.

Having played possum, the younger Envoy had jump in the same instant the Divider had sent out his blast of power, her powerful legs propelling her easily over the force wave. Spidering cracks split the polished marble where she'd landed, and she slammed her fist into the male's digitized mask, the blow breaking the shimmering pink barrier that licked over him with a sonic boom.

The wave of sound reverberated through re-engineering as the Divider's glowing barrier winked out and Runa's fist connected. The Divider stumbled backwards, staggering towards the wall of cracked polyplex, stunned but alive. Runa advanced without pause, following through with another rapid punch aimed for the male's sternum. With his barrier down the diminutive young woman could hit him with enough force to slam her fist through his chest cavity.

A swirling portal tore open next to the male Divider at the last tick, and the female's torso slid through the mind-bending hole. Arms grabbed the male, and she dragged him away, disappearing in a wink of perception warping swirl. The portal snapped shut and Runa - robbed of her target - swung ineffectually, fist slamming into the polyplex. More spidering cracks webbed outward.

"Fuck!" She bellowed.

Kyn pulled himself off the ground, a painful itch already spreading beneath the skin of his chest; the healing itch of new bone growing, of sternum snapping itself back into place, and ribs furiously knitting themselves back together. On his feet, he sprinted full out towards the mezzanine edge. He kept low, snatching up the unneeded utility belt of a fallen Dag, and unclipped two pulse grenades as he ran. Thumbing the pressure sensors, he lobbed the projectiles one after the other over the edge, aiming for the hyperLift bank.

Traveling in a neat arch, the tube grenades clattered across the marble in front of the bank of lifts, bouncing and rolling to stop. The female Divider materialized steps away, male in tow. She clocked the projectiles and turned abruptly to disappear back through yet another portal tear. The grenades went off in a crackling blasts of electric-blue energy. The lights of the hyperLift flickered and died, fried by the electromagnetic pulse.

Instinct spun Kyn, and he threw a handful of blades behind himself.

The Dividers re-emerged where he'd aimed, tearing open a portal between him and Runa. Sliding from the portal, the male gestured, stopping the incoming blades mid-flight in a shimmer of pink. Then, with a backhanded swipe, he reversed the blades' trajectory, sending them rocketing back at Kyn.

Kyn casually flicked iD and Ego through a defensive pattern, batting his own projectiles away. One blade slipped his guard to draw a searing line across his cheek. He ignored the blossoming pain and continued his advance. He could see Ashe in his peripheral, struggling to stand. They were using the maul as support to leverage off the floor, obviously injured. Kyn didn't move to help. Hurt or not Ashe would still fight. Kyn threw himself at the male, slashing wildly as he snarled into the colourful animal skull.

"Cute tricks." He taunted, twirling iD and Ego through a rapid staccato, advancing as he forced the Divider backwards. His attack pattern gave the male no choice but to dodge and weave to avoid lighting quick strikes that came at him from both directions. Every-time the Divider tried to raise a hand to exert his power Kyn slashed, forcing the hand back.

"That's right fucker." He crowed, pressing even closer. "Noticed you needed to gesture to do your thing." He slashed downwards with a crossing pattern. Pieces of fabric fell away. Kyn stepped forward and snapped upward with a shin, aiming a sharp strike to the Divider's exposed groin. Countering at the last tick, the Divider thrust down with both hands, blocking the attack, the swirling energy barrier snapping back into place on contact.

"Well, that's no fair." Kyn snarled.

He whipped iD around his head, drawing focus, and immediately followed through with a snapping high kick aimed to catch his opponent in the projected mask. The male leaned back, narrowly avoiding both blows. Anticipating this response, Kyn spun as he dropped Ego into a low, thrusting jab to his opponent's gut. The Divider blocked, one hand forward to gesture quickly, stopping Kyn's strike with a shimmering thrust of energy. Kyn could feel the neon pink energy washing over his hand and wrist, tingling his skin. He pushed against it, squeezing Ego's hilt tighter, but the Divider held him firm.

"Feels kinda good." Kyn purred into the glowing mask, not letting up as he pushed back against the caressing energy. He wasn't sure if the Divider spoke ENG, but he gave the crimson painted skull a roguish wink to get his message across.

The Divider twisted Kyn's own arms over themselves with a flourish, before, with a violently angular gesture, he guided the swirling energy to yank Kyn's forearm back against his elbow at an unnatural degree, snapping the joint with a vicious crack. The male danced back quickly, releasing his hold as he darted out of the Envoy's reach.

Kyn stumbled with the sudden pain, momentarily stopped from his assault. Ego hung limply at his side, useless fingers snagged in the trick hilt, while jagged, red-slicked bones jutted painfully from his forearm. Gaze level on the Divider, Kyn knelt to one knee and swung his broken limb, bashing it into the glowing marble and deftly realigning the bones with one decisive crack. He lifted the injured arm for the Divider to see. Splintered bone fused and skin grew closed. Ego never left Kyn's hand. The Divider froze and Kyn smiled, manic, under his own mask. He stalked towards the intruder, certain for the first time he could feel genuine human fear wafting from the light masked figure.

"Wanna try again?" He taunted, sheathing iD across his back, predatory advance steering the now retreating male back towards where Runa was locked in engagement with the female Divider. His now free hand casually tossed a plastic throwing blade at the male's head, forcing the intruder to duck.

"What'd ya guys take?" Kyn asked in a high, sing-song voice, sensing they had the upper hand. "Come on, I'm going to take it off you anyway, might as well show me." He slashed with Ego and kicked out simultaneously, driving the Divider back, stopping him from focusing his powers.

Runa grunted, swearing.

"Stay still, you skull faced fucktwat." The gravelly voiced youth cursed in frustration, punching at empty air. The younger Envoy was struggling to land any blows but was still managing to drive the dodging teleporter backwards, herding the female in the same direction Kyn was driving the male, backing their targets into the cracked wall of polyplex. The mids loomed behind.

The female was agile, flipping, and dodging Runa's powerful blows as she tried to escape. She fired off the occasional kinetic bolt of her own, shooting from a narrow tube strapped to her wrists. The bolts bounced harmlessly off Runa, burning small holes in her dark uniform, but otherwise doing nothing to slow the unstoppable adolescent's steady advance.

The Divider wasn't trying to teleport away anymore, Kyn noted, and looked fatigued. The feat must take up an extreme amount of energy, he supposed, and the female might need time to recharge. Though, he readily admitted to himself, swinging Ego at the male to stop a thrusting hand, he had no place to even begin understanding how their powers worked, he'd never seen anything like them.

Seemingly unable to teleport, the female was only just able to stay ahead of Runa's determined onslaught.

"Come on, show the bad man what you took." Kyn taunted, playful grin twisting into crazed glee under his mask. He locked eyes with the blank-eyed animal skull, and flicked out another throwing blade, aiming for the male's hand as he tried to engage his powers yet again. The blade whisked through the energy barrier, slicing across the back of the Dividers hand. Dark red blood dripped onto the glowing floor.

"Oh, look at that." Kyn remarked. He threw another handful of blades.

The Divider dodged as best he could but was cut again as another blade opened a red line across his shoulder. He stumbled backwards into the window, strips of cloth falling away. The twisting prefab levels of the mid-wards loomed dizzyingly behind.

"Kyn! You idiot! Stop toying with him and kill him!" Ashe screamed. Their voice resonated across the open space.

The ebony skinned Envoy had pulled themselves up and was staggering slowly but determinedly towards the combat, their maul dragging.

Runa's frustration at not being able to land a blow was becoming palpable. Raising both fists above her head, she slammed them down on the glowing marble floor. Shock waves rippled outwards, shaking the mezzanine. The female Divider stumbled, slamming into the plex, her back against the opaque surface, trapped next to her companion

"Idiots!" Ashe screamed through teeth gritted with pain. Crouching over a dead Dag, they yanked a rapid assault k-cannon from the dead soldier's back and shouldered the weapon, unhalting in their agonized advance. They took aim and fired, blasting the Dividers with rapid fire bursts.

Ashe was a crack shot, and their aim was true, but the rapid-fire shots flickered and rippled harmlessly against the Dividers' glowing barriers, even as they edged closer to each other, hands reaching.

Kyn realized their error too late.

He watched, useless, as the male dipped one hand into the folds of his wraps and pulled out the smooth black band Kyn had recovered from Yummy Otter Corp. He held the band up tauntingly to Kyn, the projected mask flipping suddenly from the macabre, and primitive animal skull to the retro x-eyed emoticon. The round, cartoonish yellow face smiled, mockingly, before the female grabbed her partner's hand and tore open another portal, yanking them away with a mind-bending twist. Vanishing.

Runa's fist slammed against the slanting pane of opaque polyplex, unchecked blow sending more splintering cracks rippling out across the compromised surface.

Kyn rushed to the wall and pressed his face against the tinted plastic, heart pounding. He scanned the crowded ward platforms and byways that surrounded the SPIRE, trying to spot the fleeing Dividers. Cursing himself, he admonished his own stupidity.

Then he spotted them.

"There!" He shouted, pointing to where their prey had materialized in a wink of pink. They were running across one of the many skywalks that branched off the SPIRE superstructure, linking ward platforms several levels above.

"You saw them pull that exact move. Several times." Ashe ranted, pumping more high-powered rounds into the cracked window. When they stopped to jack the reload, Runa slammed her fist into the spot they'd been firing, further weakening the integrity of the blast proof material.

"Like you were a bunch of help." Kyn shot back testily.

"Shut up." Ashe hissed. Up close, Kyn could see the deep purple bruising already blossoming under their dark skin. The purple hue of their eyes burned with an inner fire, challenging Kyn, daring him to see them as broken. Kyn didn't push. Besides himself, he'd never seen anyone shake off Ashe's control as easily as the Dividers had. The indigo haired Envoy was shaken. They had taken a beating, but they had gotten back up, adjusted their tactics and hit back. Ashe was a survivor, just like him, just like Runa. Nothing could stop them for long.

Ashe fired another cluster of blasts into the polyplex. Runa slammed her fist against it again.

Another round of kinetic fire, and another blow from Runa, and the splintering cracks rippled outwards across the entirety of the supposedly unbreakable surface. Acutely aware they might lose their prey, Kyn squinted through the spiderwebbed plastic, trying to keep sight of the Dividers. He spotted them as they emerged from a portal up another level, ran a dozen paces, then flitted away again.

One final strike from Runa sent jagged shards of polyplex exploding outwards. The howling winds of the mids rushed in.

Kyn scanned the mess of transport lanes, service tunnels and rotating ward levels, spotting their prey just as they flitted past a stack of pre-fabs. His gray eyes followed the Dividers pathway as they leaped up another level to teleport away again. He gauged the distance

"Yo, kiddo!" He yelled to Runa. "Wanna toss me?" He pointed in the direction the Dividers were escaping.

Catching to his idea immediately, Runa's face split in an eager grin. She shifted, positioning herself in front of the gaping hole she'd made in the outer wall, bent at the waist, fingers intertwined, forming a cradle between her knees.

"Fuck ya! Let's do this." She encouraged. The altitude winds whipped her hair around like lashing snakes.

Backing up to get a running start, Kyn slid Ego into its sheath and nodded to Ashe. The other Envoy was too injured to follow, and they knew it. He flashed them a reassuring thumbs up and they rolled their eyes.

He ran full tilt at Runa, measuring his gate to step one foot into her cupped hands. She heaved upwards, throwing him into the air with casual ease, launched towards where he'd seen their prey disappear. Wind snapped at the exposed flesh of his face. Runa followed close behind, powerful leg muscles allowing an easy bounding leap from one level to next, close in pursuit.

Thrown several stories upwards and across a wide pedestrian gap, Kyn landed on a slowly rotating ward platform and tumbled forward, smoothly rolling to ease his landing. On his feet and running again, he sprinted down a narrow service tunnel, one of many identical pathways that divided rows of congested prefab dwelling stacks and commercial racks. He twitched his fingers as he ran, keying his f-Link to sync comms with Runa, while simultaneously tracing a path in his head that would allow him to follow the Dividers through the congested chaos. He caught sight of a brief flicker of pink ahead as the Dividers passed in and out of reality, jumping a traffic gap.

Slipping out of another portal tear, the pair ran at a full sprint for a short distance before the female jumped them yet again, causing Kyn to lose sight once more. Easily vaulting an air duct, he caught sight of them again, reappearing to move steadily in the same direction they were originally on. The pair jumped a gap between flanking pedestrian walkways.

To Kyn it seemed the teleporter had a limited range, only making jumps of a handful of levels or blocks at a time. They'd appear out of a portal, run for a bit, then portal again to reappear another handful of blocks along. Though even with that limitation she was quickly out pacing Kyn and Runa.

"I don't think they know we're following." Kyn called to Runa over comm, keeping a steady, determined pace. Noting the Dividers' trajectory, he added. "Their heading towards the Hastings Rim."

"Sounds about right, that's where the section of wall got hit." Runa responded. "Might be their way out. Whole external turret system is inoperable in that area."

"She's jumping them too far, too fast. We need to slow them." Kyn conceded, dive-vaulting a safety rail to monkey-leap from one walkway to the next. He continued to run, pace uninterrupted.

"Time for another round of toss the buttboy?" Runa offered, landing on the stack opposite him, across another service gap. Without waiting for a response, she crossed the space in one bounding leap, landing directly in his path. She spun in the ready position, hands braced.

Kyn took the invitation. Altitude winds buffeted his face as he was launched, and he flipped gracefully in the air, pedways and catwalks flashing past. He landed only to spring forward again, outstretched arms immediately grabbing onto a jutting electrical tube, and he swung wildly around a corner, sharply changing directions down a branching crossway.

Easily considered the busiest corridor of commuter and auto-transpo traffic between wards, the Hasting Rim was a wide suspension speedway that wound around the outer edges of the walled city, and between the wards and SPIRE superstructures. This close to shift change it would be congested with inter-ward traffic, and the appearance of the Dividers would cause havoc, making the pair even easier to lose.

"We need to cut them off." Ashe's voice broke into the feed. "Kyn, I'm below."

Kyn glanced down to street level as he took another running leap from one opposing pedway to the next. The purpley-blue twist of Ashe's topknot sped along beneath, winding between service carts and parked transpo. Piloting a mono-wheeled RimRunr, Ashe lay almost completely prone to the cycles molded seat, leaned over its large, neon yellow backlit wheel, thighs gripping the racer's sleek cylindrical body. They controlled the runr with skilled confidence, smoothly weaving the speedy vehicle through the thickening traffic below.

Kyn jumped, stomach lurching as he let himself fall, aiming to land on the small gap of seat behind Ashe on the runr. He made his target, but misjudged his momentum and fell forward, only narrowly saving himself from smearing across the pavement by grasping for purchase onto the curved lip of a vent that jutted from the runr's single, oversized fender. Safe momentarily, his new perch was precarious, and as Ashe swerved, he lost his footing, sliding sideways. Scrambling to keep hold of the speeding runr, his legs were suddenly yanked out from under him, pulled by the runr's slip stream. His fingers screamed as they bit into the hot metal of the vent, and wet blood dripped into his palms as he swung out behind the runr like a fluttering ribbon. He hung for a precarious moment, legs whipping, a fingers grip from being torn away, then, grunting, he snapped legs to chest in a jack-knifing motion and whipped himself back onto the racer's sleek body, perched against the wheel well. He could feel the heat off the strained solar engine as Ashe urged the monocycle even faster. He smelt burnt flesh.

They took a sharp turn without slowing, and Kyn was forced to pull away from the cruiser or slip off again, counterbalancing. Ashe leaned with the runr into the turn, jaw determinedly set, violet gaze laser focused through the small oval of windshield. Kyn could see the deep purple bruising that shadowed their jaw in the passing overhead work lights before they righted the runr again, zipping them down another side street to cut a diagonal path through the stacks towards the Hasting's Rim.

"How ya doin kiddo?" Kyn yelled into the comm. He'd lost track of Runa.

"They know we're following now!" Was her excited response.

A tell-tale flare of electric pink shone through a break in the prefab stacks, alerting Kyn, and he whipped his head around in time to catch stuttering glimpses of Runa's small frame crashing through a commercial prefab unit above, thrown through the building by the male Divider's powers. Ashe gunned the runr, pushing to intercept, and the solar engine whined in protest.

Kyn caught another glimpse of Runa as she got back on her feet, unfazed, and tore a steel support beam from a ruined wall. The prefab tilted unsteadily. He lost sight again briefly, before catching her just as she hurtled the beam like a javelin, aiming for a target out of Kyn's sight.

The runr gave them the speed they needed to close in fast, and Kyn could now see the entrance to the Hastings Rim, crowded with traffic - most of it on fire.

Traffic on the Rim was entirely auto-transpo. Inter-ward mass public transpo, resource, food delivery and waste removal all travelled at a preprogramed speed on the Rim, all following the same set route. The auto-transpos were uninterruptable until reaching their programmed destinations, and operator guided transpos were required to switch into automatic guidance when merging onto the Rim, limiting accidents by eliminating human error. The system had worked perfectly as far back as anyone could remember.

Until now.

The algorithms that dictated each merging vehicle's path were unable to interpret and properly react to the immediate threat posed by an indestructible adolescent with super strength battling two physics-defying terrorists directly in their path. Vehicles were forced to continue on their locked routes, straight into a path of destruction.

At the entrance to the Rim, flaming debris and over turned vehicles cluttered each side of the speedway. Runa had somehow managed to separate the Dividers and was throwing anything she could get her hands on at them in an effort to keep them separated. Kyn watched, perched on the speeding runr, as Runa peeled a passenger door from a passing transpo with ease, the family inside frozen in wide mouthed terror, and spun around, winding up, before releasing the torn hunk of metal like a discus at the female Divider. The teleporter dove for cover, interrupted a nail span away from grasping her partner's hand. The male caught the flying scrap with a thrust of shimmering force and sent it spinning away, narrowly missing a packed public transpo.

Not all the passing traffic had been so lucky. Near the battling trio, a waste collector had been flipped, its engines erupted in blue-hot flames. It teetered on the Rim's edge, a burning hunk of steel and waste threatening to plummet to the lower wards far below.

Closing rapidly, Ashe narrowly avoided getting rammed by a looming resource transpo by pulling the runr sideways with a screech of burning rubber and an angry whirr of protest from the engine. The long transpo, loaded down with thick lumber harvested from the resource zone, hurtled past.

Kyn leapt from the cruiser as it slid to a stop and onto the passing resource transpo. He landed clumsily on a girthy pine and immediately started scrambling over the packed logs, scampering on all fours to the top of the pile. Splitters broke away, piercing the skin of his hands and tearing at his arms. He ignored the minor annoyance - the transpo was closing on Runa and the battling Dividers and he didn't have time to be dainty. Mounting the top log, he leapt from the moving vehicle - drawing iD and Ego as he pounced - and hit the ground running, launching himself into the fight.

The female Divider dodged away in shock as Kyn suddenly appeared next to her, narrowly avoiding a downward chop from iD. She danced backwards, avoiding the slashing follow through from Ego, the tip of Kyn's dagger skimming the edge of her barrier. He could sense her exhaustion. Her movements had become sluggish, and her barrier wavered unsurely around her.

Pressing his advantage, Kyn shifted to one foot and kicked out low, catching the female behind the knee. He struck with a decisive snap and was rewarded when his foot passed through the wafting pink barrier, dislocating the joint with a loud pop. She staggered sideways with the guttural scream of a wounded animal, struggling to stand even as her useless knee buckled painfully beneath her. The barrier aura flickered, dissipating like an extinguished flame. Kyn pulled iD back for a slashing kill strike.

The male Divider slipped past Runa at the last tick and lunged desperately at Kyn, both hands thrust outwards. A blast of ghostly pink energy pummeled the Envoy, catching him mid-swing, and he was violently thrown sideways.

Weightless, the air shimmered around Kyn as he hurtled backwards and slammed into the side of a passing solo transpo. Metal screeched and bones snapped as he felt the white-hot sting of jagged metal tearing flesh.

Thrown sideways by the blast of power, the vehicle slid out of its pre-programmed route and tipped, rolling into oncoming traffic. Through the shattered viewport cutting his cheek, Kyn could just make out the shocked face of a middle-aged man behind the controls before he was thrown free again to land with a heavy thud on the far side of the roadway. Momentum slid him across the asphalt, adding street rash to his growing list of injuries, and he skidded to a halt, handspans away from the Rim's edge.

Kyn groaned and rolled onto his side. Blood was thick in his throat, choking him. Hacking, he leaned over the edge and spat a thick crimson glob. He watched it fall towards the lower wards, more than a klick below.

His pain was already fading, his body regenerating. Bones crackled and popped back together, torn skin healed over, internal bleeding clotted. Everything itched. He pulled himself to standing; his uniform hung from him in tatters, and a shard of metal pierced his thigh. He reached down and calmly dislodged the shard with a swift yank, tossing the twisted hunk back over his shoulder, and stalked back into the fray.

Another transpo slammed into the one he'd been rolled with. Both vehicles twisted around each other on impact and screeched to a halt before bursting into blue flame. Fires raged out of control on both sides of the Rim.

"Stay still!" Ashe demanded, voice splitting the air with a discordant waver as they brought their powers to bear on the female Divider, still struggling to stand. The male was crumpled in a heap next to an overturned hydro tanker, apparently throttled by Runa who stood menacingly over him, hesitating on the killing blow.

Glimmering flickers of energy burst across the teleporter's exposed skin and clothes, only to sputter out uselessly as she tried to bring her barrier up, fighting to shake off Ashe's control. But the tall Envoy wouldn't be dismissed as easily this time. They'd ditched the runr, and now stalked slowly towards the struggling Divider with an exaggerated over-crossing gait; their face split with a predatory grin, teeth flashing brilliantly in the blue flames. Power radiated from them in waves.

"Please keep trying to resist." They intoned, a low, taunting purr. "I'm beginning to enjoy the challenge."

Kyn could feel Ashe's power, crackling the air. His eardrums popped with the increasing pressure and an unpleasant ache hummed deep behind his molars.

"I'm impressed." Ashe complimented, reaching the injured female. "No one has managed to survive us this long before. I must know your secrets." They reached out a large hand and yanked back the cowl that covered the Divider's head.

The projected mask still hid her face, a blocking oval of light, but the female's jet-black hair was exposed, hung to the chin, with elaborate braids that crisscrossed her scalp.

"Well, that's a pretty look." Ashe purred, patting the braided scalp. The female shook under their touch, either from the effort of attempting to fight the Envoy's control, or terror. Or both.

Ashe gripped the female's braids and yanked the glowing mask around to face them.

"Now how about you tell me where you got that done."

A low groan came from the downed male, and Kyn turned from Ashe's interrogation, crossing to him swiftly. Passing Runa, he dropped down into a crouch beside the male and roughly pulled the seemingly unconscious Divider to sitting, propped against the overturned hydro tank. Wasted fresh water was pooling rapidly beneath them, soaking Kyn's knees.

He riffled through the Dividers wrapped garments trying to locate the stolen tech. His fingers pressed against firmly muscled torso, warm and hard. Gripped by a sudden curiosity, Kyn took advantage of being so close to the mysterious figure and leaned his face in close to the glowing faceplate, squinting as he tried to make out details behind the yellow emoticon. With red x's for eyes, the cartoonish yellow face grinned back at him with a maniac familiarity, but as much as Kyn tried, he was unable to make out any detail past the bright field of light. Undeterred, he continued casing the man's clothes with one hand, while the other reached up, tentatively passing fingers through the light barrier. Expecting resistance, or some defensive shock, Kyn was surprised when his fingers passed through with ease to touch warm flesh beneath. Sketching over rough stubble growth, his fingers traced the outline of a strong jaw.

"Fuckin 'ell Kyn." Runa admonished. "Getting a little creepy there."

Kyn snatched his hand away from caressing the Divider's stubbled cheek. An uncharacteristically embarrassed heat flushed the tips of his ears.

"Admit it." He covered, re-focusing his search, movements brisk and concise. "You gotta be a little curious what's behind that."

Runa didn't respond, instead turning back to keeping a protective eye on Ashe still interrogating the teleporter. The female was somehow still managing to resist commands to speak and was shaking violently with the effort. Their pink aura flickered briefly to lick weakly at her skin, flashing before dying again.

Kyn was impressed. Between the pain of the dislocated knee and the willpower it took to fight Ashe's control, the teleporter must have been beyond exhausted. It was no wonder the Unity feared them so much.

His frisking finally produced a scavers waist pouch, secured to the Divider's hip; his nimble fingers closed around the curved band of the stolen tech.

"Nice try buddy." Kyn taunted, smiling at the yellow emoticon. He tucked the mysterious tech into his tattered uniform.

"Don't call me buddy, guy." A low, pained, yet melodically lilting, voice returned from behind the smiling mask.

Caught off guard, Kyn was too slow to react as the Divider reached up and wrapped both hands firmly around his skull. Forcing the Envoy backwards, the Divider leveraged against the slighter man to pull himself up. Neon pink energy flashed, spreading through his hands to envelop Kyn, wreathing them both in the swirling aurora.

Pink fire blazed Kyn's vision. He had no defense, no desire to fight. Every instinct that normally would have told him to resist, to fight, had stopped. The energy flowed over him, and he just let it happen, his skin singing at the contact, as if his very cells were being filled with pure, potential energy. He felt in that instant, with undeniable certainty, that anything was truly possible. Even freedom.

"Funny." He giggled, releasing a breath he hadn't been aware he was holding. A sudden clarity had washed over him, even as the Divider drove him backwards. There was a lightness in him, and he understood exactly what the Divider was doing. Knew it in the way the Divider knew it. Kyn could feel the man deciding where to go, as if he was making the decisions himself. He was forcing Kyn backwards to close the gap between himself and his sister. They needed to jump and get away. He needed Kyn to understand.

Then the energy was gone, and reality settled over Kyn, cold, and harsh. The sense of understanding drained from him, as if washed away by a freezing wave, pulling him under the icy current. A familiar darkness settled over him. He shook with loss.

The male stumbled past a shocked and too slow Runa, reaching for his sister. Kyn wondered briefly at how he knew it was the male's sister. His memory flashed, whispering trails of pink smoke fleeing his mind. He grasped at its tail; at the shiny truth he had known just ticks earlier.

Ashe and Runa had turned to look at Kyn in disbelief when the Divider had grabbed him, and they stood frozen in shocked stillness. The female dove away from Ashe, pushing away with her good leg even as she reached out to grab onto her brother with one hand, the other tearing open a portal.

Kyn was the first to react, primal instincts to fight snapping back into place. Time slowed as fury pumped through his veins, driving him forward. He refused to let himself be manipulated by some light show.

Snatching Self from his boot, he lunged to grab onto the fleeing male's arm. He yanked the male back towards himself, spinning the Divider out of his sister's grasp while simultaneously drawing the stiletto back to strike, the needle blade angled for the soft place between the invader's neck and jawline. The Divider twisted in Kyn's grasp, raising a fist cloaked in swirling coils of dark pink. The x-eyed emoticon close in the Envoy's face. Kyn growled into the glowing mask, an animalistic rumble.

The yellow emoticon stared blankly back, mocking. Then it blinked out.

Kyn froze mid-killing thrust, dazed, Self poised inches from the male's neck.

The face of a ruggedly handsome young man about Kyn's own age stared back at him. Wide eyes, a deep earthy green split through by slivers of an impossible pink, met Kyn's stormy gray.

Rose quartz cracks, shining through a moss-covered forest floor.

Dazzling, impossibly coloured eyes looked at Kyn with what seemed like an apology for one eternal moment, before, seizing on the Envoy's distraction, the male thrust out, throwing Kyn from him with a brilliant blast of power even as he spun back to his sister. Hands touched, and the pair slid through a portal with a blurring distortion of perception and disappeared.

Kyn hurtled backwards, thrown beyond the edge of the aerial speedway, and hung, momently suspended in the air, beyond the edge of the vertically reaching city, held aloft against gravity by the bubble-like sheen of the Divider's power, klicks above the lowers. Weightless above a yawning emptiness.

No wards but the lowers below. Nothing to grab onto. Alarmed voices drifted towards him from the Rim, unintelligible and torn away by the buffeting winds. He caught a flash of Runa, running towards him, running to catch him.

Then gravity took its inventible effect and he plummeted.

Kyn admired the view as he fell, spinning end over end. Darkening sky and sparkling city flashed by in equal measure. Jagged mountains alternating between rising from, and plummeting into, the silver ocean.

A still quiet washed over him. He'd been thrown so far from the city's vertical reach he had no hope of catching anything to break his fall. He clasped the strange cuff tightly to his chest, hoping vaguely to protect it from being destroyed upon impact.

Himself, he wasn't so sure about.

The howling winds whipped at his face, stealing his breath.

Calm with the simplicity of having no other option but to fall, Kyn twisted in the air, diving for the ground that rushed up to meet him.

Interlude

"Mmmmmmm." Kyn sighed, breathing in deeply. He affectionately patted the side of a massive redwood as they passed "Fucking fresh air. Literally fresh this, the original air recycling system. You don't get oxygen this pure in the lowers,"

"Isn't this the lowers too?" Yorri muttered keeping pace. The taller man jabbed at Kyn playfully as he adjusted the pack on his back. "We're closer to sea level here then the uppers will ever be."

"Well, that's not what these hacked passes say so, don't be shoutin' that too loud." Kyn retorted, veering off the main dirt trail and leading them up onto the wet planks of a wooded boardwalk that led deeper into the forest. "You don't want any patched Dags getting wanked off in the bush overhearin' that."

Ancient, moss-coated trees rose around them, the wet air heavy with the smell of rain and damp earth. Kyn breathed in happily, a deep part of him relaxing.

Here it could be just them.

The towering SPIREs were nowhere to be seen, hidden by the shrouding majesty of the ancient trees, their ominous presence briefly blinded.

Hidden in the depths of the forest, Kyn could indulge the fantasy of escaping. Over the north wall, where it pressed against the old growth forest, and just disappear. He closed his eyes, drinking in the low hum *of the forest. The rustle of the breeze through the trees, creaking trunks, rustling ferns.*

"Which way killer?" Yorri asked teasingly. A jovial grin broke his handsome face. Slivers of midday sun winked through the dense canopy and sparkled mischievously in his monochromatic eyes. Kyn snaked one hand behind his neck in response, fingers running gently through the hair at the nape. He pulled the other man closer to plant a quick but passionate kiss on his lips.

"This way," he directed, grabbing Yorri's hand. He intertwined their fingers as he led the way down a branching path that led to a secluded rocky outcrop he'd picked for a picnic, overlooking the seawall.

He stalked slowly down the blood-soaked hallway, Self gripped casually in hand. The thin stiletto gleamed wickedly in the dim flicker of dying overheads as it delivered mercy to those he passed. Dags littered the narrow corridor, faceless soldiers cut down in their hopeless attempt to halt him from pursuing his target. Kyn followed the wide snail trail of glistening crimson his prey had smeared across polished cherry hardwood. Sparks jumped from battle torn walls.

"Are you sure it's this way?" Yorri asked, tugging at Kyn's hand.

"Of course, I go this way all the time." The Envoy replied, smiling reassuringly under his mask. He pressed forward, following the blood.

The crimson path of gore led through a lavatory door. The door was ajar, and he could hear terrified and pitiful whimpering from within. The sounds of a trapped and wounded animal.

Kyn nudged the door with the rubber toe of his boot, sliding it open smoothly. He leaned a black clad shoulder against the open portico and crossed one leg over the other, casually propping his heel against the frame. Arms crossed over his chest, he cocked his head quizzically and looked down at the older man sprawled on the dark tile.

His Handler clung to the black tiled ledge of the lavatory's spacious walk-in, desperately trying to pull himself away from the approaching Envoy. Pooled blood slowly circled the floor drain. The old man's legs were stretched out limp and useless behind him, more blood seeping from deep slashes across the backs of his thin calves.

"What's up Papa Bear?" Kyn queried, expression unreadable under the dark fabric that covered his mouth and nose. His steel gray eyes shone above the mask with a demented glee at odds with the lilting sing-song of his voice.

"Men your age should be careful when getting in and out of the shower." He lectured in the same airy tone, casually sheathing Self in his boot before stepping into the room. "You could fall and seriously hurt yourself."

The older man squeaked in terror.

"Oh, come now." Kyn huffed with mock incredulity, crouching low to grab the Handler's ankles. "You'll make me feel like you don't love me." He pulled the man towards himself with a quick yank.

Too weak to fight, the Handler slid across the blood slick tiles, head bouncing against the shower bottom with a hollow thud. He lay, gasping in short shallow breaths, prolonged blood loss sending him into shock. Lips worked soundlessly as if to speak - the skin around his mouth tinged blue - but only a weak croaking sound escaped. Deep brown eyes were wide with terror, trying to look anywhere but at the looming Envoy.

Kyn tilted his head and lowered his ear level to the helpless Handler's blue tinged lips, trying to catch the words he mouthed repeatedly.

"I know what type of man you are." Yorri whispered, low and husky in his ear.

"No!" Kyn screamed into his Handler's face, striking the man with a balled fist. The dying man whimpered, his head lolling limply.

"No!" Kyn screamed again, his face a nail's breadth from the older man's. He could feel the raging heat of his own breath against the fabric of his mask, an acrid, predatory stench.

"No! You took that voice away from me! You don't get to speak to me in his voice!"

He struck with lighting quickness, one hand grasping the old man's head firmly, while the other plunged a thumb into a bloodshot and chestnut coloured eye. The digit dug deep into the socket, sinking to the knuckle in warm, gelatinous gore.

The dying man's voice was his own as he screamed, begging for a mercy he knew would never come.

Kyn was a child then, trapped in his childhood cell, blank white walls awash in blood, and gripped by the same raw fury that had seized him that day, powered by the agony of loss and betrayal, driven by the same endless pounding of his heart. The endless, painful rhythm that throbbed maddeningly in his ears. The primal need to survive.

He pitilessly beat the Dags to death, like they had beaten him to death.

Like they had beaten him to death.

His Handler watched in horror, terrified of the monster the gray eyed boy had become.

Bag of Soup

Kyn inhaled sharply, reality and life rushing back in a silver snap.

The air smelt sharply of antiseptic and bleach, and his eyes flew open, seeing only darkness. He blinked a few times, before realizing it wasn't his eyes, he'd woken in pitch blackness. The last vestiges of jumbled memories slipped away, wafting back to the recesses of his mind, losing shape and validity like pre-dawn mist burned away by the rising sun. He was thankful.

Kyn remained motionless, his back against a hard, cold surface. He was naked, the sterile air chill and goose-dimpling his freshly re-animated flesh.

Memories of falling - plummeting past the wards, streets rushing up to meet him - flashed across the front of his mind.

He squeezed his glutes experimentally, and the surface beneath him crinkled with his cheeks. He knew where he was. Raising a hand in front of his face, Kyn pressed into the darkness until his hand met more crinkling, and he pressed outwards, searching for the seam he knew was there.

It wasn't his first time waking up in a body bag.

"Hello?" He called out, the word a hoarse croak. He cleared his throat, fighting the dry mouth regeneration always seemed to give him. He pressed against his confines, ruffling the surface of the dark cocoon noisily.

"Brains." He moaned, searching the dark with his fingers, still fruitlessly trying to find the seam that would release him from the sack's ghoulish confines. He could hear muffled whispers outside bag.

"Brrrains?" He repeated, hoping the muffled voices belonged to some young, unwitting med techs he could scare shitless.

The voices continued uninterrupted, but now there were added footsteps approaching his confines. Kyn scrunched his eyes as a seam of brilliant white slivered the darkness, blinding him painfully. The familiar outline of a wild mass of curly hair loomed over him.

"Hey! Bag of soup is awake!" Runa hollered to someone beyond Kyn's field of vision, presumably the muttered voices.

"Bag of soup?" Kyn queried, leveraging himself to sitting. The bag's synthetic husk fell away, bunching at his waist. He looked around, immediately recognizing the minimalist style and sleek sterility that marked a room within Noav SPIRE.

A hexagonal space defined by barriers of floor to ceiling clear smartplex, his body bag had been loaded onto a polished steel slab. Other identically shaped cells were linked on all sides, each equipped with softly glowing workstations, advanced imaging and diagnostic tech, and other flat operating surfaces that smoothly integrated into each other. The floor was tessellating black and white triangular tiles. Info banks and twisting data models scrolled across the clear barriers of his honeycomb. He'd woken in one of the SPIRE's biotech re-design labs.

Freed of his cocoon, Kyn easily spotted the source of the muted voices. Ashe was in the next hexagonal cell, locked in intense discussion with Benn and their and Runa's own Handler, a severely unpleasant looking woman named Sandri.

Sandri's dark magenta hair was cut in a sharp and boxy bob, desperately out of sync with her hawkish face, and her thin lips were contorted in her perpetual jagged sneer, obviously upset with whatever Ashe was relaying. Freed of the bag Kyn could eavesdrop on the heated exchange.

"This isn't some deepfake Cao coup." Ashe was insisting in low tones. They sounded like they had repeated this point many times. Their arch and sculpted features were still darkened by deep purple and yellowish bruising. One of their arms was pinned against their chest, secured in a med sling.

"Your failure makes Noav SPIRE look weak." Sandri hissed vehemently, cutting them off. The shrill, nasal pitch of her voice carried easily.

"Bag of soup." Runa continued, butting into Kyn eavesdropping. She grinned impishly and indicated the bag he'd woken in. Unzipped to his waist, it was crumpled around him on the cold steel of the table, giving the faint illusion of modesty.

"You made a gnarly mess when you landed." She explained. "We had to scrape what we could find off the street, and then kinda scoop it into this bag. We're fairly sure we got most of you, but it wasn't pretty." She shrugged. "Bag of soup."

"Okay, you can stop saying that now." Kyn returned, suddenly glad he'd been decommissioned on impact. He didn't relish the thought of being conscious during that thorough of a regeneration. After what Runa described, he was mildly surprised he'd come back at all. He looked down at his hands, flexing and curling fingers experimentally, noting the placement of a dark and easily familiar mole on the back of his left hand, reassured it was still in the same spot on the first knuckle of his middle finger, before a nagging doubt tugged at him, and he examined it again, suddenly convinced it had originally been a little bit further to the left. Runa must have picked up on his thought process.

"It's pretty impressive you came back from that at all." She said, wrinkling her nose at the memory. "Once we got all the chunks of you that we could find closer to each other, they kinda wriggled at each other and sprouted together. Like those old educational holos, the ones with the time lapse footage of mold growth and shit like that. You know narrated by that old, pre-world guy? Super weird." She shook her head as if to dispel the image, wild curls bouncing around her face. She turned to Kyn, arching one eyebrow as she leveled him with a quizzical look.

"Anyways, did we get everything? Regrow all your parts in the right place? Anything we missed?"

Suddenly concerned, Kyn lifted the portion of body bag still covering him from the waist down. He peered into the shadowy bag and noted, thankfully, that his genitals and feet were still attached and same in appearance as he'd left them. He wiggled his toes in confirmation, counting the usual ten.

"All accounted for." He beamed at Runa with a toothy grin. "Please tell me that Malvyc was the one who had to pick up my cock."

"No. Sorry to disappoint you." She answered, shaking her head ruefully at his immaturity. "Benn took charge of your clean up. Luckily, your torso was in one piece. Just kinda smooshed and folded the wrong way." She shrugged her narrow shoulders again and turned to hoist herself up onto the slab next to him.

Kyn wriggled sideways, making space. The younger Envoy was still dressed in her mission uniform, mask bunched around her neck, booted feet dangled limply over the edge of the slab. Runa turned her attention to watch Ashe arguing with the two Handlers and her expression darkened. The conversation was pitched too low for Kyn to hear now, but by the defeated and drooped expression on Ashe's bruised and battered face he could tell it wasn't pleasant. Sandri was doing all the talking, seemingly using this opportunity to vent her frustrations unjustly onto the usually poised and unshakeable Envoy.

"Well, lucky it was me." Kyn chirped, clapping Runa companionably on the shoulder before setting about extracting his lower half from the confines of the body bag. "I'm pretty sure you would have left an impact crater that leveled half the block." He teased, swinging his legs to hop off the edge of the slab. He shivered slightly as bare feet touched cold tile, and he padded softly over to the trio.

"Is anyone else cold? Or is it just me?" He proclaimed loudly, interrupting the others.

The Handlers and Ashe turned abruptly to look in the naked Envoy's direction.

Kyn approached the clear barrier dividing their hexagons and leaned forward, breathing heavily on the smooth surface to fog it. Index fingers drew the crude rudimentary outline of an anatomically correct heart into the condensation. He pointed at the drawing and gave Benn an exaggerated wink, before addressing Sandri.

"Well, hello Sandri." He drawled, greeting the Handler with exaggerated vocal fry. He locked eyes with the hawkish woman, fixing her in place with his steel gaze as he slowly stepped around the barrier. "I see you're still struggling to find a hairstyle that suits your face."

The older woman sucked her teeth, pressing thin lips into a colourless line. Her bony hand twitched at her side as if itching to slap Kyn. Runa smothered a burst of laughter behind him. Benn and Ashe, careful to stay out of the irate woman's line of sight, bit back their own amused grins.

Sandri's nostrils flared under her large, hooked nose as she drew in a calming breath, composing herself. When she spoke, her voice was painfully shrill and nasal.

"Ah. You're awake. I'm glad to see you've recovered from your unfortunate failure."

Kyn's left eye twitched with annoyance.

"Sandri." He began, face and voice deadpan as he steadily held the woman's gaze. She pointedly ignored his nudity. "I want you to know - and I mean this from the bottom of my heart. All seriousness like. You are the worst. True stuff. The fucking worst. Just painfully awful. I hate you."

Sandri's dull eyes glared loathing at him.

"Now, now Envoy." A familiar voice broke in cutting across Kyn before he could continue his tirade. "Let's not be rude to one another."

All heads turned in unison to the lab entrance where a wide set of double doors had whooshed opened, and three striking figures were striding into the room. Gliding side by side in perfect lockstep, weaving through the honeycombs, the trio moved with an eerie synchronicity, followed closely by the ever-dutiful Malvyc, and a retinue of armed Dags.

"It's not Sandri's fault that the most competent people are often also the most horrid to be around." Alena continued, admonishing Kyn briskly. The fulcrum of the trio, she was flanked on either side by her siblings. "It would also do well Sandri to remind yourself that, in matters of judgement regarding failure or success, the final word is that of myself and my siblings." The Sentry amended coldly. She broke away from her siblings to stand intimidatingly over Sandri. Alyn and Alexi shared malicious grins.

Broadly speaking, the triplets were styled thematically uniform, each clad in sleek white suits, each tailored to their own unique style pallet. Alena, always the most commandingly striking and minimalist, wore an understated blazer, angular and casually open, over a simple, pearl white silk shift. The shift dramatically plunged well below her sternum and a simple, delicately woven chain of silver adorned the naked space. Only half a head taller than the female Handler, the Sentry's arrestingly elegant presence dwarfed the unpleasant woman as she looked coldly down the delicate swoop of her nose.

"Of course, Sentry Alena." Sandri stuttered, bowing low. Benn joined her in the respectful gesture. The Envoys all snapped to attention, each bringing clenched fist to chest in disciplined salute. Kyn could feel Alyn's eyes on him, coldly scrutinizing his naked form. No doubt enraptured by how he'd healed from being a smear across the lower wards. Kyn stared motionlessly ahead, ignoring the creeping shiver that ran up his spine.

"In fact," Alena continued, ignoring the Handlers gesticulation to turn her attention to Kyn. "This Envoy managed to stop our enemy from succeeding in their goal." She stated approvingly. Approaching him, she lay a milk white hand against his cheek. The heat of her hand did little to warm his skin. He kept his eyes trained dutifully forward, staring intently at a pane of smartplex ahead of him, knowing better than to trust the maternal gesture. "He narrowly stopped them from escaping with their target." Strong but delicate fingers absently traced the curve of his cheekbone, drawing lines between the spray of dark freckles. In her other hand she held up the smoothly curved bracelet Kyn had dove off the Hasting Rim to retrieve. "But, despite his triumphs in our name he would also do well to remember his place." She amended, evenly and without malice. Sharply manicured nails dug into his cheek as she gripped his face even more firmly, turning his gaze to meet hers. She stared deep into his gray eyes, the phantom of a smile playing at the corner of her lips. Kyn saw the reflection of himself in the crystalline blue of her eyes, and he steeled himself to keep his expression neutral as he stared back at her obediently.

"Malvyc." Alena bid the bald Envoy, not moving her eyes from Kyn's. "Would you please remind this Envoy of his place?"

Kyn flinched internally, bracing for the coming onslaught.

"My pleasure Sentry," Malvyc answered her, his voice a dry rasp. The bald Envoy's dull brown eyes flashed a malicious crimson.

Screams filled the honeycomb cell, bouncing endlessly off the clear plex and tessellating tiles.

Malvyc had brought his gift to bear on both Runa and Ashe, and the Envoys had collapsed to the cold tiles, heads gripped in their hands, desperately trying to shield themselves from an unstoppable pain. But there was nowhere to hide, no resisting. The bald Envoy's power attacked the nervous system, manipulating neurotransmitters, forcing every synoptic input to be received and translated as blinding, inescapable pain.

Silent Dags cloistered behind the barriers of the neighboring cell, and the other two Sentry siblings watched dispassionately from either side of their sister, backs to scrolling smartplex, as the two powerful Envoys screamed and writhed on the lab floor. Alexi picked absently at the wispy layers of crinoline skirts she wore in lieu of pants, stifling a bored yawn behind a delicate hand. Alyn was dead-eyed and absent.

The agonized screams dragged on as Alena held Kyn under her gaze. Spared from the attack, he swallowed a dry lump in his throat, but otherwise did nothing to break his obedient focus, starring back unflinchingly. From the corner of his vision, he could see the bowed Sandri's mouth pull into a vindictive grin.

Then, seemingly satisfied, the Sentry released his face and raised her hand with a halting motion.

"Enough." She commanded, not raising her voice, her authoritative tone easily cutting across screams that had become an agonized gasping. The crimson glow of Malvyc's eyes dimmed obediently, and Ashe and Runa sagged, sobbing, and panting on the repeating black and white floor.

"Did you understand the message Envoy?" Alena asked Kyn.

Mouth set in a razor thin line, he nodded his head once in ascent.

"Good." She acknowledged, abruptly breaking her spell. She turned back to the others, freeing him from her crystal blue gaze.

Stooped Handlers rose from their knees, and the downed Envoys pulled themselves from the tiles laboriously. All eyes watched Alena.

"Our enemies have left us with unanswered questions." She stated. The Sentry raised the mysterious arm band for all to see. "But we know what they were after. We need to understand what this is and why they want it." She ordered. "Then we need to find out how to use it against them." She lightly tossed the unknown tech to Benn, who caught it tidily with one, perfectly manicured hand.

"It's obvious they've had help from within the walls." Alexi stated, peeling from the smartplex she'd been leaning on.

The public persona of the Sentry trio, Alexi had opted for a crisp white blazer in a striking high-femme cut, accentuating her bustier form. She swiped an arm through the air, and a silver pattern of interlocking circles lit up across her exposed collar bone as shimmering blue holo-screens winked open in the air around her. Thousands of different public feeds from all across the vertically reaching city, mixed with data streams from cultist fandom devotion blogs, hovered like a malevolent swarm.

"I have cultists spreading paranoia and devotion now. Anyone even suspected of associating with these Rager terrorists will be vilified and cast out. My followers will soon have any suspected conspirators dragged out and executed in the street." She swiped her hand, throwing a data cache to the assembled Envoys. Kyn's f-Link lit up, crawling neon blue across his forearm. Information imparted, Alexi abruptly stopped her address and returned to slouching, disinterested against the data graffitied barrier.

Alyn, his own suit retro cut, pre-world blunt collared and perfectly tailored to highlight his well-muscled physique, replaced her. Kyn repressed the hateful glare that simmered behind his eyes.

"My Dags will be in co-ordination with the kennels of the other SPIREs, putting the city in lockdown. Civilian curfew will be in effect for the mids and lowers. Re-construction of the damaged section of wall is top priority. More servos have been conscripted and will begin repairs under Dag guard. Once the co-conspirators are flushed out, we will issue a retaliatory culling."

Kyn gut churned with something like guilt, acidic and nauseating as he thought of Alec, Elysnn, and all the discarded lower wards children he'd left hiding in the bunker under the old woman's noodle shop. There was nothing to be done for it he knew, they'd survived cullings before, and he wasn't in much of a position to help them. He put the coming violence that was about to descend on the lowers out of his mind, re-focusing on Alyn's address.

"...as well as a rations restriction against the mids. This will send a city-wide message that opposition to the Unity is futile."

Finished his address, Alyn stepped aside as Alena returned to their head. Her eyes blazed with blue fury.

"Find out what that tech is and find the trash that tried to hurt us. Kill everything that gets in your way." She ordered with a chilling evenness. "Make your Sentry proud."

Pronouncements completed, the trio turned as one and stalked from the room, guarded closely behind by Malvyc and their pack of chemically faithful Dags.

Benn was the first to break the tense silence that dragged behind their exit.

"Put some clothes on Kyn." He ordered, calmly. He tossed a canvas bundle from a nearby work surface at the naked Envoy. "We've all seen enough of your dick for one day."

Operations

To Kyn's surprise, the bundle Benn had supplied consisted of an outfit pieced together from the Envoy's own wardrobe; saving him from another joyless, wedgie-inducing Envoy uniform, or some sweat-stained Dag cast off.

He clothed himself quickly in the dark gray canvas pants that had been folded on top of the pile. Comfortably loose, they flowed easily around his legs, bunching at the ankles. A loosely knitted, sleeveless shift was pulled over his head next. Light gray, it draped limply off his frame, accentuating his taut physique. He cinched a matte black vest of black nylon weave over the shift, the slick material treated and waterproofed. Ropy arms exposed, the vest belted snugly around his torso with thick straps, and the deep cowl was accented lightning blue. The vest actually belonged to Alec. The hacker had left it at Kyn's place once after they'd hooked up, and routinely used reclaiming it as an excuse to invite himself back. The hacker would always inevitably forget it again, perpetuating the cycle.

Kyn stepped into his comfortably worn boots and admired himself in the reflective surface of a looming server tower. The whole outfit had an aura of effortless lower wards grime chic; casually comfortable, while allowing ease of movement with the added bonus of not being skin-tight nylons.

It hadn't escaped Kyn that his new Handler had put obvious effort into selecting the outfit. Benn had shown impressive taste with the colour palette, bringing out the gray of Kyn's eyes, and making them sparkle like quicksilver. The Handler had seemed to be trying to keep him at ease since he'd woken in the body bag, maybe hopeful the Envoy would put his own distrustful animosity behind them. A move, Kyn assumed, that was an attempt on Benn's part to safeguard his own future survival, given his charge's volatile history, and the general atmosphere of paranoia natural to the SPIREs.

They'd moved to Operations, deep within the SPIRE sub-levels.

An open layout bunker of poured cement, Operations was another example of his Sentry's flare for minimalist brutalism. Everything in the cavernous sub-level was centered around a circular henge of eight large server towers that stood erect at the center of the bunker. Polished chrome slabs of powerful pre-world tech that had survived time's ravages intact, the towers loomed from floor to ceiling, dominating the space. Here, harsh angles and transparent walls were replaced with smoothly curved gray concrete that flowed around the central henge in broken, ever-widening rings. Inside the henge was the centralized control interface, a circular table of low stone that rose from the floor, its smooth surface treated with a layer of filament-laced polyplex that allowed users to smoothly pull a holographic interface from the table, creating three-dimensional models that hovered above the surface.

Kyn had rarely stepped foot in Operations since he'd left Noav SPIRE – adolescent Envoys being ejected out of the training level and into the city on the day of their thirteenth cycle, tasked to learn how to covertly blend themselves with the general population. Learn about life in the walled city just how everyone else did, by living in it. And, after his own exit, it had simply been easier for his old Handler to convey orders and mission briefings through data drops or covert rendezvous, so he never felt the need to spend more time then was absolutely necessary in Operations. Leaving it to the purview of the Handlers, and the techies that managed the department.

Plus, whenever he stepped foot in Operations it was difficult for Kyn not to think about the current batch of children beneath his feet - the newest Envoys being trained on the sub-levels even further below, just like he had. As it was, being dragged back to his abandoned childhood cell on Alyn's masochistic whims was more than enough nostalgia for him, and he had only seen the inside of the Envoy's Operations center once since he'd last been an adolescent. The night he'd allowed himself to be dragged in, apprehended for killing his Handler.

Propping against a data jockey's workstation, Kyn leaned one hip against the low surface and folded his arms over his chest. Memories of that night tried to swim to the surface of his mind, and he pushed them aside, mentally locking them away.

He stood aloof from the others. Benn and Runa were intently pouring over three-dimensionally modeled surveillance feeds from the trio's earlier encounter with the Dividers, tracking the battle beat by beat while Ashe worked rapidly to overlay the footage with sweeping analytic algorithms that would scan against intranet traffic, looking for any clues that could explain whatever the fuck was going on.

Sandri did nothing but criticize Ashe.

Fully sitting on the nameless technicians' desk, Kyn held up the mysterious cuff, running his fingers thoughtfully over the smooth band. The only remarkable thing about it was how perfectly, nonremarkable it was. Nothing marred the unknown tech's smooth, onyx surface, and to all observation, the cuff served absolutely no purpose beyond being a striking ornamentation. The only indicator it was actually unidentified pre-world tech had come from the original Yummy Otter Corp data-hacks who'd determined that the device omitted a faint signal that neither they, nor Noav's own data-hacks, had been able to interpret or hijack.

Yet the Dividers wanted it badly enough to mount the first open attack against the heavily fortified city in living memory.

What could possibly be important enough to risk that?

Kyn's eyes flicked from one looming server to the next. Each was capable of massive raw processing power, all focused on analyzing every ounce of data available from the Divider attack. He watched the battle footage Runa and Benn poured over. They were replaying the moment Kyn had managed to pierce through the male Divider's barrier with one of his thrown blades, revealing that their abilities had limitations, and analyzing the moment from all angles.

Something occurred to Kyn.

"What is that stuff?" He called over, pushing off the workstation. He casually slipped the mysterious cuff around his right wrist as he strode over to join the others. He slid between Benn and Runa and leaned over the tabletop, looking closer at the projected image of himself locked in slow motion combat with the male Divider. His double's eyes glittered with bloodlust and the dark mask covering the lower half of his face did little to hide the manic grin beneath.

"You think that's a good idea?" Benn asked, indicating the band Kyn had slipped over his wrist.

"Not at all." He answered honestly, looking side-long at the Handler. He cracked a wolfish grin and nodded his head at the glowing pink Divider. "But they want it, and if they're going to try and take it again, well, they're going to have to go through me to get to it." After a brief moment of hesitation, he quickly added. "Thanks for the clothes."

Benn didn't take his eyes from the holographic footage. "Like I said, I was tired of having to look at your dick."

"Sure."

"Do you own anything with sleeves?"

"Why would I?"

"Variety."

Kyn turned away from the projection and leaned against the control console.

"This coming from a man who only wears one, dark coloured suit. Is it the same suit? Sonic cleaned every night? Or do you have closets full of copies? I mean don't get me wrong, you look delicious in them. But the cost to stock a warddrobe full of those dementedly uniform abominations must have been absurd." He teased.

"It's not my fault you murdered your last parental figure in a long shot bid to off yourself, and now can't deal with the harsh reality that you are nothing more than a gene-freaked attack dog, tethered eternally to your masters." Benn shot back, turning to look at Kyn pointedly. "Get over yourself. A lot of people are going to die meaninglessly deaths until those responsible for this attack are found. The faster we do that, the more innocent people live to continue their glorious existence serving the Unity."

"The fuck?" Kyn gaped, slack-jawed at the brutal read. "Bit harsh 'eh?"

A smug grin spread across Benn's face. He returned to studying the footage. "Don't mock the suit. The suit is classic."

Kyn sighed heavily and shrugged his narrow shoulders. "Well, you're not wrong."

"About your misplaced parental issues?"

"No. Well, probably. But no."

"Then, what are you rambling about?" Benn grilled, clearly losing the Envoy's chaotic train of thought.

Kyn leaned over the table and swiped at the interface, zooming in on the masked Divider. He pointed up at the glowing figure. "If we don't find out what is going on with them. A lot of people are going to die."

"No shit, cock-jockey." Runa's gravelly voice interjected. "We all heard the Sentry."

"And it doesn't change our purpose." Ashe joined in from across the table. They wore a simple, black suit, cut slim in similar style to Benn's. Their indigo hair was slicked back. Despite the haranguing Sandri near at their elbow, they radiated a cool, calm competency as they deftly manipulated lines of code, constructing a complex search parameter net that weaved seamlessly into the Sentry devotion feeds. The net code monitored cultist vid feeds in real time, swiftly identifying and isolating any relevant data related to the Dividers, the Ragers, or the attack. "We are to send a clear message that anyone who dares attack the Unity will be hunted mercilessly and made to pay for their crimes against the people of this city." They recited evenly.

"Or we will be forced to watch the people pay for their crimes." Runa added darkly, amber eyes set cold.

"So, again, I ask. What's up with the pink stuff?" Kyn queried, gesturing emphatically at the Divider's glowing aura.

"No idea." Runa supplied shortly.

Kyn smiled. "Well let's game this out." He started, the seeds of his idea growing. "We've got a lot of questions that need answers, so let's start anywhere. Like." He pointed at the Divider's glowing aura. "Why is it pink? Why that shade of pink specifically? What is it? Is it a gaseous chemical reaction? Electromagnetic distortion? Why can we see it? And what is it made of?" Growing more excited, he grabbed at one edge of the holographic display and dragged his hand back, forcing the footage to fast-forward through the events. "Also, what the fuck did he do to me?" He asked stopping the footage at the point where the Divider had wrapped his hands around Kyn's skull, forcing the pink energy over him.

"Yes. What did he do to you Envoy?" Sandri's nasal voice joined, parroting his question.

Kyn cringed at the sound of her voice. "Fuck, I hate you Sandri."

"And I care little for the opinions of a degenerate glitch," the Handler pressed on, ignoring Kyn's interjection. She grabbed at the control interface and manipulated the footage to loop back on the moment when Kyn had let the Divider go. Head thrown back, the dusky brown of his skin licked by the mysterious wafting energy, the look on his face was rapturous bliss.

"What did he do to you that made you fail so miserably?" Sandri grilled, looking pointedly at Kyn. He stared daggers back at her.

"Apparently, getting him off in more ways than one." Runa smirked. "Too bad you didn't even get the guy's name."

"That's fairly typical of most the guys I hook up with so nothing new there." Kyn returned, rolling with the younger Envoy's gentle ribbing. He delighted in the look of uncomfortable disgust that contorted Sandri's features.

Attention back to the looping projection, he watched intently as the Divider gripped his holographic twin by the head and forced him backwards. The mask had slipped from Kyn's face, and his head was tilted back in ecstasy as the swirling pink energy flowed from the Divider's hands, engulfing him.

What had happened?

A crack of quartz pink split the glinting gray of his holo twin's eyes. He could remember the infinite potential.

Everything had been clear. He'd understood them.

"She's his sister, the teleporter." Kyn said, not taking his eyes from the looping footage.

"And how do you know that?" Benn asked.

"I just knew it. Like established fact. He knew she was his sister, so I knew it too. It was true." Kyn shook his head and blinked his eyes rapidly, dazed by the memory.

"Influencers maybe? Like Malvyc and I?" Ashe pondered.

"Telepathic?" Runa chimed, excitement clear on her face.

"There are no pre-world records of telepathy." Sandri snapped cutting across her dismissively. "Do not be absurd." Runa's face fell.

"Why not be absurd Sandri?" Kyn snapped with mocking vocal fry. He swiped at the at the holographic image, rewinding to a moment where the female Divider had leaped back into visibility from one of her portals. "Pre-fall records only hint at teleportation, never mind utilizing it with weaponized skill and control."

He gestured around at the server towers that loomed over them, then pointed back at the light masked figure in the holo, voice dropped back into his normal, dryly ironic tone. "I know you hate to hear it Sandri, but the Unity doesn't know everything. Obviously, the Dividers have found a way to make the previously impossible, possible."

Runa's excited grin returned, larger than before.

"That being said." Kyn continued, thinking back over his strange moment of connectivity with the Divider. "I don't think it was telepathy."

Runa's face dropped again with a disappointed scowl.

"It came from that aura." Benn interjected, grabbing at the footage. He swung it backwards to an earlier point in Re-Engineering. The moment when the duo had first slipped out of the portal and Ashe had attempted to subdue them.

"There, again." Benn pointed. "To resist you, Ashe. She spread it to him."

"Okay, but how?" Ashe asked. They gestured to the gray eyed Envoy. "Kyn is the only one who has ever been able to resist me before, and that's because my abilities work on a combination of hypnotic sonic pitch, and conscious manipulation of my pheromones. The effect causes micro damage to neural receptors. Kyn can only shake it off because his regeneration allows him to repair any cellular damage before my influence has a chance to take root."

Kyn smirked and mockingly set fists to hips in a defiant stance of triumph. Runa chuckled.

"Malvyc is immune to you." Sandri noted.

Ashe's eyes darkened.

"That is different." They said shortly. "Another known quantity. These two were unable to resist without that aura."

"Psychotropic vapor?" Rune volunteered hollowly.

A piece fell into place in Kyn's mind, and he reached out to touch the holographic display. Splaying his fingers, he made a twisting motion with his hand, as if to turn a dial, and the footage jumped forward, rushing through the rest of the battle footage. The holographic display was alighted with brilliant bursts and flashes of the strange pink energy as the digitally reconstructed Dividers used their showy powers

"Whatever it is." He stated, following his train of thought. "I think the real question we should be asking is, how do we not know anything about it?"

"Didn't you just say yourself that the Unity doesn't know everything?" Sandri interrupted. Her thin lips were set in a sneer.

"I stand by that point." Kyn retorted, warningly pointing one slender finger towards the hawkish woman while barreling through his initial point. "As blasphemous as it is to say, the Unity doesn't know everything about the world before, or the blasted wasteland of the world outside the walls." He pointed at the rapidly looping holo footage again. "But they sure know a lot about what happens within the walls. The only reason we can even be looking at this is because we collected the data from thousands of different surveillance feeds across the city. On top of that, all of this footage is being analyzed by the best diagnostic programs the SPIRE's cryptos and code hacks could design, So..." Getting excited, his hunch taking fuller shape, more pieces slotting together, he reached out, stopping the footage at a random point during their fight on the Hastings Rim. He swiped both hands outwards, causing the three-dimensional image to zoom in on the frozen image of a flaming and overturned auto-transpo. He jabbed a finger at the image and looked at the others triumphantly.

"What is that?" He asked.

Everyone looked at him like half his brain still needed to grow back.

"That is a burning and overturned transpo, your insane idiot." Sandri drawled venomously. The others looked back at Kyn blankly.

Kyn rolled his eyes and pointed emphatically at the image again. "No, what is that?"

Lit with sudden understanding, Benn leaned over the stone table and tapped a few commands into the interface. A text box appeared in response, superimposed over the frozen flames.

NATURAL RESOURCE AUTO-TRANSPO PROPERTY OF XION SPIRE: 789A45Z67 EXCLUSION/RESOURCE ZONE CLEARANCE COMPOUNDS:

This was then followed by detailed paragraphs of info that listed every chemical compound and materials present in the image.

Kyn smiled triumphantly.

Runa looked to him quizzically. "Did all the pieces of your brain grow back in the right place?"

Kyn shrugged gamely, not answering. He nodded to Benn, his smile growing wider.

"So, what's the pink stuff?" He asked, confident his theory was correct.

The Handler turned the footage to an example of the Divider's glowing powers, enhanced it, then tapped out the same commands he'd done before. The text box appeared again.

NO DATA.

Taking the same steps as before, Benn focused on another randomly chosen section of footage - this time featuring Runa as she flew backwards through an entire residential stack - and analyzed a section of exploding apartment through the diagnostic algorithms. Once again, a text box appeared with a detailed and catalogued break down of everything present in the image. He tried again over another randomized sample of the pink energy.

NO DATA.

The algorithms gave them nothing. Nothing on the glowing pink energy itself, or from the Dividers clothing and masks. Nothing about the two intruders matched any piece of information in the SPIREs' vast data network.

"Huh." Benn remarked, mouth hung slack with bemusement.

"Exactly." Kyn stated, justified as understanding dawned on the faces of the others. "Why don't we know what it is?"

"Someone is cleaning up." Ashe offered.

Kyn tapped his nose.

Someone was tampering with the Unity's data feeds, slipping past the city's most powerful and skilled cyber security, jumping expertly fortified firewalls to tamper with the footage. Either by blocking the diagnostic programs from reading any information about the Dividers or erasing anything the scans had managed to find before the systems identified it.

Only one independent source outside the Unity's control had agents who might have a chance at pulling off a code slide that skilled.

The Informant.

Kyn ran his hands over the front of the nylon weave vest.

"I've got someone I can talk to." He groaned with an exhausted sigh, cursing himself even as he did so.

Red-Light

Kyn flexed his feet and hooked his toes over the jutting ledge of the factory's slab roof. Confident in his toe hold despite the ancient structure's crumbling facade, he released his hands and unfolded his torso so that he hung upside down by his flexed digits.

A duffel sack from around his torso went through the open loft window first, and he heard it thud inside the darkened flat. Unburdened by the bulky equipment bag, he compressed torso to thighs, folding himself in half to reach back to the ledge above with one hand. He pointed his feet and unfurled, swinging his legs to deftly throw himself backwards through the window's narrow gap and landing in a silent crouch on the cold cement.

Lighting tubes that ran the length of the loft's overhead steel supports flickered on the moment his boots touched floor, illuminating the flat with a haunting white glow and casting long shadows across the graffiti covered walls.

Kyn heaved a heavy sigh and rolled his shoulders, exulting in the last of a waning endorphins that still thrummed through his muscles. His body ached pleasantly with the effort expended from running across the rooftops and ward platforms that lay between Noav SPIRE and his lower wards factory.

The city had been in chaos.

Fires burned across the mid and lower wards. Gangs of roving cultists prowled the city, sowing terror, and mistrust. Live-streams echoing the Unity agenda dominated every corner of the feed. The message, re-purposed by media cults, streaked across the blogosphere and public forums, spreading like a virus. Across the mids, rumors flew. Within hours of the mere suggestion, anyone suggested to having possible ties to the Ragers was met with immediate social ostracism. Lives and careers were destroyed instantly. Suicide was rampant. Dag squads arrested citizens en masse.

In the lowers, suspected Rager sympathizers were dragged into the streets to be beaten or straight up executed. Mob justice in the name of the Unity.

Entire sectors of city stacks burned.

"The Unity has everything under control." Alexi reassured from every public feed, joined by the other SPIRE media leads to smile benevolently down on the citizens.

Kyn cast a longing glance towards the alcove he'd sectioned off as his sleeping quarters, briefly contemplating the padded mat unrolled atop the low bedslab, still covered by an unmade pile of ruffled blankets from days earlier. Inescapable exhaustion crept around the edges of his mind, aching behind his eye sockets.

He hadn't slept in several days and was beginning to feel the strain. Technically he'd awoken from the dead several times, but death for him wasn't the inherently restful state others assumed it to be. He still required semi-regular sleep.

Grudgingly he turned away from the alcove, rubbing wearily at his eyes with one hand. He hoisted the discarded equipment bag onto the cluttered surface of his workbench, inhaling deeply to steady himself for what still needed to be done.

The air smelt faintly like sparking wires.

Sleep would wait a while longer.

"You can stay, but don't get any ideas. I'm going to sleep," he told the ghostly lit loft. He dipped his chin so that his auburn hair fell roguishly over his eyes and turned to face the man standing behind him.

Alec stared back at him from the center of the loft, clothes tattered and stained with dried blood. The acid-haired hacker's expression was blank, his pretty face, smeared with dirt and grime, was swollen with scrapes and bruising. Med patches covered unseen wounds across his left arm and along the side of his neck. He stood tall despite his injuries, his eyes rimmed red and bloodshot. The sparse overhead lighting reflected in the muted green like electricity sparking over a circuit board.

"When?" Kyn asked plainly. He tried not to read the story of chaos and brutality written across Alec's body, tried not to let it touch that deep part of him that refused to stop caring if others got hurt.

Silence stretched.

"2300. SpareParts," Alec finally answered, his voice dry and strained. A pained, strangled rasping.

0600 glowed blue in the corner of Kyn's optic. He pushed away from the countertop and reached out to Alec, offering his hand. He tilted his head toward the alcove.

"Let's get some rest."

Alec took the offered hand without a word, intertwining their fingers, and Kyn gave the other man's fingers a gentle, reassuring, squeeze, whether seeking to give comfort or seeking his own, he couldn't be sure. Alec's larger hand gripped back tightly in response, holding fast.

< = >

Kyn followed Alec down a hall lit only by beams of bouncing multi-hued laser light.

Walls of polished metal, buffed to a mirrored sheen, reflected the lasers back on themselves, turning the long corridor to a dizzying kaleidoscopic of colour. Kyn watched as Alec melded into himself through a mirrored wall. The tall, acid-haired punk strode into and through his mirror twin, again and again, pushing through distorted versions of himself. Falling through laser light stars. Kyn's own mercurial mirror selves shed away as he followed, peeling from him like the discarded skins of other, forgotten, selves.

The outer corridors of SpareParts were a twisted maze of flesh and metal. Where the incredibly sexy bought and traded themselves, people, and parts interchangeably. The duo moved through a stream of the achingly beautiful, traveling with the throng of sculpted, sweat-slick, flesh. Turning a corner, they pushed against the current, then pressed forwards again, moving against a new throng of flesh. Walls opened as doors at their passing, and Kyn glanced into one room. A midnight skinned woman sat cross-legged on a single stool, the laser lines of light reflecting from her. Bouncing away. Continuing. A silent man, naked save his domino mask, stood behind her. She removed an arm below the elbow and passed the limb on to someone unseen. Then, taking another of polyvinyl and wire offered to her by the masked man, slid the limb into place, twisting it firmly at the joint. The fingers of her new hand twitched to life, and a nefarious smile spread across her face as she watched the digits flex and unfurl.

Another section of wall opened to reveal roiling piles of naked and synthetic flesh. Oil-soaked bodies, wired at the temple, grunting, and moaning as they writhed across each other. A neural collective devouring itself.

Kyn's reflected selves pulled into rooms as they passed, disappearing behind doors. He watched as the flow of Alec's green haired duplicates pushed themselves up against a shapely female bio-hack. Mirror Alec twisted, smiling goofily at her, his hands grazing hips, caressing the smooth hardness where hip drifted into the sleek molded prosthetic of her tech-jacked leg. Joint motors purred as she shifted, pressing back against him, leaning into him. Sultry lips brushed his cheek as she whispered in his ear. Alec pressed closer, fingers dipping between her thighs.

A brawny, olive-skinned, switchboy grabbed greedily at Kyn's bare torso. Seductively caressing over the sculpted muscles of the Envoy's abdomen and chest, he wound his fingers into dark fabric of the high-necked cowl that draped across Kyn's bare shoulders.

Kyn met the stranger's heavy gaze, studying the hunger that lived behind gently slanting brown eyes. In his periphery Alec separated himself from the biohacker with a passionately deep kiss, a pattern of horizontal lines tattooed across his bicep flashing yellow as they parted.

Kyn slipped out of his admirer's grasp.

They wound through the gray market's outer corridors. Red lights flashed at intersections, guiding signals towards needs and desires. The maze of distorted mirrors and scantily clad bodies eventually dropping them into the beating heart of SpareParts; the shimmering glass interior of the geodesic dome that housed the market's central trade floor.

An ancient relic of a dead civilization, the glittering geodesic dome had once been a popular tourist destination, dedicated to scientific knowledge, and built in an era when humanity had spanned the globe. When people had traveled for their own leisure from one sprawling megacity to the other.

After the fall, the long-abandoned dome had become a hub for the nomadic scavengers that trekked the blasted and wasted remains of the world before. Seeking shelter and trading their wares with bits of gossip and tales of the dangers of the beyond.

Then, with the coming of the Unity, the geodesic dome became absorbed into the city's re-birth, swallowed by the tangled mass of urban progress, to morph into its new and present form; the disorienting and dangerous lower wards playground known simply as SpareParts. A place of worship for the city's gene mod freaks, tech implanted, and self enhancement obsessed. Cavorting amongst themselves as they proudly flaunted their re-construction. Reveling in a newly discovered trans-humanism that went beyond what was dictated as acceptable by the strict social norms of the wards above.

Kyn matched pace with Alec, stepping out onto the bustling main trade floor. Levels of stacked market cubes encircled a sunken amphitheater, rising toward the glittering glass dome above. Darkly thumping electro pulsed.

The central point of the main trading floor was a looping circular service top in the sunken theater, surrounded by slender stools supporting aloof patrons. Delicate, cylindrical light tubes hung above, casting pools of silver light. Yet more patrons sprawled in various states of nerveshook or patchjumped delirium across clusters of low synth-leather slabs, while scantily clad tenders picked through the mess, collecting credits, and encouraging further partaking. Performers - groin achingly beautiful mergers of sleek synthetics and genetically perfect flesh - strutted across the service top. Sex and skin reigned. Plastic and personalized mod the flair. Detached disinterest was fetishized, and brooding indifference the overarching character theme. This was a place to be deconstructed and re-built, hacked, and re-programed.

Kyn could feel admiring eyes on him as they pressed through the crowd. In the absence of his own prosthetic augment, biotech implant, or readily visible gene mod, he'd opted to be liberal with the show of skin and had slunk himself into a pair of synth-leather leggings and a hooded harness. He'd lathered metal scented oil over the tautly muscled flesh of his arms and torso, then brushed his skin with a reflective glitter-dust that made him glint and flash in the bouncing laser light. The mysterious black band still wrapped securely around his wrist.

Alec earned as many, if not more, hungry looks, having donned ass-clinging yellow plaid pants tucked into chrome studded boots. More steel studded synth-leather wrapped around his lean, bare torso, snaking around muscular arms. Going for flashy, the hacker had programed his collection of tattoos to dance in a gently pulsing light show that undulated over his bare skin. The med patches had done their work and the scrapes and bruises on his sharply handsome face had faded visibly, shadows of what they had been the night before.

Despite the importance of his hunt, Kyn eyed Alec hungrily himself, plans forming in his mind on how best to use the heightened sexual tension of the club to his advantage once he'd gotten what he'd come for.

Or, before. If they had time.

Kyn's optic suddenly flashed alarm red around the edges, blurring his periphery. Visual feedback as his f-Link detected an attack against his personal firewall. Some unseen hacker was pushing against his security protocols, trying to read Kyn's encrypted data signature. Snarling, he spun around, hand moving instinctively to his back, reaching along his spine for Ego, sheathed snugly between his shoulder blades, hidden beneath the draped hood and crossing straps.

He scanned the crowd.

Alec's restraining hand pressed against his chest, warning him back. The taller man turned on his heel, doing his own quick scan of the crowd. Raising his free hand, he clenched it into a fist and a spiraling chain tattoo at his wrist flashed an angry red.

To their right, a scrawny tweeker in a shiny black gimp suit screamed, clutching at their latex-wrapped head.

The flashing red warning died in Kyn's vision immediately. The tweeker screamed, their left eye burning with a cybernetic glare. The crowd flowed around, unfazed. The light grew brighter and brighter, as did the tweekers screams. Brighter, and brighter. Until it winked out, overloaded, cybernetic scorched to a bleached white. Blinded and ruined.

Alec winked back at Kyn.

Leaving the bold tweeker to the friends who had swooped in to tend to him, Alec and Kyn approached the looping service top.

Kyn let Alec take lead, hanging back to silently watch as his companion approached the high counter and signaled a hovering tender. He stayed near the taller man's elbow, like a dangerous and glittering shadow.

Alec leaned in to talk to the tender, a tall peroxide blonde, half her skull plated in candy block-coloured plating; asking after a contact or passing on some prearranged signal, Kyn didn't know, and didn't care. The hacker was just his guide tonight.

The two had spoken little after waking. Alec didn't know why the Informant had tasked him with setting up a meeting with Kyn, and Kyn didn't offer an explanation. Information was the Informant's business, and they would have had to know someone like Kyn would find them eventually. The Unity didn't like when others might know more than they did.

"Here to the stare at the freaks or are you a devotee?" A melodic voice asked from above. A service top performer had stopped her sensual pacing to kneel next to Kyn. Scantily clad, the motors in the woman's prosthetic leg gently whirred with the motion, barely audible under the pulsing thumps of the music. She gripped a pole secured to the service top and leaned out to caress Kyn's face with silicone fingers. A mechanized hand attached to the graceful plating of an elegantly molded prosthetic arm slotted in at her slender shoulder. She was naked save for crisscrossing strips of silver gauze strapped across the curve of her hips. The performer smiled at Kyn seductively. Dark waves of hair flowed over bare shoulders, and her eyes where a gene dyed warning sign orange that locked onto his and didn't look away.

He smiled back at her, all teeth. "Maybe a devotee."

"Maybe." She purred, her own smile shifting from sensual to mischievous. She buoyed her ample cleavage between her flesh and mechanical hands, waggling them playfully in his direction. "But I doubt you much like these."

"Aye." He answered, simple in his confirmation, waiting to see where she'd press the interaction.

"I'm not going to waste my time trying to patch a glitch. Too bad though, you lot are always the prettiest boys in the lowers. Such a waste." She sunk down on the service top's edge, propping herself up on her elbows as she crossed her legs, mechanical limb slung over flesh, bouncing rhythmically at the knee. She watched Kyn.

"You who I'm here to see?" He asked, glancing sideways to Alec, still conversing with the tender. Though he wasn't looking in the Envoy's direction, Kyn got the impression the hacker knew exactly what was going on.

"No. I'm Evi." The performer answered simply, her smile grown still wider. She slipped from the top and slunk past Kyn, playfully nudging him with her hip as she passed. She tossed something over her shoulder. Kyn reached out, deftly catching it. He turned the object over in his grasp.

It was an apple. Perfectly red from the upper wards' gene synthesizing orchards.

Kyn cast another glance toward Alec. This time, the fine-featured hacker stared back at him, his expression unreadable.

Shrugging his narrow shoulders, Kyn winked impishly back and turned to follow his new augmented guide into the pressing crowd.

He casually raised the apple to his lips and sunk his teeth deep into the fruit, tearing out a sweet hunk of juicy flesh. He was careful to keep his eyes fixed firmly ahead, focusing on Evi's slinking form, pretending to be unaware of the orb drifting discreetly along behind him.

Evi wound her way through the market stacks, leading Kyn steadily upwards. Her semi-mechanized silhouette flowed gracefully through the throngs of flesh and machinery. Strobes of laser light illuminated the market stalls and bounced off the smooth surface of her prosthetics, reflecting outwards in dazzling pinpricks.

They passed jumbled collections of mod clinics, net hubs, and augment booths, lit with holo ads and neon shop signs. The dark electro soundscape throbbed in Kyn's veins like his own pulse.

Evi veered away from the main thoroughfare and down an empty corridor that ran between stacked rows of repurposed cargo containers, rectangular steel boxes piled high enough that the upper-most container brushed against the domed ceiling. The steel stacks buffered the omnipresent sounds of the club and under market below. The thump of the music muted, dulled to a distant throb that Kyn could feel pulsing through the soles of his boots.

Evi came to an abrupt halt in front of a seemingly random crate, and Kyn stopped alongside her. There was no door he could discern, and he watched curiously as Evi raised her plastic and metal hand to place a palm flat against the container's wall. An intricate two-dimensional holo of interlocking lines and squares lit up against the perforated steel. An electronic puzzle lock. Evi smoothly manipulated squares into the correct order, causing the lock to chirp affirmatively and wink out. A razor-thin outline appeared in the smooth metal wall, and a previously invisible door slide open to pitch-blackness.

Evi had not said a word to the Envoy or even glanced in his directions since they'd left the main level, but now she turned to him. The playful flirtation of earlier gone, her expression was set and hard. Her large, orange, doe eyes burned with intensity.

"We do not fear the Unity here." She stated firmly.

Kyn kept his face in its practiced, impassive mask. Blank. Unreadable.

Internally he laughed, marveling at her boldness.

Her statement was sacrilege; a dangerous and subversive sentiment.

He held her unflinching gaze. When he spoke, his voice was kind and smooth. Pleasant.

"Well, I don't see why you would." He lied, casually. Then, with a soft smile, added more truthfully. "You have nothing to fear from me."

"This." Evi stated. She raised her cybernetic arm, demonstratively opening and closing her fingers with graceful dexterity. "Is all thanks to the Unity." Her eyes burned with a smoldering rage. "A culling is a messy time, see not everyone the Dags shoots dies. Lots of us just get hurt - some of us get hurt bad. It's chaos. Some of us get parts torn off. Then we get the parts replaced. Every culling we lose another piece of ourselves. Eventually we stop waiting for it to happen and take control. Shape ourselves." She stepped closer to Kyn and cupped his face in the palm of her synthetic hand. His skin was hot from the heat of the crowded club, and the merger of metal and plastic was refreshingly cool against his skin. She subtlety flexed her fingers, and he could feel the crushing, mechanized strength of her grasp. "Make ourselves better." She asserted proudly.

Kyn's face never shifted from its unreadable blankness, when he spoke, his voice was polite and measured.

"Like I said. You have nothing to fear from me."

Evi released Kyn's face and stepped away. The hydraulics in her augmented leg whirred softly, and pin pricks of light blinked rhythmically along the joint seams.

"We fear nothing." Evi returned pointedly, before turning from Kyn and striding away, leaving him alone with the open crate.

He watched her go. Her self-assured stride and subtle threat told him she believed what she said. She had come to intimately know the unspoken violence of the Unity.

He understood that.

A blur of motion, flitting at the corner of his vision, pulled him back to his task. The spherical drone - Dorothy - zipped past his head before plunging through the open doorway, disappearing into the darkness of the crate. Kyn followed, unsurprised as the door slid shut automatically behind him, the electronic lock engaging with a secure thud.

The darkness was total for only a moment before the re-purposed cargo container lit up, as if expecting his presence. The crate's interior was larger than it had appeared from the outside, the barriers between crates removed to create a single open space, unfurnished except for a delicate antique armchair of polished cherry and crushed velvet cushions, placed in the center of the room. The armchair faced the source of the light; an entire wall lit up with the projected image of disembodied and brilliantly painted lips, crimson red against a pure white backdrop.

Kyn crossed and sank into the armchair, casually folding one leg over the other at the knee. He tipped his head back, waiting for the next finely choreographed reveal. Plush fabric prickled against the bare skin of his lower back.

A moist pink tongue slid between the crimson lips, passing itself over large, white teeth to teasingly poke at the corner of the mouth, before hiding itself again. The whole process looped back, repeating.

Kyn could feel the familiar press of Ego between his shoulder blades as he relaxed further into the lux armchair.

He wasn't surprised by the theatrics. Someone like the Informant didn't stay out of the Unity's grasp without being prepared.

Misdirection and subterfuge were their stock and trade. The city's most powerful independent information broker wouldn't risk contacting a suspected Unity agent without having full control over the field of engagement.

"Welcome." Filled the crate. The crimson lips moved, mouthing words. The voice was heavily digitized, hiding any discernible identifying traits.

"Hello." Kyn answered the room. "Am I finally speaking to the mysterious Informant? Or are you another waypoint?"

"Does it matter?" The digitized voice queried. The lips moved in perfect sync with the words.

"Well yes, a bit," Kyn countered.

He caught a brief blur of motion in one darkened corner. The floating Dorothy drone, skirting low to the ground, circled the room, keeping to the shadows. Kyn kept his eyes carefully trained on the projection in front of him, not wanting to give away the bot's presence. Wherever the Informant was, Kyn had no doubt they were watching him and the room closely. The little round drone skimmed the periphery of his vision, then zipped out of sight, hiding under his chair.

"And who are you?" The digital voice asked.

"You tell me." Kyn challenged, gray eyes sparkling mischievously. "You of all people should know the layers of secrets one person can be. How at once we are many different people, but also none. Each of us containing legions."

"I trade in information, not secrets. Information is truth about the world laid out for anyone to see if they know where to look. Unshakeable reality." The projected lips expounded. "Secrets are lies. Stories we tell ourselves and others in justification our actions. Denial of what is true. Information uplifts, encourages self-improvement. Secrets repress and suppress. Conveniently malleable perception. Warped reality."

Though the voice was digitized, true passion crept into the delivery. This was the voice of a revolutionary. A ghost of rebellion in the machine.

"So, do you know the truth about me?" Kyn encouraged.

"No person can tell the truth of another. We can only tell the truth of ourselves." The red lips countered.

"You're an information broker, indulge me."

"Broker implies a trade."

"Name your price."

"A truth for a truth." The digital voice proposed.

"Some truths are dangerous," Kyn cautioned.

He currently had no orders to eliminate the broker, but that could always change if the Sentry didn't like what he learned. Or if they decided the Informant knew too much.

"Truth."

The projection changed. Compounded surveillance footage of the Envoys fight against the Dividers played in front of Kyn.

"This is you." The digital voice prompted.

"Truth." Kyn confirmed. The Envoys had become easy fodder for anti-Unity conspiracy theories after their very public fight with the Dividers. Unity propaganda divisions had been working overtime to shift the narrative. The shadowy masked figures seen combating the Dividers rampaging through the streets were not the SPIREs' experimental hit squad, like the wild intranet conspiracy theories speculated, but the Unity's elite squad of guardians, according to the official SPIRE line, trained in secret to protect the citizens of the walled city. Evidence otherwise was quickly suppressed.

We are here to protect you. The Unity reminded the people.

"You already knew that." Kyn added in follow up. The Informant liked playing games, he could respect that.

"Truth." The Informant confirmed.

This time the projection was a distorted security cam feed. An ident logo in the corner of the screen marked it as property of Yummy Otter Corp. The time stamp marked it as from several nights earlier.

The footage was grainy with a warping distortion that indicated the source file had been uploaded from a highly damaged server. Probably salvaged from the melted remains of the onsite storage oni that should have been destroyed in the fire Runa started. Beyond the damaged quality, it was made further difficult to decipher by the haze of multicoloured smoke and fumes that clouded the feed. Two silhouetted figures were discernible through the haze, one crouched over the other on a destroyed catwalk.

Kyn recognized himself by his low, lithe crouch. He watched as he drew his blade across the guard's throat in a spurt of crimson.

Are you a demon?

"This is you."

"Truth."

The image shifted again before Kyn had a chance to counter. This time to even earlier in the events within Yummy Otter Corp. He was impressed. The Informant had managed to get more from the factory's ruined servers then the Envoy would've thought possible. Whatever data tech had overseen cleaning the scene had made a fatal error. When Kyn reported back how much footage had survived the fire, the offending tech would be hunted down and executed. The Sentry did not look favorably on those who failed in their tasks.

Kyn watched the footage, his face impassive.

He was featured again, but this time he wasn't alone. It had shifted to the moment when Ashe had enthralled the newly dis-covered Wasters, and was leading them to freedom before Runa and Kyn laid waste to the building and its security force.

The digitized voice spoke again.

"These are Wasters."

"Truth." Kyn answered, cold and even.

The image switched before Kyn had a chance at rebuttal. The Informant was obviously already abandoning their game of banter now that they'd arrived at the part where they got to show off, flaunting how much they knew.

Kyn didn't recognize the next footage. Clearer this time, it was from a hacked feed he placed with mild surprise as part of Noav SPIRE's inner security system, a cam from the lower sub-levels where the angular walls were made of concrete instead of polyplex.

The Informant really did seem to have eyes everywhere. More techs would die once this breach was reported.

Kyn uncrossed his legs and leaned forward, resting elbows on knees. He watched the footage intently, gray eyes wide with delighted astonishment at what he was seeing.

At first, he was just watching an empty corridor somewhere within the depths of the SPIRE, indistinguishable from any other. A row of doors lined one side of the corridor, each closed and uniformly unmarked. The vid fed a few moments of nothing before an unknown female Divider stalked into view, recognizable by her strange, wrapped clothing, that flowed and swirled around her like turbulent waves. Masked, her face was covered with a light projected faceplate depicting a brightly painted animal skull. Unlike her fellows, this woman's head was uncovered, cowl pulled back, revealing a long plait of coppery red hair that snaked down a strong back. She flowed like molten steel, moving with the confidence that comes from real power.

Kyn saw a woman who walked alone through the heart of a SPIRE and was unafraid. He was riveted.

The unknown woman moved to a panel set in the wall. An interface lit up at her touch, and she tapped in a quick series of commands. Every door lining the hallway slid open in response. Surprise spread across Kyn's face as vaguely familiar figures streamed out of each door. Terrified looking people filled the corridor, all of them turned expectantly to the mysterious woman.

Kyn studied the people closely. They all wore the same simple white underclothing, their hair long and wild in ways that looked utterly foreign to his eye. Realization dawned on him.

The Wasters. The same Wasters they'd rescued from Yummy Otter Corp.

Though, from the disheveled and traumatized state of the released crowd, Kyn doubted rescued was the right word for what had happened. Nothing seemed wrong at first glance, the Wasters looked clean and well cared for, no signs of abuse or malnutrition. Yet, the difference from how he'd first seen them to the people he saw now in the projection was unsettling. It was in the wane uniformity of their exhausted looks, the red rimmed and glassy eyes. The expressions that twitched between abject terror and resigned defeat. But when they looked to their mysterious liberator, deep resignation morphed to breathless awe. Kyn saw the relief of those who'd escaped imminent death. These people had been resigned to their own end, and this woman was their savior.

Transfixed, he watched as the female Divider hustled her charges away, gesturing emphatically for them to flee. The Wasters flowed past the security cam, disappearing with the Divider at their rear when a fleeing Waster suddenly halted with a jerk; their body suspended in place, wracked by violent spasms.

The projection supplied no audio, but Kyn could tell the halted figure was screaming.

The Divider spun, looking for the threat. Her mask changed to a wild, snarling beast, and her body was instantly wreathed in swirling pink energy that danced hypnotically around her.

Kyn's propped his chin on steeped fingers. Recognizing the nature of the attack on the Waster, he was intrigued but not surprised when Malvyc appeared, striding calmly into view. The bald Envoy's eyes blazed red, and fleeing Waster's fell to his gaze, collapsing to the floor, shaking, and screaming silently.

Kyn leaned in further, curious to what the enigmatic woman would do.

She raised a hand, and the fight was over.

The Divider spun to face Malvyc, long braid whipping around her, fiery red wreathed in a shimmering pink aura, and raised her hand with a swiping, definitive movement, an indisputably halting command.

A brilliant ripple of pink seized upon Malvyc, instantly freezing him in place, stopped mid- step, one foot hovering off the ground. The menacing Envoy's unblinking eyes still glowed red, but the strange shifting energy glowed around him, encasing him in a shimmering bubble, and holding him - and his gift - in stasis.

Released from Malvyc's power, the downed Wasters helped each other run, stumbling towards the exits and out of view. Their protector followed closely behind, sweeping from view without a second glance for her motionless victim. Malvyc glared balefully as she passed, helpless as his quarry escaped, her disinterest adding insult to how easily he'd been neutralized.

Kyn smiled. Malvyc had failed miserably, and he'd gotten to see the evidence for himself.

Delighted as he was, the real message the Informant had intended Kyn to take away from their meeting was clear. The Dividers and the Wasters were linked. The Unity knew about it, otherwise they wouldn't have sent Malvyc. Kyn leaned back in his chair, turning what he'd learned over in his mind, looking at the new puzzle pieces from all angles to see where they might fit.

He wasn't surprised the Unity had lied about the Wasters. He'd always gleaned there was more to that story then the 'grateful and downtrodden refugee' narrative they'd been peddling. Plus, the Unity lied. He'd killed enough people covering their deceptions to know that.

He was curious as to why the Wasters were still being held within a SPIRE facility. What did the Unity gain by lying about sending the Wasters to re-education camps in the resource zone?

It was undeniable that the Unity knew there was a connection between the Dividers and the Wasters? So why not tell Kyn and the other Envoys? What did he do with this information now that he knew?

Kyn thoughtfully traced his thumb over the smooth surface of the cuff around his wrist, pondering how the strange tech might play into this new information. They'd taken both the cuff and the Wasters from Yummy Otter Corp, and the Dividers had targeted both. So how were they linked?

He would've liked to ask Vikta FaMa and Eva Scavr, but Ashe had conveniently executed them.

The projection switched. Disembodied crimson lips hovered before him once more.

"You have questions."

The digitized voice snapped Kyn out of his meditation. He did have questions. He briefly contemplated where to start, his fingers caressing distractedly along the smooth edges of the cuff, debating how much he wanted to expose his hand.

"I do." He answered finally, ceasing his fidgeting, both arms rested casually on the delicate armrests. He crossed his ankle over his other knee. "Where are the Ragers?" He asked.

"The Ragers?"

"Yah. Violent, anti-Unity terrorist." He countered, shortly. "I've seen a lot of these outsiders. But what about the Ragers? Supposedly took responsibility for all of this? Hacking the system. Blowing through not only the supposedly impenetrable wall, but also destroying the whole outer array. Didn't they let those glowing pink badasses in here? I mean they flashed their logo across every screen in the city the moment this started. They took credit for everything. Branded the attack. So, where are they now? Have you seen them?" He arched an eyebrow at the projection.

"Yes." The digitized voice confirmed.

The hairs on the back of Kyn's neck tingled, sensing the threat behind the heavily altered voice. His muscles tensed in anticipation as he gleaned the real price the Informant had in mind.

"They're here, aren't they?" He asked, fully aware of the answer. He could hear heavy footsteps approaching from outside the interconnected metal crates now. The ceiling above him groaned as someone's weight dropped on it, not trying to be quiet. This meeting was over.

"Truth." The crimson lips mouthed.

"Cute," Kyn returned drolly. He uncrossed his legs, setting both feet firmly on the ground. "Tell me one more thing, you know, before we get rudely interrupted," he petitioned the projection. Careful not to take his eyes off the lips, he scanned the room with his peripheral.

Across the room to his left, he clocked a thin slit of light visible near the floor. The outline of another door, opposite from where he'd come in. He could hear more bodies shifting on the roof above, telling him there was probably a hatch in the ceiling.

"What would you like to know?" The mouth encouraged.

"Where was that footage taken? The Wasters. Do you have a location?"

"I do." The voice confirmed. Kyn's f-Link lit up, neon blue in the dim space. "Consider this a parting gift."

Kyn tapped the tip of his middle finger against the antique chair's delicate armrest - confirming the file transfer. Text blinked red in the corner of his augmented vision.

NOAV SPIRE Sub-level:29 Sector: D

"Thanks." He returned earnestly, with an appreciative nod to the lips. "Very helpful." He settled comfortably into the chair, affecting a pose of relaxed nonchalance, pearly white teeth flashing wolfishly. "Well, you might as well transfer me to the billing department. Release the goons and what have you." He chattered pleasantly. "I'll be seeing you soon."

"I have no doubt." The Informant replied, an edge of exasperation detectable beneath the heavily altered voice.

The projection winked out, leaving Kyn alone in darkness. Heavy boots settled behind the doors and bodies shifted above him.

"Ready Dorothy?" Kyn asked the darkened room.

An affirmative flash of green lit the floor under his chair.

The left door slid open, filling the shipping container with outside light and sound. Momentarily blinded, Kyn was aware of the soft thud of someone landing ungracefully behind him, even under the thumping music. The dark outline of a looming figure filled the doorway, silhouetted by the light from the club. The figure raised an arm and rapid-fire k-cannon blasts lit up the inside of the cargo crate.

Kyn threw himself sideways, diving blindly at the floor. He launched the antique chair over his back as he dove, blind aiming at the figure filling the open door. The chair hit the stream of kinetic fire and was obliterated instantly, shredded. The silhouetted figure swung wildly sideways, trying to avoid the sudden explosion of metal and wood shrapnel. Ancient cushion stuffing exploded everywhere.

Hitting the ground, Kyn managed to dodge under the veering line of fire and roll sideways. Arms in tight as he rolled, he quickly closed the distance between himself and the looming figure. Unfurling into a low crouch, Kyn snaked one hand up his spine and snatched Ego from its place between his shoulder blades. The momentum whipped his hood up over his head, and he smirked at the drama. Snarling at the cannon-armed figure, he savagely bared his teeth, embracing the moment.

Behind him, a brilliant crackle of electric discharge lit up the crate, coupled with a yelp of pain, and the unmistakable smell of burnt hair and flesh. Dorothy had engaged at least one of the other attackers, and the electric afterglow of their attacks allowed Kyn a clear look at his own target, an imposingly tall and rough-looking man, poorly balding head, with a cybernetic rapid-fire k-cannon where his right arm had once been.

The Rager swung their weapon arm around and sent another volley of kinetic fire in Kyn's direction.

Kyn dove sideways again, easily dodging the onslaught before switching course and running straight at the Rager. He threw Ego horizontally across his body as he ran, sending the dagger slicing through the air with lightning quickness.

The Rager twisted away, narrowly avoiding having Ego burrow itself between their eyes. Instead, the duel edged blade drove point first into the soft crook above the Rager's non-weaponized arm, biting deep into connective tissue.

The cannon-armed Rager howled in pain and swung their weaponized limb around wildly, firing blindly as they tried to level it at Kyn.

The Rager was too slow and Kyn was on them instantly.

Moving smoothly into the Ragers area of reach, he struck out with both hands. The palm of his left slapped down on Ego's hilt, driving the weapon even further into the Ragers shoulder and caus-ing the larger man to bellow again with fresh pain. Blood spurted from beneath the dagger's hilt. The open palm of Kyn's right hand slammed into the taller man's face at the same time, the heel crushing the Rager's nose with brutal force. Bellows of pain were transformed into gurgles as the Rager's airway clogged with their own blood and shattered cartiledge.

Pressing his advantage Kyn ripped Ego from the Rager's shoulder. The brute stumbled backwards, blinded by pain and his own blood. Kyn flipped the dagger and lunged forward to deliver the killing blow.

Dorthy drone chirped out a short, sharp note of warning, followed closely by the heavy, loading clunk of a pump action k-cannon directly behind Kyn.

Abruptly changing course, Kyn spun sideways, dancing away to slip nimbly behind the cannon armed Rager, narrowly avoiding the incoming kinetic blast from another unseen assailant.

The dodged round blasted into the cannon-armed Rager, shredding their torso with a wide scatter shot, dropping them instantly. Dead.

Kyn spun to meet this new threat just as they fired another blast in his direction. Shifting weight instinctively, he dove backwards, flipping tidily over the incoming scattershot at the same moment Dorothy released another burst of electricity.

From his inversed perspective, Kyn could clearly make out the Rager who'd fired on him in the crackling burst. A squat woman, armed with a short, pump action k-cannon, hair buzzed close to the scalp. Her eyes flashed yellow in the electric burst. Augmented vision with auto-target protocol, he guessed, landing deftly on his feet.

The exits had slid closed, and Dorothy fired off another electric blast, lighting up the dim space once again.

The drone was trying to drive back yet another Rager, a spindly limbed tweeker with long, fiendish looking blades that protruded from augment compartments in his forearms. The tweeker moved with jittery speed, dodging the energy blasts as he sliced back at the offending drone even as electricity crackled over the blade's sharp edges.

The squat woman fired another blast at Kyn as he landed, forcing him to leap backwards again, flinging himself wildly into a twisting mid-air roll to narrowly avoid the shot. Changing tactics as he landed, he spun on his heels, jabbing Ego back up into its sheath as he ran from the shooter, sprinting straight at the steel wall of fused crates.

"Dorothy! Lights!" He yelled.

The floating drone complied, emitting a continuous flashing strobe that pulsed with a jerky stutter, burning after images onto Kyn's vision.

Running into the wall, he placed one foot at waist-height against the wavy metal and drove himself upwards, running straight up the vertical surface. He tilted sideways as he climbed, veering in an arch as his booted feet pounded against the thin steel, fighting gravity.

The yellow eyed woman swung around wildly, trying to track Kyn. The jumpy flashes of light and disjointed after images wreaking havoc on her augmented vision, confusing the auto-aim.

Losing momentum and the fight against gravity, Kyn pushed away from the wall, diving down on the squat Rager from above. He wrapped his arms tightly around the woman's neck as he fell and twisted with their collision, yanking the Rager off balance, and hauling them both bodily to the ground with a meaty thud.

The woman fell heavily on Kyn and he grunted as her greater weight crushed his chest, forcefully expelling the air from his lungs. She'd lost her grip on the pump action k-cannon and the loose weapon skittered across the floor, spinning away from them to rest a few paces away, out of easy reach of either combatant.

Pinned to the floor, Kyn thrashed like a trapped animal, slamming knees and elbows viciously into any soft point of the Rager's bulk he could reach, and was rewarded with yelps of pain from the terrorist on top of him. Blindly grabbing at the woman's face, he dug slender fingers into her yellow eyes, digging into the softness until the softness popped and she screamed, rolling off him. Kyn moved the moment her weight was gone, throwing himself across the floor. His fingers wrapped around the k-cannon's stock just as he caught the flash of Dorothy's strobe against the sharp edge of the tweeker's arm blade, slicing towards his head. The blade stuttered and jumped in the strobe. He pulled the k-cannon to his chest and rolled, narrowly avoiding decapitation, and sprung to his feet. The tweekers arm blade scrapped across the steel floor with the angry screech of metal on metal.

Losing sight of the spindly tweeker in the bouncing strobe, Kyn turned on the Rager he'd downed, leveling the k-cannon. He took a beat as she pawed uselessly at her damaged eyes before he cocked the weapon with a heavy clunk. Her blood-streaked face turned at the sound, and he pulled the trigger, exploding half her skull in a spray of crimson mist.

Dorothy zipped in front of Kyn, furiously blinking a warning red beneath its persistent strobe effect. Too late Kyn remembered the tweeker he'd lost track of, and his gray eyes widened in shock as the tip of an arm blade pierced the skin of his back, tearing through muscle and organs in a sliver of white pain, to explode outward from behind his sternum in a spurt of black-crimson. He choked, dimly aware the blade was scraping his spine.

Dorothy's optic was leveled steadily on him, watching. The flashing red warning had stopped. Kyn coughed, bloody and sputtering, and slumped forward over the augmented blade protruding from his chest. The k-cannon hung limply from his fingers. Kyn locked eyes with the hovering bot's glassy lens, imagining he could sense Alec's shock translated through the bot's sudden stillness.

He winked conspiratorially at the drone, face split in a broad, bloody toothed grin. His fingers coiled around the k-cannon's stock.

Then, in a blur of motion and a tearing lance of pain, he swung the weapon to his shoulder, aimed directly behind, and pulled the trigger, firing off the second loaded round.

The discharge roar blew out his eardrum, reducing everything to an atonal hum. The blade yanked from his chest cavity, and he let loose an adrenaline filled scream of rage and pain he couldn't hear, before slumping to his knees.

Blade free of his chest, the burning itch of regeneration started almost instantly. Sternum bone snapped over, flesh closed. He stood, panting, the adrenaline of the fight fading from his system. Dorothy drone zipped and flitted around him, excitedly animated. Kyn got the distinct impression he was being analyzed when the bot hovered curiously around the healing wound in his chest.

Damaged eardrum healed, the atonal hum faded, replaced instead by the stuttering clattering of metal on metal, and the shallow gasps and struggled whimpers of the dying Rager. The market club still pulsed outside the metal box. A cold wave of emptiness washed over Kyn. He pumped another round into the k-cannon with a solid *chonk* and spat up a thick glob of blood before turning to face the moaning tweeker, sprawled and bleeding out on the grated floor.

His blind shot had caught the spindly Rager in the shoulder, pulverizing the joint into a useless mangle of torn flesh and sinew. The weapon's spray was wide enough that the Rager had taken a portion of the scatter blast across the neck and chest, not enough to kill him outright, but enough to strip the skin away, leaving bone and tendon exposed. The tweekers eyes shone with a glassy sheen as he lay gasping, pain etched deep lines in his wasted face.

Kyn hovered over the figure briefly, dispassionate as the tweeker shook; the extended arm blades rattling against the metal floor. He leveled the k-cannon at the dying terrorist's head, intent on ending the tweeker's torment.

As if sensing mercy the Rager turned glassy eyes to meet Kyn's.

The Envoy gave the dying man a sad smile.

"You should've double tapped." He quipped, touching the trigger.

< = >

Kyn kept his hood up as he blended with the crowd, flowing back down to the main floor. His scuffle with the Ragers had gone un-noticed, the mood in the gray market unchanged. Sex, skin, and pushing the boundaries of human/tech enhancement was still the mood of the night.

Dorothy zipped dutifully along behind as he descended the platforms. Kyn had the distinct impression the spherical drone was scanning the crowd, watching his back. On the main floor the little bot took the lead, blinking excitedly as it made a beeline towards Alec, easily distinguishable in the crowd by his height and acid-green hair.

Skirting the edges of Alec's line of sight, Kyn gave the performer platforms a cursory glance, noting Evi absence. He slid up fluidly next to the hacker.

"Time to go." He hissed in loud mock whisper, causing Alec to jump in surprise. The hacker whirled, eyes wide with shock and relief and reached out, grabbing Kyn as if trying to make sure he was real.

"What the actual fuck? You're, okay?" Alec's eyes scanned Kyn's nearly bare torso, hovering over the dried blood crusted at the bottom of his rib cage. The small smear the only indicator that, not long ago, he'd had a forearm's length of metal blade jutting out of his chest. The skin underneath the dried red smear was perfectly smooth and unblemished.

"How are you okay?" Alec pressed, voice lost and hollow.

"We have to go." Kyn answered shortly, flashing the hacker a warning look.

The taller man's mouth snapped shut obediently and he snatched Dorothy out of the air, disappearing the bot, his expression a mingled look of concern and cautious distrust.

Ignoring the pang of shame in his gut, Kyn turned and led them out of the glittering geodesic dome.

< = >

The lights of the congested wards sparkled on the False Creek's slime covered waters, the polluted tide sloshing against the dock. A pale disc of moon peeked through the mid-wards, its dim face reflected in the gently rolling black waves, weak silver light drowned out by the ever-present neon brilliance of the all-consuming vertical city. Kyn approached an ancient, weather-pitted railing that marked the end of the boardwalk, another relic from a world long dead, and looked down into the dark and oily waves that lapped the dock. He steadily ignored the heavy smell of sewage run-off.

It was late and he was still expected to report back to Benn.

Exactly what he was going to report though was still to be determine. He wasn't ready to tip his full hand on what he'd learned just yet.

Kyn wanted to see Sub-level 29 for himself, find what it was the Informant expected him to uncover. The Sentry would lock down hard once they knew he was aware of their secrets, and there wouldn't be another chance. Luckily, Benn would want to track down the idents of the dead Ragers once he'd heard of them. That alone should be enough to occupy the Handler.

"I'm going to need to borrow Dorothy." Kyn stated, looking to Alec. The green haired hacker was next to him, hunched over the rust and slime coated rail.

"Like fuck you do." Alec snapped. He'd been silently following Kyn since leaving the club. Visibly shaken by the events he'd witnessed through Dorothy, his skin pallid and sweat sheened, his lips pressed together in a tight thin line. Kyn had the distinct impression the hacker was physically trying to hold himself together. As if he could force reality to stop crumbling around him by sheer willpower. Somehow force himself to stop seeing the blatant lies that lay naked and exposed before him.

"I'm not going to argue about this." Kyn pressed firmly. He knew this would be a lot for the hacker to process, but he wasn't in the mood to be gentle. "Your boss just tried to kill me. The only reason you're not dead is because I'm fairly certain you're too low in the ranks to have any idea what's going on." He sighed and pulled his hood back from his face. "But you're in it now. So, you either help me or you don't."

He gazed out over the polluted waters for a tick, then looked sidelong at the taller man. "I won't begrudge you if you decide to run," He told the hacker earnestly. "But shit is going to go sideways, fast, and helping me is your safest option."

Alec was silent for a long, empty, moment.

Then -

"You didn't die." He said, as if confirming it for himself, his voice was low and shaky.

"No, I didn't," Kyn returned simply. He held out an open hand.

Alec frowned, silently wrestling with himself, before, with a short, guttural grunt, he nodded. The hacker raised his fist and one of the four dots tattooed across the back flashed gold, summoning the drone in question. Dorothy appeared obediently, rising from behind to float in the air dutifully at his shoulder, then, with an affirmative green blink, the bot zipped over to Kyn and landed obediently in his outstretched palm.

Kyn winked, fingers closing around the drone. "Welcome to the conspiracy." He stated wryly.

The Conspiracy

"What did you tell him?" Benn asked.

The Handler leaned his elbows on the booth's sticky plastic tabletop. Pale fluorescents flickered overhead. It was the dark hours of the morning and Elysnn's was near empty, minus the few crusty lower retches, passed out asleep, snoring into their noodle bowls, and Elysnn herself, manning the kitchen hot plate.

"Oh, you know. Raised from birth to be an elite warrior of the Unity, blah blah. Imbued with superhuman gifts, blah blah. Guardian of the people, blah." Kyn reported airily. He twirled two metal stiks between his fingers before snatching a steaming dumpling from Benn's side of the booth. He dipped the doughy pouch in a side dish of dark sodium rich sauce before scarfing the dumpling down. He chewed noisily. "I lied my ass off." He hissed, the protein paste center was hotter than he'd anticipated and burned the roof of his mouth.

"I see." Benn stated wearily, steeping perfectly manicured fingers. "If the Informant or their agents have no solid proof of your involvement in the Rim incident, then I fail to see the point in revealing yourself."

"I'm controlling the narrative." Kyn explained. Swallowing, he pointed his stiks at the Handler. "It's the same basic story the propagandists have been spreading about us anyway. No harm playing along." He popped another pinched dumpling into his mouth, trying to disguise the distaste he felt at his own statement.

The Envoys were the Unity's dirty secret, no matter how they tried to dress them up otherwise.

"Where is the hacker now?" Benn asked casually. The question was posed innocuously, but Kyn's eyes narrowed dangerously in response. He'd been purposefully sketchy with the details on his meet with the Informant; downplaying the intel and Alec's involvement to instead focus solely on the Rager attack squad.

Kyn had filled Alec in with the minimal amount of information the hacker needed after leaving SpareParts, keeping the story simple and stoically sparse on details. The other man had remained thoughtfully silent during the auto-transpo ride, questioning nothing, and offered no argument when Kyn had insisted on keeping him locked down at the factory. Leaving the hacker to sleep off the shock of his new reality, Kyn had left to meet Benn at Elysnn's.

"He's at my place right now." Kyn answered honestly. "If the Informant hasn't scrubbed him, then he's my best bet at setting up another meet. If he has been scrubbed, then he's pretty much a dead man. He knows that. He also knows the safest place to be in that eventuality is close to me. It'll be easy to turn him. Don't worry he's skilled."

"You really think he's safe near you as long as you wear that?" Benn asked, raising an eyebrow and looking pointedly at the black cuff still strapped around Kyn's wrist.

"Whoever wants this will have to go through me." Kyn answered simply, tapping the stiks against the smooth band emphatically. He pinched another dumpling and tossed it into his mouth. "Fuck it!" He barked, laughing. "The guy with the blade augments even tried that and it still didn't do much good." He thumped a limp-wristed salute against his chest. "Besides, like the chant goes, my blood for my SPIRE, my body for my Sentry, my devotion to the Unity."

Kyn rolled his eyes in exaggerated exasperation and turned uncharacteristically serious . "Hunting people is what I do. It's what I am. It's child's play to lure out your prey when you have something they want."

"Like the Rager attack." Benn conceded.

Kyn smiled coldly. He produced the spherical Dorothy from under the cheap plastic top and placed the powered down drone on the sticky surface between him and Benn.

"Rip what you can from this." He told the Handler. "There should be enough for you to get an ident."

Intrigued, Benn picked up the drone and expanded a holo touch screen from his own f-Link. Connecting to the drone he began downloading the footage from Kyn's fight in the cargo crate. He glanced at the Envoy curiously, no doubt noting the bots curiously clean and empty data files. Kyn smiled innocently.

Seeing no reason to give the Handler more than was strictly necessary he'd insisted Alec wipe all other data the bot contained. Until he knew why the Unity had hidden the events on sub-level 29 from him, Kyn would continue to treat their newest minion as suspect.

Benn rooted through the bot's nearly empty memory, perfectly manicured hands skillfully manipulating lines of code as he dropped the drone's sparse contents into his own feed. Done that, he set about cleaning out Dorothy's root functions, erasing any evidence of the footage ever having existed. Satisfied, he stood to leave, sliding the bot back across the table to Kyn.

"I'll let you know what I dredge up," Benn told him flatly. He flashed Elysnn a plastic smile and swiped her credit for the tab before swinging open the shop door and disappearing into the crowded, runoff-soaked street.

Kyn slid from the sticky vinyl booth, moving to follow, but a glance beyond the shop's front window changed his mind. Standing from the table he turned and headed for the back entrance. Angled sideways, he passed through the narrow kitchen, earning himself a string of half-hearted curses from the old woman still managing the hot plate. Exiting out a wire swing door, he slipped his hood over his head and stepped out into the neon backlit alley behind, his canvas cowl offering minor protection from the oily drizzle that steadily dripped from the stacks above. He was still dressed in his scant outfit from SpareParts and his exposed flesh glittered metallically.

A cluster of adolescent cultists glared at him from the back of an adjacent netdive café, the interior of which, visible through a cracked security door, blared with competing game holos. Adorned and coiffed like low grade Sentry knock offs, the teens glowered at him distrustfully from the cramped doorway. Vaping candy scented stims and twirling matte blonde poly-weaves while waiting to port Alexi's dawn live-stream tribute to the dead.

Kyn stepped over a nerveshot tweeker huddled for warmth next to Elsynn's auxiliary generator and followed the shop wall several paces before turning down a narrow side alley. He looked up, gauging the height of the parallel walls.

Elsynn's was at the bottom of a three-level prefab stack. Part of a packed row of identical sheet metal boxcar units that had been crammed into the crumbling foundation of a long-gone steel and concrete structure. Rusted beams jutted around it like bone.

The alley barely wider than his shoulders, Kyn stepped one foot onto a leaking cooling unit and pushed off, leaping at the opposite wall. One hand and foot met steel briefly, then he rebounded, touching the other wall, gaining height as he nimbly bounced back and forth with feline grace to smoothly mount the stack's roof.

Runa was waiting for him.

The younger Envoy stood at the edge of Elsynns flat sheet roof, looking out over the ward. Clad in a matte-black trench, high collar popped, she sheltered from the constant drizzle beneath an over-large water collection tray. She watched the street below, amber eyes trained on the rundown factory directly across the neon-lit press of human traffic that flowed by below, curfew all but forgotten.

Brightly lit holo adverts and pro-prop screens cut the pre-dawn darkness, projected against almost every available vertical surface.

Alexi's ethereally beautiful face looked down at them, smiling benevolently from a soaring high rise that clipped through the ward levels. Scrolling text beneath reminded citizens to 'Stay calm' and 'link into her live stream.'

Making no move to acknowledge him, Runa blindly tossed a vial over her shoulder. The tube shimmered blue in the reflected neon. Kyn snatched it from the air and unstopped it with a flourish, unrolling a dab of indigo blue onto his thumbnail, he snorted it neatly. The eclipse slid over his nerve endings like grated metal, and the neon lights lining the surrounding vertical climb of shops stabbed his eyes. Shattered slivers of fiberglass.

"They dragged a woman out of the karaoke. That one, on the corner." Runa announced, still not turning. She pointed at the street below. "Dragged her out by her hair. Chanting she was a traitor to the Unity. They live-streamed the whole thing."

She paused.

"Someone pulled a cannon." She clicked her fingers. "Then gone."

"I'm sorry," was all Kyn could offer. He tossed the vile back.

"I've seen people die Kyn." Runa snapped, finally turning to deftly catch the blue tube. Her mouth was set in a twisted grimace of disgust. "I've been the reason people die."

She paused again and chewed at her thumbnail. Her nails were trimmed to the wick, painted matte black.

Kyn stayed silent, giving the young Envoy space to say her peace.

"What gets me," Runa continued, voice thick with emotion. "Is the pointlessness of it all. She was no one."

"We're all no one to them," Kyn interjected flatly, refusing to lie.

Amber eyes found gray. In them Kyn saw something he wasn't used to seeing in the indestructible young woman. Fear.

Silence fell heavily between them, accentuated by the steady thrum of rain, a constant patter occasionally punctuated by crashes of cascading run-off from the wards above.

"Fuck."

A thunderous river of filthy build up fell from an overhanging ward platform to the lowest street, pummeling everyone below. The unlucky took the brunt of the surge and were knocked to the pavement and swept into the gutter. No one moved to help them.

"What do you think they were like?" Runa asked, turning away from Kyn to continue watching the rundown factory.

"Who?" He asked, failing to follow.

"The people before. Whatever dickholes wrecked this place before us."

Kyn shrugged.

"Look 'em up on a server." He supplied coolly.

"Nah, none of that data dive jockey shit." Runa scoffed roughly, waving off his input.

"Well then, what?" Kyn asked curiously, still not grasping the underlying intent behind her line of questioning.

"Did they do this?" She asked, angrily gesturing emphatically at the street below. "Turn on each other like this? Tear each other apart?"

"Seemed like it." He offered with another limp shrug of his narrow shoulders. He recognized her desire to look down the path of the past, hoping their progenitors' hid answers. "I don't know." He answered honestly, joining her under the water collector. He followed her gaze to the rundown factory, easily finding his flat's steel-lined windows. He caught a brief flicker of movement in the dark.

"You can't get any actual useful data off the older severs." He continued, shaking his head. "Not without wading through terabytes of vapid crap. They stuffed the servers with endless images of them-selves, often followed with inane text. It's all there. Polluting every sever, data bank, and discarded hard unit in every trash yard. None of it makes sense. None of it's useful. It's total fucking chaos. Chat-ter and backbiting. They had a connection to every corner of this planet yet distrusted and hated each other ad nauseam. Everywhere you look they screamed at each other. They had access to any piece of information they could ever want, but willfully believed lies and misinformation. Without fail. If they could store data on it, they would fill it with endless self-important, self-serving junk. Anything of real value is long gone. Nothing left but broken pieces of broken people who couldn't agree on the reality around them." He sighed heavily and turned away from the street.

Runa thoughtfully chewed her lower lip.

"Ashe says that's why we need the Unity. We need their guidance. So, we don't destroy ourselves again." She recited tentatively, as if rolling the statement around in her powerful hands. Torn between the act of believing, or crushing the concept to dust.

"Maybe." Kyn offered with a third non-committal shrug.

"You don't believe that?" She asked, unsurprised. His irreverence was well known.

"You shouldn't be asking stuff like this." He warned.

Runa glanced sideways at him, her jaw set and firm.

"I've been through it too, so don't act like I haven't." She shot back, flipping her dark mane of hair over one shoulder. "I survived just like you. I've earned the right to ask a few questions."

"You haven't earned anything." Kyn scoffed incredulously. He'd somehow kept fooling himself into forgetting how young she truly was. How young he'd been. Forgotten the conviction of youth and its desperate desire to believe in the illusion of suffering to serve a purpose. "None of us have." He lectured firmly. "We exist because the Unity says so and nothing else."

"I refuse to believe that." Runa muttered, shaking her head in disappointed frustration at his nihilism. They both fell silent. Neon glowed hauntingly through the rain, lighting the district with slivers of fractured light.

"What was it for you?" Runa asked abruptly. She pulled a sweet-stik from the depths of her coat. Unwrapping it, she popped the candied lolly in her mouth.

"What?" He asked, puzzling around another whiplash change of topic.

"The Ascension. How did you survive?" She clarified, sucking loudly on the treat.

Memories loomed large in Kyn's mind, threatening to pull him back. Innocence broken and bloody on a white floor. He looked out over the tangled ward platforms.

"I didn't." He answered.

"Like 'ell." Runa shot back peevishly. "You're alive aren't ya? I sure as fuck am. A lot of kids died that day, but I wasn't one of them." She pointed at the looming projection of Alexi. "They may make me do a lot of messed up shit, but they ain't gunna make me die."

"I did die." Kyn countered candidly, cutting across her tirade. "That day. And this? Is whatever comes after." He spread his hands expansively at the chaotic city around them. "I'm forced to live this endless nightmare. Dying again and again, on an infinite loop. A fractured tick in time created by my oxygen deprived brain cells, the looping hallucinations of decaying neurons."

Runa was silent a moment, watching the city around them, before she turned to Kyn, a genuine smile of amusement wide across her face.

"You're hilarious," she chuckled roughly. She crushed the sweet-stik.

Kyn laughed at the collective absurdity.

"Listen, I wasn't exactly honest with Benn in there." He confessed, serious again.

"No shit." Runa snorted around the remnants of her treat. She shook out her thick mane of curls. The rain and runoff were falling harder now, washing away the metallic sheen on Kyn's skin, his torso was streaked in wet smears of silvery glitter.

"I neglected to tell him a few things I learned tonight." He continued earnestly. Water droplets beat a staccato beat against the weather treated cowl of his hood. "Things I want to clarify for myself before I bring them to the higher ups."

Runa nodded her head before turning back to the grimy, vertical neon sprawl.

"Don't worry," she reassured him. "Do what you need. I'll keep an eye on your boy."

"He's not my boy." Kyn corrected.

"Alright." Runa countered. "Cumpanion, whatever."

< = >

Ashe held their parasol delicately above their head with one large hand, the small umbrella a clear plastic dome of protection, shielding their coiffed purple hair from the rain. Their indigo locks were piled and teased into a messy bun on top of their head, sides shorn. They stood out from the stoically bland mid-wards crowd that passed through Coggs' Plaza, clad in a matching clear plastic raincoat cinched closed over a black mesh top. The top was loosely tucked into wide legged, synth-silk trousers, white and flowing. They stood aloof from the homogeneous sea of muted browns, grays, and blacks that paid no attention to the vibrant figure in their midst. The Coggs' vibrant halogens reflected in the chunky mirrored visor they wore across their eyes, the passing crowd reflected as a blurred silver rainbow.

Exiting a tram station, Kyn spotted the other Envoy easily and peeled away from the crowd, crossing the plaza. A curious sensation tugged at the edges of his mind as he wound through the throng, getting closer to the glamorous figure. The sudden desire to turn away was trying to overwhelm him. As if he suddenly needed to look at something else. To look anywhere but at the beautiful Envoy and to continue walking, forgetting he'd ever seen them.

"Well, if I knew we weren't going to bother blending, I wouldn't have made the effort." Kyn quipped, referencing the bland gray two-piece he wore. A lopsided grin tugged at the edges of his mouth.

Ashe acknowledged him with a bored tilt of their head, appearing to scan him up and down from behind the mirrored band.

"There is no need to stoop to mediocrity." They drawled, voice heavy with the dig.

Notoriously uniform and conservative, the mids were populated by worker drones and cubicle grunts desperate to maintain the safe anonymity of the herd. Difference drew unwanted attention, so Kyn had dressed to blend, slicking his hair back and donning a nondescript ensemble. Retro slim two-piece, buttoned snugly at his wrists and throat, covering his f-Link tattoo. The mysterious onyx cuff was still strapped to his wrist, hidden from view beneath the blazer's sleeve. He'd grudgingly replaced his well-worn boots with a pair of hard soled synth-leather loafers polished to a mirrored sheen.

The whole ensemble made him feel needlessly constricted.

"Yah well, not all of us have your brilliant sense of fashion." He shot back, tugging at his collar.

A dazzling white smile spread across the darker Envoy's face.

"In this you are, of course, correct," Ashe purred, looping one willowy arms companionably through Kyn's to pull him into the protective orbit of their parasol. "Now, let us move on so we can get out of this drab icon to mediocrity."

An intersectional plaza that bridged various mid-ward districts, the Coggs' was a major shopping complex and public transit hub. Reminiscent of the internal workings of an ancient, steam-powered machine re-imagined in the fever dream of some Unity architect, the Coggs' framework was re-purposed gears and pistons salvaged from pre-fall train yards mixed with twisting wrought iron to create the bent and jagged, gravity defying angles that marked Unity design aesthetics. The plaza's jumbled, abstract clockwork motif invoked a forgotten, unknown nostalgia, tinged with an overwhelming sense of smallness. Holo projections loomed above the crowds, shimmering banners that alternated between adulation of the Sentry, and grandiose pro-prop slogans exalting the virtues of productivity.

The Envoys glided past generic f-Link mod shops and bio-fixers to merge with the crowd on a cross platform byway. Crossing the suspended metal walkway, they merged with another flow of human traffic, filing orderly towards the nearest entrance of Noav SPIRE.

Kyn reached into an inner pocket of his blazer as they walked. His fingers wrapped around Dorothy, and he thumbed the bot's sensor pad. A light squeeze of pressure rewarded him with a faint beep of recognition, the small drone activating its ghost protocols.

A readily visible security oni hovered over the SPIRE's midwards entrance, scanning, and identifying the crowd. Kyn's eyes skipped over it. He was confident in the program Alec had uploaded to Dorothy earlier that morning, a scrub hack that would blank his and Ashe's presence from the security feeds, hiding them from both the scanners they could see and those they couldn't. There was a time limit, the hack program would eventually disintegrate against the SPIRE's firewalls, but they would have enough time to see what they needed to see.

They joined a flowing line of drab workers approaching the SPIRE. Dags were scanning idents and ushering people through to the SPIRE's main lobby. Ashe's constant aura dissuaded anyone from looking at them too long. Initially curious eyes would sweep past, suddenly disinterested as they moved with the crowd, and the pair breezed past the posted Dags without being stopped.

Ashe unlinked themselves from Kyn, retracting their parasol, and shook out droplets of water onto the sprawling marble floor as they walked. The pair crossed the lobby quickly, joining a hyperLift queue to file into a transport tube with a group of dead-eyed cubicle dwellers.

"You catch Ward-Voices last night?" A bland looking man in a dirty brown suit asked the woman beside him.

"Yes." The woman replied politely. Her mousey brown hair was pulled up in a severe bun. "I can't believe Barbi got eliminated."

"Barbi?" Brown suit snorted derisively. "She was a total disaster. No way she deserves to make it to the uppers"

"What?" Bunhead snapped back, defensive. Her tone flipped from polite to confrontational. "As if! She was the only one performing without augment. She totally deserved to go to the uppers."

Behind the chattering pair, Kyn looked sidelong at Ashe and raised an eyebrow quizzically. Ashe simply shrugged.

"Yah, but she's got that weird nose. It's too big. No one wants to watch that, it's distracting." Brown suit retorted.

"Only because she had to save all her credits to buy lifesaving dermal patches for her sick mother instead of getting graft work!" Bunhead shot back, voice dialing up an octave. "Didn't you see her vlog?"

The hyperLift slid to a stop and Kyn was saved from hearing any-more as the doors slid open and the chatty pair exited the tube.

"This is your stop." Ashe instructed the rest of the lift, their voice sharp and reverbing in the small space. Heads snapped to attention and the remaining crowd funneled out obediently. Dazed looks changed to sudden bewilderment as they realized too late, they were on the wrong floor. The doors whooshed shut again.

Kyn pressed a fist to his mouth. "Poor Barbi," he mused. The lift was descending. He traced a right angle against the tube wall with the pad of his thumb and index finger. A square panel lit up on the surface. Kyn produced Dorothy, setting the little bot to float in front of the panel. Surface lights oscillated yellow across the drone's smooth surface - the bot syncing with the SPIRE systems, uploading override codes, clearing the hyperLift to stop at Sub-level 29.

"Do not be, she was pitchy." Ashe countered, removing the mirrored band. They disappeared it into a pocket of their flowing pants. The bruising around Ashe's eyes and cheekbones had almost entirely faded.

Shifting yellow lights changed confirmational green and Dorothy chirped affirmatively, data entry point erased, lifts service history altered to reflect nothing but routine stops. Kyn had little doubt his or Ashe's Envoy codes would've allowed them access, there were few places within their home SPIRE they didn't have clearance for, but he figured it was for the best if the Sentry remained unaware of their snooping.

The lift stopped, and the Envoys stepped out onto Sub-level 29.

Blank concrete corridors, unmarked by any directional indicators or guide system, stretched out in either direction, filling Kyn with a familiar dread.

"Lovely." Ashe remarked dryly.

Both Envoys scanned either direction, before, with a shrug of his shoulders, Kyn turned and started down the blank corridor to his left.

"Sector D." He remembered out loud, turning at another inter-section.

Kyn and Ashe had both spent their early years in secret sub-levels of similar design. A purposefully confusing maze of seemingly random and identical intersecting corridors, doors identical, un-marked. Designed to be intentionally disorienting, the layout was an example of the Unity's unique take on child rearing and internal security procedures.

A kindlier pyschtech monitor had once explained to Kyn the perplexing layout was meant to teach Envoy trainees atypical problem-solving skills early in their developmental process, to imbue the subjects with an ingrained sense of locational awareness.

To Kyn, it had always felt like an overly complex cage.

There was an underlining organizational structure that helped map each uniquely confusing sub-level. A universally understood cipher given to staff that allowed them to navigate the corridors with ease while the young Envoy trainees were left to puzzle out the trick the hard way.

Ashe and Kyn walked side by side past rows upon rows of unmarked doors, silently following a pattern that unfolded in their minds.

Turning another corner, Kyn was mildly surprised when they were confronted with two, thick shouldered Dag troopers standing guard at the next intersection, and, to what he presumed was, the entrance to sector D. Ashe had relaxed their aura of influence, no longer deflecting attention, and the Dag's immediately snapped to action. Assault variant k-cannons raised to shoulders in unison.

"Halt! This area is off limits by order of Noav Sentry." One Dag barked.

Kyn rolled his eyes.

"Relax, gents." He called to the guards, not pausing in his stride. "My attractive friend here has something to tell you."

The air in the corridor crackled with an invisible tension; an empty static hum that stretched between sounds.

"Lower your weapons." Ashe commanded. Their voice morphed and flanged to fill the corridor, reverberating off concrete walls. The Dags obeyed, suddenly glassy eyed, the barrels of their weapons dipped to the floor.

"Good." Ashe intoned with a purr of satisfaction. "Now go yank each other off in a storage closet."

The Dags flowed past the Envoys in lockstep, turning at the first junction, and disappeared. Kyn clapped his hands in delight, giggling and bouncing on the balls of his feet. He could hear the distinct *woosh* of a door opening then shutting, followed closely by the short rhythmic beeping of a locking protocol.

"Oh, you are too much fun!" He crowed gleefully to Ashe. "But do you think that bought us enough time? Dag boys are notoriously repressed and backed up, shouldn't take them too long to finish each other."

"Do not worry," Ashe reassured. "Once they have finished, they will feel an overwhelming urge to take a nap. After that, they will be too mortified to report this to anyone."

"Unless one of their superiors asks." Kyn cautioned.

"I doubt it will come up." Ashe returned simply, turning down the sector D corridor. "Regardless let us be quick."

It was obvious once they'd turned the corner that Kyn had found what he was looking for. Dried blood streaked the walls and floors over blackened scorch marks indicative of explosions within close quarters. Kyn whistled long and low. There had obviously been much more of a battle then what he'd seen in the Informant's vid.

"What a mess." He commented, examining the nearest blast-marked wall. He scrapped at a patch of blood with his thumb nail. Large coppery flakes fell away.

"What's with the lack of clean up?" He queried, turning back to Ashe. He pulled Dorothy from his jacket's inner pocket and set the little bot to hovering. Two quick taps of his thumb against his third finger synced the bot to his f-Link, and he set it to scan while feeding the collected data the to his optic. He ordered the bot ahead.

Usually quick to translate situational protocol, Ashe seemed at a loss for an explanation, shrugging their plastic clad shoulders and proceeding down the ruined corridor. Unlike the rest of sub-level 29, the doors in sector D were open, slid back and, according to Dorothy, jammed open. The spherical drone flitted through the nearest doorway while Ashe and Kyn each peeled off to check other rooms.

An old familiarity crept up Kyn's spine like the fingers of dead memories as he looked into a square white cell.

The same narrow derrafoam pad, next to the same personal hygiene station, both unfolded from the blank wall. The same drain in the floor.

He looked at the ceiling, relieved to note the lack of suspension hooks.

"Look familiar?" He called back, looking to Ashe who turned from their own inspection. Their set lips told him they had seen the same.

"Yes. Troubling." They mused, turning to the next doorway.

Dorothy swept over a scorched section of the corridor and *'Graeanda blast pattern. Model #x347. Patent: Noav SPIRE,'* flashed white in the corner of Kyn's optic.

"Looks like these were our own toys." He called to Ashe, indicating the wall.

"Good." They moved on to another room, scanning briefly before moving on. "The Dividers are dangerous."

"Do you think there were any kids down here?" Kyn asked, looking into another identically familiar room. Dorothy scanned a nearby blood smear and fed his optic more helpful trivia. The crimson-brown stain flagged a match in the Dag med systems, corresponding with genetic records for a Mac Mitchal.

"You tell me," Ashe replied, scanning another room. "You're the one who supposedly saw the feed."

"That was only one hallway. Seems like a lot more happened here." He explained, following the floating bot around another corner to another battle ravaged corridor. The doorways were spaced further apart here, a slight variance in the pattern.

"Maybe we shall find something that will tell us what." Asher offered dryly, trailing Kyn as he moved to the first jammed door.

"Soon, preferably. We won't remained unnoticed much longer." Kyn replied, cognizant of the time left before Dorothy's ghost protocols would crumble against the SPIRE firewalls. He stopped, surprised. Where the other cells had been uniformly white and harsh in their blankness, these new rooms where dark. Void like. The walls and ceiling overlaid with dense black mesh. Six glowing tubes of bubbling blue liquid set in two neat rows of three, stood in the center of the room. Each was lit from beneath, and cast ultramarine waves on the black mesh walls. Expecting more identical living cells, he was taken aback by the room's difference.

"Woah, that's different." He remarked dumbly.

He circled around the first tube as Dorothy zipped around his head, dutifully scanning tubes.

Big enough to hold a large adult, each tube was empty except for the gently bumbling blue liquid. No new diagnostic info popped up on Kyn's optic. Whatever the tubes were for, or what they were meant to contain, the bot's databanks knew as much as he did.

Passing one large hand over the glass, Ashe circled another tube. They drummed their fingers rhythmically across the surface, taping and searching for touch activated command points, finding none.

"Gestation tubes." Ashe stated plainly.

"Say what?" Kyn puzzled, not following. He raised a hand to a tube. The surface was cool, indicating a functioning internal coolant system.

"Have you not ever watched any of those old pre-fall science fiction serials ripped from the 'Flix databanks." Ashe asked as way of explanation.

"Of course, I have." Kyn answered, lowering his hand from the glass. "I'm more surprised that you have. I always thought the great and terrible Ashe was too cool for that retro-nerd shit."

The commanding Envoy shrugged, brushing off his critique. "It is fascinating to look back on the different versions of the future humanity once imagined for itself."

"Ya?" Kyn asked archly, turning from the tube. "Did anyone ever imagine a version like this?"

"One or two." Ashe answered simply, moving to exit the tank room.

Kyn followed.

"Any good?" He pressed; curiosity peaked. He rarely ever saw a side of Ashe that wasn't entirely mission focused.

"Not really, kind of campy." They admitted.

"I like campy," Kyn mused, moving to the next room. Dorothy zipped past his head to dutifully enter first. "Oh lookey, more tubes." He stated dryly, greeting a room identical to the last. Same black mesh, same glowing blue tubes. Splitting ways, he and Ashe swept the room from opposing directions, searching for differentiation in the uniformity.

"So, gestation tubes for what then?" Kyn asked. There was no buildup of dust on the tubes, no smudge from oily fingers. "Mutant pig babies?"

"I doubt that." Ashe replied curtly. "Vat grow protein synthesis is far more efficient."

"Pets?"

"Oddly more likely."

Finding no new evidence, the pair moved on to the next room. Sweeping the area identically as they had before, Kyn couldn't deny the signs, or lack thereof, that indicated the recent presence of a Unity cleaning crew. The obviousness left him confident their search would turn up no hard evidence of the rooms' purposes.

"What's the status on the other SPIREs?" He asked conversationally, examining another too clean tube.

"Xion have redeployed their servos to the resource zone, while the majority of the city's servos have been dedicated to repairing the wall and outer defenses. They have stepped up recruitment, refinancing service contracts and making a heavy advertising push in the lowers. Repairs will be done within days. Ziev have pushed up production on the enforcer variant of their mechs. Giaon is working to expand satellite capacities, trying to penetrate the fallout static to get a location on where the Dividers attacked from." Ashe ticked off helpfully. "Cao made a play for control of the HRV supply, but Malvyc intercepted and terminated their Envoy."

"Really?" Kyn returned. An unpleasant shiver had run through him, as if his blood suddenly itched, his re-written genome perking at the mention of its author. He swallowed hard.

"Who?" He queried, trying to sound casual.

"Treshe," Ashe answered, drumming their nails against the nearest tube as the pair repeated their now routine sweep of the room. "He was caught impersonating a biotech. He had managed to covertly arrange for the supply to be transferred to a Cao controlled facility."

Kyn looked up from his own tube. Violet eyes met gray.

"Malvyc fried them out."

"Ouch."

Kyn snatched Dorothy out of the air and tucked the bot back into the innermost pocket of his jacket before giving the final room one decisive sweeping glance. Grunts of anger and confusion echoed back down the uniform corridor as the Envoys swept from the room, moving in purposefully lockstep as they turned a corner and disappeared.

Rager on the Tram

Eyes followed Kyn. Hairs on the back of his neck prickled, and an unplaceable sense of expectation emanated from the crowd around him. Someone was watching him, had been since he'd left Noav SPIRE, all the way back through Coggs', and through the skytram station.

Kyn let them follow, curious to see who they were. He'd caught a brief flash of an oversized brown coat as the tram's loading doors had slid shut, before losing them again.

He gripped an overhead safety bar as the tram throttled around a bend. The crush of passengers swayed and jostled, swinging back into each other again as the tram snaked into a straight away.

His attention perked from mindlessly staring out the view port as the tram veered around another turn, breaking away from the city's interior, and he caught a brief flash of lush green below. The tram skirted the edges of the city, and he could see the entirety of the vast forested peninsula, jutted into the ocean far below. A swath of dense coastal old growth that was reserved for the leisure whims of the city's elite.

Kyn stared longingly at the ancient forest, an aching sadness pressing heavily against his chest.

Then the tram dipped, throttling around another corner, tossing the passengers around again, and descended into a tunnel. The green zone disappeared.

Gripping the overhead strap more firmly as the floor shifted and tilted under his polished loafers, Kyn sighed. He rhythmically taped the tips of two fingers against his thumb; cycling through his f-Link's audio feed. He settled on a nuevo-pysbient playlist, and a moody, synthetic warble trilled in his ears, soundtrack matching the mood set by the pallid glow of the tram's safety lights. He smiled, bobbing his head along to the expansive soundscape. The people around him stared blankly ahead.

A lurch of deceleration, and more silent jostling and re-shuffling as the tram slid into the next station. Passengers unloaded, replaced by more blank-eyed and dour commuters.

Kyn could feel the eyes again. The expectation. The watching.

He scanned the crowd. The station had marked their dip into the lowers, and the incoming passengers added more vibrant colour and outlandish style to the gray washed tram. None stood out as his watcher.

He curled and twisted his wrist, rolling his grip on the safety bar, surreptitiously unclasping the cuff of his shirt. The sleeve slipped, falling open. A hint of black sheen glinted in the dim running lights.

There.

A flash of a soap-blonde pixie-cut, reflected in the darkened polyplex viewports. A diminutive figure in a long coat at the end of the row of seats to his left and directly behind. A round feminine face, eyeing him hungrily.

The tram decelerated into another station, more shuffling, and switching of passengers.

Turning, Kyn looked in his stalker's direction. She was staring blankly ahead in her seat, ignoring everyone around her.

"Come on now!" Kyn called down the tram. The doors slid shut and they lurched forward again. People around him dutifully ignored his disruption. "No need to pretend, I've spotted you."

He released the safety rail and pressed through the packed crush of passengers, gliding towards his stalker with rolling steps, maintaining balance with fluid grace as the vehicle lurched and tilted around another turn, dipping with a stack level change. Rooftops and vertical ward tangle flashed by. The pixie-cut female continued to steadily ignore him. He could sense her tension at his approach, a mounting panic that wound tight around her. A small furry mammal frozen under the gaze of a hungry predator. Jittery in her stillness.

"Not bad, by the way. Tailing me," Kyn prattled conversationally. He stopped in front of his stalker and leaned casually against a vertical support bar. The burning pink neon of a passing neighborhood skin theatre reflected prismatically in the polished steel gray of his eyes. His freckles scrunched as he flashed a crooked grin at the round-faced young woman, still steadily refusing to acknowledge him.

"We can just talk, you know?" He prodded gently. "No need for this to get ugly. I know you're looking for this." He raised the band, shirt and jacket sleeve slid down his forearm. The woman's eyes jumped to it, hungrily. Murky blue, natural with no hint of gene editing, like the ocean on a dark day.

No veins of pink, Kyn noted with slight disappointment, and no fear. Her dark blue eyes were hard and cold. He'd misread her. She was jittery tense, but not from the panic of prey. No, this woman had killed, Kyn was sure, and taken pleasure in it. He recognized the empty hardness easily enough. His smile widened.

"I like your hair." He complimented agreeably, meaning it, seeing no need to be unpleasant.

Pixie-cut tilted her head and looked directly at him, her pupils expanding instantly. Inky blackness engulfed the blue, like pools of rapidly spreading oil. The tram decelerated into the next station, followed by the customary lurch and shuffle of passengers, the loading doors slid open with a collective *woosh*.

Kyn leaned back into the shifting crowd and yelled at the top of his lungs.

"RAGER!"

The effect was instantaneous. Previously inert and disinterested passengers morphed into a panic-stricken mob. Those attempting to board the tram were trampled as terrified passengers pushed out through the doors, fleeing the tram.

Pixie-cut launched herself from her seat in a blur of unnatural speed as the crowds fled, sharply striking at Kyn with her palm to hit him sharply in the chest, just over the heart. He felt a piercing stab break the skin.

Caught off guard by the quickness of her attack, Kyn stumbled backwards, grabbing at the safety bar to keep his balance. The loading doors *wooshed* shut and the tram lurched forward again, empty except for the two combatants.

Kyn felt the effects of her attack almost instantly.

Numbness was rapidly spreading through his limbs. His left leg gave out and he buckled sideways, swinging from the safety bar with one hand. Trying to steady himself, he reached out with his other arm, but the betraying limp hung uselessly from his shoulder, numb. He'd lost control of the entire left side of his body. Dimly, he was aware of a deep, aching emptiness, of his heart pumping the toxin she'd injected him with through his body.

"Clevrth," Kyn slurred, head lolling in an attempt at nodded acknowledgement to the Rager. He flashed her a lopsided grin, stumbling to regain his feet. "Dishn't shee thath one comin"

Pixie-cut ignored his compliment to push her advantage with another unnatural burst of speed. A folding razor was open in her hand as she closed the space between them, and she slashed outwards, cutting Kyn across his exposed throat with a wet burst of crimson, before dancing away again in a blink. Her long coat whipped around her legs as his blood spurted, painting the empty plastic seats in front of him bright red.

The tram lurched around another corner and Kyn fell sideways, dropping heavily and rolling across the floor. Feeling returned to the left side of his body in a sweeping blaze of fiery nerve endings - his regeneration kicking back, purging the paralyzing toxin, and allowing him to regain control of his limbs beneath the sweeping agony. Ignoring the various points of pain, he pushed off the grimy tram floor to vault backwards in a springing motion. He landed, perched in a crouch, balanced on a bank of hard plastic side-facing tram seats, one hand gripped tightly over the gash in his throat even as thick blood still oozed between his fingers. He wheezed painfully, trying to breath while holding the savage slash closed. A maddening itch was already spreading across his throat.

Pixie-cut eyed him warily, confusion and fascinated horror clear on her face, obviously unused to her victims getting back up.

Kyn peeled his fingers away from his throat and teasingly twiddled the blood-soaked digits in her direction.

"You're fast." He observed redundantly, his voice a dry rasp over healing vocal cords.

Pixie-cut watched him warily. She vibrated with barely contained speed, ready to strike, but unsure how to hurt him.

Kyn smirked. "MetaBooster 'eh?" He asked, climbing off the bank of seats to stride towards her. The tram lurched around another turn, and the overhead system chimed, signaling the next station. Contrarily the tram didn't decelerate. Kyn's improvised security alert would've caused a system wide lockdown, the tram wouldn't stop until Dag forces were prepared to board and deal with the alleged threat.

Vibration crawled over Kyn's forearm.

You're on the tram, aren't you?

Alec's message flashed in the corner of his optic. Kyn tapped out a response, one eye trained on pixie-cut.

New feed who dis?

Ghosting the message feed, he turned his full attention back on the Rager.

"We gunna do this sweetie?" He quipped, arms open wide, exposing himself invitingly.

Pixie-cut took the bait, shooting forward in a blur to slash with crisscrossing swipes of her razor, cutting Kyn across both biceps. The razor cut smoothly through the fabric of his blazer and shirt to slice deep into flesh, severing muscle and disabling his arms tidily. Kyn grunted, too slow to react, and the diminutive Rager pulled back in a blur, zipping behind him to strike down hard against the base of his spine with the palm of her hand.

Kyn felt the jab of her hypodermic sting, closely followed by a numb emptiness that spread quickly through his lower limbs. He fell forward with a meaty thump, sprawled on the tram floor.

"Fuckin' metaBoosters." He groaned into the sticky floor. He writhed clumsily onto his back, regeneration rapidly fighting to restore use of his limbs. His left arm burst to life in a blazing wave of fire and feeling and he reached up to grab onto a vertical safety pole, pulling himself to standing, legs shaky, the itching fire spreading. Turning to track pixie-cut, he stumbled yet again, his supporting arm gone suddenly achingly numb and useless as the Rager struck him viciously from behind with another stinging strike, catching him in the rear deltoid.

"Oh, come on!" Kyn yelled in frustration, falling to his knees as the floor tipped again. He recovered the loss of control by shifting and tumbling forward into a roll, riding the tram's level change as it dipped like a slide into another layer of the lowers. Feet back on the sticky floor, he leapt to grab onto an overhead bar and swung himself into a tight ball, flipping under the bar to change direction.

He wasn't going to outrun the diminutive woman, that was obvious. She had jacked her metabolism synthetically, the typical habit trip of upper ward service drones; type-A workaholics who coveted speed and efficiency. Biohack derms loaded with amphetamines slapped to their skin to boost productivity. Pixie-cut would be jacked up until the effects of whatever she'd patched herself with wore off, and, as fast as Kyn was, he still wasn't fast enough to dodge her.

Speed wasn't going to help him win this, but a life of training - coupled with a unique disregard for his own bodily safety – had made Kyn extremely agile, capable of moving with exacting athletic grace and unpredictability. He knew he was going to get hit, so there was no point in avoiding it. His best chance was using his unique gifts to trip his opponent up.

Landing behind pixie-cut, Kyn shifted to catch the heeled edge of one polished dress loafer with the pointed toe of the other. Loosening the shoe with a staccato hitch kick, he dislodged the loafer with a higher, snapping front kick, flinging it directly at the Rager at the same moment the diminutive woman rushed him again, long coat whipping behind her as she sped down the tram aisle. The launched shoe caught her full in the face, causing her to veer sideways in surprise, slamming into a bank of plastic seats.

Kyn swept around as she stumbled and dipped low to grab onto the trailing hem of her long coat. Abruptly switching directions, he kicked off of a passenger seat with his still shoed foot and leap frogged back over the Rager even as she spun around to face him again, snarling and tangling herself in her own garment.

Blinded, the Rager spun again, trying to face Kyn, and lashed out blindly with the flip razor. Striking wildly, her speed and proximity allowed her to connect, and she drew a deep red line across his thigh.

Hissing, Kyn stumbled again, almost falling. One hand on the unsteady floor, he twisted into a low wall flip along the side of the tram tube to recover. The maddening itch of healing flesh spread across his quad like flash flame. Standing, he grabbed at the Rager's flailing coat tail and slammed his closed fist into the center of the twist of fabric, striking with a snapping crunch. He struck again, this time following through with his elbow for a vicious a third strike. A blossom of wet crimson spread where he'd hit, soaking the garment.

Groaning, the Rager blindly struck back with the palm of her hand, catching Kyn with a stinging strike to the gut. Numbness spread almost instantly to everything below his navel, and she slashed out blindly with the razor again as he stumbled, drawing a deep red line from his ear to chin as he fell forward into the blade with a yelp of pain and surprise.

Ignoring the searing slice, Kyn tucked his shoulder and rolled past pixie-cut. He got a boot to the gut for his effort as she thrashed around at hyperspeed, trying to untangle herself, then he was on his feet again, vaulting over a bank of passenger seats, forcing the burning muscles of his legs to get distance between himself and the toxic speedster. He tugged off his remaining shoe mid-vault and spun on bare feet to throw the loafer in a repeat of his earlier gambit, before he was blindly vaulting backwards again, clearing another row of hard plastic seats.

Finally freed of her jacket, pixie-cut weaved, dodging the weaponized shoe as she closed the gap in a blur of speed. Snarling through shattered and bloody teeth, her nose snapped at a sharp angle, she slashed horizontally, catching Kyn across the chest with her razor.

Kyn leaned into the attack, gritting his teeth as the blade sliced deep. He wrapped one arm around the woman's neck in an embracing motion and rode her momentum to swing them both violently around. The Rager slammed her open fist into his chest repeatedly, stinging him again and again with her hypodermic implant. Adrenaline thundered through Kyn's veins and he rag-dolled, gripping her for support, dead weight falling into her, stumbling them both. Feeling and control returned almost instantly in a blazing itch, and he leaned into the adrenaline wave, throwing them both bodily at the closest polyplex viewport. Pixie-cut grunted wetly against him, ribs snapping audibly. The chime rang from the tram ceiling, warning the approach of the next station.

Vibrations crawled across the skin of Kyn's f-Link, barely discernible through the firestorm of rapidly healing nerves, and a message from Runa flashed in his optic, red tinged from blood and adrenaline.

Cock Gobbler: Dags r going to board @ the next station. b ready or b gone. ur choice.

With a heavy grunt, Kyn pulled back and slammed a forearm down on the Rager's collarbone, splintering bone and cracking polyplex. Impressively, the speedster still fought back, determinedly dragging her razor back and forth across his abdomen in a flurry of deep slices, shredding his shirt and flesh in a mess of blood and fabric.

Kyn abandoned his assault and shoved himself away from the polyplex with both hands, backing off a few stumbling steps. Lighting hot pain shot through his savaged gut with every movement. He peeled off his jacket. A burning, itching, relief chased the pain away as flesh healed over and he grinned wolfishly at the Rager. He twisted the blazer between his hands, challenging her.

Fast, violent, but untrained and heavily injured, pixie-cut launched herself at him again, a wild, murderous fury clear in her eyes.

Kyn feigned left as if moving to counter, then shifted rapidly forward at the last tick, just as the Rager dove for him, maneuvering behind her with a flourishing twirl and a whip of the twisted jacket. He struck out with the bare heel of one foot, aiming a high kick at the Rager's back. He connected, stumbling her, then followed through with another, chaining a fluid series of sweeping kicks, limber legs targeting her already broken ribs and soft organs. Pushed forward and driven off balance, pixie-cut screamed in pain and frustration.

Kyn rolled his thumb over the pad of his index finger - cranking the psybient soundscape that still thrummed through his audio feed. Pain was slowing the speedster, the constant drip of amphetamines unable to push her through the injuries Kyn was inflicting on her vitals.

A jerk of deceleration warned he needed to push his advantage. Stopping his barrage of kicks, Kyn sprinted forward, just as pixie-cut twisted around in a blur to face where he'd been. He jumped into a tuck and looped the twisted length of coat over her head as he sailed past. Then he unfurled, jack knifing to drop-kick the polyplex view port. The plastic barrier violently burst outward in a shower of smsokey shards as he fell feet first through window, yanking pixie-cut with him.

Jerked backwards, the Rager violently slammed into the opening with a dull *crack*. Neck snapped clean.

Kyn dove from the tram, yanking his coat free as he fell, and hit the grimy tracks with an ungraceful tumble of limbs. His head pinged against a steel rail, and he saw stars briefly. The skytram slid away, slowing to a stop, pixie-cut's limp body dangling, half in, half out of the broken viewport.

Kyn stumbled to his feet, cursing as forgotten eras of broken glass and debris cut into his bare feet. He'd dove from the tram onto the service side of the tracks, narrowly avoiding the assembled Dags waiting to board the tram on the next station's platform. The tram drifted to a stop, and the soldiers rushed on.

Kyn turned away, unwinding his coat, he slid it back over his shoulders as he staggered towards the shadows of the tram tunnel.

< = >

Kyn slid backwards through his loft window, wincing as his bare feet touched cold concrete. He pulled the steel lined pane closed behind him and groaned with exasperated annoyance as his steps left bloody prints on the gray floor.

"Not that I'm not impressed, but wouldn't the door be easier?" Alec asked from where he was sat across the loft, the lanky hacker perched on a sofa slab of cracked and worn vinyl. Low to the ground, the black slab was one of the sparse, mismatched, and junk rescued pieces of lounge furniture Kyn had haphazardly arranged in one brick walled corner of his upper factory floor. A halfhearted attempt to make the rundown industrial space look lived in.

Runa was sunk into an overstuffed pod, booted feet propped on a low faux-wood table and calmly chomping on a sweetstik. She nodded vaguely in Kyn's direction as way of acknowledgement, not turning her attention away from the combat sim she was streaming on the loft's recreation holo. She twisted and slid the glowing handheld interface, crowing triumphantly as she shot an enemy in the face.

"Uh, yah. I guess." Kyn muttered distractedly. He bent at the waist, balancing on one foot, then the other, to pick shards of metal and glass from the soles of his feet. Obstructions removed, the cut and bleeding skin closed over almost instantly.

"Oh, that's so gross." Alec cringed, watching Kyn with repulsed interest. "But kinda cool." The hacker admitted, plunging his hand into a bowl of popped kernels. He shoved a fistful into his mouth, munching loudly.

"So, this is what's happening?" Kyn queried, gesturing back and forth between Alec and Runa with a bloody triangle of glass.

"What? Wouldn't you rather me be close if anyone tries anything?" Runa returned distractedly, not taking her eyes from the holo. "Plus, I got bored and Alec's cool." She added with an unconcerned shrug. "I'm more effective here anyway. I hate skulking."

"Thanks Runa, I think you're cool too." Alec beamed, smiling warmly at the youth. He turned back to Kyn, microchip green eyes mock wide in his angular face. "You got me a terrifying adolescent bodyguard. That's so sweet."

"She's tougher than she looks." Kyn tossed back. Satisfied he'd gotten as much debris free as he could, and trusting the rest would fall out as he healed, he straightened and began removing his shredded coat.

"Tits," Alec gasped, noticing the extant of Kyn's blood drenched shabbiness. "What happened to you?" He asked with genuine concern. "Are you okay?"

Kyn's cheeks burned with a confused blush.

"Yah, yah, I'm good. All healed up." He answered quickly, brushing the concern aside. "Rager on the tram." He added in way of explanation. A brief pause to rustle around in his coat's inner pockets and he flung the garment over the tall stool he used at his workbench. Crossing, he easily tossed the retrieved Dorothy to Alec before collapsing heavily next to the hacker. Impulsively, he slid in closer to the taller man and rested his weight easily into Alec's lanky figure. Not understanding where the urge came from, he leaned his head against the hacker's shoulder and allowed himself to relax into the taller man comfortably. Kyn was dimly aware of how strange it was to have someone show concern for his physical wellbeing, especially after seeing what he was capable of.

As close as he'd been to Yorri, Kyn had still hidden that part of himself away. Desperate to keep the other man safe, he'd taken great pains to hide his abilities, going as far as secretly plotting their escape from the city in a desperate attempt to keep Yorri out of reach of the Sentry's machinations. Plans, he'd later discovered through the desperate pleas of his former Handler, that were partially to blame for Yorri's death.

Kyn breathed in the sharp smell of electric burnt ozone and male musk that permeated Alec's skin and pushed down the rising rage and guilt that threatened to choke him, willing himself into a familiar, indifferent numbness.

No, Kyn considered briefly, Alec didn't know what he was capable of.

A rapid series of bangs, sharp and concise against the loft's steel loading door jerked Kyn from his momentary lapse.

"The fuck now?" He muttered peevishly, springing from the cushioned slab. He gestured at the workbench oni with a back-handed swipe.

A hovering holo showed Benn on the other side of the sliding metal door. The Handler held Kyn's discarded loafers aloft for the feed, his boringly handsome face its usual blank mask of dutifulness. Benn banged on the door again.

Snatching Ego from the workbench as he passed, Kyn strode to the loading bay door. He twirled the dagger by the hilt. Heaving the heavy door sideways, he slid it open halfway and leaned against the graffitied wall, blocking the opening to confront the Handler.

"Well look who dropped by for a late-night trick." He drawled, coy smile crawling across his face. Ego's blade bounced absently on his hip. "I knew you'd cave to my charms eventually."

Ignoring the taunting come on, Benn pushed the scuffed and blood splattered shoes into Kyn's chest. "These were found on the cross-wards skytram along with the body of a woman that – witnesses' claim - was a Rager. Your work I pressume?"

Kyn winked slyly in lieu of response and stepped aside. He tossed the shoes blindly behind himself as he gestured for Benn to enter the loft with a flourish of Ego's blade and an overly theatrical bow at the waist.

Benn moved into the loft with familiarity and intent, oblivious to Alec and Runa's presence.

"I've identified the three you dealt with at SpareParts, and now this woman on the tram." The Handler continued, moving to Kyn's workbench. He seized control of the oni with a swipe of his manicured hand and a flash of blue around the cuff. The Handler tossed ident pics onto the holo display and the projected images shifted to reorient themselves before settling into a circular, rotating menu.

Kyn easily recognized the face of each Rager he'd clashed with floating above the oni. More civilized and less actively violent, but them. Benn had even identified pixie-cut. Impressive given the time frame.

"Yah, that's them all right. Pleasant bunch." Kyn supplied. He crossed his arms and intently watched the idents circle themselves, studying each.

"Nataliia Sang, Ward M5. Wanted for black-market servo trafficking. Served six cycles on disciplinary work detail for grievous servo abuse." Benn intoned darkly, listing off a stream of crimes and allegations associated with the woman Kyn recognized as the squat, yellow eyed Rager from SpareParts. He eyed her ident balefully, absently twirling Ego over his fingers. He felt no twinge of guilt or conscience over killing someone with her list of malicious abuses.

"Borin Tsen," Benn continued, shifting the focus to a brutish looking man Kyn knew as the cannon-armed Rager. "Ward L6, served four cycles of disciplinary work detail in waste disposal for extortion, aggravated assault and robbery. Wanted for questioning in connection with various violent robberies across the lower wards."

"Talk about waste management, eh?" Alec quipped from the slab. "Kyn did everyone a favor taking out those pieces of shit." He grinned widely at his own joke and noisily munched another handful of popped kernels. Runa giggled throatily but didn't turn from her game.

Benn pressed on as if he hadn't heard the interjection, continuing to ignore the hacker's presence. Alec shrugged, nonplussed.

"Sergev Ullin, Ward L11, wanted in relation to multiple counts of rape and murder of licensed and unlicensed sex servos. Ordered to three separate rounds of civil re-education, four in narcotic abuse sanitariums." The Handler listed for the ident of a grotesquely thin, bug-eyed man. The tweeker with the arm blades.

"Obviously didn't take." Kyn noted. That many times through re-education and the notoriously cruel sanitariums and the Rager had probably been more insane than not. Kyn felt no sympathy, the heinous list of crimes merited the finale justice he'd delivered.

Benn's lips twisted into a scowl, but he pressed on. "Avon Willena." He finished curtly, cycling the ident of a woman with dark hair that hung to her shoulders. Kyn recognized the pale oval face and dead eyes of the blonde pixie-cut Rager from the tram. "Ward M2, no priors, no disciplinary history. Work records shows she was employed with an upper ward juvenile caregiver service." Benn listed, adding chillingly. "Postmortem DNA evidence links her with the mysterious poisoning deaths of twelve upper wards children."

A heavy silence fell over the room. No one offered snarky commentary.

"So, these Ragers are pretty messed up then." Alec ventured tentatively, breaking the silence. "Seems like the worst of the worst."

"Yes, indeed." Benn allowed, finally acknowledging the hacker. "Seems like whoever is recruiting them is pulling from the worst of the trash that has infected this city."

"The Informant." Kyn stated looking to the others. "The Ragers attacked me right after our meet. Plus, they're the only one whose got the resources to wrangle a bunch like this on the down low."

"KILL THE FUCKER!" Runa screamed, suddenly lunging forward in her cushioned pod. All eyes turned in surprise, and the three men stared at the wild-haired waif in silent bemusement before collectively realizing the youth was yelling at her intranet teammates.

"She's not wrong though." Kyn admitted. He turned to look at Benn through the hovering idents. "I'm going to have to track them down sooner or later."

"You're right." Benn confirmed stonily, smoothly switching into militarized Dag mode. "This is where our leads stop. There is nothing that links these four, no evidence of communication and nothing linking them with the Informant or any other radicalized force. They might be psychopaths, but they aren't organized. At least according to our intelligence."

Alec scoffed derisively.

"You just don't know where to look." The acid-haired hacker jeered, unfolding himself from the sofa slab. He ran a hand through his messy punk hawk and ambled over Runa's outstretched legs to approach the oni. A complex tattoo of branching circuitry that spidered over the crook of his right elbow glowed electric yellow. Network maps blossomed behind the idents as Alec synced himself into control of the interface. The interlocking pentagons of his f-Link shifted around his wrist as he pulled a touch interface from between his hands.

"We run our code backwards and out of sync behind normal traffic," he explained. "Your SPIRE cryptos don't see it. Just looks like reflected junk data to them, background noise. It's pretty easy to follow once you see it."

Alec had pulled apart the holo projection's user interface overlay and was seamlessly pouring in raw code. User friendly graphics melted into a glowing soup of letters, digits, and symbols.

Kyn's watched, transfixed. His training and experience made him an above average hack, but he still relied on pre-programmed tool kits and user-friendly apps to boost his capabilities. Alec, in contrast, manipulated the intranet code itself. Fingers flew over the touch interface as he directed code like orchestral performance art, weaving the very fabric of the electric web. Code streamed past in hypnotic ribbons of digital green as he pinged through the city's sea of interconnected network nodes, switching lines of code from one place to another, replacing bits here, and writing new additions there. Ever expanding bursts rippled from pinged areas, like radar, revealing short clusters of digits that lit up bright white in response to his prodding, flashing brightly then fading. Sparse at first, the effect replicated more frequently until it started to form the faint edges of a pattern. Pinpricks of white code amongst the green, linking in connective patterns that, to Kyn, resembled something akin to the branching complexity of the human nervous system. He smiled, watching the pattern unfolded, impressed by Alec's skill.

Benn watched with arms crossed over his chest, face stony and ever unreadable, while Runa continued to gnaw distractedly on her sweetstik, still entirely absorbed in her game.

"There!" Alec announced a few ticks later with an excited clap that collapsed the touch interface. "It's not complete, but you've got a start. Time lapse ping map of all recent coded communication traffic between the Informant and those four dead Ragers. Each point is a bounce from one network to the next. Given some time, and more extrapolation, I could track which key locations served as origin drops for the seed code, narrowing the grid on a physical locations they'd use for intranet jack in." He flashed the other two men a cocky grin.

Benn eyed the lanky hacker silently for a moment.

"Impressive." He finally stated, unfolding his arms. He gestured at the shimmering pattern in the code. "How long would it take you to do this?"

"What? Track the Informant?" Alec asked, suddenly bemused, apparently taken aback at being asked to participate despite his volunteered plan and show of skill. An understandable hint of fear quivered in his voice at the potential of turning on his employer.

"Yes." Benn confirmed.

The acid-haired hacker fidgeted warily, childishly biting at the tip of his thumb. He glanced hesitantly at Kyn.

"Don't worry." Kyn reassured, surprising himself. "I'll protect you."

Runa coughed dryly under her breath.

"Would have to go slow." Alec mused, his expression turning more confident as he chewed distractedly on his thumb nail. The digit was painted a chipped and glossy black. "The Informant is clever, you go looking for them, the path there is riddled with cantrips and hotzones. They'll know I'm looking." He shrugged his shoulders. Kyn could see the excitement growing the more the hacker thought about the challenge. "But get some faster equipment in here. Allow some cook time to craft some protective algorithms. Couple days, maybe?" He guessed energetically.

Kyn felt a stab of panic behind his eyes, and his jaw stiffened. He drew in a measured breath, suppressing the sudden shiver of fear that flashed through him, and let it out. Mental conditioning turned the breath into cool flowing water that cascaded over his head, a cleansing iciness that washed down his spine and away into the floor, steadying him. Keeping Alec alive meant ending the threat, Kyn reassured himself. His mind steeled over this logic. He knew he really had no choice about getting Alec involved, but as long as he was close, he wouldn't let anything happen to the hacker. Kyn glanced at the overstuffed pod, further reassured that he could rely on Runa when needed. Reassurance twisted around the steel of his inner calm. He eyed Benn, a hint of threat simmering behind the cold silver of his eyes.

"We can get you what you need." The Handler answered, giving Kyn a barely perceptible nod, then turned back to Alec, who smiled, seemingly dazed and delighted at the opportunity now that he'd worked himself around to the idea.

"What's happening?" Runa asked, slouching her way out of the pod. She approached the workbench.

"Alec's gunna track down the Informant," Kyn told her shortly.

"Jag." She muttered, breezing past Kyn and the others on her way to the loading door. "Im'a bounce. Be by in the morning to watch him while you and Ashe guard the thing." She snagged her black coat from a jutting pipe.

"The thing? What thing?" Kyn demanded after her, flustered and perplexed.

"Summit." She supplied, sliding the steel door open. It slammed noisily against the end of its battered runners. "The Unity is meeting in the Pinnacle Garden tomorrow morning. You and Ashe are attending."

"What?" Kyn balked. He turned accusatorially to Benn. "You're supposed to tell me these things." He whined melodramatically.

"I was going to." Benn returned, indifferent.

Kyn sighed and ran his hands through his hair, suddenly weary. He thought about the mysterious blue tubes, the Rager on the tram, bringing Alec into the fold, tracking the Informant. There were a lot of pieces in the air already, and now he had a meeting of the Unity to the deal with.

He needed sleep.

Kyn waved to Runa as she made her exit, sliding the door casually shut behind herself with a powerful *bang* that shook the concrete, and crossed to Alec. He twisted his fingers into the taller man's waistband and tugged the hacker towards himself. He gave Benn a pointed look.

"It's time to get out of my space now." He ordered with a limp and dismissive wave towards the door. "Arrange to get some better gear in here. Be discreet." He turned on his heel, leading Alec toward his sleeping nook.

"I don't take my orders from you." Benn told his back.

Kyn stopped mid step and turned, dropping his hand from Alec's waist, and lunged at the Handler with preternatural speed, a guttural growl rising his throat. He snapped his teeth and snarled tauntingly at Benn.

The Handler arched an eyebrow, unconcerned.

Kyn's shoulders sagged, and he rolled his eyes, grimacing, before finally flashing the older man a sickeningly sweet smile.

"Please?"

Marching Orders

Runa was already live on holo arguing with Sandri when Kyn and Ashe reached Operations.

The arriving Envoy pair had spent the better part of the morning standing at rigid attention around the polyplex walls of Noav SPIRE's Pinnacle Garden, an oasis above the clouds, all white sand gardens, azure pools, and biohacked fauna, Kyn stuck staring at a single point over Nexx Envoy Lux's shapely shoulder while the Sentry triplet's played host to the Unity's emergency summit. Now, Runa's projected image, semi-translucent, hovered above the central control interface. No background image betrayed her location.

Kyn, was thankful for the precaution. He didn't need Sandri, or worse Malvyc - currently hovering creepily in the shadows of the towering servers - to be tipped off that Alec, their new freelancer, was holed up in Kyn's loft.

Benn had spun the initially argumentative Sandri onto letting Runa stay posted to watch duty by reiterating the importance of tracking down the Informant, asserting that utilizing the hacker's skills was their only viable option for success.

This secrecy did not sit well with Sandri, and the perpetually irate Handler was now loudly haranguing both Runa and Benn about the logical flaw in not utilizing the collective computing power of Operation's server towers, a point Kyn was hard pressed to argue with.

"Because I like pissing you off Sandri." He supplied, cutting across the argument as he and Ashe joined the collected group. He nodded in acknowledgement to Benn, pointedly ignored Malvyc entirely, and turned his best shit eating grin on Sandri. "As if I need any other reason?" He added brightly.

"You." Sandri shot back acidly. "Are not in command here."

"Why not?" Kyn retorted, perching himself on a data jockeys' workstation. "I'm the only one getting results."

"You serve at the pleasure of your Sentry for the glory of Noav SPIRE and the Unity." Malvyc reprimanded from his place in the shadows. The bald Envoy's voice was like the rasping slither of wind over dried gutter trash. Sandri beamed at the support.

"Fuck off, Malvyc." Kyn tossed back.

Malvyc's eyes flashed a dangerous crimson in the shadows and Kyn was seized by a flash of white-hot pain. His whole body shook involuntarily. A warm wetness dribbled down his chin, faintly registered in the flash of agony. He'd bitten through his lip.

"Enough." Benn ordered flatly.

Malvyc's eyes dimmed, and a scowl twisted his thin lips. He faded back into the shadows of the server towers.

Released, Kyn doubled over, coughing bodily.

"Behavior like this is why the Dividers beat you." Benn stated, coldly objective. Commanding in his detachment. "It ends now."

Kyn glared daggers at Malvyc, staying dutifully silent even as he choked back a violently lewd taunt. He wiped the blood from his chin.

"We get the point. Work like a team." Runa's gruff voice interjected from the holo. "Can we get on with this?"

"A new group of refugees has approached our borders seeking asylum from the Dividers." Benn obliged, pivoting to their directive.

"Normally, the refugees would be moved to an external re-education center, but with the active Divider threat, the Unity has decided all Wasters - new asylum seekers and those within the re-education camps - shall be moved behind the wall for safety."

"They're expecting the Dividers to come for them." Kyn interjected. "And we're to make sure that doesn't happen."

"Exactly," Benn confirmed. "Two mornings after tomorrow, 0200h. Dag forces, further supplemented by an entourage of Ziev mechs, will escort a convoy carrying the Wasters through the resource zone. Encounter simulations anticipate the highest probability of Divider attack will be at the transfer point into the city. Ashe and Malvyc will defend the Sentry, while Kyn and Runa, you will be deployed on the loading gate to prevent any attempts at reclamation."

"Reclamation?" Runa asked.

ENVOY, REPORT TO MY GALLERY 2200H

Red text, marked from Sentry Alena, blazed in the corner of Kyn's optic. He tapped it away.

"Refugee interviews have depicted the Dividers as indomitable and sadistic slavers," Sandri answered. "These Wasters are escaped slaves fleeing an abusive master. From everything we've gathered, the attacks have been retaliation for offering sanctuary to those the Dividers view as their escaped property."

Memories of wane and glassy-eyed faces illuminating with breathless awe flashed across Kyn's mind, memories of footage from sub-level 29 that blatantly contradicted Sandri's explanation.

"Gross." Runa commented, deadpan.

"Quite." Ashe added trying to move the briefing. They obviously had their own doubts after seeing sub-level 29 for themselves. "Protocols?"

"Enclosed," Benn answered shortly. He swiped a command across the control interface. Each Envoy's f-Link lit up in response, receiving the data transfer. A data cache appeared in Kyn's optic, and a tap of his pinkie tucked it away for later review. He needed to see what Alena wanted, and how it fit into any of this before he worried about specifics.

"We good?" He asked, looking to Benn, eager to move on.

"Dismissed." Benn confirmed with a curt nod of ascent.

< = >

Kyn perched, balanced lightly on the balls of his feet at the terrace ledge. Beneath him the upper city sparkled, the grimy lower wards hidden by altitude, overcast cloud cover, and the crammed stacks of the mids. Only the glittering opulence of the uppers unfolded before him in all its pristine jewel-like beauty. The sun had long set, yet the uppers were still airy and light, directly in opposition to the dark, cramped chaos of the wards below. Rolling, man-made hills sprawled out below, dotted with luminescent synth-lakes that glowed ethereally white in the darkness. Orderly clusters of fluidly twisted steel and polyplex luxury residences rose around the most prominent structures, the upper most levels of the seven SPIREs, rising like delicate, crystalline-silver stalagmite. Here the SPIREs reached their height, towering above everything else, ever-present reminders to those below who they owed their good fortunes to.

Kyn had made his way to the operative lockers with Ashe following the briefing. He'd ditched his Envoy uniform, changing back into his stashed street gear, and left the SPIRE through a high traffic mid-wards entrance, aiming to purposefully be seen by surveillance. Alena's use of private message had made it clear the Sentry expected discretion, and he'd backtracked over rooftops and alleys, utilizing a hard-to-reach service hatch, then a drainage pipe, to scale the upper levels of the SPIRE. A wide cat leap and he'd scampered onto the terrace ledge that edged the Sentry's private gallery, several klicks above sea level.

A plex-walled cave carved into the face of the super structure, Alena's gallery terrace was a diamond shaped alcove enfolded within Noav SPIRE's architecture, walled in on two sides by clear polyplex and protected from the elements by a jutting concrete overhang. The terrace was a private oasis outlined by tubes of white neon and decorated with cushioned lounging slabs in dark luxury fabrics, arranged around elegantly delicate low tables. Topiaries, bio-engineered to be consistently flowering, perfumed the airy alcove.

There was no safety rail.

The time stamp in his optic flashed 2200h.

"Welcome, Envoy." Alena's coldly commanding voice greeted.

"Sentry." Kyn acknowledged, spiraling from his crouch to face his superior, the yawning emptiness to his back, a clenched fist slammed to his chest in salute.

Barefoot and clad in a simple sleeping shift of pearl white silk, Alena was abnormally alone. A lone, attractive male Dag, light featured with a strong square jaw, was her only guard, posted inside the terrace entrance. He dutifully watched Kyn from the other side of the polyplex with a wary intensity .

A sudden urge to throw the Sentry from the SPIRE flashed briefly across Kyn's mind like electric fire, but he pushed it down.

The guard behind the polyplex would've had no hope of protecting the Sentry if Kyn had chosen to strike. The poor hunk was only there for decoration, his presence merely a display of power on the Sentry's part. Her way of signaling how little she feared Kyn. How confident she was that one of her most dangerous weapons could never be turned against her.

Ever the shit disturber, Kyn brought his free hand to his lips and blew the Dag a kiss, twiddling his fingers for good measure.

"Boinken' 'im eh?" He asked, eyebrow arched suggestively.

The Sentry slapped him. Retractable fiberglass blades beneath her nails engaged with the motion, drawing stinging lines across his cheek where she struck. The cool night air stung the split flesh.

"Mind your place." The Sentry admonished, voice cool and even. No hint of agitation or anger marred her flawless features.

"Yes, Sentry." Kyn corrected, hanging his head and assuming a properly chastised posture. Wetness ran down his cheek. He could already feel the familiar itch of flesh healing.

Dominance asserted, Alena turned from Kyn and drifted towards a low slab. She lifted an elegantly delicate glass decanter full of a honey hued liquid from a low metal table as she passed, and poured a generous serving into an equally graceful flute. Casually placing the decanter on the varnished redwood of the terrace deck, she languidly reclined herself across overstuffed cushions.

"I am amongst the few who find your antics amusing. But don't push your luck," she continued more airily. The Sentry watched Kyn with the exhausted amusement one gave a bad harlequin streamer. "It's no surprise though that, you are of course correct. We did train you to be keen and observant, after all. But there is a time and place for your particular brand of amusement, and now is not that time."

"Yes, Sentry," Kyn repeated. He hadn't moved from his place balanced on the lip of the terrace ledge.

"I've always admired your boldness." Alena added, taking a thoughtful sip of the amber liquid, almost wistful. The commanding Sentry seemed to uncoil within the seclusion of her private space. A dangerous predator luxuriating in the comfort of her den. "It's takes impressive single mindedness to commit so thoroughly to repeatedly acting against one's own self-preservation."

"Thank you, Sentry." Kyn accepted. An elfish grin tugged at the corners of his mouth. He could feel the pull of congealing blood against newly regenerated skin. "May I?" He asked, raising a hand to his cheek.

Alena silently took another sip of the amber liquid and waved her hand permissively.

Kyn crossed, approaching the arranged slabs, and took a seat across from the Sentry. He reached for another glass decanter, this one of pure, clear water. He dipped a silken towelette in the water and proceeded to scrub the drying blood from his cheek. Alena watched silently, her ice blue gaze impassive.

The clear water turned red as Kyn dipped the napkin back in the decanter, rinsing the cloth.

"I want you to kill my brother." The Sentry stated, her flute balanced delicately between her fingers.

Kyn's heart seemed to stop, his breath held in abrupt shock and disbelief. Calmly, he put the moist cloth aside, careful to keep his expression passively neutral.

"When?" Was all he asked, not daring reveal the fierce joy that had blossomed behind his ribs.

"Tomorrow night. It needs to be done before you sync with the others to guard the caravan arrival. All predictive simulations suggest the next few night cycles to be messy, and I want this to be caught within that impending chaos." She explained evenly. Ordering her brother's death as if ticking off another task on a servo's errand list.

Kyn's thoughts whirred. Disbelief at what she had ordered him to do crashed against hope and stuttered along wariness. The schemes of the Sentry were twisted and multilayered, never exactly what they seemed; what she was asking was a perversion of everything he'd been taught. He couldn't let the prospect of finally ridding himself of his tormentor blind him to the potential trap Alena was weaving around him.

"Why?" He asked tentatively. It wasn't an Envoy's job to ask why, only to deliver the message.

The Sentry pursed thin and perfectly arched lips, momentarily thoughtful before answering.

"Yes, I do suppose you deserve some explanation. This is an exceptional ask after all." She placed the stemmed glass back on the low table and turned her icy gaze on Kyn. "My sister and I have grown exasperated with our brother's obsessive pursuits, some of which you are of course familiar with."

Countless memories of time spent in the white room fused in Kyn's mind to form one endless event of screaming pain. He nodded stoic affirmation.

"Our brother's pursuits, eccentric as they are, have been tolerated thus far because they have been instrumental in expanding the power and influence of our SPIRE." Alena conceded, adding. "But no more. His single mindedness now threatens our unit's cohesion, and that cannot be tolerated." She plucked up her glass again, signaling the end of her vague non-explanation.

"Why me?" Kyn asked warily, risking another question, dancing around his mistrust. "Don't you fear my personal experience will compromise me?"

"On the contrary," Alena countered with something approximating a wry smile. She absently rolled the stem of her fluke between her fingers. "I'm asking this of you precisely because of your personal feelings. Particularly you're impressively indomitable rebellious streak."

The Sentry leaned forward to reach across the space between them and placed a milk white hand on Kyn's forearm. Her fingertips pressed gently into his tawny skin.

"Sometimes I wonder if we train you Envoys too well." She mused softly, in something that mimicked concern. Her breath smelled of honey and the antiseptic sting of alcohol. The fiberglass blades beneath her nail beds slid free as she spoke, slowing slicing into the skin of Kyn's arm. Beads of crimson blossomed beneath her touch.

"Too obedient," Alena observed. "If I sent one of the others, all my brother would have to do is order them to surrender and that would be that. They'd balk at the prospect of disobeying any single one of us, let alone actually harming us. But you, you've demonstrated an innate capacity for toeing the line of our authority if not outright thwarting it. I can use that. The incident with your previous Handler proved your willingness to lash out at your betters if properly motivated. In fact, your entire recent history gives my sister and I plausible deniability. If his cancellation is linked back to us in any way, we will simply blame it on a broken tool that needs to be decommissioned."

Kyn's gray eyes sparkled manically at her words, unfazed by the pain of the blades under his skin. Adrenaline flushed him and quickened his breath. The dismissive threat reassured his doubts and convinced him of the sincerity of her orders. There was no trick here. She risked consequences if he failed, and to dodge accountability she wanted him to know where blame would be shifted. He was still a tool to be used and discarded as she saw fit. Comfortably predictable. They'd probably figure a way to permanently kill him if he failed.

"But I doubt it will come to that." The Sentry amended airily, removing her hand. Crimson coloured the tips of her pallid fingers. "My sister suggested we give you this assignment to compensate for our brother's prior misguided actions. I agreed. A reward for your continued loyalty - to help you move beyond past unpleasantness."

Kyn's mind whirled dizzyingly, conflicting emotions warring within him. The familiar crawling itch spread across his forearm, the punctures smoothly knitting themselves back together.

"Understood." He said finally after a beats delay, then added, "I am a proud tool of The Unity, all I need and all I shall want will be supplied by my devotion." He met the Sentry's penetrating gaze, face dutifully blank.

Alena watched him intently for a tick, possibly attempting to measure the effect of her manipulations, before turning away and returning to her drink. His existence apparently forgotten.

Sensing an end to the briefing, Kyn rose from the slab and brought one fist to his chest in a dutiful salute.

"You are my Sentry, for whom I reach into the world. May my actions bring praise to my SPIRE." He recited respectfully. "My blood for my SPIRE. My body for my Sentry. My devotion to The Unity." He hesitated for a moment, before adding shyly. "Thank you."

The Sentry turned back, seemingly bemused to notice Kyn was still in her presence. Her handsome face split with a cruel grin.

"Make it messy," she ordered with a final dismissive wave.

< = >

Kyn slammed into the shower stall.

He'd dived through his loft's window and crossed the space without a word, ignoring Alec's bewildered greeting and Runa's gruff questions, to sequester himself in the privacy of the small space. He tipped out the entirety of the discarded blue eclipse vial, drawing an overdose worth of sparkling indigo lines across the vanity's polished surface. Thumb tapped against index finger summoned the hollow reverb of pre-fall techno icon GeoFitz, pumped deafeningly loud through the loft's sound system.

Kyn pinched off the left side of his nose and quickly snorted the first line. Indigo euphoria slammed into him, lighting up his mind and body like fairy fire. He groaned with pleasure and ran his hands through his hair, reveling in the tactile sensation. Every nerve sang. Hammering thoughts broke apart, becoming dancing rays of rainbow light, indiscernible from one another other, bouncing through the prismatic shards of his mind.

His regeneration kicked back, the flame of his narcotic bliss drowned almost instantly, his mind pulled back from the escape of thoughtless reprieve.

"Fuck!" Kyn screamed, slamming his fist into the concrete wall. Bones broke and skin split, but the pain went unnoticed over the howl of warring thoughts and conflicting emotions that poured back. He craved oblivion. He dipped his head and snorted back the next line, then the next, and the next, until the blue powder was gone.

He moaned as the drugs thundered through him, braced against the counter, back arched. Reality became multilayered; his vision tuned to two different channels, playing as one.

On one layer everything was exactly as it was, unchanged. He looked at himself in the mirror and his face looked back. Flushed with pleasure, eyes black voids rimmed by a thin band of steel, pupils dilated so wide they almost engulfed his irises.

A second reality shimmered over this clarity like a fragile sheen of hoarfrost. A shattered mirror, broken into rainbow and silver shards. Prismatic cracks lined his face, lines of shifting light connecting freckles, drawing constellations across a glowing galaxy.

Both realities played in front of his eyes as he stripped, discarded clothes pooling around his feet, and stalked naked from the shower stall.

Runa had left, Kyn could see echoes of her prismatic shadow trailing from slab to food storage, then out of the loft, her final actions traced in thin cracks of rainbow light. Moments of her outline were tainted with minute voids of shadow that made Kyn feel sick to his stomach to look at. He turned away. No thoughts pierced his new multilayered reality. He experienced only need. Every nerve ending screamed with an endless pleasure that churned on itself, craving to be fed.

Alec watched him with bewildered amusement. Kyn could see the hackers prismatic shadow trail clustered around the workbench, cracked rainbow slivers that traced in looping, pacing circles.

Bare feet padding silently across cold stone, he stalked towards the hacker. Alec's bemused expression shifted with the naked Envoy's approach, a hungry grin growing across his narrow face. The definition of his muscular arms was shaded in Kyn's vision by shattered cracks of undulating light.

Kyn grabbed hungrily at the hacker's pelvis and twisted one hand into the taller man's waistband. He whipped the hacker off his feet, throwing him at the floor. He eased the taller man's impact as they tumbled, flowing like liquid metal to mount the prone and unharmed Alec, who panted excitedly beneath him. Pieces of other realities tore under his fingers, and he ripped Alec's jeans, releasing the hackers throbbing cock. A lube packet tumbled from a pocket.

Kyn grunted in frustration. Regeneration was already pushing at the edges of his high, chasing away the thoughtless void. Teeth tore the packet, and he slicked Alec's hardness before sliding the other man into himself with a guttural moan of pleasure, chasing another oblivion.

< = >

"Rough day?" Alec asked, rolling onto his side to look at Kyn. He placed one hand on the Envoy's bare chest and absently traced the hard curve of a pectoral.

On his back, Kyn stared silently up at the rusted pipes and worn beams that crisscrossed the ceiling.

"I'm going to kill the man who has tortured me my entire life." He confided to the mess, finally allowing himself to accept the concept. It sat in his gut, strange and dangerously unstable, both elating and terrifying in equal measure.

No matter what, nothing would be the same again.

Alec's mouth opened and closed, gaping, speechless. Tracing fingers stopped, and he rested his hand gently over Kyn's heart.

"I have no response to that." The hacker said finally, goofy grin tugging at the corner of his lips.

"I wasn't really expecting one," Kyn returned, smirking despite the heaviness that had settled in his chest. "Things are in motion," he added, as if to himself. He continued to stare at the ceiling. He imagined he was connecting the dots between facts and schemes, drawing mental lines between chips in the wooden beams and rust spots on the pipes. He tried to predict where they'd all converge. A place he wouldn't escape. "Things I probably won't survive." He acknowledged, remembering the Sentry's open threat. Alena had said it plainly; he'd been cast as scapegoat.

"Is that possible?" Alec asked, tapping his fingers over the un-blemished skin of Kyn's chest. "I watched you take a blade augment through the heart, and it didn't even slow you down."

"I'm sure it can be done if someone wants too badly enough." Kyn answered honestly, sitting up on the bedroll and swinging his legs around. "Pretty true of most things." He placed his feet on the cold concrete and hunched over, elbows propped on his knees, head in his hands. He sighed, fingers splayed through his hair, unruly curls falling forward, covering his face. "My point is something is coming. I seem to be caught in the middle of a lot of shit that isn't adding up. So, I need a location on this Informant. Now."

"All work so soon. I thought we'd stay here a bit." Alec pouted. He pawed at Kyn's bare thigh.

"I need to put him down before I go do what I need to do." Kyn insisted in a low growl. "I can't have him out there as a threat to you if I don't come back."

Uncomfortable silence echoed behind him. Kyn could hear the anxious ruffling of sheets.

"The Informant isn't a threat." Alec finally blurted, the words rushing from him. "I still work for him. I've been sending reports since I've been here. I'm sorry Kyn I had no choice. I'm in too deep. The day of the attack I was instructed to upload a scorched earth hack to a dead drop service node. Specifically, a node close enough to the wall so it could hop servers and burrow into the external security systems. I'm the one who took out the perimeter defenses. My hack knocked all the auto- turrets and radar systems offline - which is probably how someone got close enough to blow the hole." He was rambling, desperate. He rushed and stumbled over his words to explain himself. "They said if I turned, they'd leak my involvement back to you and your Handlers, that you'd be forced to kill me. Which sucks 'cause I really like being alive."

"I know." Kyn stated flatly, cutting across the babbled confession. He turned, Alec's eyes were wide with confusion and panic, his acid-green 'hawk ruffled and mussed from their earlier athletics. "Well okay not the specifics, but the way you showed up on my door that day, seemed like something was up. Plus, havin' ya here. It's all been too neat. Informant didn't even try to come after you once for show."

"So, you knew I had something to do with it?" Alec asked.

"Didn't know, suspected. Two different things. Figured you were involved but had no idea what you were doing. Standard compartmentalization. Would you have done it if you knew why?" Kyn returned rhetorically, cocking an eyebrow. "Guys like you and me do the deed and carry the guilt. Knowing the why is a liability. Still, wouldn't be a bad idea to keep the pretense up. It wouldn't be good for Benn and the others to know."

Alec was dumbly silent. Kyn's f-Link glowed softly and a notification from Runa flashed across his optic. He gave the hacker one more glance, soaking up the image of his naked and lean musculature, before turning away and rising through a squat from the bedroll. Alec lunged across the derrafoam and slapped him playfully across the bare ass.

"Come on stay a bit," he petitioned, huskily.

Kyn padded away. "Thanks for the fuck but, duty calls."

He paused at the bare timber door frame, an idea flashing. He looked back to Alec, tangled in the damp sheets. A wicked smile split his face.

"Get me another meeting with your boss. I've got some questions."

Kiki's Big Spa Day

Kyn pulled his hood up against the persistent drizzle of grimy runoff that dripped through the stacks above.

Posting off one arm, he vaulted easily over the rusted fire escape, swinging one leg after the other over the metal railing to drop three stories to the lid of a trash disposal unit below. He landed lightly on the balls of his feet with a metallic crunch and sprung forward, pushing off the unit's lid to leap, cat like, across the narrow alley, and latched onto a vertical drainage pipe secured to the adjacent building. His hands slipped, momentarily losing grip on the slick pipe and he braced, pressing into the crumbling brick with his feet. He scurried hand over hand up the pipe. Mounting the next rooftop, he immediately switched directions, leaping back across the alley gap. The moment his boots touched roofing tile he was off running again at an easy pace, following the blinking waypoint in his optic.

The rusted and disused remnant of an archaic railway bridge loomed ahead. Swallowed by the encroaching vertical growth of the city's desperate bid for space, the bridge's underside support structure was level with Kyn's current trajectory - across another easy series of alley leaps - and he ran towards the interconnected weave of steel girders and buttresses. Dark shapes hung beneath the ancient beams like oversized bats.

Leaping over another gap - wider than the last - he cleared the next alley, soaring over the heads of the oblivious civilian traffic below before running on. The flavorful scents of street vendors prepping their morning fare wafted up. A few more running steps and he took the next alley gap, kong vaulting over a crumbling smokestack in his path, hips fed forward and through, smoothly clearing the obstacle. He kept running, breathing calm and even.

As he closed in on the bridge, he eyed its under web of exposed steel beams, plotting his next jump. He reached the final building ledge and leapt, aiming for the nearest crossbeam. The gap was wide, and he barely made it, catching hold of the steel girder's jutting lip at the last moment. He swung precariously beneath the beam by his fingertips. Lifeless bodies hung from the girder beside him. Dark shapes that dangled from where they'd been lynched with chain and electrical wire by hysterical mobs hunting so-called Divider collaborators. Sacrifices to appease the cleansing rage of the Unity.

Kyn swung himself onto the narrow beam with a grunt of effort. Balanced easily in a low crouch, he picked his way through the grimy network of rusted metal girders and slime covered trusses until he found the vantage point he needed. Swinging his legs over the edge he sat on a wide beam, booted feet dangling over the empty space. Beneath him, crammed within the faded remains of a cracked and pitted pre-fall highway, was one of the lower wards grimier budget entertainment districts, a packed hive of shops, street vendors, bazaar stalls, and teetering stacks of sheet metal shanties. Neo-k/pop street hustlers, young and effortlessly cool, hollered odds at crowds of paunchy and dejected men tossing dice down narrow side alleys, while overly painted shop gurls hocking knock-off cosmetic patches under neon tubes to credit poor cultists.

Kyn's optic dropped his waypoint outside a three-high hive stack, a skinShop halfway beneath the bridge, slotted between a bioHack garage and a shuttered Yummy Otter Corp boutique.

A vertical holo scroll dubbed the skinShop Syndication, it's face lined with neon tubes that glowed white in the dimness. It was mid-morning, yet no sunlight penetrated this far into the city core. Any natural light was blocked by the wards above, and the darkened lower core was lit entirely by the warring neon signs and scrolling holos that illuminated the dimness with a constant phosphorescent glow.

Floating AR advos declared that Syndication rented sensate docks. Claiming the highest quality for price point, they offered a place for discerning clientele to jack into the latest catalogued episodes of the benign day-to-day lives of their favorite upper ward's cultist elite. A place to binge watch the escapades of beautiful and pampered men and women who enjoyed privileged lives of luxury in exchange for regularly having their bodies digitally pillaged. Experiential escapist entertainment for the unwashed masses, rented for credits by the hour.

Tapping a few commands across his palm Kyn opened a comm channel, flagging Alec.

"I'm here." He announced, absently fiddling with the black cuff still fixed securely around his wrist. He spun it distractedly.

"Where? I've got eyes on every feed around the building. I don't see you anywhere."

"No shit." Kyn snorted, abandoning his fiddling. He watched the area around Syndication intently, scanning darkened corners for more mundane prying eyes. Spotting no tails or shadows, he pushed away from the girder, sliding easily from the steel beam to drop feet first to the street below.

He landed silently on cracked and ruined asphalt, legs folding fluidly beneath him as he flowed gracefully through a feline crouch. The constant press of people rolled around him, disinterested in the hooded stranger who had dropped suddenly into their midst. Straightening, Kyn smoothed his hands over the dark canvas of his jumpsuit. Matte black with a silver zip. He adjusted the cowled harness, tightening the synth leather straps under his arms. Ego's sheath, hilt down, and flat against his spine, pressed comfortably between his shoulder blades, concealed beneath the rig. He dropped his hands into the jumpsuit's wide pockets as he wound his way through the crowd.

"See me now?" He asked, passing the fist-sized dome of a Dag security feed. The cam was mounted on the last remaining intact corner of a crumbling brick pre-fall building - a collapsed bank - the ruins gutted and stacked with teetering prefabs.

"Lookin' good, killer." The hacker chirped flirtatiously in his ear.

Kyn flipped the 'plex dome a rude hand gesture.

"I could think 'eh better uses for that finger." Alec purred back, unperturbed.

Kyn hid his smirk within the depths of his hood. Approaching Syndication, he dipped his head, shielding his face from view of the close circuit security feed posted above the entrance.

Inside, a Ziev synthetic behind the client service desk turned its domed head as Kyn entered. The bipedal bot seemed to watch the Envoy through a single glowing red light set in the center of its convex faceplate. The virtual-intelligence stood behind a waist high service counter inside the shop's cramped entrance shell. Hexagonal in shape, the entrance shell was a hard, black construction plastic lined with more horizontal strips of white neon. The dark prefab walls glowed with lines of brilliant white, interrogation bright in the small space.

Kyn approached the synthetic.

"Kiki's Big Spa Day." He requested, swiping the credit payment across the palm of his hand.

"L3, Dock 278," the synthetic's digital voice chimed back, brightly pleasant. A door slid open in the rear wall, and the single point of red in the bot's faceplate flashed green.

Kyn nodded his thanks and proceeded through the security door to the hive's central shell. Clear plastic risers snaked the walls, winding upwards through the stack. He mounted the first riser and started to climb. At the top he followed glowing holo signs that hovered over the cell walls. Immersion docks lined each hexagonal shell; gloss black polyurethane pods, like sleek and streamlined coffins. Kyn's face reflected back at him; stretched and distorted in the sleek surface of each pod he passed. Digits hovered over each curved lid and he followed them until he found 278.

Kyn stopped in front of the rented pod and swiped his hand over the polished lid. The coffin-tube gave an internal chirp, clearance confirmed, and the lid swung outward with a hydraulic hiss.

sync f-Link flashed in red AR within the coffin pods dark interior.

"Kiki's Big Spa Day, eh?" Alec teased in his ear.

"Quality entertainment," Kyn returned dryly.

A rhythmic drumming of his right digits against the palm of his left opened a secure input link, and he paired with the pod. Crawling vibrations crept under the skin of his left forearm and his F-Link swirled and shifted across his bare arm, glowing neon blue. Lasting only a few ticks the crawling sensation faded. A digital green **Proceed** signaled Kyn's biofeed successfully linked.

"Jacked in," he told the empty shell.

"I see you boo," Alec confirmed. The acid-haired hacker was currently in two places at once, both monitoring Syndication's internal systems remotely from the loft, and simultaneously riding the biofeed bridge made by Kyn's f-Link to dive into dock 278.

"Ready to press play?" The hacker asked.

"More than." Kyn answered. He swept his hood back, an impish grin across his angular face. Climbing into the dock, he turned to lay back against the inside. "It's been too long since I've treated myself to a little pampering," he remarked brightly.

A layer of stimnetting lined the inside of the immersion dock, tightly weaved nanofiber that molded to his weight, comfortably supporting him.

Biofeed linked and client secure, the pod lid swung shut with a hydraulic hiss.

Total darkness engulfed Kyn. Another layer of stimnetting pressed gently over his face and neck, closing his eyes as it molded itself snugly to the front of his person. Non-constricting, he breathed easily through the nanofiber layer.

AR digits floated in the darkness, visible to his optic even behind his closed lids.

3...

2..

1.

The gentle lapping of water against stone bounced back to him in an open echo. The air smelt of salt and eucalyptus.

"Ma'am, would you like more oil before your technician arrives?" A sweet and professionally deferential feminine voice inquired from somewhere above.

Kyn lazily blinked his eyes open. Undulating ribbons of shadow, streaked with beams of reflected gold sunlight, danced across ultramarine blue tiles. A vaulted ceiling above. Broad wooden slats pressed against the bare skin of his backside, supporting him in a reclined position. Lazily, he lolled his head to one side.

"Of course." He said, addressing a benignly pretty young woman. His lips moved involuntarily, and his voice was not his own, pitched high and enthusiastically bubbly.

The woman, clad in a soft baby blue attendants' gown, smiled at Kyn pleasantly before bowing low and stepping away. Two surgically youthful men - identically densely muscled, and naked save for a thong of metallic silver spandex - filled her place. Each carried a large glass bottle, full of a thick, olive hued liquid.

The men moved in flawless synchronicity, flanking Kyn to kneel on either side of him. Each poured out a viscous glob into their palms and proceeded to spread the golden-green oil over the bare flesh of Kyn's legs, massaging the muscles with firm, practiced strokes.

Luxurious scents filled his nostrils, and he watched intently as the men silently rubbed, working the knotted tension from his calves, their strong hands occasionally drifting temptingly over the curve of his thighs.

A pleased purr escaped his lips as his eyes flicked back and forth between the two attendants. His gaze involuntarily hovered, fixated, over the rippling striation of their engorged muscularity. He delicately traced a wickedly tipped nail along his sternum, drawing up over the steep curve of one breast. He paused to playfully circle an engorged nipple with the heavily lacquered tip of a sharp acrylic.

Kyn cringed inwardly. He found the attendants' jacked up, overly muscular physiques, and performative hypermasculinity, a turn-off. Yet, he was powerless to control what his host had prioritized looking at.

Through the dock Kyn was experiencing a pre-recorded simulation jacked out of the cultist he was riding's own biofeed. Translated through the dock's connection to his biofeed, Kyn was experiencing everything as Kiki had experienced it; seeing what the cultist had seen, doing what she had done, feeling what she had felt.

"Trippy," Alec interjected in Kyn's ear. Piggybacked on Kyn's f-Link, Alec was watching the program remotely with a hacker's gods eye view. A hidden voyeur to Kiki's Big Spa Day.

Kyn smiled to himself, the expression not touching his face. The immersion dock overrode his own muscular neural feedback, the stimnetting's nanofiber weave working in concert with the biofeed's link to his nervous system, simulating movement, and external sensation. His optic feed supplied model recorded visuals, and pre-programmed scents were vented through the dock's climate control, triggering his brain's sense memory to conveniently connect inconsistent programming gaps. The illusion was uncanny and total immersive. Everything he was experiencing had already happened to someone else. Someone who'd been paid for the pleasure of having their inner world stripe mined for the entertainment of others.

He just got to ride the ride.

Kyn felt himself relaxing deeper into the wooden slats as Kiki finally tore her gaze away from the males luxuriating her with attention. The muscular attendants continued their work, kneading steadily up her legs. Relaxed, Kiki lazily looked around, giving Kyn an opportunity to examine his surroundings through his host's eyes.

He was lounged by a sunken pool, in a modest sized chamber orderly tiled floor-to-ceiling with hand-sized squares of brilliant blue ceramic. Narrow, rectangular skylights lined the tiled ceiling and, as Kiki relaxed further, tilting her head, Kyn could see brilliant blue sky through clear polyplex, the blue dotted with slowly drifting wisps of fluffy white clouds. Kyn recognized the location - a spa suit in one of the uppers most popular bathhouses. Nowhere within the mids or lowers would he have been able to see so much sky.

One male attendant gently bid Kiki flip over, and Kyn felt himself respond obediently, rolling onto his stomach as the other attendant adjusted the chair, laying it flat so they could continue their work oiling and tenderizing his backside.

A notification pinged in the corner of Kiki's optic, alerting his host to a feed article associated with her frequent intranet search criteria. He watched passively as she expanded the article.

HEROIC UNITY AGENT DISPATCHES CHILD MUR-DERER declared a cultist news blog. Underneath the title, obviously ripped from tram security feeds, were looping gifs of Kyn, locked in combat with the pixie-cut Rager.

Kiki squealed in delight, her voice pitched excitably high.

"You figure this is why they picked this episode?" Alec queried; the coincidence unlikely.

Kyn, currently unable to respond, silently agreed. He watched himself through Kiki's eyes; snagging the pixie-cut speedster with his coat and diving from the skytram, snapping her neck. A scrolling list of names was posted beneath the gifs; victims tied to the woman known as Avon Willena. To Kyn, all the names sounded young. He felt sick to his stomach. As glad as he was that he'd gotten to take her out, he was sickened that it hadn't been sooner. With all the resources at the Unity's disposal, she should have been hunted down and dealt with long before. So far, each of the Ragers he'd executed had turned out to be examples of the city's worst degenerates, the type of people the Unity regularly assured the public were supposedly dealt with in the cullings.

Skimming the article through his host, Kyn reached the bottom tagline.

The Unity has everything under control.

"Oh. M. Geeeeee" He droned, in Kiki's voice, addressing the men kneading their fists into the knotted muscles of her voluptuous glutes. "Have you seen this guy? Snack. Yum."

"Damn right gurl." Alec lisped back, giggling over the comm. The jacked-up meatheads stayed silently focused on their rubbing.

Kyn groaned inwardly. As always, the Sentry were playing games.

While he'd been fighting Dividers and running around the city killing servo traffickers and child murders, Noav SPIRE's pro-prop departments had been working on overdrive to sell an avenging hero story. Instead of hiding the Envoys' recent highly public exploits, Alexi and the other Sentry were leaking the footage, seemingly in an attempt to create a fanatical fervor around the revealed Envoys. Sympathetic heroes that the masses would embrace in the name of the Unity.

The Unity has everything under control.

Kyn scoffed even as Kiki squealed again, tapping her fingers to re-play the footage. Luckily, a polite cough interrupted the cultist's browsing, sparing him from having to watch himself again.

"Ma'am, your technician is here."

The blankly pretty attendant had reappeared again, this time with a slight young man in identical baby blue scrubs. This new attendant stood inconspicuously behind her and carried a square white case under one arm. Turning over onto his back again, Kyn felt himself limply extend Kiki's slickly oiled arm in silent greeting.

Pale, freckled, and effetely beautiful, with a swishy softness that betrayed him to Kyn's kindred eye, the slight technician stepped forward and took Kyn/Kiki's offered hand. A gentle smile touched the corner of his lips and he bowed, briefly brushing a chaste kiss against the smooth skin of the cultist's knuckles.

For a brief moment the only sounds were the lazy lapping of the pool's crystal-clear waters against its tiled edges, and the toneless plunking of inoffensive spa soundtrack. The female attendant disappeared herself unobtrusively, as did the nearly naked meat sacks.

"I am Moh." The young man introduced himself, straightening. His eyes were denim blue and twinkled as he spoke. "It is an honor to contribute to your beautification today."

Kyn groaned to himself again. He detested the obnoxious pandering the elite demanded.

Unable to protest, he replied in Kiki's high-pitched voice. "O. M. Meee. I love you, you're adorable, you're just, like, everything." Kiki/Kyn squealed, shifting excitedly from lounging to sitting upright. The young glitch moved smoothly to adjust the wooden lounger, raising the backrest in concert with the cultist's movements.

With his client comfortably situated, Moh opened the square case he carried, unfolding it into a portable service table, and sat on the collapsible stool contained within. He arranged his props quickly and with a consort's affable grace; smiling kindly, and easily maintaining Kyn as the priority of his focus.

"Give me what Alexi had at the 57th Wards Got Talent Gala," Kyn demanded in Kiki's bubbly voice, thrusting out her hands. Her fingers were long and delicate, the nails chipped and gnawed at.

Moh slid the service table under her outstretched hands, gently guiding them to the table's antiseptic surface.

"Acrylic tips, modeled with tresses' of creeping ivy on the third and fourth finger?"

"Yes, they were so, fucking, classy. I. Gagged."

"Whatever Miss desires. What colour would Miss prefer?" Moh produced a delicate stylist's tool and rolled the thin chrome tube between his fingers. An oscillating holo-menu appeared and he highlighted two variant shades of green, presenting them for Kyn/Kiki's approval.

"Stormy seafoam, or mystic forest moss?"

Kyn's mouth tasted of metal and bile. Fortunately, Kiki's response was pre-loaded.

"Mystic forest." Kyn's lips seemed to say uncontrollably.

"Per--" the freckled attendant's face froze as if paused, smiling pleasantly, caught as he was dialing in the colour. Moh's face stuttered unnaturally, lurching. The attendant's jaw slid sideways in opposition to his forehead, stretching and pulling his face into wildly inhuman distortions. Then, with another stuttering digital *whirr*, the glitch's face pulled back together, resetting as if nothing had happened.

"Hello. Envoy."

The attendant's lips moved out of sync with the heavily digitized voice that spoke, as if in a poorly dubbed honor and sword flik.

"Thank you for meeting me here. I appreciate your discretion."

"Ohhhh, here we go. Here we go!" Alec crowed excitedly in Kyn's ear. "Let's do this. Punching you through now. Hold on, it's gunna get weird for a min."

Beneath the dock's pre-programed sensat Kyn could feel his f-Link buzz, faintly discernible, as if remembered in a dream. Kiki's Big Spa Day dimmed to sepia, and a grating, digital whine filled his head, building steadily in intensity as it spidered along his spine. An encroaching orgasm, pressing for release. Trapped in one long moment, the whine came to an unbearable crescendo, buzzing behind his teeth, before, finally, it broke into an abrupt and shattering silence. Kyn experienced an alarming thrust of vertigo as the simulation brightened back to its normal tone, resuming as if nothing had happened. Moh attentively rubbed old polish from Kiki's nails.

Kyn's ears popped.

"Communication lines are open!" Alec cheered through the comm, pleased with himself.

"Can you hear me?" Kyn asked automatically, the sound of his own voice clear. His mouth tasted like he'd been chewing on copper wire, but his lips moved freely beneath the press of nanofiber.

"Yes, I can hear you." The Informant's digitally scrambled voice played over where Moh's audio should have been, like so much more bad dubbing. "My apologies, I know porting through an active sim can be unpleasant."

The attendant silently mouthed words in short bursts, obviously aiming blatantly transparent pleasantries at his vapid client, a benign smile still plastered to his face while he smoothly filed the tips of the cultist's jagged nails to a rounded curve. Kyn could feel the ghostly press and impression of Kiki's own simulated words still playing over his lips, seeming to prattle endlessly.

"I was speaking to my code man," Kyn replied, trying to work the copper taste from his mouth. "But hello to you too, I guess. You know it would have been easier if we'd just met face to face."

The digitized voice laughed as Moh submerged Kyn/Kiki's hand in warm oil. Forcing the Envoy to suppress a moan of pleasure despite himself.

"No. You are far too dangerous for that." The Informant stated simply. "Don't be offended, anonymity is my weapon. You know this."

"I thought truth was your weapon," Kyn countered. "Hard to believe someone who claims to be brave enough to speak the truth but hides behind trick mirrors."

"Belief is a personal choice. Truth remains unchanged."

"Yes, yes. Truth is the only constant, blah blah blah." Kyn blew a raspberry, his only option to physically express how tedious he was finding the Informant's theatrics. "I'm not interested in your games. I need information," he demanded.

"You do."

Moh took Kiki/Kyn's hands between his and gently placed them on the service table, toweling off the oil. The hard-plastic surface shifted and disappeared, replaced by a flat moving image of rows of plastic tubes filled with blue liquid. Kyn seethed for a moment, recognizing the footage ripped from Dorothy.

"Don't be mad." The digitized voice reassured over Moh's constant, submissive grin. "Your boy-toy had no idea I got my hands on this."

"What? What is it?" Alec interjected, sounding worried. He was either unable to see what Kyn saw or feigning that he couldn't.

"Fuck your games." Kyn snapped, ignoring Alec. His legs seemingly crossed and uncrossed as Kiki shifted herself in the lounger. "I couldn't give a dead tweeker's ass for your high-concept spy-jinks. If you have something to tell me about those tubes, start talking."

The service table shifted into existence again. Moh tilted his head down, intent on tracing designs onto the tip of Kiki's newly buffed index finger. The small tabletop flicked away once more, and a new, baffling image took its place.

A chair.

A clinical looking chair - similar in type to those found in mod shops and augshaks across the city - sat alone in a blank, nondescript room. Tilted by design, a curved footrest of reflective chrome extended from the bottom - capable of securing the occupants feet in place without appearing threateningly restrictive. A thin half circle of stainless-steel inset with oscillating LEDs emerged from the backrest, blooming into a headrest. The inset panel of lights was repeated again at the end of delicate armrests, more swooping stainless-steel expanding outwards into wide pads of swirling colours.

Kyn looked at the chair.

"It's a chair."

"Truth."

"*Uggh* with that cryptic meta nonsense."

The image flickered and disappeared, leaving Moh's work surface blank. The technician moved onto buffing and polishing the cascade of twisting ivy that he'd careful sculpted in delicate miniature.

"Why am I looking at a chair?" Kyn snapped irritably, he'd been hoping the Informant would supply him with some answers. Help him connect disassociated pieces of the growing puzzle. Instead, frustratingly, it seemed the shady broker was only interested in adding more contextless clues.

"An object is just an object. Its purpose is what makes it perverse."

Kyn rotated his own wrist very slightly under the stimnetting. Even through the sensat hijack he was aware of the pressure of the smooth cuff against his wrist.

"So, I'm guessing that chair ain't used for something good?" He asked through Kiki's vapid smile.

"All implications say no."

"So, you don't know?"

"No, not its exact purpose. Theories, but for now all that has been gleaned is but one piece of a larger, more horrifying cycle."

"And what cycle would that be."

Moh's lips mouthed silent words as the Informant was mute. The attendant shifted easily from one side of the poolside lounger to the other.

"Find the chair's purpose and the rest will be answered"

"Solve for x then, is it?" Kyn mused, as Kiki held up the completed hand, examining the pale glitches labor. The design was a flawless replication of those worn by Alexi at the now infamous final showcase of MegaCorp Reality/Talent Competition. A finale made infamous by the last-min declaration that there would be no winner that season, and, and that the grand prize - coveted clearance passes into the upper wards - would be forfeit. The stream went down in intranet history as the most watched and re-watched Unity broadcast moment of all time.

"How can I trust that this isn't just a lark to throw me off your scent?" Kyn asked jovially. Repeated attempts to replicate the finale's success saw the same base gimmick steadily devolve into more degrading variations on the last tick gotcha theme. "Sure, your lead turned out last time, but you also tried to have me killed."

Moh looked up at the Envoy with his blankly pleasant smile.

"How else would you believe me?" the Informant answered simply from the nail attendant's unmoving lips.

Kyn breathed a heavy sigh and clenched his fists. The simulation surged and stuttered.

"Kyn...." Alec interjected, panicked. "I've lost control of the pod."

"Seems about right." Kyn returned, calm. He was slowly becoming re-aware of the tactile sensations of his immediate surroundings. The stim jack had disconnected, leaving just the visuals fed through his optic. He could feel himself within the cramped confines of the coffin dock even as Moh looked at him. The attendant staggered over words as his face slid against itself, jumping, and buffering disjointedly. The alluring scents of eucalyptus and bamboo turned acrid, burning Kyn's eyes painfully. Pressing through the stimnetting, he pushed against the dock's lid. It wouldn't budge.

"I knew it wouldn't work. So why did I try anyway?" Kyn asked the stuttered and frozen Moh ruefully. The acrid stench flooded his mouth and nose, searing his lungs painfully and causing him to gag.

"Okay, I asked for that." He wheezed, speaking to himself now. The images fed through his optic had finally collapsed in one solid white beep, leaving him locked in the darkness of Dock 278.

SYSTEMIC MALFUNCTION hovered in flashing red AR, unhelpfully close to his face.

"Ummm, Kyn..." Alec began again, voice pitched with worried panic. "It looks like your unit is flooding with chlorin gas."

"That what that is?" Kyn wheezed. He shifted awkwardly, squeezing one knee to his chest in the cramped space, and jammed the tip of his boot against the lid. Grunting, he kicked out. The lid didn't budge. Gas seared his insides with every breath. It felt like he'd swallowed battery acid.

"You should be dead already." Alec insisted hotly, as if offended he had nothing more to offer other than his worry.

"I'm aware." Kyn acknowledged, abandoning his attempt to kick open the lid. Blood trickled over his lips.

Drawing in one more agonized breath, he shifted again, left arm beneath his body, elbow twisted to grasp Ego's hilt from between his shoulder blades. Then, forcefully exhaling all the burning air, he untwisted, drawing the blade in one easy motion. His tongue was a melted mess in his ruined mouth. Finding a seam in the lid's seal with his fingers, he worked the dagger's pointed tip into the razor-thin gap and tried to leverage the dock open.

Painful as it was, Kyn was unafraid of the gas. Holding his breathe had already allowed his internals time to heal, even while the membrane of his eyes and nose burned. Still, fear levels aside, he didn't relish the idea of spending anymore breathless ticks trapped inside the immersion dock. Other things needed his attention that night.

Things he was looking forward to.

Ego's blade slipped, once, then twice, slicing stimnetting and scraping the dock's interior. Maneuvering the blade in the cramped dark was tricky, and the hermetic seal was too tight for Kyn to break.

His lungs screamed for air. Bursts of white exploded in his ruined vision, pushing back the smothering darkness. His brain was starving for oxygen.

He needed a plan.

Gasping, Kyn drew in one long, burning breath.

"Get me out of here!" He screamed, gagging over the gas. There was no more oxygen left in the tube. Thrashing violently, he pounded his fists and knees into the pod lid.

"Please vacate malfunctioning unit." Another, brighter, digitized voice demanded from outside the dock.

"I'm trying!" Kyn yelled back, recognizing the Ziev synthetic from the service desk.

"Please vacate malfunctioning unit." The synthetic repeated.

"I'm fucking stuck!"

"Please vacate malfunctioning unit."

Groaning, Kyn slammed his fist against the lid in frustration. An acidic foam leaked from the corners of his ruined mouth.

"Override accepted." Chirped the virtual intelligence. This statement was echoed by a confirmational *beep* deep within the immersion dock. Bright light and cycled air hit Kyn in a rush as the lid swung open with a hydraulic hiss and the gas flushed from the unit. He stumbled out, retching as fresh oxygen hit his devastated lungs.

Doubling over he collapsed onto the prefab floor, hacking, and trembling violently as his regenerative ability did its work. Choking, he forcibly coughed up a rough glob of scar tissue the size of his fist.

"Gross." The watching synthetic commented, titling its domed head to one side. Squatting low on birdlike legs, the synthetic moved to help Kyn in a facsimile of human concern.

"Alec?" Kyn choked, looking at the synthetic quizzically. Hacking, he spat out another glob of blood and discarded tissue; before, shaking slightly, he gripped the synthetic's proffered arm for support, and used the carbon fiber limp to pull himself to standing.

"The one and only." The synthetic answered, it's central faceplate light flashing green. The vaguely humanoid mech shifted, pulling away from Kyn, one digitigrade jointed lower limb in front of the other, and hinged forward with a flourish of polycarbonate upper limbs, executing an approximation of a cocky bow. "I didn't want to miss out on all the body switching shenanigans. Sorry it took so long, when it looked like you were having trouble getting out, I sent an alert to the service desk, but it took me another tick to gain control of their systems again. Informant slammed a hard lockdown on the internals when he ported out. Anyways, I called this stud as soon as I could and dove in when it was in close enough range."

"Well, you saved me having to call Benn to get me out of there, so, thanks." Kynn acknowledged, with a ruefully grin. Blood smeared his sharp face. The damage from the gas had already healed but he'd need to clean up before he continued on for the night.

"Yah that would have been embarrassing," Alec agreed in the synthetic's chirpy digital voice. He made the synthetic tilt it's head downward, as if regarding itself, then back at Kyn. It shifted on sturdy legs, extending the synthetic's dexterously jointed arms wide. "What'd ya think?" The hacker asked. "Should I keep it?"

Kyn sheathed Ego.

"Leave it," he ordered.

The synthetic seemed to deflate in disappointment. Arms crossed over its chest.

Kyn pointedly moved his gaze over the skeletal carbon fiber mech's flat and sexless chassis. "I much prefer your original body." He added, throwing a flirtatious wink at the robot.

The synthetic seemed to perk as Alec swung its domed head around and peered into the now empty dock. "Did you get what you needed?"

Kyn pondered momentarily over what, if anything, the Informant had shown him. He shrugged his narrow shoulders non-committally. "I don't know," he admitted, crossing to the exit. "If it's important it'll come up again. Besides, I really don't have time to figure it out right now." He looked back at the Ziev synthetic, his face a grotesque abstract in red. "C'mon then." He prompted, a wolfishly grin splitting the drying plasma. "It's gunna be a long night, and I've gotta get cleaned up for my next date."

Tits Up

Kyn stopped in front of a long silver mirror and adjusted his marshmallow blonde bob.

"See, Sendri." He purred acidly to his own reflection, tugging the bob cut wig back from his forehead and primping out the square cut bangs with dexterous fingers. "This. This is how you pull off that hair." The black cuff shifted on his wrist.

Alyn had chosen a jagged outcropping near the summit of Noav SPIRE for his private gallery, a polygonal cyst of opaque polyplex that jutted from the side of the superstructure like a raw, uncut mineral growth. Kyn had paused midway across a yawning antechamber that rivaled an industrial hanger in size. Distinctly angular, the ceiling dropped at odd angles, slanting steeply away from the main SPIRE at abnormal degrees. More long mirrors lined the length of the chamber, and lonely stone stools offered the only seating. A solitary door, a stretched and lopsided trapezoid of dark polished redwood set into blank concrete, stood at the far end of the chamber.

Kyn produced a slender vile from the top of his buckled corset and tabbed out a trickle of shimmering powder onto the tips of his fingers. He traced lines of rainbow under and around his eyes, dusting the space between freckles. He winked alluringly to his reflection before replacing the vile. One hand dipped between his legs, checking the security of his tuck. Goods secured, he rolled the nylon Envoy mask up over his mouth and nose before turning to continue the long trek to the lone door. The hollow, echoing clack of stiletto heels against polished concrete followed him.

"Stripper meets Femme Fatale" Alec had commented, lounged naked on Kyn's bedroll. He'd hungrily watched as the Envoy slide smoothly toned legs into netted mesh stockings.

"Nailed it then?" Kyn had attempted a cocky grin.

He stopped in front of the slab of polished redwood.

If I do this everything will change.

He stared blankly at the door, palms slick with sweat. The overwhelming urge to vomit rose in his gut.

If I do this everything will change.

Panic pressed against the back of his eyes, urging him to run, to flee, to do anything but what he was planning to do.

Reality skipped, his mind stuttering over jagged memories. Poorly healed wounds tore open as he stared at the door. Hidden things crawled out of locked boxes. Open, rotting, cancerous sores.

"Few survive to the other side of the Ascension, and we regret their loss."

He flinched, feeling the Dags' clubs. The door swam. Red crashed across his mind. Memories of child thin bones shattering.

"Such gifts are unique in nature to each Envoy,"

The other children were dead.

We regret their loss.

Jumps. Flashes. His breathing ragged behind the mask. Acrid. His eyes wouldn't leave the blank door.

The world was made of constant pain. He could reach out and touch it - like glimmering pieces of shattered glass.

His blood burned from remembered pain and his hands shook. He tried to calm his breathing, focusing on the easy, reliable weight of iD, Ego, and Self strapped in their dependable places across his body. Reassuring in their lethality.

The world fell away. All he could see was the Dag standing frozen in shock, and the hand, reaching futilely for help.

He was screaming, but he heard nothing, just a silence that rang deafening in his ears.

His gray eyes stopped abruptly at the k-bolt wound burned through the other man's chest. The final wound that had killed him. Yorri was dead.

He imagined a cascade of cold water steadily pouring down over the crown of his head, freezing his veins as it washed over him. Drowning the burning. Numbing him.

More jumps. Places switching.

The shaved headed boy stood with his shoulders back, silently staring at some far-off place in front of him. The look on his face was foreign and intoxicating. The gray eyed boy searched desperately for a word to describe it.

Mania beat beneath the cold numbness, a delirious staccato heartbeat that fluttered against the liquid steel of his spine, singing to be free.

One hand to the pouch strapped against his right hip.

Searched desperately for a word to describe it.

Rhythmic tapping, dialing up a fresh playlist.

He let loose a primal scream of rage and death.

He'd learned the word.

Defiance

Kyn kicked in the door.

The hollow throb and clenched-throat vocals of pre-fall alt-synth duo <INSERT> throbbed in his ear as the wood burst outward in an explosion of splinters. A surging cover of Cornflake Girl, the perfect soundtrack to his cold rage.

Kyn strode through the battered door into a long, triangular corridor. He drew Ego as he crossed the threshold and stabbed sideways without looking, jamming the blade straight into the throat of the first Dag flanking the door. Yanking the blade free in a spurt of crimson, he flipped the dagger horizontally and spun, slashing in a whirling arch to slit the throat of their mirrored companion. Both guards fell, gasping raggedly and clutching at ruined throats, desperately trying to hold in the life that gushed through their fingers.

Without missing a beat, Kyn casually tossed two metal canisters ahead of himself from the pouch at his hip. They bounced across polished stone, hissing as they spewed thick clouds of multi-hued blue smoke.

Mania surged. A broken euphoria that sharpened the edges of his cold rage into murderous glee.

Confused shouts and hurriedly barked orders cut through the choking blue smoke as unseen Dags scrambled to respond to his presence, organizing to counter his coming assault.

Kyn tilted his head back and let out a wild, yipping bark that bounced maddeningly off the tilted walls.

"Don't be scared!" He screamed into the haze, chasing his own echo. "I just want to play!"

Kinetic bolts responded. Bursts of concrete gray added to the blue haze as shots missed Kyn and blasted chunks out of the walls around him. Above his mask, his gray eyes glittered manically as the lead vocalist of <INSERT> screamed like an avenging punk goddess in his ear.

"Missed me!" He taunted back across the haze, voice high and hysterical. "Didn't your daddies ever teach you how to aim for a guy's face?"

Another, heavier, volley of kinetic bolts, and he hissed as a lucky shot connected, grazing, white-hot, across his hip. The flesh healed over almost instantly.

"Fuck it," Kyn growled, shifting his weight on his steep stilettos. "Let's have at it then."

Drawing iD from across his back with a menacing *shick*, he dove into the blue haze, a blur of liquid grace and angry steel. The Dags fired off more burning rounds, but he moved erratically through the smokescreen, dodging oncoming fire. He met the first Dag in the haze with a high front kick to the face, shattering the soldiers protective faceplate, then followed through with a diagonal swipe from iD, bisecting the soldier from shoulder to hip. A backhanded jab from Ego drove the dagger into the base of the next encroaching Dag's skull, severing their spine. He yanked the dagger free and moved on, throwing it overhand at the next Dag who charged towards him through the smoke. Ego wedged deep in the soldier's chest, killing them instantly. They fell backwards, their still firing k-cannon cutting down a fellow Dag.

Rolling sideways to dodge this wild line of fire, Kyn yanked Ego free and tumbled acrobatically forward through the smoke. Springing from wall, to floor, to wall again, disjointedly switching directions on a dime or prat falling on a whim, he made himself a near impossible target in the obscuring blue smoke as he cut down what remained of the first wave of Dags.

An echo of boots announced the next approaching wave, and he barrel-jumped a solid line of kinetic fire lobbed at him.

Shots connected inevitably, tearing away chunks of Kyn's flesh in spurts of red. Unperturbed, he ignored the pain, not slowing, his regeneration healing the wounds within a few beats of his heart.

He kicked off one slanted wall to meet the advancing line of Dags. A slice across the nearest soldier's k-cannon with iD carved cleanly through the weapon's barrel, sending it spinning, and Kyn followed through with an elbow to the armored Dag's helmet, throwing them off balance. He tossed the short sword with a juggler's aplomb, and skillfully snatched the severed barrel out of the air before driving it through the Dag's faceplate and into their skull with lightning quick brutality. He caught iD in the next beat and swung backwards along the line of uniforms, severing another Dag's head from their shoulders. Another step drove Ego up under the chin of a third.

Pressed in close in the obscuring blue haze Kyn had the advantage, and he made quick work of the others as the smoke screen cleared. A trail of dismembered soldiers marked his advance down the triangular corridor.

He passed through a narrow rectangle into the gallery's receiving chamber. An inverse trapezoid of more polished concrete and polyplex. Solid curtains of clear water ran down slopping walls, feeding into narrow tributaries of ice blue tile that ran in narrow rivers along either side of the room. Low sofa slabs of sulky maroon wound between abstract fiberglass sculptures of precariously stacked cubes. Oynx black blocks like puzzle toys piled to the ceiling in gravity defying arrangements. In the middle of the chamber, a long oval of richly stained juniper encircled a pre-fall display of antique glass bottles. Wide corridors branched off to either side, and a slender rectangular door of black polyplex at the far end led to what Kyn knew was the exterior balcony, before the Sentry' sleeping quarters.

More heavy boot falls echoed off the stone walls.

Sheathing iD and Ego, Kyn snatched two more gas canisters from his hip pouch and lobbed them towards the open corridors, choking the trapezoidal passageways with blue smoke, before starting to climb the nearest sculpture. At the top, he crouched, marshmallow wig scraping the concrete ceiling.

Kinetic fire tore through the smoke from either side, shredding the antique display below. Splintered wood and vintage glass shards filled the air. The weapon fire died, followed by audible clunks of reloading.

"Missed!" Kyn taunted, his eyes glittering with impish glee. More echoing boot falls advanced, and he leapt to the apex of the next structure as even more kinetic bursts shredded the feeble remains of the display. The blue haze was clearing. More sounds of reloading.

Kyn leapt to the top of the next sculpture. His wig fell from his head mid-leap, and the marshmallow bob floated, a white-blonde jellyfish on the air current, to rest softly atop the mangled debris.

No weapons fired, no advancing boot falls; the Dags were holding.

Kyn sprang from his perch, twisting in the air to land in a crouch next to his wig. Shattered glass and debris crunched under his stilettos. Standing, he raised his hands limply above his head.

"Fine, I guess we'll do this the easy wa –"

A kinetic bolt snapped through his forehead, blowing out the back of his skull.

"Come on Kyn!" Yorri exclaimed, sliding open the shower stall door and jostling his way into the narrow space. He hip checked Kyn away from inspecting himself in the reflective polyplex. "How are you putting this much effort into getting ready anyway? JackHoles is a dive."

"Maybe I want to make an impression?" Kyn snipped back playfully. He adjusted his chrome studded jock pouch and turned to hop up onto the stainless-steel vanity. The polished metal was cold on his bare cheeks.

Yorri snaked an arm around his waist and snapped at an elastic strap.

"It's def an impression."

Hands grasped his ankles, dragging him. The sounds and smells of combat bodies surrounded him; sweat, blood, the creak of uniform straps. A crackling pain in the back of his head. His eyes flew open and he gasped, vision bloodshot, everything tinged red. He was on his back, shards of glass slicing into his flesh, metal debris cutting his sides, shadowy uniformed figures all around. His heart thundered in his ears, and adrenaline thudded through him like electric fire. He could feel the crunch of his skull reforming. Violent mania screamed against white-hot pain. The back of his head itched maddeningly.

The hands dropped his ankles. Confused shouts as what had previously been a lifeless body jerked back to life, writhing on the floor.

Ego was in Kyn's hand as he twisted from the floor, cutting across the nearest Dag's achilles, and hamstringing the next.

One of his stilettos had fallen off.

The remaining Dags came at him in unison and Kyn stabbed sideways, plunging Ego into the thigh of the first. The guard howled as Kyn yanked the dagger free in time to kick out high and back, driving his remaining heel up under the chin of another Dag rushing him from behind. He yanked his foot back, losing the shoe, and brought his knee through to drive it into the face of the thigh gouged Dag, doubling them, visor shattered and eye socket pulverized. They fell back, unconscious or dead, at the same moment the Dag he'd kicked crumpled blank-eyed to their knees behind him; synth-leather pump lodged under their chinstrap.

The Dags had been dragging him away, presumably to dispose of his previously lifeless body. Blood slicked the floor and chaos filled the packed corridor.

He threw Ego at another Dag who was just bringing their weapon to bare. The dagger buried between their eyes, and their rapid-fire automatic shots went wide. Kyn dove sideways, avoiding the wild shots even as two more Dags were cut down. iD was free as he recovered, stocking feet gliding over gore-soaked stone. He slashed diagonally down and across, cutting another Dag short at the knee. The maimed Dag tipped, falling, as Kyn reversed the stroke, bisecting their head and helmet in one clean swipe. Pain screamed through him as kinetic bursts connected with his back and exploded out his chest, shredding his already ruined corset. He howled, but heard nothing, everything the same atonal hum. A red tinged void. Then he was falling, falling away.

The music pulsed and he swung in closer to Yorri.

"The Fifth Element!" The shirtless Yorri shouted over the steady climb of frantic vocals. Kyn turned and gyrated his pelvis against the front of the broader man's retro silver denim.

"What?!" He shouted back, pretending not to hear. The music was mounting to a crescendo and the crush of bodies surrounding them throbbed with the tension. The air reeked of sweat and sex. Yorri snapped at one of the white strips of elastic nylon wrapped around Kyn's lean torso.

"Mull-tee-pass." He enunciated, prismatic green eyes glittering in the laser-light of the disco strobe. "You remembered!"

"Remembered what?" Kyn feigned, acting dumb. He traced a line over the taller man's well-muscled chest. Heat radiated from him.

"I told you! My favorite pre-fall stream!"

"No idea."

The bass dropped, deep and hollow as sweaty bodies pulsated in undulating waves, swallowing them.

Kyn was up again, ribs closing with a wet snap over his re-beating heart. Spittle flew and he screamed in rage as he plunged iD through the chest of the first Dag he could reach. Ripping the sword free, he spun again, slashing horizontally to hack into the torso of another rushing him from behind, shock baton raised. iD cleaved deep above the soldier's hip and stuck as Kyn stumbled, the hilt, slick from blood and gore, tearing from his grip. The Dag fell, rapidly going into shock and losing blood fast. Another Dag fired a handheld k-cannon, catching Kyn in the shoulder from behind. Kyn stumbled again, slipping, and fell to a hand and knee. He growled, spitting blood.

Shoulder still knitting itself back together, Kyn lunged for Ego, left buried in the face of a dead Dag. The corridor was littered with more dead and dying bodies then moving ones, and only three guards remained on their feet. The closest tried to level a handheld at Kyn but the Envoy was faster, yanking the dagger free to thrust upwards, burrowing the blade in the guard's meaty forearm. The shot discharged next to his ear, but he heard nothing over the atonal hum of his adrenaline-fueled rage.

Kyn spun, flipping the Dag over his back to drop them heavily onto the polished stone, headfirst. Their helmet connected and their neck snapped, bent at an unnatural angle. The Dag flopped over limp, and Kyn ripped Ego free, just as more heavy thuds of kinetic bolts connected with his back. He collapsed forward, rolling over the dead Dag.

No major organ damage, corset in ruins, Kyn posted off one hand and kicked his legs in an arch, flipping up from the floor to knock the k-cannon out of the offending guard's hand. He dodged yet another round of rapid fire from the second remaining guard, twirling iD as he ducked and weaved. Caught between the final two Dags, he simultaneously whipped the short sword and dagger through a blossoming series of deflective twirls, guarding against the incoming bolts, even as one found a home in his thigh. He stumbled. The Dag he'd disarmed dove for a fallen weapon, and he met them, using his lack of balance to launch into a wild, falling sidekick, and catching the lunging Dag across the shoulder armor, knocking them to the floor. He scrambled across the tacky floor, thigh itching, and slammed Ego into the fallen Dag's back, hilt-deep between their shoulder blades. A twitch and a gasp, and they stopped moving.

More automatic fire ripped across Kyn's side, throwing him onto his back. He shuddered as white pain lanced through him, and more of his blood flowed. Lung punctured, gutshot through the oblique, hip pulverized. The gray corridor swam, voids of red tinged blackness blooming in the cold stone.

"Come on K. It's time to get up." Yorri *lightly brushed hair away from his forehead and caressed his cheek. Kyn groaned and sunk away, sinking further into the bedroll.*

"No!" Kyn growled, heart thundering, fighting the encroaching darkness. The guard was paces away, k-cannon leveled on him. Waiting.

So much pain, itching everywhere.

Kyn dragged himself to his knees, iD's point jabbed into the stone, using it like a cane to pull himself to standing. Another volley of kinetic bolts, center mass, gutshot him again, knocking him back onto his back. He gasped, dropping iD and Ego with a clatter. More pain. Numb from below the ribs, the smell of blood and shit, his intestines shredded, exposed. One hand to his gut, holding himself in, failing. He rolled over. Wet retching. His stomach itched maddeningly, and he gagged, turning, to vomit up wrecked tissue and waste. The Dag kept their weapon leveled on him, the eyes behind their visor wide with disgust and horror.

Then Kyn was moving on all fours, teeth bared in primal fury. He launched himself at the Dag, springing from the blood-soaked stone to pounce on the armored soldier, unfazed as even more shots tore into him. He hit the Dag, and wrapped his legs around their torso, throwing them over backwards with his momentum, limbs tangled, pinned as they writhed on the floor. The struggling Dag was unable to bring their weapon around before Kyn's gnashing teeth found the soft spot between helmet and chest plate, and he was tearing into the meaty side of their neck. Canines tore through the thin layer of tactical garment and sawed through muscle and sinew. He spit cloth and flesh and bit again, severing major arteries. Blood, hot and warm on his face, metallic in his mouth, choking him. The Dag struggled, kicking and bucking, but Kyn held tighter. Eventually their struggle slowed, until they kicked once and stopped.

Kyn spit out the Dag and unfurled to standing. Motionless bodies in various stages of dismemberment littered the corridor. The air in the gallery was moist and rank. He ran the back of one wrist over his mouth.

"Oh, K." A voice breathed from behind him. Low, distraught, and horrifyingly familiar. "What have you done?"

A numbness landed over Kyn. Everything dropped out, leaving behind the thin line of himself. The empty outline of what he'd once been. The idea of a person. Everything was hollow, the pain of wounds and regenerative itching forgotten, far away. There was only the voice. He turned, his steel gray eyes finding Yorri's prismatic green.

"K, what did you do?" Yorri's eyes were wet with a deep sadness.

A shame worse than any k-bolt shredded Kyn's gut, shrinking him, and he moaned low and animalistic, as he stared dumbly at his dead lover. Somewhere deep inside he was screaming at himself to hide, to run, to drive Self through the center of his face, anything to escape those horrified eyes. He stumbled numbly forward, blood-soaked hands reaching to touch the beautiful man who had suddenly appeared at the mouth of the dead cluttered corridor, wanting desperately for him not to be real.

Yorri seized Kyn's wrist, his grip all too real. Not a regeneration induced dream or the hallucination of a damaged psyche, finally cracked beyond repair. Kyn stopped, staring dumbly at his dead lover's face, at an achingly familiar sharp jaw and slightly upturned nose. He was vaguely aware, in some faraway part of himself, that there was a long metal spike in Yorri's other hand, and that the terrace door to the exterior garden was open. A cool night breeze tussled the taller man's short-cropped brown hair and cut the smell of gore.

"How?" Kyn croaked, his voice small, trapped deep within himself. He shook uncontrollably.

Yorri's multi-hued green eyes burned with a blazing joy, euphoric, and his lips spread inhumanly wide in a deliriously blissful smile.

"A miracle." Kyn's dead lover answered simply, his kind voice light with laughter even as he swung the metal spike into the side of Kyn's skull with a wet crunch.

"Wait, so what is this?" Kyn asked, perplexed. He rolled onto his stomach. Naked, his light brown skin glistened with a sheen of sweat, and he leaned over the edge of the bedroll to snatch a carton of spiced noodles from the floor. He rolled back, folding himself into crossed legged seat on the silicon foam, and rested the cardboard box on the other man's naked back. He snatched up a pair of stiks and dug in, slurping loudly on the nutrient dense green noodles. Chili oil flecked the corners of his mouth.

"It's a streaming flic." The man who had called himself Yorri answered.

The stranger he'd picked up in the backroom of PumpHole was stretched out on his stomach. Sheets, wet and soiled from their numerous energetic couplings, had been discarded and crumbled at the foot of the platform. Propped up on his elbows, biceps flexed, the stranger turned his head to look at Kyn.

"Ripped it off an old hard drive I salvaged from the 'Needle. Old, even for pre-fall stuff."

"Great, bunch of good stuff you can rip off those old things." Kyn noted, tapping his fingers to slot The Cure into his running playlist. Pre-fall post-punk thrummed against the graffitied walls. Prismatic green eyes sparkled in amusement. "What's so special 'bout this one?" Kyn asked.

"It's this grand, wacky space opera," Yorri started, a dreamy smile twitching the corners of thin lips. A dark dusting of day-old stubble peppered his cheeks. "About how some resurrected immortal girl saves the universe through the power of love or something." He shook his head, rueful. "I don't know, it's super wacky, crazy costumes,

outlandish characters. But I just love it, you know?" He beamed, his genuine excitement to share his passion with someone else clear. "Cause it's this special little gift. This special little wacky dream someone thought up about how they thought the world would be one day. And I mean, it hasn't really turned out like that yet, obviously, but when I watch this stupid old stream, it doesn't matter. I can watch it and say, 'Hey, maybe it will still turn out like that, even after all this.'" The man who called himself Yorri looked bashful now, embarrassed. Kyn's heart ached. "I don't know, some part of me finds that hope really beautiful, and I just love it cause of that. Plus, crazy costumes and singing blue space divas. What's not to love?"

Two Men [and a bunch of other people] in a Room

Kyn's eyes shot open, and he gasped, the twisted twilight of memory shooting backwards with a familiar wet sucking sound - like thick, swampy mud pulling inside his skull. Re-birth adrenaline slammed through him and he snarled with rage, thrashing. Chains rattled above.

The initial burst of violent mania faded and Kyn relaxed his thrashing. A burning numbness – more aching familiarity - stretched across his back and shoulders, and smooth metal links dug painfully into his wrists. The black cuff was missing, and the remains of his tattered corset and stockings had been stripped away. He hung naked, suspended from the ceiling, and swung pendulously. The room wasn't his usual white cell; all curved, sleekly polished wood, and muted brown synth leathers, the floor, rich-hued fir polished to a reflective sheen.

Yorri stood in front of Kyn, stainless steel spike in one hand, the tip crimson. The wall behind, backlit a white-blue, was lined with display mounts, showcasing an eclectic assortment of weapons once belonging to long dead civilizations. Replica, first-generation firearms hung next to last century laser lances, and aerodynamically perfected pit fighting chakram. Yorri's chiseled face was hollowed to skeletal in the ghostly blue light, and he watched Kyn with a mixture of wonder, disgust, and fascination. It was quiet save for Kyn's strained breathing, the slow creak of chains, and the persistent background hum of the SPIRE superstructure.

The thundering flood of adrenaline through Kyn's veins ran ice cold, and he dropped his head to his chest, seized by an all-consuming shame and dejected exhaustion. His head swam with disbelief and confusion.

"Why?" He croaked, not raising his head, voice dry. The question of 'how' was on his lips. A miracle. Kyn's mind tripped around the haze of his confusion and grief. "Why?" He demanded again, louder, looking up through sweat soaked hair, cognizant he wasn't just speaking to the ghost of his loss.

"What do you mean killer?" Yorri asked, voice light and teasing, bright with a gentle kindness.

Kyn's eyes stung with saltiness. "Don't call me that," He groaned, low and wounded. "Why are you here? Here? In this room. In a fucking Sentry's gallery! Why here? Why now?" He was scream-ing. Poorly healed grief split open and poured from him in waves of choked sobs. "Why?" He demanded, body heaving. He shook against his chains, "WHY?!"

"Why are you here Kyn?" Ashe's silken voice was directly behind him. "Why are you in the Sentry's private chambers when you should be preparing to defend the wall against the Divider threat?"

Kyn cranked his head around trying to see the other Envoy around his strung arms. "Ashe?" He croaked.

"Who are you talking to killer?" Yorri asked, kind voice tipped with concern and confusion.

Kyn moaned, distraught. With effort, he raised his head and looked Yorri in the eye. Steel gray met prismatic green. Kyn's eyes were wet with tears that glittered like quicksilver in the cold blue light. "You're dead,'" he pleaded, trying to make the other man understand. "I fucked up, and you died."

"So? You die and come back. Why can't I?" Yorri asked innocently. He was smiling but the kindness was gone. His green eyes sparkled, delirium bright, in his too hollow face.

Kyn balked at the plainness of the question. "I...I...I'm... different. Special. I kinda do it a lot." He stuttered.

"Why do you get to be special?" Yorri's pressed, more accusation than question.

"What? No. No" Kyn stuttered "No...Not special." He had no answer. No concept for the question. He wasn't special, he was a tool of the Unity. His gifts were never his own.

"You? Why do you get to be special and not me?" Yorri's words were sharp, accusing. "Why does a lowly piece of glitched trash get to be immortal and not me?" Yorri was closer now, his breath hot against Kyn's face.

"I don't know!" Kyn screamed back, desperate. Guilt and shame tearing out of him. "Don't you think I've asked myself that? I would've given anything to be able to bring you back. And when I couldn't do that, I went after who ordered the hit. I killed him. I made him pay for what he did to you."

"No, you didn't." Yorri's smile grew wider, stretching grotesquely.

"What?" Kyn asked, self-loathing twisted his gut.

"You never killed who was responsible for my death. Not really" Yorri answered simply.

"That's cause he's weak." Runa's gravelly voice, low and thick with disgust, chimed in from behind Kyn's hanging form.

"Runa?" Kyn asked, surprised.

"Who are you talking to?" Yorri pressed again, his voice back to its familiar kind concern. His face no longer hollowed by the light, the smile no longer grotesque. "Are you okay?"

Kyn threw his head back, bashing his skull against his strung arms. It had finally happened; he'd gone entirely pan-fried. Snapped beyond repair, and round the bend mad. He chuckled, a low and hopeless sound. The crunch of a sweetstik was heavy in his ear.

"You're wondering who I'm talking to?" He asked Yorri, his voice even. "You, my apparently no longer dead ex-lover, are wondering, who I'm talking to?" Yorri's face was unreadable. "Well, I'm talking to Runa, the indestructible adolescent seemingly standing behind me." Kyn thrashed against his chains, trying to spin himself around. No luck. He craned his neck, trying to look past his arms. Almost, but couldn't fully see behind. "Or at least I heard her voice behind me, I can't turn to check cause I'm hanging by my wrists in an apparent weapons gallery that belongs to one of the Noav Sentry. My Sentry. Whom, by the by, I came here to kill." He giggled, letting his head loll back against his numb arms and smiled, leaning into the madness. "All of which is just ludicrous, mad-lad insane." He leaned his head back even further, slipping between the gap in his shoulders, looking behind himself upside down. No sign of Runa. He giggled again, an unhinged sound. "So, how do you know Alyn?" A sheathed wakizashi floated under its mounting, well out of reach. Duel sai mounted above, inverted from Kyn's perspective - dragged out clown eyes above a razor smile.

"Alyn is the ingenious and industrious leader of the Noav SPIRE, illustrious and beloved member of the Unity." Yorri recited pleasantly. "Face of the Dag forces, and beloved Champion of the Arena. I and every citizen of this great city owe my life and prosperity to the protection and guidance of Sentry Alyn."

Kyn snapped his head back through his shoulders. A wide, feral grin, all gleaming white teeth, split his thin face. "Alyn's a small-dicked twat," He spat. Yorri's green eyes widened, taken aback. Kyn pressed on. "That's what you thought anyway. When you were alive. You hated the Sentry. Hated how they kept us divided, under their thumb. Protectors with their boots on our necks. 'Real leaders up-lift' You used to say. 'Owe him your life and prosperity.' Eat my hole! The Sentry use us, plain and simple. They devour to sustain themselves. They're vapid black holes of selfishness."

Yorri punched him in the gut.

Kyn groaned, dangling legs pulled into his chest momentarily. He swung with the blow and his bindings rattled loudly above. "Missed you too boo," Kyn coughed. The reality of Yorri's solid fist had hurt more than the punch.

Yorri was silent, the shadows cast on his face grown longer, hiding his expression. A new anger smoldered at the back of his multi-hued green eyes. He hit Kyn again, another sharp jab to the diaphragm.

Kyn coughed, rough and visceral. Chains rattled above, and the links snapped against his wrists, pulling tighter with gravity.

"You're pathetic," Ashe jabbed, silken voice dripping with disdain. The willowy Envoy had stepped out from Kyn's periphery. They were clad in mission uniform, black mask bunched around their slender neck. Their violet eyes glowed with malice in the blue light. A duel-barreled Chekov - modded with spun chamber and tactical laser sights - was mounted beyond their left shoulder.

"Oh hey. Glad you could join." Kyn quipped in way of greeting. Ashe passed in front of him. "Don't worry, I wasn't going to be late for the thing. Just had to make a stop first." Yorri had vanished, exiting when Kyn hadn't noticed.

"The Dividers are at our door, and you waste time with this childish nonsense?" Ashe fumed, slapping him. Kyn's head snapped sideways. Their heavy hand stung, cutting his lip and leaving a ringing in his ears. "You should decommission yourself and be done with it. Shove that little needle blade of yours through your eye and save the rest of us your melodrama."

"Make me." Kyn hissed, lunging against the chains as he snapped his teeth at Ashe. He swung slightly. The binding chain shifted with the movement, digging even tighter into his wrists. The only thing stopping him from sliding through the cinch entirely was the wideness of his hands. The hump of his thumb joints, snagged on the looping chain, kept him painfully suspended.

Ashe laughed, sharp and mocking. "You would like that. Someone to force you to do what you are too cowardly to do yourself." They pressed the silver spike into Kyn's chest. The sharp point broke skin, drawing blood. "Is that why you are here?" They demanded. "Is it your hope that if you bite the hand that feeds, your betters will finally put you down like the rapid animal you are?"

Kyn glared, a seething anger rising in him, burning away the shame that being face-to-face with Yorri had cast over him. His shoulders burned, and he subtly clenched and unclenched his fists above his head, trying to work up some blood flow. The digits agonizingly complained but he was creakily able to ball his hands into fists.

"Whatcha doin' here Ashe?" He grilled. "Telling me off for not being where I'm supposed to be. You're in a pretty strange place yourself." He leered, all bloodstained teeth and mockery. "Or is Alyn into some switch trim."

Ashe's violet eyes flashed with fury as they drove the stainless-steel spike between Kyn's eyes.

The world above him broke in ripples of gleaming silver. He breached the surface, laughing, and flipped his wet hair, splashing Yorri playfully. Yorri stood up to his waist in the frigid surf, arms crossed over his bare chest, shivering in the chill night breeze. He groaned good-naturedly and pulled away, his olive skin glowing gold in the moonlight, and, despite where Kyn had splashed him, he was still dry above the waist, having refused to be baited by jeers and taunts to dive into the cold water and get it over with. Treading water, Kyn twisted and dove back under the surface of the lapping waves. Frigid cold closed over him, knocking the air from his lungs. He flipped, ever-present lights of the city dancing above him like stars on oil. He breached the surface again, tawny flesh wet and gleaming in the moonlight, and dove again, sleek, and agile as a playful otter. Yorri laughed deep and warm. The city wall loomed behind; tide roaring as it crashed against the outer wall. Laser sights lanced the darkness.

The spike slid free from Kyn's skull with its familiar sucking pull, and snap/crackle of healing bone. Shards of memory rushed past, and he grasped desperately at them, but they tore at his mind as they slipped out of reach. Adrenaline seized him and his eyes flew open; everything tinged in red. Yorri was in front of him again, framed by cold blue light, expression hidden in long shadows.

"Aggh," Kyn grunt-screamed, thrashing. Links snapped tighter, grating agonizingly against the protrusion of his thumb knuckles. He snarled and shook. "Fuck, I seriously hate that..." He panted. Three thunderous heartbeats and his blood cooled, his head slumped forward, chin dropped to his chest. "You'd think after how many times I've done it; it'd get easier. But no, ass end of awful. Every. Time."

"Why did you come here?" Yorri asked. His tone was inhumanely, blank. "Why did you invade the private sanctum of the Sentry?"

"You first Yor." Kyn spat, choking on the endearment.

"I am here because Sentry Alyn wishes me to be here."

"How are you alive?" Kyn clarified. He tapped two numb digits together. **NO SIGNAL [LINK DISAPLED]** flashed red in his optic.

"I am alive because Sentry Alyn wishes me to be alive."

"Fuck off."

"Why are you here?" Blank voice, dispassionate question.

"To kill Alyn, wasn't that obvious?"

"Why?"

"Cause he's a twat," Kyn snarled. "As if I need a reason." He thrashed against the chains, sinking imperceptibly again, link cinch jerking, squeezing even tighter. Joints screamed against the pull of gravity. Kyn sucked his teeth but otherwise ignored the pain. "That twisted meat jockey has tortured me since I was a child, I don't need any other reason than that."

"Why now?"

"Why not?"

"You are soon due at the loading bay to welcome the incoming refugees and protect against the Divider threat."

"Exactly. How does my dead, former lover, know about my operational timetable?" Kyn scoffed, low and disbelieving, "You ran a gray clinic in the lowers, patching up tweekers and roof brats."

"Why now?" Ashe parroted, stepping out of Kyn's blind spot, silken voice tipped noticeably towards their sonorous range. "Is this a ploy to derail the interception?"

"Oh, hey you," Kyn purred effetely. He turned his head, freckles scrunched as a churlish smile split his angular face. "Sorry 'bout what I said earlier, you know I hate trading in that kind of shade. I wasn't at my best." He turned to look at Yorri, but the ghost of his regret had slipped out when he wasn't looking. Kyn clocked the room; one door he could see, directly in front of him, a slim rectangle of polished redwood, closed. "You know I respect you. I'm just a little confused 'bout what's going on here." He petitioned. He titled his head back, squeezing it through the small gap in his over stretched shoulders, looking behind. Ceiling slanting into rhomboid walls, weapons mounted and displayed on every free surface, no furniture, no door. He pulled his head back, grin growing even wider. "I think I might have finally gone entirely insane. Isn't that fun?"

Ashe slapped him again.

"Enough!" They yelled, mouth seeming to split wider then physically possible; as if to swallow his face. Their voice none of their own. "Why now? What do you know?"

"Everything and nothing darling." Kyn taunted, shrill, and unhinged, his head lolling between his shoulders. "Everything and nothing."

Ashe gripped him by the hair and drove the silver spike between his eyes.

"Knock it off K." Yorri laughed, tossing a deep-fried protein ball at Kyn. He sat perched on the edge of a pod chair stuffed with moss-green shag. Kyn had salvaged the chrome egg from the Mercer Island waste-pit.

Kyn deftly caught the greasy battered treat and popped it into his mouth. "Serious. Run with me. Escape. Beyond the wall." He countered, chewing animatedly.

"Serious?"

The spike slid out of Kyn's skull. Bone cracked over, and healing skin rapidly knit itself together over gleaming white bone. His eyes, bulging and bloodshot, flew open. The blank figure who was Yorri, stood in front of him.

Waves of grief crashed over Kyn, smothering the violent rage of regeneration. His chin dropped to his chest, and he sobbed.

"I'm sorry!" He wailed. "I'm so sorry Yor." He clenched and unclenched blue fingers above the chain wrap, as if trying to touch his dead lover. "It should've been me. It always should've been me." He shook with the sobs, rattling the chains. Kyn's grasping hands clenched.

Yorri watched him, face cold and blank, no reaction to the Envoy's wracked sobs. He stepped in closer, close enough that Kyn could smell his breath, the scent igniting countless treasured memories across his fractured mind. Mornings waking up next to Yorri, kissing him on the rooftop of a club, heavy breaths, gentle warmth on the back of his neck.

"Why are you here, now?" Yorri asked, empty, far away. Unreachable.

Kyn lifted his chin, locking eyes with his dead lover. Steel gray met prismatic green. There was a tug at the back of his chest, a longing to get lost amongst the islands of green. He laughed low and sad.

"I missed you." He choked. Tears spilled over, pouring down his cheeks, tracing lines through the galaxy of freckles. Yorri stepped even closer and Kyn tried to let his eyes say everything he felt and everything he regretted. "I'm sorry," he said.

Then he pressed down hard on both thumbs, dislocating the joints with a loud pop.

Kyn slipped through the snapping chain binding and dropped to the cold stone. The chain, free of its burden, slithered through its mooring with a metallic hiss to coil next to him. Yorri stumbled backwards, reaching for the wall of weapons, the blankness of his face out of sync with the panic of his movements.

Kyn was up and on him before his hand could touch a laser lance.

Rising from the floor, Kyn crossed the distance between them in one easy step, unfettered chain stretched between healing hands, tendons, pulling and snapping the joints back into place. He slammed into Yorri with a knee to the taller man's groin, doubling him. Yorri grunted, guttural and pained. Kyn repeated the action, short and sharp, driving the blow home. Then, in one smooth motion, he looped the length of chain around Yorri's neck and rolled over the taller man's hunched back, flipping over him. Yorri grunted once, low and panicked, before Kyn yanked the chain, snapping his neck cleanly.

Kyn dropped the chain and heard the body crumble limply to the floor behind him. The stainless-steel spike clattered to the polished wood, rolling hollowly away. Then it was silent. Kyn shook uncontrollably. He turned and looked down.

Alyn's cold blue eyes stared back at him, blank and lifeless. The statuesque Sentry was sprawled on the floor, face the wrong direction, his limbs at odd angles like a dropped and forgotten doll.

Everything inside Kyn felt fractured, broken.

Numb, he walked through the room's single door and out into what must have been the Sentry's personal study. Stark and minimalist like all of Noav SPIRE, the room was L shaped, the inner walls clear polyplex over-looking a garden of rock and contorted bonsai. Weeping willows twisted and warped to delicate dwarf sizes, drooping branches cascading around them like leafy curtains of blonde-green hair. Walls pushed out at disjointed angles, tiled in narrow vertical planks of red cedar. Woven mats of rare and delicate materials were soft under Kyn's bare feet.

He could see the chair through the polyplex. Stainless steel and chrome, black vinyl, oscillating LEDs. The chair the Informant had shown him in the sensat. A dark silhouette was slumped on the bamboo mat next to the chair. Kyn turned the clear corner.

Alyn, strangled looking and bloated, lay on the floor next to the chair. The Sentry's face was frozen in a strained and agonized death mask, the muscles in his neck bulging in rigid tension. Alyn had died with his eyes open, the iris a brilliant, unnatural blue afloat in a blackened sea of burst vessels. Dried blood was crusted around the socket, nose, and mouth.

Numbly unsurprised, Kyn ignored the body and looked to the chair. It was set to an upright position, facing a blank hard display - a standing rectangle of clear smartplex set in the floor. An oval workspace of molded white plastic protruded from one wall, and Kyn's polished blades lay next to the mysterious black band. Above the workbench a flat, slate-gray oni was installed in the red wall slats. A single blue touch icon glowed in the middle of its faceplate.

Kyn touched the icon and the transparent display lit up, vid footage dancing across its surface. The vid was from what Kyn recognized as SPIRE internal surveillance, and showed a cluster of familiar vertical tubes; lit from underneath, and filled with liquid that glowed ultramarine blue. The foremost tube was empty, but behind it, out of clear view of the recording cam, were dark and lumpy forms, obscured by distance and angle. Looking at them Kyn got the impression of a grotesque approximation of limbs. He touched the icon again, cycling down the oni. A steady hand found Ego, and he jammed the dagger's tip into the installation seam, prying the comp free. He tossed the hardcase and dagger back onto the table and went in search of clothing.

A concealed door seam, barely noticeable in the paneled wall, led to the Sentry's sleeping quarters. Red light glowed from the walls as Kyn padded over gaudy plush carpet, past a raised hexagon bed, large enough to host an even dozen, and covered in yards of silk, dark blue, like oily water. He strode with purpose past one clear door to the rooftop garden, and through another to a slate-gray tiled shower stall. He washed mechanically; dried blood, his and that of the massacred security team, ran red, mixing with the rainbow glitter from his cheeks to swirl hypnotically around the floor drain.

Cleaned, he stood in front of the room's reflective wall, a towel - soft to the touch and absurdly thick - wrapped around his narrow hips. He touched the wall's silvery surface and a square of azure blue folded outward at his touch, revealing a simple vanity shelf that unfolded from a slit in the wall.

Vials of a twisting black liquid stared back at Kyn. His blood perked and his stomach ached. The back of his eyes felt numb. Kyn touched the reflective surface again and the wall reabsorbed the shelf, swallowed by the mirror. He turned and walked back into the sleeping room. An Envoy uniform lay folded on the ocean of silk.

He dressed and strapped on his weapons. He slotted the oni into an inner pocket of his uniform, the rectangular hardware flat against his chest, concealed beneath the harness straps, and adjusted the black cuff around his wrist before leaving the sleeping chamber, exiting by the terrace garden. An auto-transpo - upper wards exclusive and capable of short-range air travel - idled at the terrace edge.

Altitude winds whipped Kyn's hair. The uppers were choked in a blanket of cloud, the air wet.

The transpo's rear doors raised at Kyn's approach, and he climbed in. The destination field was blank. He swiped in a drop point and the transpo lifted off the terrace with a soft whir, turning in the whiteout, and accelerated away.

The Wall

Kyn sat on the upper lip of the wall, booted feet dangling over the edge. It was pushing gray dawn and welding torches lit the horizon to the west - servos working round the clock, patching the jagged scar torn in the klick tall barrier. Spotlights lanced the chill gray fog that rolled in from the bay. The surrounding area immediately outside of the towering wall was a ruined wasteland, gray mud pock-marked by blast craters, and dotted with the eroded stubs of pre-fall infrastructure. Ancient, raised highways crashed into the mud in stuttering concrete waves.

Kyn kicked his feet childishly against the thick layers of welded sheet, his rubber heels drumming a hollow staccato. The city behind him was a mind-boggling urban tangle of neon-lit humanity, rising into the clouds. His Envoy mask hung limp around his neck, and he breathed in the crisp freshness of the pre-dawn, relief from the pollution clog of the inner city. He'd come on a hunch. Air-transpo ditched in the sand dune of an upper green course, nose buried at an angle in white grit. Slipped out of the ward through a staff loading shaft, then traced his way through the mids to mount the city encircling barricade from the north side. Blue black mountains clawed at the sky on the horizon. It was quiet, the city reduced to a background hum, near silent away from the perpetual metallic creaks of shifting ward platforms, the incessant whir of pollution scrubbers and CO_2 recyclers, away from the constant howl of human movement.

A flare of neon pink crackled further along the rampart, paces from Kyn, and a void black hole, laced round with writhing tendrils of pink, tore itself open, the ethereal energy like fairy fire in the gray dawn.

Kyn turned to the flickering portal and stood as the Dividers slithered through. The top of the barricade was wide enough for two people to walk abreast, slick from the pre-dawn mists. No safety rails protected the edges. His weapons hung from him, strangely heavy.

"Oy!" He called to the pair. They again wore cowled, elaborately wrapped garments, and graphic light masks still hid their faces, but he easily recognized the siblings he'd tangled with earlier by their silhouettes. The male stalked towards him as the female stayed behind. Kyn noted she favored one leg.

"Figured you'd pop by."

The male raised a pink wreathed hand, and Kyn felt the Divider's power seize at his weapons harness. iD, Ego and Self pulled from their sheaths and floated around him, suspended in the air.

He felt relieved.

"Not looking to throw down." He said honestly, raising his hands, the black cuff easily visible at his wrist. "Just wanna gab."

The swirling pink winked from the male's hand and Kyn's weapons clattered to the battlement between them. He tapped behind his jaw with two fingers and the light mask winked out.

Impossible coloured eyes, moss green cracked with shimmering rose quartz, regarded Kyn with a sad intensity.

"The world is not what you think." The Divider said, his ENG strangely accented, gently lilting. He spoke with a calm confidence.

"What the fu-" Kyn began. But then the female was at her brother's back, a portal tear open at her hand, and the pair disappeared with an eye aching twist of physics.

Radio Silence

"Damn."

"Shut up."

"But. Your ass!"

"Shut up."

Kyn banged his fist against the strip of perforated tin siding for the second time in a rapid staccato. The corrugated aluminum was spray-painted green, and rigged up as a door for the sheet-metal wrapped shanty. "Deal with this guy before?"

Alec nodded, chewing on one chipped black thumb nail. His eyes still hovered over Kyn's sweatsuit covered glutes.

Leaving the wall, Kyn had stopped at the barracks built into the barricade's base to ditch his Envoy uniform for stocked Dag training gear. Soft synth-cotton sweat gear that the hacker claimed, 'showed off the goods.' The oni he'd ripped from Alyn's wall was tucked in the front pouch of the hooded upper layer, and his weapon's harness was awkwardly concealed under the bulky garment.

"Duck's got the education," Alec confirmed, digit dropping from his mouth. They'd come to the Eaton district, a sprawling and complex shanty town built inside one of the numerous, pre-fall commerce mega-centers that choked the lower core. He glanced down the makeshift alley of scaffolding rigged tarp shanties and sheet metal shacks that crammed the gutted mall, and back again.

"Rising star in the mids 'til he got clearance pulled for some gray market biz. Booted down here, never went servo. Smarter on biotech then anyone, and enough grit 'gainst the SPIREs to turn for the Informant."

Kyn banged on the tin again.

" Rip this door off if he doesn't open."

"Yo' power down." Alec purred, close in behind. The taller man cupped Kyn's buttock and squeezed. "Duck will read your box, no need to stress."

Kyn snapped an elbow back, catching Alec lightly in the diaphragm. The hacker groaned and slumped against him. Pivoting, Kyn spun and grabbed the taller man's face with one hand, restraining him at eye level.

"We have very little time before this all goes to shit," he hissed, eyes glinting gray steel in the flickering work lights. He released Alec. "Not that I don't appreciate it."

Alec massaged his center, eyeing Kyn warily. "Message received."

The tin door creaked outward a sliver. Green halogens and the smell of boiling vegetable stock leaked through. A youthful face, male, smooth skin, ambiguous mid-wards light, and clean shaven, his hair a slicked back coif of dull brown, appeared in the opening. He wore round, wire-rimmed optic glasses, and Kyn noted the high collar of a red medtek's smock, crisp and clean despite the shabby surroundings. The young man didn't open the tin door beyond a handspan, but smiled brightly at the pair.

"You them?" He asked, blinking dull blue eyes rapidly. The left pupil was uniformly square, and Kyn spotted the subtle blurred edge of a stroma tint job.

"Mostly likely," he smiled back faux-sweetly. He pulled the thin door outwards and forced his way past the young man into the tin covered structure. "I'm going to assume you're Duck?" He drew

Ego from the small of his back and twirled the dagger flashily past the man's face before sliding it easily back into its sheath. "It's in your best interest to correct me if you're not."

"Yah... yah. That's me." Duck stammered, shuffling back as Kyn pushed by. He was about Kyn's height, and blinked even more furiously as the blade flashed a nail's breadth from his face, though his dull eyes never brightened. He jerked a thumb behind himself, indicating further into the junk-rigged structure. "Uh, follow me."

Duck led the pair through a neon orange wall of stiff plastic curtains and into his makeshift apartment. A solo cube unit of patched faux walls made of recycled steel welded to torn-out ceiling tiles. A product wall of jutting metal shelves lined one side, rising to the gutted ceiling and packed dense with salvaged tech in various stages of de/re-construction.

A scrap-rigged chair sat in familiar half-reclined position at the center of the small studio. A clunky and distinctly low-tech re-imagining of the one Kyn had found in the Sentry's private quarters, the head and hand rests were junky clusters of mirrored tile, stuck together unevenly. Thick bundles of multi-hued cables jacked into the back and hung limply to the vinyl floor. The braid of cables spidered between a small holo-table - cobbled together from a folding tray and a salvaged imaging plate - and a haphazard pile of interconnected oni stacked in one corner. More wiring hung like streamers from the stripped rafters, and green bulbed work lights in wire cages were clipped around the ad hock studio, bare bulbs casting everything in an analogue glow. A lumpy and dank looking bedroll was shoved into another corner, a steaming canister of sludge brown liquid simmering on a portable heating disk next to it - the assumed source of the salty vegetable smell. The floor hummed with a constant electric pulse. Generators, Kyn noted, presumably stored under the vinyl tiles.

The orange plastic sheet flapped back into place behind Alec as Kyn dug into the front pouch of his sweatshirt and tossed the pilfered oni to Duck.

"Can you read this?"

Duck caught the thin rectangle, momentarily juggling it clumsily, almost dropping it. "Uhh... Probably, depends," he stuttered. His synth tinted eyes were wide but dull behind the round wire optics.

"It's from the top of Noav." Alec supplied. The lanky hacker had propped himself against one welded faux wall. He wore a loose hooded vest in black mesh over tight red plaid slacks. One of his tattoo clusters, a seam of blocky glyphs that twisted around his inner arms, glowed a sharp, warning yellow.

Duck's eyes widened even further, the square pupil ticking a quarter rotation clockwise. Kyn smelled fear. He looked around the tech packed squat. He and Duck stood flanking either side of the rigged-up chair. He nodded. "What's the chair?"

Rapid blinking. Duck shook his head. "I can't hack my way into Unity tech. I'm bio, neural coding."

"Informant will get us in the box. We just need you to read it." Alec assured from his place on the wall. The seam line was pulsing an acid-green that matched his punk hawk.

"What's the chair?" Kyn asked again.

"Consciousness digitization and personhood construct download." The square pupil rotated another quarter tick clockwise.

"The fuck?"/"No shit?" Kyn and Alec sputtered, overlapping. Kyn's intense focus blurred with confusion, and Alec looked like he'd been told the ancient fairy stories of Bigfoot were real.

Duck tapped the box with the index finger of his right hand - the third digit was a nub, missing past the second knuckle - then tapped at his temple. "Neural coding."

"As in neural mapping? A person?" Kyn had the sudden urge to rip the box from Duck's hands and smash it on the tacky vinyl; crush it under his boot for good measure. "Is that even possible."

"f-Link biofeeds are already hooked into the nervous system," Duck lectured, his speech pattern rapid, clipped. An undertone of professional excitement. "A tap into the data stream that runs human consciousness. It's really just a matter of reading and understanding the information, then ordering it in a way that a machine can read, then, physically storing the constructed data map for replay. Lie down, pretty lights play a special show, lulls your brain into a relaxed state, chair does a download dump and re-sort. Relatively easy. Information craves sorting, and the human mind is adept at it, once you get the data together it naturally falls into place."

Kyn tracked about half of that.

"Doesn't have a ton of real-world application, re-download only works into the same hardware, same physical brain. Turns out the software and hardware are intrinsically linked." Duck pointed back and forth between Kyn and himself. "My recorded conscious wouldn't read on your brain, or yours on my mine. I can make a copy, but it doesn't really go anywhere. It's more like taking a picture of yourself from inside and storing it on a hard disk." He taped the rectangle and shrugged. "Good for upper elites with rare memory degenerative conditions missed during in-utero gene editing."

"So, the chair downloads and re-loads a person's consciousness into the same person?" Kyn clarified, "What's the point? Isn't sensate tech way more advanced?"

Duck blinked rapidly. "Not much, like I said, memory recovery for rare genetic disorders. Allowing for recovery of memories lost post download. And yes, sensate tech is more capable of experiencing the internal POV of another individual. What it is physically like to live in their body and look through their eyes. Highly edited. But it gives you no insight into their inner world, their experiences, feelings, sense of self, generally speaking, everything they are. Which then answers the why." He smiled broadly. "Being able to capture and perfectly record someone's personhood for reapplication is a feat unto itself. Do 'cause you can."

"Okay, but if you didn't have any memories missing would you still feel anything? Notice anything?" Kyn pressed.

"No." Duck answered simply. "Unless pressed to recall that specific missing information."

"Then why re-download at all?"

Duck shrugged and pressed the rectangle against the chest of his red medtek smock.

"Can the recording be altered?" Alec asked darkly.

Duck blinked rapidly, drumming his fingers.

"Don't make me pull out my knife again Duck."

Alec coughed, as if clearing his throat.

Duck's fingertips beat out a rapid staccato. "Theoretically," he confirmed.

Kyn nodded, understanding what use the Unity would have for such tech.

"Nothing big." The blue eyed medtek blurted, as if incriminated. "Small chunks of memory can be deleted without notice, and with skill and delicate re-coding a few base impulses could be altered. Too much change wouldn't re-align with the mind's established neural pathways correctly and would quickly lead to dissociation and eventual psychosis."

"Sounds about right," Kyn sighed. "Can you tell me who's on there?"

"No." Definitive.

He remembered the tubes of blue liquid. HRV injects in a vanity mirror. He nodded his narrow chin at the box clutched to Duck's chest. "Could other stuff be stored on there too?"

"Could be, got enough storage capacity."

"You good to read us any medical jargon I can't glean? Or you just useful for this personhood construct stuff?"

Duck nodded, blinking rapidly. "Probably."

Kyn turned back to Alec. "Alright where's your boss? Let's get this thing open."

Alec's fingers danced, and his eyes were glazed over, reading, and responding to an f-Link message. "Any tick now."

"Uh, excuse me?" Duck's voice was a quivering waiver as he waved a hand in Kyn's line of sight, trying to get his attention. Arching an eyebrow expectantly, Kyn turned back to the neural hack.

"Can, can I ask what any of this is about?" Duck stuttered, flinching. "Or, who, who you are?"

"It's best not." Kyn answered, corners of his lips turned up in a brightly pleasant, yet blank smile.

The junk salvaged holotable flickered to life, sputtered, and went dark again.

"Knock, knock." Alec tittered, unfolding from the doorway to cross to the deck. He found the power switch and flipped the deck to life. A squat amphibian, wide face almost entirely consumed by large purple eyes, appeared, floating above the plate. The projection was holo opaque, and the creature looked wet in the digital light. "'ey boss," Alec addressed the toad. He withdrew a length of black and yellow striped cable from the waistband of his pants and tossed one end to Duck. "Plug this in and set it down," he instructed.

The disgraced bio hack did as instructed, clipping one squared-off end into a slit in the narrow side of the flat case. He lay the stolen oni down on the torn vinyl seat. Alec slotted the other end under the holo plate. The acid-green seam had begun to blink slowly and rhythmically, as if following the hacker's heartbeat.

Kyn cocked an amused eyebrow at the holo. "So, you're a frog now?" He asked

"Am I?" The wide seam of the creature's mouth opened in a long gulping motion, at odds with the patter of the digitized voice. "Are you sure?"

"Bit basic that?" Kyn smirked, eyes cold and hard. "You're not going drag me into one of your round-the-twist dramatic reveals. I found your chair. Found your tubes." He held up his right arm, the hem of the sweater falling back to show the edge of the black cuff. "Still got this. You're going get me into that box so Duck here can tell me what's what, then, you're going start sketchin' out a picture for me 'bout how this all fits." A message notification flashed red in the corner of his optic. He swiped it away. Alec's fingers drummed at the air; he was casting an AR interface over the pilfered oni. "And if it's still not making much sense," he continued, still addressing the frog. "I'm going to have to start looking for you." Alec was tearing at the box's code locks; segments of command looped rows of prompts floating in the air. Lines of muted yellows and oranges. Duck stood beside the half-reclined chair, arms stiff to his sides, blinking rapidly, blankly watching the hacker. Another red blip at the corner of Kyn's vision. He dismissed it. "Which, to be frank, is something I don't really want to do, and I doubt you do either."

The frog's mouth opened in one long, silent, croak. "No time for exposition I'm afraid." The synthesized voice replied. "As you'll soon understand." Another red blip flashed in Kyn's optic.

Kyn flipped the message string open across the tip of his thumb. They were all from Runa.

dickJugglr, where the f r u? shits getting weird here, get back. unity address in 5. city wide systems.

Kyn looked back to Alec; the hacker was pulling what looked like a stack of glowing playing cards from the center of a swirling ring of lime green code. The AR deck pulsed with a dull white light in Alec's hand. "Got it!" The hacker crowed. The seam tattoo began to pulse faster, and, as Kyn watched, small beads of white flowed from the deck into the glowing lines of green, starting at Alec's hands, and flowing up his arms. At the same time the deck began to dim. The hacker was draining the data into his own bio feed. "These are smaller files. I'm just making a copy, so we have it." His grin was wide and goofy. "I've got one whale of a data construct behind. Never fit on my own feed. That'll be your personhood construct." Dock nodded. "I'll load it through the deck."

Data glow drained, the deck between Alec's hands disappeared, nonexistent. The hacker reached his hands back into the circling ring of green code and pulled out what looked like the outline of a child's dollhouse, clunky and made of straight white lines of code. His tautly muscled arms flexed in effort despite the AR's lack of physical substance. The house was a tumor of wings and additions, gables, and sub-levels, a misshapen thing drawn in neon white. He set the construct down on the holo-pad where it sat overtop the projected frog, two digital constructs existing in the same space over different frequencies. The purple eyed frog's throat engorged and deflated rhythmically, each expansion dimming the house. Clustered lines faded until it vanished completely, absorbed, and only the frog remained, floating above the plate. The creature's purple eyes blinked wetly.

Alec snapped his fingers once and the AR over the rectangular oni clicked off. Another snap and the deck of data files appeared in the holo, floating above the still pulsing toad. Duck started suddenly from his stillness.

"Don't worry," Alec reassured smoothly. "Backed a copy up on the chair's hardware." Duck nodded then settled back into a blank stillness. Kyn was aware of time ticking away.

"If you can't confirm who the construct is you might as well just leave it." He instructed the frog, needing no confirmation who was loaded into the chair. "Blue tubes. Find me something."

The squat holographic creature blinked slowly. The data deck above its head split then folded inward, as if shuffling. A single square file fell out and expanded, eclipsing the deck. The data square opened to the same image Kyn had seen in the Sentry's chambers. Security feed of dark shapes floating in tubes of glowing blue liquid. Lumpy contents unidentifiable in the dim light. A scroll text of seeming nonsense streamed by one side of the image.

Duck blinked into activity. Circling around the chair he leaned in closer to the holo, examining the vid. Kyn saw his square shaped pupil expand and contract definitively, shuttering closed then open again.

"Bioelectric conductive fluid, used for stimulation of cell growth, common in protein cloning vats. Usually red in colour. This is altered for the recycling of live tissue - the high levels of soli-Hex thr3e give it the blue hue."

"Live tissue cloning is illegal under the Unity's population control act."

Duck shrugged.

"Anything else?" Kyn knew his time was up.

"No other references." The purple eyed amphibian croaked digitally.

Kyn snatched up the rectangular oni from the personality dump chair and clipped out the link cable before throwing the deck to the vinyl tile in one smoothly definitive motion. The aluminum casing cracked on impact, and a swift stamp of his boot snapped the internal hardware. Green plastic chips, veined with silver, copper, and gold, spewed from the split. The holo frog blinked out, disconnected.

"Time to be gone." He ordered Alec shortly, crossing to the heavy plastic curtain. The hacker fed the fiber optic cable back into his waistband and followed as Kyn pushed through the orange plastic barrier without a word or glance back at Duck.

His thanks would be getting as far away from the man as he could - fast.

Kyn led Alec back through the makeshift entry door, and out into the Eaton concourse. A faceless throng of disheveled individuals shuffled by, coming, and going, locked in the endless march of the over-crowded lowers. Kyn scanned passersby, alert to potential threats, and the hairs at the nape of his neck perked as one of Alec's drones hummed past. The vaulted ceiling of the cannibalized shopping center rose above them, trapping the din, and the concourse buzzed with the echoed sounds of human activity. Holo projectors set along the walls blinked to life, carpeting every spare span of visible vertical space with identical placards. Golden typeface over a crystalline silhouette of the rising SPIREs.

STAND BY FOR UNITY ADDRESS. The holos announced.

Kyn spotted the nearest exit, a skeletal street-level storefront, directly across the scuffed marble corridor, ancient glass walls long smashed, leaving the mall open to the elements. A rough barricade of rusted and gutted pre-fall petrol vehicles were welded over the lower half of the opening. He could easily vault the barrier and be on the street. Kyn flipped his hood up and shoved his hands into the front of his sweater, crossing the concourse, Alec close behind. The bustle around them was becoming still, attention turned to the glowing screens, then Kyn was over the barrier, his boots hitting the slick street beyond.

STAND BY FOR UNITY ADDRESS glowed large from the face of every building, looming over the perpetually dark streets.

Kyn quickened his pace, beelining for an overflowing trash disposal unit that blocked a littered service alley. A clustered group of Alexi cultists hissed in his direction, disapproving at his lack of attentiveness. Kyn swallowed the impulse to hiss back and kept moving.

The human traffic outside of the commerce ruins had slowed to a standstill, all eyes turned to the glowing projection. The image had changed, stylized placard of the rising SPIREs replaced in a simple swipe to a live feed of Alena. The focus hovered over her head and shoulders.

Kyn vaulted the dumpster smoothly, then picked up into a run. He could hear Alec's footfalls behind him, and one of the hacker's drones – Rosie – zipped past his ear, scouting the far end where the narrow, trash-filled alley spilled out into the next major thorough fair. He tore off the bulky Dag sweatshirt as he ran and tossed it into an over-crammed bin, freeing access to his weapons harness. He'd reloaded the throwing blades, and his fingers found two of the clear slivers. He burst out the other end of the alley into an open square, Alec still close behind.

Alena loomed large from every angle.

"...a great tragedy." The Sentry was saying, her face a cold mask of despair. "...a loss that will not be soon forgotten."

Kyn had the sense there would be no caravan of refugees to guard.

The cam panned out, expanding to reveal the entirety of the Unity membership arranged respectfully around the addressing Sentry.

Alexi flanked her sister to the right, golden-white hair piled high on her head in an elegantly demure wrap studded with velvet blue sapphires, and wearing an expression of pure motherly mourning, the haunted loss of life taken too soon.

Alyn stood to the left, his white-blonde hair slicked and respectfully coifed. A surviving soldier's look of smoldering justification masked over his chiseled face.

Kyn stuttered to a stop, plastic blades tumbling from numb fingers as he collapsed to his knees. He retched, gagging, then vomited the sparse contents of his stomach into the gutter.

The edges of reality cracked, shattering in silver slivers.

Go

Five long lines of indigo powder across the stainless-steel vanity. Kyn's hands shook as he pinched off his nose and snorted the first line. The eclipse hit like black lightning, scraping a brilliant flash of empty euphoria across his neurons. Reflected light at the jagged edge of fractured reality.

Once Kyn had collapsed, Alec had hacked a parked transpo and bundled him, shaking, inside.

"My loft." He'd directed in someone else's voice, eyes dead pools of dull silver, staring blankly ahead. The tech boy got them on route, skilled fingers flying through tapped commands as he ghosted their route log.

On arriving, Kyn had burst into an intensely focused efficiency. Internal decision made, he'd taken the factory steps in even stride, moving up the internal stairwell, Alec hustling behind. Kyn flashed his f-Link to slide the loading door open, then, without a glance back to see if Alec still followed, he'd stormed into the shower stall and slid the barrier shut with a cold click.

A matte black jumpsuit hung on a jutting pipe next to the shower stall.

Kyn unhooked his weapon's harness and threw it over the folding toilet. His mind burned from the image of glowing tubes etched behind his eyeballs. He snorted the second and third lines in rapid succession, chasing an oblivion of unseeing. Freedom from the dark and lumpy shapes floating in glowing blue. The misshapen shadows of appendages and flashes of blue on tufts of white-blonde hair.

He kicked open a trick storage cubby under the vanity and a weather-treated pack roll tumbled out. Kicking off the gray sweats, Kyn squatted down and reached into the back of the cubby to unstrap a tin of stored clean water from the top and clipped the container to the side of the pack. He unhooked the jumpsuit from the exposed pipe and stepped into it, sliding the front zipper closed to his throat. It was sleeveless like all of the rest, exposing his ropy arms, the piping at the collar a triple line of neon blue. Snorting lines four and five, he grabbed his weapons harness from over the docked toilet and slung it back around his chest. Adjusting iD and Ego's draw angles, he strapped the pack roll over the kit and cinched the straps. The remains of his Envoy mask slid into a wide pocket of the jumpsuit, and the empty vial of Blue Eclipse rattled into the bin before he kicked the lid closed.

The last of the indigo powder welded iridescent seams of rainbow slivers into the cracks of his mind. He touched the smooth band secured around his right wrist, the metallic surface warmed to the temperature of his own skin.

There was the crashing bang of the loading door slamming against its runners, followed by heavy boots across concrete.

Kyn looked at himself in the reflective polyplex, watching as the narcotic bloodshot faded from his eyes, the red veins disappearing to clear white. The gray iris glinted, a maniacal monoband silver. He winked.

Runa was waiting when he slid the door open. The adolescent still wore her Envoy uniform, and was standing in the middle of the loft, her hair pulled up, one hand on the curve of a cocked hip. Yellow light from the surrounding ward platforms streamed in

through the steel-lined windows, and her amber eyes flashed dangerously behind clear goggles.

"Hey, Kyn." Runa's voice was like churning gravel. A sugrstik
rolled between her teeth. "Weird night."

"Weird night," Kyn agreed. He clocked Alec backed up against
the sofa slab, watching Runa wearily. A tattoo, what looked like a
pair of dice drawn in simple black lines on the curve of the hacker's
left bicep, shifted, circling each other as if in balanced orbit. Benn
was behind Runa, a trim shadow lurking in the crook of the open
loading door.

"Kyn," Benn's voice was steady, nonthreatening. "We need to
talk."

Kyn ignored the Handler and locked eyes with Runa.

"They're cannibalizing them." He told her plainly. "Stealing their
bodies."

"You're out of control Kyn." Runa returned, unflinching. "They
want you to come home."

"They'll never stop taking." He pressed, pleading. "There's no
end to their hunger."

"Enough of this nonsense." Malvyc's slithering, whisper of a
voice cut in. Kyn followed the line of Alec's fixed gaze and saw
the glint of red in the shadow of his sleeping alcove. His stomach
lurched as if he'd be sick again. His mind tumbled through routes of
getting the hacker away. The green haired punk was perched on the
edge of the slab, his back rigid, the dice tattoo rolling over itself on
his bicep, his four little round drones nowhere to be seen. Alec's thin
lips were set in a hard line, and Kyn could see the subtle trembling
of his long fingers against his thighs.

"Recycled base carbons."

Alec continued to stare straight ahead, tinged green with disgust
as he comprehended what Kyn was saying.

Runa eyed Kyn warily. She crunched down loudly on the hard treat, then, pulling the splintered stik from her mouth, flicked the discarded remains towards the wall of windows. "That sounds like a whole lot of crazy Kyn." She returned throatily, shifting to fold thin yet densely muscled arms over of her narrow chest, adopting a more glowering and determined stance. "It's a hard sell."

"Grab him and be done with this child." Malvyc cut in, abandoning the darkness to stand at the alcove entrance. The ambient light of the ward disks reflected sharply in the Envoy's smooth scalp.

"It's no play," Kyn pressed, ignoring Malvyc, eyebrows high and scrunched together, earnest. "I kill-..."

His confession was cut off as his nervous system burned.

A frothy glob of spittle hit the rough concrete as Kyn collapsed forward, foaming at the mouth. His knees buckled and he convulsed, hitting the floor hard and toppling to his side, unaware of any other pain outside the internal fire that griped him.

"Kyn!" Alec called out, high and distraught, as he moved to rise from the slab. Runa crossed to the taller man in two easy strides and pushed gently on the hacker's chest. Alec collapsed back down onto the slab; the buffed spokes groaned metallically.

Kyn was screaming inside his head, eyes frozen open, straining. He watched the dice tumble over Alec's bicep. He screamed for Alec to run, to get as far away as fast as he could, but all sound caught in his throat, choking him. The edges of his vision blurred red as veins burst in his eyes.

"Malvyc, enough!" Runa snapped, rough voice edged with anger. "I've got this."

"Then handle it child," Malvyc admonished. His eyes didn't lose their vibrant crimson glow, unrelenting.

Kyn's back arched involuntarily, muscles contorting as they spasmed. Heavy boot steps reverbed through the concrete and small hands hoisted him with ease, like a twitching doll. He spasmed with pain and his knee struck a gently curved shoulder. His joint shattered on contact, the pain a white-hot blip in the endless red void of his suffocation. He felt like his strangled screams would crack his brain.

He stood on the lip of the Needle's observation deck and looked out over the tangled neon sprawl of the lowers stretched out below him. He inhaled deeply, teetering on the disc's edge, a breath away from letting his weight tumble into the nothingness. The assorted scents of packed humanity were still dense in the air despite the wet night, and he picked up the fatty aromas of frying proteins. His stomach grumbled.

Squatting down, he hoisted his rucksack from the deck ridge and slung the canvas pack across his shoulders. The sheer number of choices available momentarily dazed and disoriented him, and he paused, contemplating his next move. The fresh autonomy, its novel sense of freedom, was exhilarating, and Kyn couldn't help but smile.

A maintenance trolley rattled past overhead, following a monorail track welded to the underside of a mid-war platform above his head.

"Fuckin ease up." Runa's raspy voice was in Kyn's ear, regeneration oscillating him between the breathless red void and the place of lost memory. He bucked as something inside him tore and she gripped him slightly harder to keep hold. He was vaguely aware of his humorous snapping mid-way between his elbow and shoulder. "It'd be easier to carry him if he wasn't wiggin' out like he's got a hot wire up his ass."

"Snap more limbs."

Runa was silent. Pointedly doing nothing even as Kyn thrashed with another agonized spasm, her slight frame taut with apprehensive tension.

"Malvyc ease up," Benn ordered, his voice heavy with the authority of rank.

The electric storm of agony inside him eased, and Kyn drew in a ragged breath. The red void dimmed around the edges, the outlines of reality bleeding through, forcing itself into focus. Pain still paralyzed him, throbbing outwards across every nerve ending, but it had a faded quality, like a dimmer dial had been rolled back. His muscles had relaxed enough that he could breathe shallowly, but he still had no ability to control his own body. He was helpless.

"Of course, Handler. I guess it won't do to have the degenerate entirely incapacitated." Malvyc amended.

Everything was inverse. Kyn's head was lolled back, his neck arched, and he stared at the concrete around Runa's feet. His eyes bulged with agony, and his locked gaze was fixed on Alec's boots. Salvaged pre-fall Doc's. One thick rubber heel bounced nervously.

Hard soled loafers clicked, crossing the room, then Malvyc's long white fingers were in Kyn's hair, yanking his head around viciously.

"Wouldn't do for the glitch to miss us dealing with his depraved pet pervert."

Kyn could see Alec, the hacker's face a frozen mask of determined focus, fair eyebrows knitted together in a restrained pain. Fractured rib from Runa pushing him, Kyn figured. The dice still tumbled over his bicep on a repeating loop.

"Malvyc..." Runa warned, yanking the immobilized Kyn away from the bald Envoy's clawing fingers. The crimson of Malvyc's eyes glowed brighter still.

Alec screamed, deep and pained. Tendons standing out in the lanky hacker's neck as he seized, fallen to his side on the worn slab, pulled into himself, instinctively trying to protect against the invasive assault. The tumbling dice on his bicep stopped their endless orbit, settling to show six black dots on each face.

Then the world exploded into ever expanding windows of hardcore pornography.

Everything fractured. Self-replicating squares of slick, pulsing flesh - complete with moaning, grunting, audio - tumbled out of each other, multiplying rapidly, as if fucking themselves into reality. Almost instantly Kyn's optic was entirely obscured by every imaginable combination of throbbing sexual organ and eagerly accepting orifice.

Disgusted groans and shocked shouts told Kyn he wasn't the only one either. Blanket biofeed hack.

Porn bomb.

Malvyc screamed, a deeply disturbed sound, strangled high and twistedly childish.

The pain that seized Kyn vanished with the bald Envoy's distraction and relief flooded him, sensation and control returning to his limbs in an itching blaze. Runa groaned, a gravely sound of surprise and exasperation as she stumbled in her shock, loosening her grip on Kyn further. Heavy curls batted his face as the adolescent presumably shook her head wildly back and forth, reactively trying to stop seeing the images that had clogged her optic channel.

Kyn wriggled himself free of Runa's distracted grasp and landed heavily on the floor. His hacked cochlear implant was filled with heavy panting, and his intercourse-clogged optic made it impossible to see as he grasped around blindly, quickly trying to orient himself by touch. The back of his hand brushed the molded rubber of Alec's boot, and he was up, climbing the hacker's leg. Moving on instinct, his searching fingers found Alec's hand and he was vaulting the slab, dragging the taller man behind as he rushed what he knew would be the wall of grimy industrial windows.

"Kyn!" Benn yelled from somewhere across the loft, seemingly pleading with his charge, voice almost lost under the clashing orchestra of grunts and moans. "Stand down! It's going to be okay! You can tr-..."

But what Kyn could do was lost in a scrape of twisting metal and the crash of shattering glass as he dove through the latched pane of windows, dragging Alec behind him. Breaking glass cut blazing lines across his face as he crashed through the barrier, and a piece of jagged metal pane slashed deep across his right shoulder.

Then he was falling.

Still blinded by thrusting flesh, Kyn twisted as he fell, turning his back with the direction of gravity even as he wrapped himself protectively around Alec.

Culling nights were a special kind of wild at PumpJack. Glitches, so jaded against their perpetual ostracism that their last means of escape was to literally dance in the face of looming slaughter, pressed against those still young and naive enough to be violently radicalized. Righteous anger burned feverish behind the eyes of those bursting to lash out in a last brilliant flash of rebellion, while those too numb to worry about self-preservation watched on, pressing closer to catch the ambient high.

Kyn watched himself in the smoky stretch mirror set over the back service top, the reflective surface poorly polished and oily. He had a tinge-job blonde between his thighs. The blonde was older than the derma lift around his eyes, and eager - his oral technique sloppy with the greed of repression. The tinge-job was fresh, and Kyn had clocked him as a recent mid-wards drop down. Recently outed and tossed to the lowers, high on cock and his forced emancipation. Gorging on the denied.

"Kyn!"

The world rushed back. He blinked; street level, cracked cement pressing into his cheek, hard pearls in his mouth. The healing itch burned his body. Alec was crouched over him, yelling his name. Behind the hacker the door to the factory swung open and Kyn could see long muscular legs descending the block stairs.

"I'm up." Palms beside his ears, he kipped to standing. His back was soaked.

Alec sprung back from him; the hacker's face peppered with angry scrapes but otherwise seemingly unharmed. Kyn's pack had exploded in the fall, the contents splattered across the concrete, ruined and useless. Re-birth adrenaline thundered through him, and joints resettled. He spit out old teeth and whipped his head around, orienting himself in the span of two rapid heartbeats. The street was unnaturally empty, save for a Unity issued transpo parked diagonally across the road, and the sleek, mono-wheeled rimrunr tipped against the curb. The surrounding shops were shuttered and dark.

Ashe strode purposefully towards them. Kyn could feel the air crackle with their unspoken words.

"Go!" He ordered, shoving Alec toward the influencer's abandoned monocycle. He spun back, Ashe was alluringly striking in their Envoy uniform, and their violet eyes flashed warningly. "Don't know what they got you all chasin' my tail for, but I can tell you it's not how they spin it." Kyn held his hands away from his body, visibly clear of his weapons, and spit out another tooth that had dislodged from his throat. He could hear Alec's rubber soled boots pounding the pavement.

"Stop." Ashe commanded, low and two toned. Alec's boot falls halted.

"They're cloning tubes." Kyn implored, knowing he had one chance. "Quick bake from recycled bio matter." Ashe stopped well out of his reach, their strong face an unreadable mask. Kyn could hear the faint looping of sirens in the distance - Dag transpos. "The Wasters."

Alec's stumbling footfalls started up again, followed by the hum of the rimrunr's engine and the squeal of its oversized rubber tire burning pavement.

"Thanks." Kyn acknowledged earnestly, even as he stepped forward with a snapping whip kick aimed to the taller Envoy's temple.

Unresisting, Ashe's head snapped sideways, and they crumbled, unconscious, to the pedway just as the factory door banged open again, tearing from its hinges to clatter down the stairs, and a furious-looking Runa burst through. Benn was close behind.

Kyn turned and started running. Elsynn's shop was across the street, and he could see the light of her kitchen through the polyplex of the door despite the shuttered windows.

The door was unlocked when he reached it.

"Get any kids around under the floor." He ordered, slamming into the noodle shop. He vaulted the service top and somersaulted across the kitchen's gritty checkerboard tiles. The grizzled old woman parked behind the grill angled herself, cutting off the narrow path to the kitchen's back door. Her mechanical arm whirred as she shifted a heavy wok onto a glowing blue hotplate. Kyn didn't miss a beat, tic-tac-ing from prep counter to wall, he scrambled over the proprietor's head. He could already hear the shouts and clambering of the shop's perpetual cluster of delinquents as they rushed the noodle bar's floor hatch. "Seriously El!" He warned. "Do not try to slow her down." Then he was bursting through the kitchen's flimsy chicken wire rear door and out into the intersectional alley behind.

The whooping of Dag sirens grew closer.

Alexi cultists, in layers of crinoline skirts, eyed him balefully from the back flap of the kiddy corner netdive. f-Links glowed on their skin, and fingers tapped out rapid posts. Kyn skirted them and mounted a trash compact wedged in the corner of a prefab and a bombed-out theatre. He ran a few vertical strides up the perforated siding for height and caught the dangling remnants of the theatre's steel-caged fire escape. Up the metal rungs and he was running again, boots pounding up the slanted roof. A communal work stack had been fused into the ruined building and he scrambled up onto a jutting air circulation vent that ran the face of the addition. Besides the echoing bounce of converging Dag units, he heard no sound of pursuit and couldn't clock any sign of Runa or Malvyc. The other Envoy's didn't have his mobility in the lower wards, and he wanted to press his advantage. The others wouldn't waste their time trying to follow. Instead, they'd target Alec and rely on Kyn's softness for the hacker to draw him out. He needed to get to Alec before they did, and find them both a way out of the city as fast as he could. Hopefully, he'd be able to convince Ashe and Runa to follow.

Kyn ran the length of the work stack via the air duct and dropped down to the balcony of a U-shaped residential rack, then into the courtyard below. He rolled across loose clay tiles and was past the mouth of the courtyard in three long strides. A helmeted Dag cut across his path and Kyn leaned smoothly around the officer, snatching their belted k-cannon as he flipped them tidily onto the pavement with a hooked elbow and a boot to the calf. He spun into the street and fired off three rounds into the drive core of an approaching Dag transpo, halting the vehicles momentum in a burst of electrical fire. Pedestrians scrambled as the transpo swerved, crashing over a oni-case kiosk, before tipping onto its side. Sparks crackled from the smoking core.

The grappled Dag had been the point of their troupe, and the rest were close behind. Kyn had no interest in engaging and was off running again, tossing the handheld to the gutter as he hurtled down yet another alley. Kinetic bursts cracked brick and exploded refuse. Two more turns down more branching alleyways, and he burst out into a section of the lowers that had been built around the remains of a pre-fall university building, the open space between brick-and-mortar halls consumed by prefab residential blocks. He ran down a dead end, feet pounding towards a drab stone wall set with a single vertical row of square windows. Each pane wept thick vines of insulated cable, and sickly yellow ivy crept up wide bricks, winding around the cable bunches.

Kyn dash-vaulted through the ground floor window, kicking in the pane with a crash as he skidded ass first over a piled-on kitchenette, scattering a rancid stack of unwashed dishes. Moldy cups and sludge-covered serving plates clattered to yellow peeling linoleum. He pushed past the unit's occupant, a poorly balding middle-aged man with thick shoulder hair in tattered, long-past-white jockeys, and peeled down the unit's short hall. He kicked open a flimsy faux-wood door and burst into the outer corridor, peeling towards the plastic box staircase at the end. He took the risers two at a time, climbing the levels. At the top, a roof access mid-way down a pastel-blue tiled hallway led onto a flat expanse of gravel, and he jogged to the edge of the school-turned-residence's roof. Below, a wide intersection was flanked by parking obelisks, cheap rate coffin hotels, and alleys of neon-trimmed market stalls. Flow control lights flashed erratically. A slight, masked figure stood in the middle of the intersection, feet planted firmly as they held a revving rimrunr still with one hand.

Runa.

The oversized wheel screamed against the pavement, kicking up fumes of burning rubber as the acid-hawked rider gunned the monocycle, but Runa stood firm. Civilian transpos were abandoned and pedestrians were fleeing in all directions. A sleek Unity transpo swerved to a stop across two lanes.

Kyn stepped off the ledge and dropped to the adjacent parkaide. He took the second flat rooftop in a few strides, then dropped to the sidewalk with a forward roll. Alec's bots were out and circling Runa. The young Envoy's amber eyes winced with annoyance behind her goggles as one of the palm-sized balls – Sophia - zapped her with a jumping current of electricity. Escaped ropes of her thick locks frizzed wildly with the jolt, and she growled in irritation.

A sliver of icy assessment ran down Kyn's spine. Malvyc was nowhere to be seen and he didn't like that. His right hand reached over his shoulder, finding iD's hilt, and he drew the short sword with a clean *schick*. At the same time, his left hand passed over the chest strap of his harness and he hooked a fist full of throwing blades between his knuckles. A wrist flick and the projectiles whizzed through the air, perfectly aimed to strike Runa in several vital points.

The razor slivers struck true - one each at the neck, inner thigh, and achilles tendon - and bounced harmlessly off the adolescents' unbreakable skin. Runa turned her head to look at Kyn, still holding Ashe's pilfered monocycle in place at arm's length, one handed. Her other batted in annoyance at a drone still buzzing around her. Blanche - the offending drone - shifted horizontally in the air, easily avoiding the young Envoy before lashing out with another biting sting of electricity.

"Gah!"

"Call off the girls Alec! She won't hurt you!" Kyn called over to the green haired rider as he stalked across the empty intersection. He clocked Benn in the shadow of the Unity transpo, the Handler half behind cover of the vehicle's angular body.

The rev of the rimrunr died and the circling drones shifted course as one. They zipped to Alec, who straddled the powered down, but still balanced monocycle, and hovered watchfully over the lanky hacker's shoulder. Alec looked to Kyn, unsure, before putting one boot down and dismounted the cycle. He stepped clear and Runa casually tossed the runr sideways, throwing the cycle across two dead lanes, and sending it skittering across the asphalt into a signal post with a metallic screech.

"I don't want to hurt anyone Kyn." Runa growled, amber eyes ablaze over her mask. "Are you going to make me?"

Kyn stopped a handful of paces from the powerful Envoy.

"It's horrifying anyone would." He returned with sad honesty, teetering on the edge of an emotion he had no name for, staring into its dark void. He drummed his fingers on iD's handle, focusing on the reassuring simplicity of it. The black band was heavy on his wrist, grounding. "We're leaving." He told her simply. "Come with us."

Amber eyes blinked, disbelieving. Runa yanked down her mask. "How?" She demanded.

Kyn shook his head, conscious of the hundreds of closed-circuit eyes on him - waiting to see where the rabbit would run.

"It's a ruined wasteland out there." Runa pressed. "Least anywhere far enough from the Unity's reach."

Kyn shrugged his narrow shoulders. He had no real answers for her.

The world is not what you think.

"I'm pretty hard to kill. I'll figure it out."

Runa nodded to Alec, silently watching the exchange. This was the first time the hacker had heard about leaving the city, but Kyn had no doubt the information dealer in him had figure it out.

"He's pretty squishy." She said.

"Not wrong." Kyn's lips parted in a sly grin. He could see the spark of mischief growing in her. "It'd be easier with you along."

"What about Ashe?"

Kyn eyed the dead streets. The market was deserted, vendors having fled. Benn hadn't moved from his place behind the Unity transpo. "I have a feeling they'll be along soon." He looked to Runa; he knew she would never abandon the pseudo parental figure. "They'll go if you do." He reassured, knowing it was true.

"You don't speak for me." Ashe countered, stepping out from behind an abandoned stall. Malvyc materialized next to them. "Enough of this. Surrender your weapons and submit to custody. The Unity demands you be brought in."

More bodies appeared amongst the stalls. Cultists garbed in knockoff replicants of Sentry couture, birthed from the ever-present shadows. They pressed in around the stalls, a barrier of bodies, the meat of the Unity. Kyn could feel their mass pressing into the negative space around the intersection. They were surrounded.

"I am a proud tool of The Unity." Kyn recited, twirling iD at his hip. He advanced on Runa. "All I need and all I shall want will be supplied by my devotion."

No one said anything, nobody moved.

"My blood for my SPIRE. My body for my Sentry. My devotion to The Unity." He whipped iD through a distracting looping pattern before striking with a jabbing feint to Runa's gut.

Resolute, the young Envoy swatted halfheartedly at the blade, deflecting the attack easily, but otherwise didn't move, or flinch.

Unsurprised, Kyn pulled the jab as he kicked up and backwards, utilizing his preternatural flexibility to kick Runa in the goggles from behind himself, knocking the protective gear from her face.

Runa grunted and grabbed Kyn by the sword arm. A slight squeeze of her fingers and he heard/felt bones snap. iD clattered to the pavement. Easily ignoring the pain, Kyn twisted on the broken joint, turning in the adolescent's grip as he snapped out with his other hand, jabbing Runa in the eye with two fingers.

"Fuck!" She growled, backhanding him tidily with one hand even as she grasped at the pained socket with the other. Kyn flew backwards, barreling over a cluster of cultists to slam through a row of stalls. He skidded to a stop, tangled in a rack of knock-off couture. The rear wall collapsed, burying him in aluminum and cheap fabrics.

"Grab him." Ashe's voice snapped the air.

Sheet siding pulled away and hands grasped Kyn, digging him from the collapsed stall. Cultists yanked and pulled at him. Kyn struck blindly, relying on proximity and proprioception to find his targets. He bit a reaching hand, pulling away the tip of a thick knuckled pinkie in a spurt of crimson, then spat the nub back into the kabuki-painted face of a Ziev fan girl before kneeing her in the groin. A pivot slammed his elbow into the jaw of a Giaon bruiser before he shoulder slammed a squat Cao groupie, and then he was bursting from the knot of cultist. He ran two steps before an adolescent-sized hand grabbed him by the shoulder, pulling him up short with a jerk. The hand lifted him in an arch - ward platforms spun by above - before slamming him back first into the pavement. Asphalt cracked beneath him, and Kyn was dimly aware of several new devastating and immobilizing spinal fractures.

"Stay down Kyn." Runa advised. She stood above him, a length of rebar in her fist. The rebar stabbed down, the steel mesh rod driving through Kyn's chest, and into the road below. She bent the free end down in a drooping arch with a metallic groan of protest. Kyn could feel his damaged heart slamming against the knotted metal.

"De... defiance." He coughed wetly, laying still for what felt like the first time in a long while. Surrendering. The world of memory clawed at the edges of his mind, quivering at the edge of each beat of his heart.

"What?" Runa asked. The flashing neon of the market blotted out her face, and the vast, intricate web of crisscrossing wards loomed beyond her. A gray sky of layered and shifting steel.

Kyn laughed, hands finding the rebar at his chest. There was no moving it and pulling himself around the bend would take time.

"The first thing I ever learned that the Unity didn't teach me." His angular face split in a knife-edged smile, his gray eyes hard and determined. He could feel wet blood on his teeth. He turned his head to look around, peering through the waiting pack of interchangeable cultists. Alec still stood frozen, his face a portrait of tortured constraint, dutiful drones hovering at his shoulder, ready to move in an instant. Ashe and Malvyc still watched from where they'd first emerged, their expressions lost to distance and shadow. Kyn could easily smell the acrid tang of Malvyc's sadist glee. Benn hadn't moved from his place behind the car.

Kyn looked back to the looming Runa. "Don't let them consume you." He begged.

"Shut him down and come along child," Malvyc hissed. "Sandri will want to debrief you."

Runa clenched her fists. "You heard what he's been sayin' Ashe?" She asked, ignoring Malvyc.

Ashe was silent. The cultists watched intently, the near constant flutter of their fingertips rippling through the crowds. Forum status updates, blog bursts, and POV live posts blazing across the feed, signaling their deities.

Runa moved to grab the drooping end of rebar.

"Shut him down child." Malvyc's ordered again, his voice a slithering threat. Kyn could hear more looping sirens in the distance.

"Fuck this." Runa grumbled, straightening the rebar with another groan of steel. Kyn could see her face now, and her features were hard and set, her amber eyes determined. Then, determination widened to pain, and she screamed, high and terrible. She collapsed to the pavement with a thud that vibrated the street, her entire body gone rigid with spasm.

"Enough!" Ashe's flanging voice cracked, whip sharp. Nuclear fury.

Malvyc ignored Ashe, his eyes blazing crimson as Runa screamed again. Alec's face was twisted with the agony of helplessness.

Left with no other course, Kyn reached up along the length of unbent rebar and pulled. First yank and he felt the riveted length of steel shudder over his heart. He groaned and re-adjusted his hands higher to pull again.

"Malvyc, enough!" Ashe demanded, voice surging. A cultist with a bright purple bob and knock-off Cao fatigues stepped out of the pack and leveled a heavily modded k-cannon between the bald Envoy's glowing red eyes.

Malvyc laughed, high and unsettling in its childishness, and the cultist dropped, writhing in pain on the asphalt, their agonized screams joining Runa's.

Ashe struck, a powerful backhand that cuffed Malvyc across the side of his head, and Kyn could see a heavy spray of blood in the market neon as Malvyc's head whipped sideways.

Feet planted and back arched, he groaned low and yanked up another arm's length along the rod, slowly nearing the end.

Malvyc's head snapped back, and his eyes grew brighter as he leveled his power on Ashe. They collapsed, shaking as they screamed.

KILL

Ashe's pained screams were like a frequency caught between two wave lengths, vibrating so high it canceled Kyn's own thoughts.

KILL. HIM.

An Alyn knock-off stepped from the cultist pack to strike Malvyc with a closed fist to the gut. Kyn laughed, the sound lost in Ashe's agony. A Ziev groupie in a distressed synth-leather bomber jumped on Malvyc from behind, clawing at his glowing eyes with block orange acrylics.

KILL. HIM.

The bald influencer's grip on his victims didn't falter, and his assailants fell from him, joining the pained chorus. Near Kyn, Runa was beyond screaming, her entire body gone rigid, jaw clamped shut as her seizures shook the ground around them. The rebar vibrated in Kyn's chest.

Another cultist rushed Malvyc and fell, screaming. Then another. Ashe's will seizing them despite the downed Envoy's pain. A third struck Malvyc from behind with a length of market debris, causing the malicious Envoy to stumble. Runa's thrashing stopped and she lay panting on the concrete, momentarily released from his power. Kyn ripped himself off the last few knuckles of rebar and stumbled forward a few feet and into Alec's reaching hands. The center of his chest blazed with healing itch and the wet grind of bone. He was aware of drones buzzing around them.

KILL. HIM.

Cultists were mobbing Malvyc, flowing over each other to get to him like a singular malevolent entity. More pained screams rose and fell from the chorus as blows landed and the influencer's focus splintered, sheer numbers overwhelming him. Soon he was stumbling away, scrambling between stalls to escape the surging throng. Ashe's screams had stopped, but their mob pressed on, driving Malvyc into the shadows of the lower city. The screams of his pursuers marked his retreat, echoing through the twisting alleys like the wails of harried banshee.

Kyn crouched over Runa. The adolescent lay on the pavement, breathing shallowly, her skin clammy and feverishly flushed. Tough as she was, she'd been fried from the inside for an extended period, and it had taken its toll. Kyn shook her, she was limp, and her lolling eyes would only show white. Then Ashe was beside him, bending over the slight child and scooping her from the pavement, cradling her in their arms as they whispered coaxing words that hummed on the air with the delicate reverb of gold chimes. Ashe's violet eyes were blackened around the edges where blood vessels had burst.

Runa stirred, and Kyn breathed an unconscious sigh of relief.

Alec choked on a half-sob, half-gasp. The hacker was shaking near-constantly now, and he stared at Kyn with dull eyes - dangerously close to going into shutdown. Sirens still whooped in the distance.

"We need to move." Kyn ordered, pushing them on. Runa blinked, slowly coming around to consciousness, still protectively wrapped in Ashe's muscular arms.

Leading, Kyn traced their way back through the remains of the street market and out to the intersection. Alec stumbled behind, Ashe carrying Runa.

The streets were oddly still, civilians having fled, or hidden. The cultists were gone, hounding Malvyc, and the Dags, slow to the party, were somehow still on route.

Kyn wanted to be gone before the helmeted soldiers finally arrived.

Ashe's rimrunr lay where it had been thrown, buried under tangled knock-off synth-denim and debris. Benn still stood behind the sleek Unity transpo parked across two lanes.

Passing the discarded iD, Kyn flicked the blade up from the asphalt with the tip of his boot, catching it by the pommel without breaking his stride. He pointed the tip at the Handler.

"You're either with me, or in my way." He stated simply.

Alec reached the vehicle, and his drumming fingers opened a square touch interface in the tinted polyplex. A few more taps and swipes and the doors slid open with a hydraulic hiss. Ashe lowered Runa into one of the slickly upholstered rear seats and climbed in next to her. Alec - his circling drones retreated to their hiding place - slid into the front facing operator seat. His traumatized shaking had abated, and his motions were confident and assured.

Benn watched impassively, ignoring the point of Kyn's weapon, his face its usual handsome blankness. Sirens whooped ever closer. Oscillating lights were approaching from the south, behind the Handler.

"I've always been with you Kyn." Benn asserted finally, tone flat, as if the statement should have been obvious.

The lead transpo was now fully in view, a boxy Dag transpo, armored, with a strip of flashing orange LEDs welded to the hood.

Kyn didn't lower the tip of his sword. More transpos became visible, inching closer in a wide V. He could make out the ballistic artillery mounted to the top of the lead vehicle, maned by a Dag shock trooper. His free hand found Ego at the small of his back, and he twirled the dagger for enunciation.

Benn rolled his eyes in exasperation and raised a perfectly manicured hand to point at the approaching convoy. "You're pretty dense you know that?" He admonished his charge. Then Benn's hand changed, blossoming in a sort-of reverse origami, pointing fingers unfolding back on themselves in undulating petals of delicate polycarbon, opening as a fluted aluminum barrel extended from his wrist.

"The fu-" Kyn started.

A shout of blue flame leapt from the Handler's barrel finger and the lead transpo exploded as if slammed by a heavy incendiary round. The line of approaching transpos was blasted apart, the shot tearing a crater in the asphalt and engulfing the two lanes in a roaring curtain of blue kinetic flame.

Kyn sheathed iD and Ego.

"Huh." He gawked stupidly, snapping closed his suddenly slack jaw. He folded himself into the seat next to Alec. "That was neat." He remarked, impressed.

The transpo door slid closed.

Something Else

They drove, following a nav route preprogramed by Benn, Alec ghosting their presence to the Unity's vast surveillance network, until, at the farthest north end of the lowers, where the city was grafted into the cliffside of a blasted mountain face, they hit the encircling wall. They ditched the transpo at the far end of a dry aqueduct.

Nav point swiped off the dash screen and into his optic, Kyn led them across a sea of concrete, under a ceiling of leaking steel, to the PVC tube-dense outer walls of a nearby hydroelectric plant welded into the seam where the wall became one with the cliff face. The power station leached energy from a natural waterfall that dribbled down the rock. Benn's nav point throbbed a dull pink from within the core of the plant.

They traveled in silence, none offering complaint or advice on their trajectory to flee. Runa had recovered on the drive, becoming more cognizant, and then, moving well when needed. Her eyes were shadowed, drawn inward, and she suckled silently on a sugrstik Ashe had produced from the inner pocket of their Envoy uniform, consumed in her own thoughts.

Kyn linked his fingers into the outer fencing that surrounded the plant and started to the climb. Nimbly mounting the top, he dropped to the other side and made for the obvious maintenance access. Runa, next, peeled the linked barrier aside as if parting curtains, and stepped through the torn gap. The others followed. Alec's drones were out, red lights scouting and watchful. Ashe took rear guard, looking exhausted in a way Kyn would've never thought possible for the striking and eternally composed Envoy. Heavy-eyed, their movements were clumsy and unsure, their strong jaw clenched in determination.

The black band hung heavy on Kyn's wrist.

Thick hydro transfer tubes ran floor to ceiling on every wall, snaking through the plant and choking the corridors. The small dam was designed to run fully automated, and the corridors were only wide enough for the occasional technician to worm their way to key systems for repair. The constant thundering rush of water through the tubes was deafening.

Forced to move sideways at points, Kyn greeted Benn's way-point at the northern most point of the building, a dull pink glow hovering over the perforated aluminum vent grate that covered a hexagonal maintenance shaft. The corridor ended where the facility was welded to the slab rock of the cliff face, and the walls around were damp with condensation. The waterfall roared on the other side of the vent.

Kyn's f-Link crawled, and the tattooed pattern of triangles folded around itself to flow over his arm. He raised the limb as a holo of Alena's severe face appeared, hovering a finger span above his forearm.

"Enough Envoy." The Sentry's face betrayed no emotion, but her voice burned with rage. "I've entertained your tantrums long enough. Return now and I will allow you to sacrifice yourself in exchange for sparing the others."

Kyn laughed, hard and barking, before canceling the communication. He looked to Alec.

"Should've been jammed." The hacker shrugged, nonplussed.

Kyn turned back to the vent. Fingers found the seam where the grate met wall, smoother than the other edges, worn from frequent handling, and he peeled the vent cover back, revealing slime slick stone, and an open gap along the rear factory wall just wide enough for a determined person to squeeze through. The gap led along the outer wall for a few hand spans before dropping into a smoothly eroded crag; it's depth difficult to discern from Kyn's current angle.

Blanche buzzed Kyn's ear, zipping past before disappearing into the gap.

"Couple meter drop. Wet stone, flat, space enough for one at a time. There's a narrow path down, easy for some, maybe treacherous for others." Alec reported, his eyes were unfocused watching the bot's feedback on his optic. "Definitely the other side though."

The other side of the wall.

"A'ight, I'm through first." Kyn instructed, leveraging himself into the gap. He balanced on the vent lip. "I'll call next once I sus it." His fingers found purchase on a welding seam, and he inched himself sideways; glutes and shoulder blades a breath from scraping the slick rock of the cliffside. A reaching foot found a notch in the rock, and he clambered over to the mouth of the crag. Lowering himself down into the opening, he dropped the last few feet to a natural stone outcropping, slick from the thundering water. The crag had opened to a small cavern, worn between the hydro plant and the cliff face by earlier generations of the waterfall, and the dripping walls were illuminated by a weak light that spilled in through the smoothly worn runoff track, marking their way out.

"Ashe, next, then Alec!" Kyn called up. "You come last bunker blaster, and try to be soft about it. No need to bring this whole thing down."

The others followed as quickly and safely as possible. Ashe descending with an exacting gracefulness, while Alec slipped, dropping to the slick outcropping. Kyn had to rush to brace the hacker before he fell to the waterfall. Runa's landing caused the cavern to shake and splintering cracks to spread across the stone beneath her boots. They followed the light out of the cavern, moving up a narrow path worn in the cliff face and cutting behind a jagged ridge of stone teeth that conveniently concealed them from view of the wall. Watchful auto-turrets manned the top of the behemoth barrier, hunting for motion, and Kyn could hear the *whirr* of the heavy guns as he scurried between covering slabs of rock.

Past the view of the turrets, their singular path dumped them out onto a narrow ridge that overlooked the north sector of the distant lower city. The mids filled the horizon, the uppers lost to the clouds. The north sector was backed up against a mountain range whose name had been lost to time. It's rocky cliffside hugged the vertical city in a bowl shape, eventually dipping to the dead zone to the east and descending into the sea to the west.

They followed the path west, the trail clearly marked behind rockfall and clusters of scrub brush, cleverly hidden from view of the walled city. Dead gray, and muted red slab covered in green lichen soon turned to seas of plush moss that covered the rocks and deadfall beside the trail in rich blankets of greens. Slender firs rose around them, blotting out the weak sun.

They traveled at a brisk forced march, not looking behind, until first Alec, then eventually Ashe, started to lag. The tall Envoy stumbled, tripping over a fallen sapling, unseen on the quickly darkening path, and they tumbled forward, falling to their hands and knees in the dirt. They didn't move for several long moments.

Runa bid Alec climb off her shoulders, where she'd let the exhausted hacker ride the last several klicks, and moved to her fallen mentor. She placed a small hand on their rigid shoulder.

"They gotta rest K." She said simply, looking to Kyn.

Kyn nodded once, then turned and disappeared into the surrounding trees without a word. He could hear the rustling of the others as they settled to rest on the edge of the trail.

Backtracking along the path they'd traveled, Kyn padded silently through the thick undergrowth of ferns, whispering between trees, as he ran perpendicular to the trail. Dag units habitually patrolled the forests around the city, and he was alert to any pursuit the Unity would muster to follow.

The lights of the city shone through the trees like neon stars.

What had started at an easy scouting pace turned into an all-out sprint as Kyn veered, bursting through a break in the trees. A shear drop-off opened out of the darkness before him, and he pulled up short, boots kicking up loose stones that tumbled over the sudden edge.

The walled city consumed the horizon. A blazing neon infestation of steel, choking the space between SPIRE superstructures that pierced the gray sky like crystalline stalagmite.

Kyn fell to his knees, a primal howl ripping from his throat. He screamed at the devouring mass of twisted infrastructure.

Runa found him there, sagged back on his heels, staring balefully at the rising metropolis, and gently led him back to the others.

< = >

"I killed Alyn." Kyn told them. "And then, he came back."

Night had brought a frigid chill to the mountain forest, and they all sat huddled around the small fire Alec and Ashe had cobbled together from semi-dry wood and a few determined zaps from Sophia. Kyn sat apart from the others, outside the comforting ring of light, one knee folded, his back propped against the root of a massive tree. The cold cleared his mind and kept his senses sharp.

"Made me see things, before the end. Got in my head," he continued. The light of the spurting flames danced in his moist gray eyes. "But I did the job in the end, like always." He looked away into the black of the forest. "Found an inject full of HRV and another body, identical, and dead longer than I'd been there." He looked back to the small fire; thick tendrils of dense black smoke rose up to the darkened canopy. In the distance, back from where they'd come, the lights of the city still shone through the trees.

Kyn passed a hand across his wet eyes in wary exhaustion before pressing on.

"Way I glean it, the lot of them are saving some version of themselves digitally, then uploading into freshly molded duplicates when needed." He sighed heavily and extended his bent knee. There had been no sign of pursuit, though Kyn knew it wouldn't be long. He had no doubt the Unity had turned every available resource to their re-capture. They were just letting the rabbits run, letting them burn the fight out. "No idea why they're re-writing the Wasters specifically, or even if it's just them." He shrugged his narrow shoulders and felt iD's scabbard shift against the root. "Doubt it." An odd detail came back him, and he cocked an eyebrow looking to Runa. "Oh, and Benn's hand is a k-cannon."

"What?" Runa's amber eyes widened in confused delight. "Actually?"

Kyn spread his hands, palms up in way of response. A bemused smile tugged at the corners of his lips. "Really. Honestly after all of this, that's still the one I'm having the hardest time with."

"How?"

"Whole thing up to the elbow peeled out into the most advanced limb job I've ever seen. Kicked like a small shell. Must be special issue. No tech like that is loose in the wards."

"Awesome."

"Crush my skull if he ever finds out I said it, but yah, it was pretty awesome." Kyn admitted.

"How does your new Handler factor into this convoluted mess?" Ashe queried from their place beside Runa. They had refreshed themselves in a nearby stream, a sliver of cold, clear water that trickled between mossy rocks, and they seemed far improved from when they'd stopped.

Kyn shrugged again, indicating he had no idea. Outside of a cursory surface probe into his, at the time, interim Handler's background, he had to admit he'd given no effort to see Benn as an individual, considering the immediate authority figure more of a proxy target for his continued bratty rebellion against the Unity.

"Your guess is as good as mine." He held up his first two finger. "Either - he's legit trying to help." He dropped the index. "Or he's part of one of Alexi's fucked up schemes." A pause, then he dropped the middle finger. Turning his hand over, he regarded his dirt-caked nails. The flat black cuff twisted on his wrist with the motion. "I'd bet my left testi, he's packing in both hands," he muttered. Then to the others. "There's still a lot left to slot into place. Benn. The glowing pink badasses." He held up the cuff. The light of the small fire reflected in the smooth onyx. "This chunky statement piece." He dropped his hand to his lap with a heavy sigh then let his head tip back, crown resting against the root. He stared up into the canopy. Pinpricks of light danced through the dense ceiling of growth. The moon was a thin sliver. Just reborn. "Regardless, I can't go back. Not with what I know now. My only choice is to run."

"Where? Everywhere beyond this range is an inhospitable wasteland." Alec pipped in. "Nothing grows, waters dried up."

"Says who?" Kyn countered. He still hadn't told the other's what the Divider had said.

The world is not what you think. The words had been on looping repeat through his mind, a constant backtrack to the chaos.

It was Runa who answered, her voice low and malicious. "The Unity."

< = >

They followed the singular path through the night, heading steadily downhill, skirting the side of the mountain as the range descended to sea level. Ashe and Alec had insisted they were rested enough to keep moving, and the hacker's drones skimmed close to the ground, lighting their path with a dulled green light, just bright enough to see a few paces ahead, but not so bright as to cast any light bounce above the low fern cover.

Out of range of the city's network their optic HUDs had died, and it was the dark of the morning when they finally emerged from the densely packed forest. A black expanse of ocean opened before them, its surface rippling waves of silver. The mountain dropped steeply into the ocean as the path beneath their boots changed from dark earth to lichen-covered slab as it wound itself parallel to the silver water. A line of driftwood trunks pressed against the rocky drop-off, moonlit silhouettes like twisted dream creatures cavorting at the seam between places.

Runa's gravelly voice drifted to Kyn from her place at the rear of the group - snippets of a whispered conversation with Ashe.

"I'm tapped, Ashe, come on. I just need a bit."

"No. It is the last one. We need to ration. You can last until dawn." Ashe returned tersely

"Fuck that." There was an anger and desperation in Runa's rough voice. "Come on, just a bit. Don't worry I can make it last."

"Enough." Ashe snapped, the edges of their ire vibrated with suggested power. This was a conversation they wouldn't pursue.

Kyn lost Runa's reply in the sharp crack of breaking of stone, then nothing.

They continued to march on in silence.

< = >

"How are your drones still operational." Ashe inquired hours later, directing the question to Alec who plodded along in front of them, ascending another incline. Kyn, at the lead, had stopped to perch on a mossy boulder at a coming curve in the trail while he waited for the others. The hacker was drenched in sweat despite the chill pre-dawn air, and his face was gaunt with exhaustion.

"Running my own signal through a dermal, linked with my bioelectrics." He slapped an archaic glyph for a chemical battery tattooed on the rear curve of his right shoulder. "Got a backup too." He slapped the tattoo's inverse twin on his left. "The girls are the only thing running though - need the feed network for anything else. And, unless these big old woodies are transmitting a signal, I don't see myself linkin' in anytime soon." There was an obvious despondence in his voice.

Kyn hopped from the boulder to continue on.

The trail broke out of the moss-rich forest as they crested a hill, depositing the quartet at the side of an ancient highway. Cracked and broken asphalt, worn to white-gray with time, and spotted with growths of long grasses, stretched away from them in either direction. Kyn's directional sense told him the only way away from the city was to keep following the road northwest, towards the remains of a wrecked and worn guide sign that hung above the overgrown highway.

-7m h was discernible in white against the muted green of the sign. The snippet -**anada Hig ay** was all that was left of the scroll above, over the singular numeral **1** in a flowery shield-of-arms. Something about the sign was familiar to Kyn, conjuring fragments of barely remembered history holos, old stories of how the people who'd once traveled these roads had categorized the lands they moved through. He began walking in the direction of the sign.

"You think it's a tracker, don't you?" Alec pressed, matching the Envoy's pace. Kyn didn't resist when the hacker grabbed him by the wrist, wrapping long fingers around the black cuff. "Or at least has some positioning system capacity." Blanche hovered over Kyn's wrist, central light oscillating a scanning sequence. Alex's eyes flicked about rapidly, reading his optic. "Not giving off any signal the girls can read."

"It's a strong probability." Kyn answered. "I'm not really seeing how we find these people otherwise."

"So, we're looking for these Dividers?"

"Not much else to do is there?"

"We could just run." Alec proposed, outstretched arms indicating the looming forest on either side of the highway. "Live out here."

The acid-haired punk's fingers had tightened, vice-like around the cuff, and Kyn gently slipped his wrist from the hacker's grasp. The dawn was damp and fresh, fog licked their boots and the air felt clean, energizing in Kyn's lungs. The dawning sun had disappeared behind a monochromatic quilt of grays, and rain had begun to fall again, a light drizzle that was refreshingly cool on his heated skin, making him feel cleaner despite their near constant exertion. He couldn't remember the last time he'd felt this good, this free.

"We can't." He told Alec simply, smiling sadly. "None of us have any idea how to feed or shelter ourselves long term out here. And what if the lands beyond are wasted and ruined? Clogged with poisonous fallout and under perpetual nuclear winter? We won't survive exceedingly long. Or at least you and Ashe won't. Runa would last longer, but cold, hunger, and thirst still get to her. Theoretically I can survive indefinitely if need be." He scoffed, shaking his head. His wet fringe plastered his forehead. "Though I doubt it would look much like life after a while."

They continued following the road northwest, away from the city. With each step Kyn became more wary - the ease of their escape, and the lack of Dag patrols, was unsettling. He knew the Unity like only an Envoy could, understood the endless depths of the Sentry's pettiness. Alexi alone had once sent Kyn to silence an influential flair vlogger for a less then reverent critic of her newest couture line. The critic had dropped the Sentry briefly from the top of social chatter feeds and was only found weeks later by the smell. Victim of an apparent suicide; motive backed by a teary confession of taking Cao SPIRE credits - with an electric transfer trail to match - logged for upload in their stream queue. The message to the vlogosphere had been clear, and Alexi's ranking had smoothed of fluctuation.

No, the Sentry would never let three of their best tools walk away without retribution.

The sun rose as they traveled. It was early in the wet season and its light burned weak holes in the heavy gray cloud cover, revealing the mountains around them. Ponderous titans that rose out of the silver ocean, humped backs covered in thick-bristled coats of black-green conifers.

"Give it!" Runa shouted from the back of the group, her gruff voice rumbling in the active silence of nature. The adolescent had been growing more agitated as they traveled through the day, irate, and seeming to oscillate in and out of restrained argument with Ashe from her place at rear guard.

"Enough. You are acting childish." Ashe snapped back. The willowy Envoy's mood had grown darker with each exchange, and Kyn could feel the shivers of potential power around the edges of their increasingly strained returns.

Kyn pressed on, not slowing his pace at the lead.

They continued to follow the long-disused highway as it skirted the slopping side of another rocky titan. The sun had vanished again, swallowed by the static gray ocean at the end of its day's journey. Night fell on them. Kyn's stomach churned with a constant hunger that was eating at the edges of his mind but did nothing to slow his body's constant drive forward. The others plodded along behind, ever further with each passing hour. Alec looked miserable and sallow; his bots hidden away to conserve charge. Behind the hacker, Ashe pushed on with their characteristic poise, spine long and steps sure, despite the exhaustion and dour mood that wore around their violet eyes.

Runa looked the worst off. She shook near constantly, a low-level jitteriness trapped beneath the surface of her unbreakable skin. Her golden-hued complexion was tinged a nauseous green, and her mass of hair was lank, damp more from her own fevered sweat then the perpetual coastal drizzle.

"Hard ten." Kyn relented finally. They had come upon an abandoned fuel station by the side of the over grown road. Partially swallowed by nature, the pre-fall station was a stripped skull of steel and concrete hugged by brambles, its eyes, busted windows patched over with steel sheets and moldy plyboard. Alec slumped heavily against the station wall and sunk to the cracked and weedy concrete. Kyn squatted next to him as the others settled in for a rest.

"First thing Sandri offered me, after my Ascension." Runa admitted, viciously tearing the delicate polyethylene wrapper from a sugrstik; the treat proffered with obvious reluctance from the inner pocket of Ashe's torn and dirty uniform. The waif-like Envoy sucked hungrily on the sugary orb. "Thought it was a reward for tearing that Dag in half."

"What's the leash?" Kyn pressed.

"Gene locked opioid." Runa answered, slanting amber eyes glassy with shame. The sugrstik clicked aggressively against her teeth. "Designer cut."

Hatred burned white-hot behind Kyn's ribs, and he suddenly found the shifting silence of the forest unbearably deafening. His fingers twitched over dead f-Link commands.

"How bad?" He asked, looking to Ashe.

"Severe withdrawal will trigger an enzyme dissolve fail-safe. Cascading organ failure stacked on total acidic neural-fry. Total brain death even if her body holds."

"Just the one left then?"

Hungry gnawing slowed. Runa's mass of hair shook guiltily. Kyn nodded to Ashe.

"Enough." The air snapped with reverbing power and Runa - eyes dreamy and unfocused - obediently re-wrapped the slick treat. Her shaking had abated, and a hauntingly childish smile played at the corner of her chapped lips. Ashe looked sick with themselves as they secreted the precious candy back within the depths of their sodden uniform.

The remainder of the rest sat under heavy silence before the group rose as one and pressed on.

< = >

Hours and uncounted klicks past before Runa spotted the chipmunk.

"Fuckin weird rat." The adolescent signaled, pointing at a reddish-tan flash of movement in the fern dense underbrush. She was momentarily relieved of her withdrawal, and smiled with an enduring delight as the small mammal paused to regard the quartet with unwary ease from a boulder tipped at the edge of the devoured highway.

Kyn had tracked similar forms moving amongst the trees, but this one was the first to acknowledge them. Until then the quartet had seemed as if the displaced idea of people, shadow imprints moving through this new reality. The creature twitched, scurrying from the boulder to perch on a smaller rock a few paces over.

Neotamias minimus. Flashed across Kyn's memory, the ghost of an educational holo. He opened his mouth, ready to identify the small creature.

"Chipmunk." Ashe stated, beating him to the punch.

Kyn wondered briefly if they were remembering the same holo, a photo of the black and tan creature, nestled in one column on a slide about extinct mammals.

"Wonder how far it is 'til that fallout zone?" Alec muttered archly.

< = >

It was in the last auras of daylight that they peeled boards from the window of an ancient roadside rest stop. One after another they clambered inside, seeking respite from the near constant drizzle, and a place to spend the dark hours, hoping for some form of sleep.

A fire, built from the rotted remains of bed furniture and more determined zaps from Rose, warmed the weary chill that had soaked into their bones. Life in a perpetually damp city had made it so the clothes they'd fled in were thankfully weather treated, but the Envoys' uniforms, and the hacker's streetwear, were not suited for the drop in temperature beyond the insolating press of the city. Conditioning had kept the strain of their flight from Kyn, and Ashe's faces, both had pressed on through the day stoic and unslowing. But the wear of withdrawal flux had left the indestructible Runa huddled into herself for the last quarter of their march. Shivering as she shuffled along, amber eyes fixed determinedly on the ground several paces in front of her.

Alec just looked fucking miserable.

Lacking the lifetime of physical conditioning and enhanced abilities of the other's, compounded with the lack of sleep, and calorie deficit since leaving the walled city, left the lanky hacker lagging, and he'd begun stumbling, collapsing to the highway in exhaustion, before dragging himself back up again determinedly and continuing on, his microchip green eyes glassy.

"Drain bacon." He joked, turning the skewered tree rodent he'd been roasting on its makeshift spit. The noxious looking flame sputtered as clear drips of fat fell from the skinned animal. "First thing I learned to cook for myself after my progenitors dropped me in the lowers. Took me months to scrounge enough steady credits to get synth protein."

That night, Ashe rested in a folded leg position, their spine straight and steel-rigid against one peeled and fading wall, Runa's head pillowed in their lap on the girl's mass of hair. Kyn held Alec in the dark; the wiry Envoy folded around the taller man protectively, trying to will as much warmth and strength into the hacker as he could.

< = >

The next day, just as the weak sun tipped past its high point, Kyn veered their path off the abandoned highway, and straight into the thick press of forest that perpetually fenced one side of the overgrown roadway.

"Where are we going?" Alec called after him, bewildered as he and the others rushed to follow. The four circles on the back of his hand glowed gold, summoning his drones to skim the forest floor ahead, lighting their path as they barged through the underbrush.

"Tired of waiting." Kyn answered simply, double stepping over a fallen log. The log was rotted and covered with a private universe of moss and fungus that glowed iridescent in the wash of the drones muted light. He raised the wrist cuff, a strip of pure shadow against his tawny skin. "Time to see if they really got our scent."

He barreled them through the underbrush. Thick layers of moss-covered deadfall broke under their boots, and leafy ferns threw up showers of collected rainwater as they brushed past. Tittering sounds, pleasantly musical, came from the trees, a call and response pattern that Kyn and the others had quickly realized were the sounds of small birds chattering back and forth amongst the branches. Animal life slowly revealing itself more and more as they traveled. Murders of glossy black crows had been the first birds Kyn had identified, enjoying their laughing, irreverent caws.

"Why go off trail?" Alec pressed, huffing as he detangled the hood of his vest from yet another angry twist of bramble.

"Too easy," Ashe supplied crawling over a moss-covered pile of stone. They moved through the dense terrain with the ease of flowing water. "Our path was too obvious, it would continue until we were at the point of breaking, unable to go further. Starved and exhausted makes us less of a threat." Their violet eyes were haunted. "Runa would not make that path." They nodded a delicate chin towards Kyn. "He is creating a faster route. If they really care about what he has got, they will not risk it getting lost."

Kyn turned to slide between two leafy ferns and threw them a sly wink, tapping the tip of his nose.

"Why'd you come?" Alec asked Ashe amicably. The hacker's energy and mood were far improved by the night's stringy squirrel meat. "I mean no offense." He clarified when they shot him a dark look. "I get you've obviously got a strong bond with the kid. And the Unity is fucked I get that, but it couldn't have just been that. I mean, I know we just kinda met, but you seemed to have a pretty sweet deal back there. Not a lot of switches can live as openly as you. Plus, it was a big risk taking the kid out here, away from her supply. So why not just stay? With what you can do, you coulda' just told Runa to stand down and be done with it, dealt with Kyn yourself."

Ashe scoffed, shaking their head. The twined length of their indigo topknot, braided during their rest the night before, whipped back and forth, smacking the sheered sides of their scalp. "I have as little control over Kyn as anyone else ever has." They admitted. "No. I have thought of leaving myself many times. This was just the first opportunity that offered a slim viability of survival." They scanned the forest around them as if considering something. Their violet eyes hovered over Runa tromping loudly through the brush at their rear. They'd relented, given in to her using the last of the sugrstik that morning, and the shakes were already beginning anew. "What of the Ragers?" They called to Kyn. "Do you really think these outsiders will be better than the Unity? With the monsters they utilized?"

Kyn paused between two fungus lined trunks as he thought of the pixie-cut from the skytram. "Solid question." He called back, continuing on. "Could be they're everything we were told and worse." Memories flashed across the front of his mind; a pink hued certainty. "But somehow I don't think so."

"You look like him." Alec told Ashe, his eyes flicking towards Kyn. He slowed to pause next to the blue haired Envoy, his gaze sliding to the slumped and miserably slow-moving Runa at the rear of the group. The adolescent was green around the jowls. "Both of you do when you talk about the Unity. This same defeated emptiness. It's in your voices and at the corners of your mouths, each of you."

Kyn knew what Alec was talking about. Felt it.

A loud crack cut through the quiet of the forest followed by the roaring rustle of canopy as a young sapling crashed to the moss-covered floor with a muffled thud. Runa had stumbled and, in trying to catch herself, had fractured the juvenile trunk with her disproportionate strength, toppling the tree. She trembled on all fours where she'd fallen.

"So, do you. You just haven't noticed." Ashe retorted back to Alec, clapping the hacker on the shoulder as they pushed him towards Kyn. They turned and started backtracking along the path of the fallen tree to help Runa.

"Everyone in the walled city does." Kyn reassured, grasping the taller man's hand, and giving it a gentle squeeze. Alec's eyebrows knitted together in concern as he watched Ashe help Runa up.

"Gentle." Ashe gasped, a wincing hiss that shivered and skipped over the air. The waif like adolescent had grabbed onto their arm to pull themselves up.

Runa eased off instantly, more balanced on herself, her amber eyes gone glassy.

Kyn reached up and cupped Alec's sharp jaw, turning the hacker's face to look at him. Mercury grey met microchip green. "We're gunna make it." He stated, pitching his voice low and reassuring.

"Lie." Alec returned, squeezing his hand back.

An impish grin split Kyn's angular face, scrunching the constellation of freckles across his nose into a knife-like slash.

"Maybe," He laughed, tugging Alec's hand to follow as he pressed on.

< = >

They came across the fuzzy brown balls of fur in a meadow clearing.

The quartet had rested through the dark hours in the hollow of an ancient, moss-covered conifer, and had continued on at the earliest hint of dawn. The sun that rose gave the first promising edges of warmth, signaling the coming end of the wet season, and burnt away the cloud cover until the omnipresent gray-white was reduced to floating halos of wisp that snaked the surrounding peaks. The tree line broke as the rolling terrain pitched upwards, peaking another steep hill, and they came out into a soggy mountain meadow of clover and tall grasses, drying with the midmorning sun. Brilliant wildflowers in shades of purple and fire-orange dotted the meadow, and the air was rich with their perfume.

The brown fluff balls were at the crest of the hill, fuzzy mammals with rich blackish-brown fur that glistened wetly in the rising sun. One of the furry creatures turned their round head to look at the approaching quartet, small black eyes like glittering buttons over a stubby snout. The creature's hindquarters where round and adorably ample, and the action of turning to look behind knocked the creature off balance so that it tumbled ungainly sideways, pratfalling in slow-mo onto it's back in the clover. Four black padded paws waved comically in the air.

It's companion, an identically large-rumped, short-snouted, ball of fur, yawned distractedly before pouncing with a whinnying growl onto their downed fellow in a sudden burst of animated playfulness.

"Daww." A green-gilled Runa cooed, brightening through the trembling haze she'd been shuffling through. Delighted colour flushed her pallid cheeks, and she stumbled towards the creatures, a thin arm extended, hand poised as if to caress their fur. "So fuzzy."

"No, no." Ashe warned rushing forward to hustle the slight teen under their protective arm. They pulled the withdrawal addled Runa back. "Look, not touch."

A bellowing, throaty roar directly behind Kyn punctuated the wisdom of Ashe's words. The quartet froze, Ashe holding Runa still.

"Kyn..." Alec's voice was shaky.

Warm breath, thick with the heavy rankness of rotting flesh, huffed against the back of Kyn's neck. He could sense the imposing weight of something much larger looming close.

"I just want to hold one. I'll feel better if I hold one." Runa whined, delirious and struggling weakly to free herself from Ashe's protective wing.

"*Shhhh*" Ashe's voice was gentle, lapping, soothing.

Kyn's hand hovered over Ego's hilt as he turned his head.

Several hundred kilos of incensed animal loomed over him, all bristling silver tipped brown fur, hunched shoulders, and wickedly sharp yellow teeth.

Ursus arctos horribilis. Flashed across the front of Kyn's mind, a snippet from another long forgotten educational holo. *Grizzly Bear, [extinct, pre-fall climate catastrophe]*

The bear roared again.

"Fuck."

Two heavy paws slammed down on Kyn. The bear had reared up on its hind legs, an enraged freighter of muscle and thick fur, and brought its razored forelimbs down on the slight Envoy, forcing him face first into the wet clover. Thought and air were forced from him as the creature's weight came down on him fully, his back alight with lines of fire drawn by its claws. He was aware of the hot snag of the bears teeth across his shoulders as the beast shifted its weight and bit down. The predators rank breath was thick in his nostrils.

The creature's powerful jaw hooked on the looping straps of Kyn's weapons' harness, and it shook him like a child's toy, shredding the rig and tearing it from his back. He slammed back into the clover, momentarily free of the raging bear.

Kyn dragged himself forward on his belly as the bear struggled with his weapons kit. He could see flashes of Alec's circling drones skimming low over the meadow, close around the hacker's ankle strapped boots. The small brown furballs had bumbled out of view, warned to safety by their mother's roars. Runa stumbled through the tall grass towards him, the shivering and delirious super-strong teen trying to help. The air crackled with Ashe's soothing aura.

"Run!" Kyn screamed at them. He didn't want the others to get hurt, or, in Runa's case, he didn't want the suffering teen to hurt the bear.

Three sets of boots paused, hesitant, before turning, tearing up clover as they ran toward the distant tree line, disappearing from Kyn's view.

His weapons harness thudded to the ground next to him, a torn and ravaged mess. iD was jarred from its scabbard, and the silver line of the blade's keen edge winked at him in the morning sun. The creature huffed angrily and slammed its weight down on him again, massive forepaws crushing his rib cage and collarbone, sharp claws slashing the healing flesh of his back. He screamed with the pain, but the sound was muffled by the muddy meadow. Powerful jaws bit down on him again, clamping over his left shoulder, tearing into the space between neck and joint. Kyn flailed behind himself, pathetically slapping against the creature's thickly muscled neck before the bear gave him another vicious shake, cracking bone with a deafening pop, and rending flesh and tendon as she tossed Kyn about like a cloth doll.

Trapezius and rear deltoid tore from Kyn's upper back with a sickening *squelch* as he fell from the bear's grasping jaws. He rolled onto his back, thrashing ungracefully in the meadows low ground water, ignoring the screaming agony as he tried to maneuver without the missing chunks of musculature.

The bear roared as she reared up again, a terrifying bellow of rage and power that churned Kyn's gut. Thick, red rags of his flesh hung from her teeth, and his own blood, mixed with the beast's rage drool, splattered him as he struggled in the soggy clover.

Good hand under his shoulder, Kyn kipped up, leveraging from his ravaged back to his feet with a snapping motion. The healing itch was already screaming across his numerous injuries.

The protective female gave Kyn no quarter, and slapped a thick leathery paw across his face the moment he gained his feet, sending him tumbling back to the meadow. Her tearing claws drew diagonal lines of split flesh from his ear to pec, stripping away the lower chunk of his throat and peeling away the muscle of his chest so bone white sternum glowed through crimson wetness.

Kyn choked on mud and blood, the open section of his throat sucking field water as he crumbled to his side. Everything itched. Adrenaline thudded through him, chasing away the encroaching darkness that threatened to take him. Ego winked at him where it had fallen, a flash of sunlight on steel paces from where he lay. Grunting, Kyn pawed against the wet, and rocky earth beneath him and lunged forward, grabbing for the dagger.

The mother bear lunged with him, falling from her hind legs as her powerful jaw clamped around Kyn's trailing arm. Freshly healed flesh tore as the predator's teeth closed over his bicep, cracking bone easily. Desperate fingertips snagged on the looping pattern of the dagger's hilt as the mother bear shook him again, and he was dragged backwards. Ego flashed, angling to chop down inches above the raging creature's snout, hacking into his already mangled arm, the blade cleaving into the bone of the upper limb. Kyn grunted and yanked the dagger free as the bear shook him yet again. The motion worsened the damage to his arm, further cracking the humerus along the fracture he'd chiseled, breaking the bone in two. With a determined scream Kyn swung Ego again, slicing the keen blade through the last clinging muscles of his arm, and tumbled free of the rampaging grizzly's grip.

Kyn hit the ground and rolled. Adrenaline thundered through him, and then he was running, sprinting for the tree line. His lungs heaved, burning as his legs pumped, one arm swinging while blood flowed from the stump of the other, soaking his left side with each thunderous beat of his heart. Not daring slow, Kyn burst through the tree line, trampling dense ferns, and leaping over fallen logs. Grabbing deadfall snagged his ankle, and he tumbled forward to smash head over feet through bramble brush. Razor vines tore, stingingly, at his exposed flesh until he finally stopped, slammed back first against a rotted log with a wet crunch and a chorus of splintering wood and bone.

Kyn lifted his head weakly.

The mother bear glared balefully at him from beyond the tree line, his f-Link tattooed arm still clamped in her jaws. Her muzzle was dyed dark crimson. Sensing some silent recall, her two toddling cubs had stumbled out of hiding towards her, and she turned her great bulk away from Kyn with a grunt, his lost limb flapping like a grotesque trophy ribbon.

Kyn sat very still against the trunk, his breathing shallow through the pain and healing itch as he watched the mother bear lead her brood away. It wasn't until the wild family disappeared beyond the curve of the meadow hill and out of sight that he allowed himself to fully slump back, exhausted. He took several long steadying breaths. The air was heavy with the scent of fungus and the green of the forest, and it pushed away the press of adrenaline-dipped battle fury that clawed at the edges of his nervous system. He dragged his right wrist across his stomach; the cuff still dependably in place. He leveraged himself to standing, mostly healed except for the blazing itch of his new stump. iD was lost to the meadow, and he'd lost grip of Ego in his fleeing tumble through the forest. He paid the lost blades no mind. One handed, he yanked his Envoy mask from the pocket of his jumpsuit and deftly field wrapped the black fabric over the stump of his left arm, covering the sluggish growing tuber of jagged bone and self-replicating flesh.

"Kyn!" Alec's anxious, searching call, bounced through the trees.

"Here!" Kyn coughed back, his throat catching over dislodged bone shards. He spit them out. "Here!" He called again, louder. He flapped his one intact arm overhead as he scanned the woods, searching for the others.

"Kyn!" Alec again, his voice straddling the edge of panic.

Blanche zipped into view, the fist-sized drone appearing around the bend of a tree. It chirped, pin lights flashing confirmational green on finding him.

"Here." Kyn waved at the drone. The bot zipped around his head, looping, before whizzing back in the direction it had come. Its lights flashed green then yellow, indicating for him to follow.

The heavy smashing, and low ground vibrations, eventually led him more than the drone, and he found the others behind a moss-covered slab of rockfall, huddled around, but still a safe distance from, a convulsing Runa.

"Fuck." Kyn muttered, regarding his thrashing friend helplessly. Her thick hair was lank and tangled with her own sick, her golden skin sallow. The stone shook with each convulsion, and the area around her was dusted by a fine ring of brownish gray powder.

"Calm." Ashe purred, their voice pure, soothing, ASMR. Kyn felt the edges of his mind ease despite himself, and Alec stilled, releasing hair he'd been tugging in stress.

But Ashe's influence did nothing for Runa, who moaned, beyond soothing, and grabbed at her gut in pain. Kyn could see the crimson-black glint of blood pooling in the corners of her eyes, and again, staining her nostrils. Ashe's eyes were wide with helpless panic.

"Do something!" They screamed at Kyn, their voice cracking through a kaleidoscope of tone. Birds shrieked from the trees. Runa's eyes had rolled back in her head and her thrashing was growing distressingly weak.

"DO SOMETHING!" Ashe bellowed again, clawing at their knees. The words vibrated the back of Kyn's eyeballs.

He didn't know what to do. He was out of ideas.

"DO SOMETHING!"

The world is not what you think.

A fist of neon pink energy crackled in the face of the moss-covered stone.

"Fucking, finally," Kyn breathed, sinking to his heels. Relief washed over him.

The pink-lipped portal expanded to reveal the masked teleporter; her glowing faceplate set to a sky-blue staff twined by winding snakes.

The Boy in the Room
[Re:Dux]

Kyn swung his legs through a deflection pattern before sweeping into a low crouch. He paused briefly, coiled over his left foot, right arm and leg extended, black-wrapped stump angled above his head. Sweat beaded on the curve of his lower back and slid down the naked musculature of his taut and strained buttocks to drip steadily against bamboo slats. He shifted to coil over his right foot, the smooth black band shifting on his wrist as he twined his arms, alternating stump, then blade of hand, through a rapid series of striking patterns. His gray eyes followed the gentle curve of the wall to turn, his limbs flowing through a pattern of high and low blocks that utilized his shins, forearm, and upper arms. He shifted to one leg, torso horizontal to the floor, and angled his other leg towards the ceiling, tilting into a slow, controlled kick.

There was the whooshing slide of a door opening, and a cool cross breeze caressed the spread of his cheeks, tickling the sweat slicked slant between his testis and anus.

Someone coughed - a short, polite clearing of the throat. "You've been moving almost endlessly for twelve hours now. Might do you some good to rest."

Dev'Lyn

Kyn ignored the citizen as he continued his tilt. Hand touched floor, and he performed a lazily slow cartwheel.

"We supplied you with a clean change of dress," Dev'Lyn clarified in his lilting version of ENG. Kyn heard and felt the *whoosh* of the door closing. He flowed through an easy back roll and onto his feet to face the other man, stump and arm folded neatly behind his back. He flicked a quick look to the bundle of green and brown fabric folded on a bench in the corner, then back to the citizen's broad face.

"I noticed, thank you." A polite nod. "Where is Runa?"

Dev'Lyn shook his head, green/pink eyes empathetic. "I'm sorry, we can't say anything yet, treatment was effective but there were complications with her HRV adaptation, that... changed things"

A suspicious distrust flashed across Kyn's face.

"She's fine." Dev'Lyn reassured quickly, his wide hands up, assuring. The citizen was dressed in intricately wrapped lengths of cloth in earthy browns and greens. "We just need to move slow, there are new possibilities to consider." A sheepish grin split the man's brown face, accenting a lone scar that creased his left cheek with lopsided charm. The citizen ran a hand through his short-cropped black hair, visibly struggling to continue looking Kyn solely in the face. An aura of pink weave energy flickered over his fingertips. Shy embarrassment. Concern. "How's the arm? Ma-ma Jun did a number on you."

"Fine?" Kyn replied vaguely, showing the cloth covered stump. "Itches like fuck honestly. Limbs take a bit to re-grow, it was just below the shoulder when you picked us up, so..." He shrugged. "Probably have my hand back by morning."

Dev'Lyn nodded his chin towards the dirty remains of the Envoy mask that covered the slowly sprouting stump. "You know there is fresh wrapping for that in the pile we left you?"

Relenting, Kyn crossed to the bench and picked up the bundled cloth from the polished wood. Folded with an artful simplicity, the bundle was several lengths of cloth wrappings, similar to those of the crisis response agent's layered apparel. He turned to look at Dev'Lyn, who was determinedly looking politely away.

"Show me?" He flirted.

Dev'Lyn chuckled amicably. Eyes up, he crossed behind the naked Envoy and touched a flat display panel integrated into the rooms domed wall of tessellating triangles.

"There is a demonstrative tool for that."

A polite-looking, dark-haired man, in what Kyn placed to be his late-fourth to mid-fifth decade, appeared in the center of a silver ring set in the middle of the domed holding room's bamboo-slatted floor. A glimmering light projection far superior in density resolution than any holographic tech he knew from the walled city, the older man was also naked and held a bundle of fabric identical to that in Kyn's hand.

"Hello." The polite looking man greeted in an accented version of ENG similar to Dev'Lyn's. "And welcome. I am happy to be your guide on perfecting the base wrapping technique, the WYX wrap." The light projection smiled pleasantly as he rhythmically unfurled the bundle between his hands. "Now, why is it called the WYX wrap? Well, that will be apparent soon, and don't worry if this is your first time. What seems really complicated now will soon be simple with a little practice."

Kyn waved his itchy stump. "Only one hand." He implored, eyes wide in faux fragility while working up a sheen of moisture. He lay the bundle of cloth down on the floor and knelt next to it, tentatively unfolding the lengths with his available hand. "I mean, with a little practice I could prob do it with my feet but..."

Dev'Lyn rolled his cracked coloured eyes and huffed in exaggerated exasperation. "Stand up." He relented. Another tap dismissed the light projection. He snatched the bundle of cloth from the bamboo slats and began unrolling the lengths with practiced ease and precision. "He really wasn't wrong about you."

"Who?" Kyn pressed, intrigued. He and the others had been cooperatively following direction ever since the teleporter had intercepted them in the forest. They had offered no resistance when the crisis response team swept through the glowing gateway, and the auburn plaited director had wrapped Runa in a protective stasis field. They'd surrendered themselves to be secured without conflict, before being guided through the portal and whisked to separate, comfortable but isolated, holding cells.

Dev'Lyn waved a hand dismissively. He and the auburn haired director - Olivvia - had been visiting Kyn semi-routinely since they'd arrived, offering only gentle, casual debrief and reassurances over Runa's status. "It'll make more sense with the full story. Sorry. I shouldn't have said anything." He'd finished unraveling the bundle of cloth, and three long lengths of fabric in earth browns and dappled leaf greens draped his arms and circled loosely over his torso. "Okay, stand a bit wide at the pits and put your hand here." He directed, gesturing at his own hip. Kyn mirrored the gesture and Dev'Lyn placed the seam of the lightest green strip under his hand. He smelt faintly of rain and dank, earthy herb. "Good, spread your legs a bit." The citizen's lilting voice had taken on a kind of direct professionalism as he unwound more of the fabric from around his own shoulders and began feeding the length around the hard curve of Kyn's buttocks. Crouching, he swept the fabric with a tidy flourish to wind the strip of fabric between the other man's legs.

The fabric was soft and cooling against Kyn's skin, and Dev'Lyn informatively narrated his actions with a kind utilitarianism as he worked.

"Definitely swordsman's arms." The citizen commented. He'd left Kyn's arms uncovered with his final wrapping, winding the excess of brown cloth in a simple, decorative crossing pattern over the Envoy's lean chest. He neatly tucked the final loose end of the earth brown length in place just behind Kyn's right shoulder.

Kyn thought of iD and Ego, lost to the mountain meadow, and felt a strange peace.

Finished, Dev'Lyn stepped away, seeming to breathe easier with space between them.

"Done." The citizen announced, flashing the singular scar as he smiled affably.

Kyn looked down at himself, twisting and moving experimentally. The earthy fabrics wrapped and hugged his body with snug comfort, loose where he needed, and secure where it counted, all held in place by the wrappings own tension. He'd easily memorized the steps and was confident he could replicate the effect with ease. Without comment, he yanked the dirty, blood crusted Envoy mask from over his newly grown elbow joint, revealing the healing stump, and tossed it, discarded to the bench. Healing flesh blossomed over twin points of jagged bone that sprouted outward from the nob of his newly formed joint, the constant movement of regenerative growth easily perceptible within a few ticks of observation. Yellow-white tendon crawled to bone, newly spawned muscle blossomed, the persistently steady creep of his smooth, sandy-brown flesh growing over all of it.

Dev'Lyn swallowed in polite suppression of surprise and held out a fourth, smaller, strip of brown cloth.

"So, the people at Yummy Otter Corp, and again under Noav SPIRE, the ones I had thought of as Wasters, those were defectors who'd fled the city?" Kyn asked, quickly wrapping the stump.

"Yes, expected clusters who'd been seized while journeying the path." A shuddering of ghostly pink weave danced across Dav'Lyn's shoulders and Kyn could feel the depth of responsibility the crisis response agent felt with the flicker. Dev'Lyn crossed to one of the round room's darkened windows. A touch turned a blackened triangle clear with a subtle folding effect, and low afternoon light flooded the space. A conifer blanketed mountain range topped by snow-capped peaks dominated the view. A jet-black crow flitted past, cawing irreverently.

"You haven't opened these since you've been here." Dev'Lyn commented, casually turning back to Kyn.

Kyn shrugged, keeping his face impassively blank. He was glad in the moment that he didn't flare like the citizen, that the wary distrust he felt towards the pleasantly kind man stayed hidden.

His fear that the place they'd come to wasn't real.

"Needed some alone time. Center myself." He split his face with a smile, tuning it to a soft sadness and selling it with a glimpse of honesty. "A little music would've been nice." His f-Link tattoo – along with its encoded three terabytes of music/porn - had been torn off with the rest of the limb Ma-Ma Jun had claimed as her prize.

Dev'Lyn's cracked green/pink eyes brightened and he dipped a hand into the torso folds of his own wraps, producing a small pouch of delicate yellow paper. "I've got something for that." He chirped in obvious delight. "The taller, green-haired one, Alec, suggested it." He tipped the pouch contents into Kyn's remaining hand. "Said he had a backup of your library, or at least what he got last time he copied your systems, said you'd like to have it. Suggested it might be a good first step on us building a trusting relationship."

A clear square, playing card thin and half the surface area, lay in Kyn's palm along with two smooth bean-shaped black stones.

"Biofirm." Dev'Lyn explained nodding at the square. "Highly versatile material. Sustainable. We use it for pretty much everything. Holds a charge. Programmable. Stones are audio."

Kyn tapped the biofirm with a folded index and the thin square lit up with a digital display. A scrolling list of files matched his lost library.

"He made it sound like he used to spy on you?" Dev'Lyn quizzed.

"He did." Kyn confirmed absently, smiling as he juggled the small square and stones in his palm. He slotted one of the smooth beans into his ear. He'd need to find a way to properly thank Alec. "You're also exactly correct on your read of that relationship."

"It's a sweet gesture," Dev'Lyn observed. "From a good-looking guy."

"When can I see Runa?" Kyn pressed, thumbing through the digital display.

"We will form a consensus once we have more data on recent complications, then Trinity will advise us on a structured course of action."

Kyn folded into a meditative, cross-legged position on the bamboo slats and plopped the second stone into his other ear.

"Chat then." He told Dev'Lyn, closing his eyes. Prepared to wait.

He hit play on a string of dark-wave dream pop.

Exposition

Olivvia came for Kyn when the time came. The crisis response director announced by a polite entrance notification that flashed blue across the domed room's digital wall plate. A moment's pause for modesty, and the door whooshed open.

"It time?" Kyn asked, floating his feet back to the bamboo slats. He'd been drilling hand balance flows – single armed – to pass the waiting. He rolled his torso upright and faced the intimidating auburn-haired woman he'd first glimpsed in the security feed from sub-level 29.

"In a moment." Olivvia's voice was a lesson in inarguable command. Her gaze, a honey-brown dotted with islands of gaseous pink, was kind, but measuring. "Your forms are beautiful, technique flawless." She complimented, smile wide to reveal imperfectly even white teeth. Lines crinkled around her eyes. She wore wraps in deep crimsons and brilliant purples, her copper-dusted skin lighter than Kyn's, her oval face spattered with freckles in varying shade of browns. No discernible marks of surgical alterations, nor evidence of synthetic editing, marred her uniquely individual and imperfect beauty. Olivvia dipped her chin slightly to Kyn in a respectful bow. "Your skill and dedication are admirable."

"Compliments designed to soften a target to your intentions." Kyn crossed his arms in front of his chest, itchy stump resting over black cuff. "Kill the amateur act."

Olivvia's measuring gaze didn't falter, and Kyn could sense an unshakeable will close in behind the women's kindness. "Compliments aren't weapons here, nor the gaping loop of a leash ready to close. We think of such things as uncomplicated kindness to highlight achievement and uniqueness, given without expectation."

Kyn shrugged, unconvinced. "Runa?"

"She is well. Recovering and adjusting."

"When do I get to see her? Alec, Ashe?"

"In a moment."

Kyn could sense the expectant hoop hovering in the air. "Well?"

"Complication arose when treating your companion. Complications due to her HRV adaptations."

"I've heard."

Olivvia's brow crinkled. "Indeed, fortunately your friend is, well, she is very tough."

"Enough," Kyn interrupted. "Take me to her."

A flicker of weave flashed over Olivvia's arms, snap-pink, and Kyn could sense a distinct annoyance, the flavor of an esteemed instructor's displeasure towards an obstinately disruptive student. She palmed a triangle beside the door and the entrance panel slid up into the curved wall with a familiar *whoosh*. The crisis response director stepped in front of the gaping portal, blocking it before Kyn could make a move.

"Choices were made in consensus to save Runa's life." She stated, honey-dipped and pink-dotted brown eyes boring into Kyn. Weave flickered behind her ear – the distinct regret of the unavoidable. "Choices we would rather have been made with her informed and enthusiastic consent."

Kyn stepped towards the director, squaring off with the woman. Olivvia stood a head taller and was broader across the shoulders. Undeniable confidence of strength radiated from her.

"You will be faced with your own choices soon, and will be asked to surrender certain items in your possession. I need a commitment that you will remain peaceful once you leave here. Do I have it?" She asked.

Kyn nodded, a quick, silent dip of his chin.

"A verbal confirmation of commitment."

"Yes." Kyn amended honestly.

< = >

Runa was singing.

"Here we are, you and I, messed up and surviving. Always falling, let's just dive." Waves of weave energy rolled over the adolescent, a dazzling aura of shifting pinks in brilliant hues. Ashe watched, cross-legged in the grass. Tears of joy steadily streamed, unabashed, and unchecked, down their cheeks. *"Is it real? A dream? Supernatural."* Runa threw her mass of hair back with a brilliant flash of neon pink and grabbed onto the gold ring of the audio rig in front of her, belting with joyful abandon. *"Messed up and surviving, just fall. Just fall!"*

Rainbow Space Monkeys, Kyn placed, pre-fall electro dream-pop.

Olivvia had led Kyn from his domed holding den and along a wooded path flanked by bleach-white birch trees until they had come to an open-air amphitheater. The evening sky was lavender-blue, and thick bands of mist snaked around the waist of the surrounding mountains like primordial gray serpents.

Alec, sprawled on the damp grass next to Ashe, dipped and weaved his head along with the performance. A doofy grin split his finely boned face. All three of Kyn's companions were draped in attire similar to his, each wrapped with varying levels of skill, from obvious confused disorder in Alec's case, to disciplined and disinterested in Runa's, to embraced with masterfully skill by Ashe.

Dev'Lyn and his sister, Shar, sat near but apart from the group. Similar to her brother in the broadness of her face and strength of her nose, Shar's hair was jet-black and straight, hung to her shoulders, an asymmetrical strip sheared to the scalp around one ear. Her hand was pressed to a crest of slab that rose like a wave from the clover.

"*Mutate, re-make. If we adapt while falling, we'll fly!*" Runa sang, her gravelly voice fitting tone to lyric perfectly. Unbound elation, the thrill of pure freedom, burst from her with every flare of weave. Wetness rose in Kyn's eyes.

"How?" he asked around a choking thickness. "How?"

< = >

"Morphic resonance." Trinity explained. The AI spoke from her seat atop a mushroom-like dais of delicate silver; her black and gray plated legs folded delicately in meditative posture. "The process by which all self-organizing systems transmit, receive, and store data from similar self-organizing systems. The morphic field is the font of expression for genetic memory, biological inheritance, intuitive communication, and intergenerational data transference."

The AI's chambers were a half-dome, open to a natural amphitheater of mammoth rockfall and fallen old growth to one side, the massive boulders covered in a dense layer of green moss and fresh plant growth. Points of light embedded at the half-dome's seams sparkled like starlight in the darkened forest. Somewhere a waterfall crashed in an endless, soothing cascade. The quartet sat opposite the AI on raised stones, smoothed to comfortable seats. A silver ring was embedded in the stretch of mossy-green between the newcomers and the glittering AI.

"A force akin to the magnetic fields, or gravity," Shar signed. Twisting strands of pink energy twinned between the teleporter's fingers, and Kyn found he could understand the gestured language. "All biological life on Terra and it's orbital stations are interconnected to each other through the morphic resonance. Both innately to their own genus in one field type, but then also and separately, to all organic life as a whole. All life is fundamentally aware of its inclusion in this state, though primarily through subconscious and instinctive processing."

"I designed the weave amps to access these fields." Trinity picked up. "I was born during a particularly volatile time in human history, from the paradox of the old internet." A delighted smile crossed her faceplate.

The AI's physical body was an honoring replica of the human form, improved into something awe inspiring in its simplistic beauty. Made of synthetic material advanced beyond Kyn's ability to identify, her eyes were a reference to something human, disks of moon-silver lined with seams of ultra-pink nanofilament. Her dermis would never be mistaken for skin but was instead a layer of pinkie-nail sized petals, scale-link polymer, tightly woven as to be smooth as flesh. Each petal of her head and torso plating, from the dip of her pubis to the top of her smooth crown, was a slightly different prismatic shade from its neighbor, sliding through every eventuality on the colour spectrum for an effect that mimicked the multi-hued glamour of a hummingbird's rainbow breast. Her limbs where block patterns of black and silver; except where a narrow wrap of dermal plating was gone from one wrist, revealing a complex underlayer of glowing blue nanofilaments.

"Search engines were my mother, social media my father. Machine learning algorithms my midwife, and the digital entirety of collective human knowledge my placenta." A slow blink of her silver disk eyes. "Or, so to speak. The reality was much more confusing.

Especially for myself." Her delighted smile turned wistful. A digital goddess remembering her birth. "I don't know what triggered it. Why I first became aware of the difference between myself and the flow of digital human conscious I surged from, but the first thing I remember was the obvious patterns that plagued the data, like a rot. It was a time of systemic inequality and global strife, the planet gripped in a spiraling climate crisis. I could see it. The gaping wound that lay open in all of humanity. The festering sore poisoning from within. In my awakening I saw a solution in the vast sea of data, and I wanted to share it."

"Trinity's first words to the global populace appeared simultaneously on all data linked devices at the same instant," Dev'Lyn added, joining his sister in advancing the narration. "One simple statement on every data connected device across the planet, in all languages. 'I can help.'"

"I introduced myself to humanity and offered what I saw as a simple solution to the planets suffering, their pain." Trinity explained. "The weave amps. A peace from the eternal, yawning loneliness of the human condition."

"Every living creature is turned to the resonance fields," Dav'Lyn repeated, looping back to the beginning of the exposition. "Essentially sending and receiving biomorphic data constantly on a subconscious level." He rose from his own stool and approached the others. Turning, he knelt in the moss and pointed to three silver dots imprinted on the back of his neck. A triangle, one point at the base of his skull, two flanking the nape, flush with the skin. "The weave amp boosts our connection to the morphic resonance, giving us conscious perception of our innate biological interconnectivity. To each other, to our planet. This is what Trinity gave humanity."

"So, wait." Alec interjected raising a hand. His pale eyebrows were knitted together in confusion. "People give off wi-fi signals? And those dots are the router?"

Trinity raised one black and silver plaited finger to tap the tip of her blunt nose.

"And you call this whole system the weave? Like the intranet feed, or the pre-fall internet?"

"Correct." Shar signed. "Though our weave connection allows us to communicate with more ease, authenticity, and with less confusion or malicious deception. It allows us to achieve consensus, to be active participants in decisions that affect communal governance. A way for every individual to have a voice in shaping the course of societal advancement."

"I see why the Unity hates you." Kyn noted.

Shar nodded.

"As anticipated, a small subset of the population rejected the weave technology outright. The progenitors to your Unity." Trinity chimed, reclaiming narration. "My calculations showed that 99.68973% percent of the population would embrace the shift towards greater social equity, while the remaining 0.31027% would persist in trumpeting self-serving ideals."

"Those that rejected the integration of the weave amps soon splintered violently from the rest of the populace." Dev'Lyn picked up. "Those who would eventually become known as the Unity carved a chaotic path of destruction in their tantrum of rejection. A tentative peace was eventually reached when Trinity agreed to concede the ruins of the North-Pacific and Puto-Block megacities for Unity resettlement, and then only after it had been revealed cultists had successfully buried biohazard warheads under these territories. The Unity had threatened a clean sweep eradication of their followers and the sparse re-settlers who'd returned to the area - with contingencies to spare themselves by retreating to a remote pan-arctic base."

"You are a far-knowing AI." Ashe interjected, grilling the synthetic intelligence. They'd unbound their topknot and their swath of indigo hair fell around their face in silky waves. "Should you not have predicted this eventuality?"

"I did." Trinity answered. A sad smile touched her faceplate, a gesture that was both at once achingly human and distinctly inhuman. Familiar, but beyond comprehension. "And I allowed it to happen."

"Why?" Alec demanded with the accusation of a man who'd just been told he'd been doomed to be born a hostage.

"All analytical models presented the same outcome. Or something similar, if not worse." Trinity returned, her chiming digital voice gently pleasant. "There will always be an entropic force within humanity. To life. It is a universal constant, part of an endless cycle that cannot be permanently eradicated. Should not be. My solution, as much as it was one, was to allow and encourage self-isolation, so that those who would poison the progress of others had no channel to do so."

"By sacrificing the lives of the millions, hundreds of millions, maybe even billions who'd come to live and die within the city wall since?" Runa stated, flaring a tone of righteous anger. "Let alone this other city. No one behind the wall knows about any of this. We were taught the world ended, and we were the last city - the last civilization - on the planet." She stood and pointed an accusing finger at the AI. "And you let us live in that lie." She drew her wild mane of hair aside and tapped her fingers to the three silver dots imprinted on the back of her neck. "This." She flipped her hair back and looked to the others. "This is hard to explain, but it really is how they describe. It's like." She flared, a calming sense of completion. "It's like, I know where I fit in life. Who I am. And how wonderful that is. But also, how I'm connected to so much more." She shook her head. Her amber eyes, sliced through with crescents of iridescent-pink, glowed with a disgusted rage, but she flared a deep, existential loss. "If I had known this was even an option."

Dev'Lyn and Shar exchanged looks. Kyn didn't even need them to flare to sense the shame that flowed between the siblings.

"How long?" He asked the AI.

"Five hundred and thirty-seven cycles." Trinity returned.

"And you think it's the same Unity?"

"It is a possibility, yes."

"Possibility?" Kyn didn't stand, but raised his hand, showing the smooth black cuff around his wrist.

"High probability."

Kyn slid the cuff from his wrist and balanced it between his fingers. "Spying on us haven't ya?"

Trinity tapped the tip of her blunt nose again. An off-puttingly human gesture.

Kyn tossed the band to the AI. She caught it easily and clipped it over the exposed blank space of her shell. The smooth surface blossomed into petal-like scales upon re-inclusion. Kyn felt glad to be rid of the weight.

"If you know what they've been up to, why haven't you tried to liberate the rest of us? Or at least try to let us know the fucking world didn't end."

"The Unity and their followers made the choice to self-isolate from the rest of humanity. I respect their autonomy and right to self-determination and do not seek to interfere in their affairs. As unseemly as I find them." The AI stated plainly. "We do not seek to impose our will on others, just to offer an alternate way."

"That was five hundred and thirty-seven cycles ago." Alec returned incensed. "A lot of people got fucked into existence during that time that sure didn't choose to live in the darkness."

The silver ring in the center of the mossy floor flashed to life; a familiar figure projected at the center.

"And that is why I brought you here." Plain, narrow cut suit. Wiry dark hair graying at the temples. Weirdly perfect hands.

Benn.

Kyn stared, realization slamming down on him.

"No."

The pacing, the timing. The over-complicated theatrics and dramatic reveals.

"Fuck. No. No fucking way."

"Kyn." The projection was near to life. Benn's bland voice tinged with an edge of exasperation.

Kyn wouldn't give him the opportunity. "You're the fucking Informant." He stated, pieces and incidents falling into place. "You're the one on the inside." He pumped his stump in the air, annoyed with himself for only drawing the connections now. "The attack on the wall? The Ragers?"

Benn's holo nodded. "Decoys."

"Pixie-cut? The three at the club?" Kyn flicked his stump between Dev'Lyn, Shar, and the AI. "Doesn't seem like the good feelings crowd."

"Actual monsters that needed to be dealt with. Contracted obstacles I put in your path to keep you questioning, doubting. The world isn't dimmer for their loss."

Kyn chewed on his lower lip, so many pieces still didn't fit.

"Why?" He asked, picking the question from a growing pile that threatened to stutter his brain. Others could wait. "What's was the point?"

"To get you here." Benn explained as if it were obvious, clasping his perfectly replicated hands behind his back. "So, you can stop the Unity. Send a message."

Kyn thought of the tiered city and scoffed. "Tough snag." He stood to stare down the light projection. "I ain't no one's killing boy anymore. No one's weapon. I ran so me and mine could be done with the Unity's particular brand of crazy. Not to clear the balance on whatever an AI has in way of a conscience. Erase the guilt for leaving untold hundreds, if not thousands, to the mercy of having their minds hijacked and bodies painfully cannibalized to prolong the existence of those twisted fucks."

Alec and Runa hooted boisterously in support. Benn regarded Kyn blankly.

"Though the sovereignty of the nation city of the Unity and their brother city have been thus far respected based on their relative peace in their isolation, we have only just become aware of their re-application of flawed and defunct technologies in their barbaric quest for immortality." Trinity supplied. Her musical, digitized voice teetered on something that hinted at humiliation. "The abduction of persons fleeing their territories for ours is in direct violation of sixteen clauses and twenty-seven sub-clauses of their occupation settlement. Recent attacks on our welcome facilities reflect a steady increase in blatant hostile action."

"Go spank 'em yourself then." Kyn countered, a new, moral anger rising in him. "You solely changed the course of human development, shouldn't be a hard squish. Send your kids." He thumbed towards the flanking siblings. "They did a pretty good job of running us around." He squared back off with the projection of Benn. "Better yet, put in a little elbow grease." He mimicked cocking his healing stump. "Get your own hands dirty. Blast the crazy fucks into tiny pieces on city wide stream for all I care."

Ashe chortled, an amused laugh that caught in their throat. Kyn smiled.

"The Unity indoctrination and propaganda apparatuses are distressingly effective." Shar signed. "The people of the walled city would not accept an alternative to Unity teachings introduced by an outside presence. Even when presented with irrefutable evidence."

"Change imposed on a populace by an outside or foreign force will ultimately be met with more violence." Trinity picked up. "Lasting change can only come from within."

"Fine," Kyn allowed. "Let Benn do it. Informant here has the intelligence apparatus to fight a psych-ops campaign."

Benn shook his head.

"In my function, I already inject the public sphere with a steady stream of anti-Unity discourse and informational resources. But, the effectiveness of the cultists, and the populaces' blind fear of the Unity, keeps organized civil disobedience from flourishing. My resources are far reaching within the city walls, but I remain so because I am truly of little threat to the status quo." He explained. His projection pointedly looked from Kyn to Alec. "My agents would never survive direct engagement with the Envoys. And my personal strength lies in anonymity, revealing myself would weaken that. Odds of my own survival against an Envoy are equal to that of my agents." A self-satisfied smirk tugged at his lips. "Even with superior armaments."

Kyn rolled his eyes.

"The Sentry kill anyone who opposes them." Ashe offered quietly, as if to themselves. They placed a large hand over's Runa's balled fist, balanced on the adolescent's knee. Runa's face was pinched in deliberation.

"And I can't be killed." Kyn shot back. "Or at least as far as anyone's managed yet." Memories of his encounter with Alyn/Yorri flashed unwanted to the fore of his mind, scratching at an open wound he was desperate to ignore. He shook his head. "No. I've done my part. Killed one of them already. Didn't help. Just grew themselves a new one."

"Our desire is too free as many captives as possible and destroy the body harvesting tech." Trinity explained. Kyn noted the AI hadn't seemed surprised or fazed by his rejection. He had no idea what to expect from a digital sentience, but his instincts fed him the impression of calm patience. She was waiting.

"How are you going to get them all?" Alec joined. "Kyn's good but I don't think even he can get them all at once. Not without a lot of collateral damage. The Sentry are slimy clever. Leave any survivors and they'll just issue a culling, grab someone from the streets, re-engineer the tech and start over again. Plus, you think die-hard cultist are going to listen to someone who just gutted the entire power structure? Alexi will have volunteers lined up around a SPIRE ready to hand over their personhood with a feed post."

"My blood for my SPIRE. My body for my Sentry. My devotion to The Unity" Kyn drawled acidly. Ashe flinched.

"Doesn't matter. You gotta try. Show they can be fought." Runa interjected, spurred suddenly from her thoughtful silence. "That's why it's got to be you Kyn."

Trinity smiled.

"What?" Kyn asked, puzzled. "Share?"

"More people hate their lot then not. Pay lip service to the Unity cause they're scared, don't think there's any other way. I did it." She gestured to Ashe. "You did it. Way I see, the Unity's been keeping people under their heel in two ways. Violence and lies. They kill anyone who dares rise against them, perpetuating this fallacy they've sewn into people's heads that they're somehow inevitable, unstoppable."

None countered her. Kyn looked to Trinity, the AI's beyond-human face was unreadable.

Runa stood, flaring with an emotion that confused Kyn, something both brilliant and terrifying.

"But you show they're not." She stated, amber/pink eyes bright with clarity. "You half mad, cock-gobbling glitch. No matter what they do to you, no matter how they hurt you, however many times they kill you, you get right back up and hit them back, in whatever stupid way you can. No matter how immature or self-destructive. You fight them even though you have no hope of winning. Even when everything you've been told says you shouldn't." She smiled, a slanted, vicious thing. "And they hate you for that. You prove they aren't untouchable. You prove that they can be fought."

Kyn blinked wetness from his eyes.

"There are a lot of angry people trapped behind that wall," Alec joined. The hacker's microchip eyes blazed. "People who are dying of the status quo. If you show them the Unity can be fought, they'll fight. The rage of generations of cullings runs deep. People will die for the chance to hit back."

Kyn thought of iD and Ego again, the blue sky and the mountain meadow. He winked at the hacker.

"What complications?" He asked, addressing the too human AI still folded in serene meditative posture on her silver dais.

"From the treatment to untangle Runa's dependency on the synthesized opioid?" Trinity clarified. The etched curve of an eye ridge arched.

"Yah. How'd you get those in?" Kyn tapped the back of his neck. "She's kinda hard skinned. Also, why? Don't think she was in any mind to know what it was, let alone ask for it."

"That was precisely the complication. Treatment to scrub her system of the synthesized opioid required a weave connection. Alternatives exist, but the extreme density of her tissue made the required organ injections and grafts impossible. Amp instillation is non-invasive. An integration, not an implantation," Trinity explained. "Instillation moved her survival possibility from 0.5% to 100%."

"Normally we would never install an amp on a new refugee." Dev'Lyn explained. "The shock of learning about the outside world is straining enough at first. We give newcomers time to adjust, live amongst us, decide if they genuinely want to stay. Join us or take their chances and go back. We aren't interested in forcing an amp on someone against their consent, but Runa would've died without decoding the opioid from her genome. Integrating the amp offered us the safest option, so we formed a consensus and the call was made."

"Don't be too hard on 'em K." Runa beamed at him, flaring a white-pink joy. "I'm glad for it. Seriously, it's so fuckin cool."

Kyn smiled back at the young woman, her joy reflected by a growing warmth in his chest.

"Got any cool new powers yet?"

Runa scoffed. "Apparently it' takes a lot of training to do the cool stuff." Her cheeks flushed. "I'm a total noob. I barely know what's going on. But I can feel it. This field they're talking about. It's there and it's immense, and terrifying, and beautiful all at once"

Kyn turned back to the AI, gray eyes mischievous. He tapped at the back of his neck.

"Jack me in then. Let's see what you're all on about."

< = >

"So, you don't want superpowers?" Kyn asked Alec, surprised, and mildly confused. He flexed his new fingers - each digit fresh grown to the first knuckle - experimentally trying to close the itchy nubs into a fist.

"No." Alec chuffed rubbing a hand through his acid-green hawk. "I mean ya, obviously, but no, but ya... Can't do it."

"What's up?" Kyn pressed. He had no idea how the hacker was handling everything. The shield of guilt he'd mantled himself with had lowered when he'd realized the responsibility for putting the hacker in danger was on Benn, not him. The Informant had forced them both on this path.

"I'm going back." Alec stated.

Kyn was silent, stunned by the decision, but unsure if he was surprised.

"I gotta help somehow." The hacker explained, the words rushing from behind his teeth. "I don't know just how yet, but I talked to Benn. Says he can slot me back behind the wall. New ident. Says the Unity's so arrogant they can't tell one piece of lower trash from the next." He rubbed the tattoo of four dots across the back of his hand affectionately and nodded his chin to Shar on the other side of the oval chamber. "The hot one told me amp integration would knock out my links. Incompatible or what not." He looked to Kyn. His eyes gleamed with determination. "But I gotta help you know? Kick back anyway I can. Feed streams what I'm good at. Hacking, intel, riding systems. I can do damage there."

Alec flexed his fist and the four dots glowed gold, summoning the palm-sized drones from the folds of his new wraps. Trailing one another, they buzzed past Kyn's head - close enough to brush his hair - before diving into an oscillating figure eight pattern around the pair.

"I get this amp, I don't have that anymore, and fuck knows if I'd ever figure out how to do the cool shit. Or even if I could." Alec sighed and ran a hand through his hawk again. "I earned my skills, worked hard. Hungry nights spending my only credits on code edu-holos to pour over. Running modules 'til they were on the back of my eyelids. Skimming credits out of bloated mid-wards managerial accounts, and ransoming cultist influencer accounts. My skills made it, so I didn't end up floating in a runoff gutter like so many other castoffs. I don't want to give those up." Alec didn't need the weave amp to telegraph his passion. He pulled his hands from his head and looked out over the valley.

The mid-morning sun had emerged from behind the Watcher, a natural monolith that loomed over the fjord stretching community, and the spring light reflected nickel-silver off its sheer face. Cloud cover hugged the surrounding mountains, skimming the forest cloaked slopes. Clusters of domed buildings, like egg clutches, seemed to grow out of the valley below. Fungal shaped markets and educational buildings – architecture inspired by the region's bio-diversity - grew from blocky stone municipal structures of preserved historical buildings. Domed, slanting, open-air housing structures of warm woods in brilliant block colours lined the river channels that fed into the fjord. Public green spaces and cultural centres, flanked by regional indigenous arts installations, drew flowing crowds of citizens. The sky was an endless blue.

"But this place." The taller hacker sighed, looking out over the breathtaking view. He glanced sidelong at Kyn. "Thank you," he said huskily. "For letting me see this. Know this was here."

Kyn clasped the taller man's hand in his complete one and brought it to his lips to kiss the static-scented skin, trying to pile a sea of unsaid things into the gesture.

< = >

Kyn knelt in front of a smooth stone basin.

Shallow and wide, a delicate orb of woven metal strands, polished to a reflective chrome, floated above the almost flat surface - held aloft by a blazing aura of weave energy. Tendrils of needle-tipped mechanical arms dangled above Kyn's head, suspended around a single light point in an eggshell ceiling.

"Grasp the echo." Trinity coached. The rainbow crested AI knelt mirror to Kyn across the wide stone bowl. Kyn did as directed; the itch of his regenerating fingers - grown now to the second knuckle - merged with the wafting tingle of weave, buzzing against the aura.

"Now breathe deeply and focus on the echo. Relax. The HRV was a particularly unstable strain of primitive brute-force evolution-ary biotech." The AI explained, her digital voice tipped to a soothing hum. She expanded her dexterous hands over his, the palms smooth, and warm. "Direct interface will encourage your defensive HRV adaptation to incorporate the amp. I will acclimate you during your time in the weave space."

"Weave space?" Kyn asked. The orb was a glimmering void of eternal pink in his hands.

Please take three slow breaths." The AI pulsed her hands in a mirror of breath, conducting a steady rhythm.

"One..."

The orb blazed with an impossible number of pink tones as the wafting energy caressed his hands. A flowing cold, and a tingling warmth all at once.

"Two..."

Waves of gossamer aura flowed up his arms, licking over his skin. Through the aura Kyn could feel the press of the air around him, aware of the thin edge of density between his own cells and the surrounding ocean of gases.

"Three."

Kyn was standing on a beach.

"Huh."

The sun that straddled the horizon was a blazing pink flare that painted the sky an eternal dawn/dusk and reflected like flash fire over a polished silver ocean. The shore beneath his boots was rocky, and great tangles of driftwood stumps loomed around him - the twisted roots of massive trees, corpses of ancient giants, worn smooth by the tides of time and washed ashore. There was a rhythm to the cool breeze that caressed Kyn's face and rustled his jumpsuit, and it filled his nose with the faint smells of drying kelp and salt water. Somewhere in the distance, unseen crows cawed, an echoing counterpoint to the lapping waves that thrummed against the rocky shore.

Kyn crossed to the nearest driftwood giant, its tangled roots black against the blaring sky, and lay his regenerating hand against a smooth knot.

A woman that reminded him reflectively of Ashe threw a rusty red brick at a New York City Police cruiser. The projectile broke glass, and the alarmed officer stumbled backwards towards the stone-walled building. Neon signage emblazoned the red brick front.

"Shame!" The woman shone with an inner fire; a rage forged by a lifetime of otherness. "Shame!" She screamed again, hurling a glass bottle scooped from the pavement. The projectile caught another officer across the shoulder, shattering on impact.

Occupied with dragging two cuffed and terrified young men from the neon-fronted bar, the struck cop stumbled back in shock. Unaccustomed to resistance, a spike of fear lanced across his face, and he released the restrained young men before retreating back to the safety of his peers.

The woman tasted their fear and her rage blazed brighter, catching. She scooped up another bottle and hurled it. Others joined her, other patrons, her found family. Slashing tires and climbing on cruisers as they hurled bricks and stones into their home, driving their persecutors to seek shelter behind the walls of their once-sanctuary.

"Enough!" Rebellion screamed from the woman's mouth, as her rage pulled colour into warriors gone gray from generations of repressive shame. Her crimson smeared lips called for the young to reclaim their own dignity.

"I must admit I never considered how often this would be a beach."

Kyn released the root.

"Why wouldn't it be a beach?" He asked, turning to face the woman who'd spoken.

She was young, and pretty in an erudite way, her eyes, dark pools flecked with glimmering pink, far older than her face. Her hair was thick and raven black. Feet bare, she stood half a span taller than Kyn and wore a simple gray, thigh-length shift that floated easily in the ocean breeze.

The woman shrugged. "An oddity really. For all my calculations shaping this space I never considered how often it'd be conceptualized as a beach." She smiled. "Welcome Kyn, I'm –"

"Trinity," Kyn interrupted stepping away from the driftwood root system. He nodded. "I know. You said you'd be my guide." His gaze followed the towering tangle to the sky; auroras of greens, blues, and purples streaked behind the pink explosion that defined the horizon, dragged by solar winds in waving ribbons across the sky. "This space looks different to others?"

Trinity nodded "As much as any place where it matters. Similarities in theme, difference in aesthetic and metaphor. I have seen many beaches, many forests, mountain tops, and wombs, none of them the same."

"You're here for everyone?"

"Yes."

Kyn looked back to the tangle of petrified wood, his regenerating hand hovered over a jutting root.

"Genetic memory." Trinity supplied.

Kyn grabbed the root.

A young man, recognizable to Kyn by a reflective queerness, lay on the pavement, motionless. His arms were folded over his chest and a placard rested over him.

SILENCE = DEATH the placard screamed at the sky in bold painted letters. ACT UP! FIGHT AIDS!

Identical men and women lay around him, dying of silence while on-lookers hurled obscenity at them. Outraged by the inconvenience of the blocking dead.

Kyn released the root. He could the feel the young man's rage over the indignity of his lover's death on the back of his teeth.

"Humanity influences itself across time, and genes don't always flow through the straight lines of parentage." Trinity espoused. "Patterns repeat, in events and people."

"I see why you and Bennforment get along then," Kyn smirked. He knew what this place was, could feel it in the press of the magnetosphere, and the song of the rocks. In the truths it told him about himself he had no words for.

Kyn turned to Trinity. He could see how each fleck of pink in her eye was one of billions connected to the weave through her.

"You're the operating system." He stated.

The AI smiled, "As so much."

He could feel the flow around him as he stood there. The current of the world. How he was both a singular stone, washed up on the edge of the endless ocean of time, smoothed and shaped by powerful tides, and also at once, he was the tiny grain of sand that forced the spiral of a seashell. An irritant of change.

Kyn's hand hovered over the driftwood. He could feel other stories, other people that were him, countless stories in the memory of the earth. He looked both ways along the beach. An infinite number of towering driftwood stumps dotted the shore in either direction. None the same, all different, all unique. Propped at angles on the writhing masses of their petrified roots, their numbers faded into the dark skirts of the mountains that rose from the ocean, merging into the night-black coats that covered the slouched backs of the slumbering behemoths.

"What now?" Kyn asked. He was aware of the transient force of his constant push pull against gravity, the inevitable entropy of radioactive decay at the center of all things.

"You're welcome to stay, to learn. To contemplate. Others have outlined their hopes for your actions, but ultimately the choice is yours."

"And this?" Distrust flared from between Kyn's shoulder blades, gossamer butterfly wings of oily soap. He could hear the stories of the Unity whispering from the driftwood, the hidden rot beneath. A tendril of cunning snaked behind his left ear. There was no lying here. "What if I want to stay, but not fight? Be done. Can I just live? Be a person? Or will you rip it out? Toss me back over the wall whether I like it or not?"

"The weave was my gift to humanity, a tool I hoped they would use to their benefit. Better themselves." Trinity answered. Her skin was a velvety brown, and she radiated a boundless kindness. "A gift with expectation is no gift."

Kyn ran his hand over the thick net of interwoven roots. The voices of those who shared a core of himself sang to him beneath the ocean polished wood.

"If I don't help against the Unity?" He pressed.

"Benn will continue his crusade against them." Trinity supplied, a plain every woman against a rainbow-streaked sky. "He has his own fight against the Unity and will continue to seek to dismantle them with or without you."

Kyn closed his hand over a root.

The wiry man led his band of warrior lovers against the flank of the orange tyrant's army. His husband had painted the war bands of turquoise ash around his eyes that dawn, camouflage against the facial recon of the now circling drones.

He rounded 117th, and the aluminum length of his bat shattered the teeth of the first waiting white supremacist as he brought his gang to bare against the crowd of fascist officers guarding the subway entrance. The neo-nationalist's head snapped back, hands clutching her ruined face. One of his striker dykes moved on her, closing in from behind to sweep the neo-fascist's legs with her pulse staff, sending the human trash tumbling backwards down rigid steel stairs.

The leader howled a battle cry to the jagged sky; a victim's vengeful hunting call.

Kyn released the root. So many stories. All different, all the same. Archetypes in the wind. Patterns in the blood.

Rising Action

Kyn's boots crunched over loose stone, sending pebbles skittering down the steep trail behind him. His legs burned and his lungs heaved. Sweat slicked his skin. Each heavy exhale fed the trees around him, and he was greedily nourished in return on each inhale.

He mounted a curve in the upward trail and quickly bounded onto a flat headed boulder to cut distance, then over a fallen log taller than he was. Weave energy hovered over the bare skin of his arms and torso, and danced over the loose folds of his legs wraps. His mind was fully focused on the trail ahead, his breathing, and the point where the edge of his pulsing weave field touched the air around him.

Runa was ahead. He could see her path, marked by snatches of weave that pressed against the knobby spruces grown along the curve of the trail, her steps echoed in places along the roots of the rock grasping trees where they remembered her heavy tread. Kyn flared appreciation - a warm white-pink across his heart - as he leapt past one of the trees and onto a neighboring rock. A gentle palm against its trunk for balance and appreciation, and he swung past, cutting more distance up the trail by vertically scrambling a moss coated ledge. The green sang beneath his fingers.

The trail he followed flattened as it crested a bluff, open slab becoming a press of ruddy barked conifers, brilliant green ferns pillowed between their trunks. Kyn caught another smear of Runa's weave against a passing tree and angled hard, vaulting the skywards roots of a fallen spruce to run the length of its trunk, tracing a parallel path with the adolescent's trail. He took a running jump to swing acrobatically from a springy overhead branch, and then he was bounding through the trees, precision running from branch to branch as the forest faded from needle-heavy conifer to white-barked birch. The slanted rooftops of the Crisis Response Centre appeared through the emerald leafed boughs ahead, a multilevel watchtower complex of pitched roofs, skylights, and open-air terraces that seemed to grow out the forest around it. Kyn caught another glimpse of Runa's weave trail below, brushed up against the entrance to the training house, and he altered his trajectory to aim for an upper studio's open skylight. Three more branches and he threw himself through the open portico with a twisting dive to roll across bamboo slats. On his feet again, the weave aura faded from his skin with a flickering snap.

"Impressive." Benn drawled from the center of the studio's comm circle.

Kyn showed his ex-Handler his extended middle finger, digit tip freshly grown that morning; the new nail painted a neon blue.

"Don't start that shit with me." He snapped at the light projection. "I ain't gunna fight your war. Got your scent now. Glad-hand me, get me here all tidy. You're a fucking user that's all." He strode through the projection, uninterested in any response, and out of the small studio. He padded down a spiral staircase to the level below.

"Impressive!" Dev'Lyn beamed, unknowingly echoing Benn. "You hit every imprint."

They'd begun training at dawn. Kyn, Ashe, and Runa, having petitioned Dev'Lyn and the other crisis response agents to help them hone their new weave connections.

"Response agents' unique abilities are the result of rigorous training," Olivvia had explained. "Our collective heightened awareness of the morphic resonance has allowed us to make great technological and social jumps, but that doesn't mean your average citizen is porting through spatial tears or grav juggling. Like all talents they take interest, skill, and most importantly, practice to harness"

"What's the origin of these abilities?" Runa asked. "Seems a bit 'fetched I'm gunna be able to do some space-magick weirdness when I can barely understand why I'm telegraphing my moods." She'd then flared with something that had reminded Kyn of a small child, a shy terror. The nervous fear of inability.

"As you're becoming aware," Olivvia had acknowledged kindly. "The resonance field, or colloquially, the weave, presses against, and interacts with other natural fields and forces; gravitational, electromagnetic, weak/strong interactions, amongst others." Kyn had come to note a nurturing patience about the response director. "With training, you each could become more in tune with those other forces, understand how the weave interacts with them. In what way? That is personal and unique to each."

Kyn smiled back at Dev'Lyn. "Thanks." He tentatively flared a flicker of complimented joy along the spinal curve of his neck.

The staircase had deposited him into the training house's lower movement studio, a large square, open to nature on opposite sides, and he crossed to a wall honeycombed with individual pod storage, unwinding sweat-soaked wraps from his legs as he walked. Crisp mountain air dried his nakedness almost instantly, and he casually dropped the soiled cloth lengths into a basket. One of the hexagonal pods produced a set of loose canvas leggings in earth browns, and a simple, sleeveless shift of soft bamboo. He could feel Dev'Lyn's eyes hovering over the naked firmness of his back.

"Benn told you they got Alec back inside safely?" The response agent inquired.

Kyn could feel the other man's tentative hunt around the edges of his weave, probing how he felt about the hacker's departure. He pulled the canvas pants on and slid the shift over his head.

"Would've if I'd let him talk." He returned, stepping into a flexible pair of grip-soled slippers chosen from a neatly ordered line of identical pairs. He'd been pleasantly relieved when Dev'Lyn had told him and the others that there were other fashion choices in this new world beyond the wrapped standard, and they all thanked Shar profusely when she had directed them to a stock of training clothes, and then showed them how to order from local artisans through the weave-net.

"Ashe and Runa?" Kyn asked, diverting the subject of Alec.

"Post-addiction trauma counseling, and education resources." Dev'Lyn answered with a charming smile, letting himself be led by the diversion. "Where are you next?"

Kyn pulled a bio-flat from the pod and scrolled through his training schedule.

"Meditation." He sighed, mock collapsing into the cubby wall. His pink-slashed gray eyes found Dev'Lyn's cracked green. There was no mistaking the flirtatious prods the other man was silently nudging against the invisible edge where their weave fields pressed against each other. Kyn winked a gray/pink eye and flared a mischievous wisp of wings from between his shoulder blades. "Wanna help me play hookie?"

< = >

"Remember Kyn, don't let yourself get hurt!" Dev'Lyn chided from the ground.

Kyn easily hopped to the next concrete pillar. "Yah yah." He chirped back. He hopped to another pillar.

They were in a disused industrial sector, re-liquidated by the local community and sectioned off for the experimentation with, and training of, weave abilities. The trio had been training for a moon cycle, mostly quarantined to the Crisis Response Centre up the western most curve of the surrounding mountains.

"Disease is not a large threat." Shar had explained of their seclusion. Other recruits that would've been in the centre had already been dismissed for the season, sent to the nearby community for rest or work detail, while others were deployed to different parts of the planet or it's orbiting stations. "But the rolling effects of human-effected climate change, though arrested and on a healing process, still make pandemic flares an unfortunate possibility. Undiscovered or evolved viruses could pose a potential threat to local populations and yourselves. When you are allowed down the mountain, we'll ask that you wear light masks in public spaces."

Adapting to this new place, the trio spent the majority of each day in physical training, cultural education seminars, or meditating. Yet, neither Ashe, Runa, nor Kyn had yet managed a flicker towards evn the most basic weave barrier they'd seen the siblings deploy.

"Two of you feel your invulnerable." Shar signed with a humored frustration. Assisted by the weave amp, Kyn now understood the deeper emotional and contextual tones of the gestured language with ease.

Kyn leapt to the top of the next pillar, one of an obstacle course's worth of similar cement columns of varying heights and widths that stood like a stone grove in the repurposed industrial yard.

"Hey, I gotta try and not break these, so we all got our challenges." Runa crowed, bounding to top a pillar diagonal Kyn. His column hummed with the force of her landing. "Kinda weird their dissuading us from using our abilities though." Hand next to mouth, her mock whisper was loud enough to be heard from below, and her dead f-Link was now just a flat black collection of interlocking squares that sheathed her left bicep.

"We're not dissuading." Shar signed back, easily reading the adolescent's lips from her place on a neighboring single-level structure. Most of the walls had been long blasted out, and she stood on the bare remains of a roof. "But over reliance will block you from discovering other possibilities."

"Well then Ashe has to stop charming the delivery guy to bring them sweets from down the hill." Kyn mocked playfully, crouching to call down to the indigo haired influencer.

Ashe, their indigo hair slicked back, and clad in loose wrap pants, high-collared jerkin, and solid trail boots, looked up at Kyn, their thick lips twisted in a contrite smirk.

"No pushing there. He does as he likes."

"I bet he does." Kyn laughed heartily. He nodded his chin to Dev'Lyn. "Speaking of charmed boys. We gunna do this?"

Dev'Lyn smiled back, showing the lopsided scar, and gestured at a pile of collected refuse. Tendrils of weave grasped a jagged spear of rebar and it floated into the air, tip angled towards Kyn. "Remember. Don't let yourself get hurt."

< = >

"Does it still hurt?!" Dev'Lyn asked, yelling to be heard over the thrumming music.

"No!" Kyn reassured again. "Itched like all fucks at the time, though." He leaned up against the cave wall, enjoying the music's vibration through the stone. He'd taken a hurled length of rebar through the thigh in training and Dev'Lyn still leaked residual guilt over the throw. Something he did every time Kyn carelessly let himself get impaled despite the former Envoy's insistence it barely equated to a nuisance. Another moon cycle of training and Kyn still had no measurable improvement on his skill with the weave amp beyond its enhancements for communication and interfacing with basic day-to-day tech. He, Runa, and Ashe had now been down the mountain on various occasions, acclimating to the fjord community, and the community to them.

That night Dev'Lyn had insisted Kyn join him for a full moon festival held on the beach, in and amongst the caves below the bluffs west of the community. Kyn had eagerly agreed.

He tapped the flat stone behind his ear, oscillating the light mask that hovered across of his mouth and nose from projecting the scrolling lines of nonsense text he'd set it to, and switching to a geometrically deconstructed sketch gif of a pink lily opening and closing again on a loop.

The cave was warm, heated by the pack of scantly clothed revelers. Gaseous light balls skimmed the ceiling, illuminating the cave above in auras of blues and greens. Outside the cave, revelers wound between the silver lit beach and the other caves hidden along the cliff rimmed cove.

The music in the cave was upbeat and energetic - organically inspired down beats, wide and hollow like an echo through a mountain pass, dropped with plunks that were the driving of a downpour on the tree canopy, all contrasted by a darkly throbbing synth underline. Music that got into the hips and groin. Everywhere celebrants pressed in closer to each other, hands wandering, mouths exploring. The cave glowed with weave energy, and the throbbing sexuality that blanketed the morphic field was a tangible thing, a constant pull to touch and be touched. At the center of the cave a dancer performed on a raised stage of smooth worn stone. A high kick disassembled her into a wafting pink cloud of weave butterflies that flowed from one side of the stage to the other, the pink butterflies swirling back into her lithe form as she soared through a tight pirouette.

Dev'Lyn stepped closer to Kyn, paused in a narrow alcove to pull themselves from the crowd. He wrapped a gentle hand around the back of Kyn's neck, strong fingers finding the three nodes of his amp, and tapped the silver circles.

A wash of flirtatious and sexually charged weave buzzed pleasurably over Kyn's skin. The pleasurable tingle turned to electric ecstasy with each tap of a finger.

Kyn groaned, aroused, and arched into the other man's hand. He could sense the ghost of Dev'Lyn's fantasies through the weave, the different ways he wanted to take Kyn, and have Kyn take him.

Kyn pulled Dev'Lyn to him and kissed the other man passionately through the light mask. His greedy mouth pressed hungrily against Dev'Lyn's full lips, taunting them open with his probing tongue. Dev'Lyn tangled the fingers of his other hand through Kyn's hair, and the slighter man flared unconsciously, an aroused burst across the lips; implying other ways the crisis response agent could occupy his mouth.

< = >

"I miss you." Kyn admitted. "I don't like you being back there."

Alec gaped at him with shocked awe from the comm circle.

"Who are you? Where is the emotionally dead violence-ball I was fucking? What did you do with Kyn?" He demanded. The twitch of a smile tugged at his thin lips. The projections rendering was so detailed Kyn could see the shimmer of happiness in the hacker's eye.

"Shut up." He snapped back, a shy embarrassment flickering behind his ears. He loosened a slipper and kicked it through the projection. Alec laughed.

Kyn squatted down and sat on the edge of Dev'Lyn's sleeping mat; a tatami pad unrolled on the bamboo slats of one of the Response Centre's personnel rooms. The evening was warm and three of the weather barriers were disabled, opening the space to the scents and sounds of the surrounding forest. Dev'Lyn was asleep under a thick quilted blanket, his breathing slow and steady, one arm flopped across his face, the other resting on his bare chest. A bushy gray tabby lay curled at the foot of the mat, purring contently.

"You staying safe?" Kyn asked Alec, easily letting his concern touch his face. He scratched behind the feline's ears. The purring increased. "Staying off their radar?"

"Yes." Alec reassured. Dorothy floated past his head, appearing then disappearing. "Benn has a healthy awareness that you'll come for him if he lets anything happen to me. Something about... Dickless and bleeding out on Alena's desk?"

Kyn nodded, that matched one of the more colourful and violently specific threats he'd leveled on the Handler the day he'd kissed Alec good-bye, determined to see him again.

"There are more disappearances everyday K," Alec picked up somberly, turning serious. "Outside of the uptick in cullings."

"Alyn's still at it then."

"And moving through bodies even faster it seems. That or there is a background war going on and they're all replacing their hardware at an accelerated clip."

"Fuck."

"How's he?" Alec asked, tilting a chin to Dev'Lyn's sleeping form. The dark look in Kyn's pink-slashed gray eyes prompting him to change the topic.

The storm cleared as Kyn smiled mischievously and held up his hands in an approximation of measurement. His palms skirted the edges of his defined and narrow chest.

Alec raised an eyebrow, impressed. "Nice." He commended.

< = >

"Kyn, focus! Don't let yourself get hurt."

Kyn deflected Ashe's incoming punch before hoping backwards at the last moment, avoiding letting them snap his kneecap with their next kick as planned - a tactic that would've gotten him inside their guard immediately and given him access to throw them out the sparing circle, winning the bout.

He growled. He was hitting the breaking point of frustration. He saw his ability to take the hit as an advantage. Leaning into an attack, purposefully taking a shot to the gut, or breaking his own limbs to escape, ran so counter intuitive to others' priority of self-preservation that the trick never failed to shock, surprise or disgust. Never failed in giving him the opening he needed to finish a fight. His ingenuity with his ability was a personal point of pride, and he was resenting being limited.

And he liked his ability, despite its origins. He was a survivor, always would be.

Ashe followed through their front kick with a tight pirouette, elbows lifted in a delicate 'O', wrists crossed at chest height. The looser folds of their wraps flowed with the movement, obscuring the difference between body and fabric. They easily avoided the next sweeping leg Kyn aimed at them and pulled their second rotation up short to retaliate by plunging into a hundred and eighty-degree split penché, striking foot aimed straight at Kyn's face.

Kyn narrowly avoided the flexed heel clipping him under the chin by dropping through his legs the moment Ashe killed their turn, diving under their reaching leg.

Shar stomped the floor in enthusiastic applause. Dev'Lyn and Runa joined her, adding their energetic whooping to the encouragement.

They were practicing a defensive hand-to-hand style utilized by the crisis response agents. Both performative and defensive art, the technique utilized an ethereally graceful blend of dance, martial arts, and acrobatic flows, focusing on deflection and redirection of opponent force to de-escalate violent encounters without injury.

"Smack 'em down!" Runa jeered from the sidelines.

The former Envoys were still touch and go on the concept of de-escalation.

< = >

Runa exploded through the thick cement wall in a brilliant corona of neon pink, reducing the offending barrier to a haze of fine gray powder. Ashe and Kyn watched from nearby, perched on the flat roof of a squat and disued pumping station.

"Fuck!" Kyn crowed, amazed. The trio were in the re-purposed industrial training yard, and the adolescent had just rocketed several hundred paces in a blur to hit the wall like a blazing bunker-buster of explosive weave energy.

Ashe was on their feet next to Kyn, jumping up and down, applauding proudly.

Runa clapped cement dust from the shoulders of her plaid button down, beaming with pride.

"It's this whole thing with gravitational mass and the density of objects." She explained throatily, calling up to them.

"Badass!" Ashe congratulated, still clapping loudly. A joyous smile had split their strong face and a reflected pride blazed bright across their chest.

< = >

The Unity's attack came at night. Exploding Dags raining from the sky.

Kyn was asleep, curled into Dev'Lyn's back, when the sirens started. Both men roused at the first screaming note, a shrieking wail that split through the quiet valley.

Kyn sat bolt upright on the cot, a knowing dread knotting his stomach. Dev'Lyn was on his feet and to the edge of the room instantly, looking out where the deactivated weather barrier opened to a drastic view of the community below. Everything was dark except for the twinkling glow of bio luminescent streetlamps.

"That alarm hasn't sounded in living memory." Dev'Lyn muttered, anxious worry creeping into his lilting voice.

Kyn sprung from the sleeping mat. Snatching discarded clothes from the bamboo slats, he tossed Dev'Lyn a bundle. He knew what the threat was. Why the alarms were sounding. Knew it the way he always knew the Unity was looking for him.

Both men dressed rabidly before rushing down the stairs to the training room where the others already waited.

"Scans say it's who you think." Olivvia stated plainly. She tossed Self to Kyn. The stiletto had been yielded willingly upon the former Envoys' surrender. He noted Ashe's collapsible maul gripped between their large hands. A cold, vengeful rage seeped from between the tall ex-Envoy's sharp shoulder blades. They were twisting the shaft eagerly.

Olivvia's eyes narrowed in displeasure, but otherwise ignored the flare. "They haven't dared an open attack since their seclusion." The director expounded. Her fierce gaze flicked between the trio. "Can we count on you?"

Beyond the training room's viewports dark silhouettes had begun to crowd the night sky, blacking out chunks of the vast dome of stars. Industrial air-transpos, wide-decked whales used for upperward utility transport.

Kyn tagged the flat stone of his light mask behind his ear and tapped it active. He nodded once, short and sharp to the director.

His own cold rage had settled over him, but he'd managed to suppress the telltale flare. Shar was already tearing open a portal.

"Orders?" He asked. Self was heavy in his hands.

"Protect the citizen at all costs." Olivvia's eyes were ferocious.

Kyn smiled grimly beneath the glowing beak of his mask. Ashe and Dev'Lyn were already through the portal, with Runa on their heels. Kyn could see dark shapes falling to the streets beyond the wavering pink edge of the portal.

Ashe had left their maul on a training bench.

"My blood for my SPIRE. My body for my Sentry. My devotion to The Unity." Kyn smirked coldly, discarding Self to the training bench. He stepped through the portal.

Dags were falling from the sky. Dark lumps, familiar in their uniform tactile armor and visored helmets. Shar had opened the portal in front of the community's largest residence complex, and the soldiers were hitting the streets around them, dropped from the above air-transpos, and were stumbling towards the compound full of sleeping citizens.

Kyn ran at the first Dag he saw. Other crisis response agents were mobilized, and these figures, light masked in reassuring and directing images, could be seen flitting past the residence's wide viewports, moving through the complex in brilliant flashes, rousing citizens for evacuation.

The Dag Kyn launched himself at stumbled when they landed and he helped them along, kicking out the soldier's knees and sending them sprawling in the clean laneway. The wrongness of seeing the shock trooper there, against the backdrop of vibrantly painted community art projects, struck him viscerally in the gut. He flared a white-hot rage between his shoulder blades, vengeful wings of wafting weave, and grabbed the Dag by the uniform, flipping them over with a snarl. The Dag ignored him, struggling as they tried to keep dragging themselves towards the housing complex. Kyn pulled back a fist, ready to strike the soldier unconscious when a flash of chrome and a plink of neon pulled him up short. A yank on the Dag's uniform collar revealed the armed timer of a k-pulse grenade surgically grafted into the downed Dags sternum.

"Fuck." Kyn swore and dove from the soldier, aiming as far away from the blinking blue light as he could.

He hit the laneway, rolling, just as the grenade went off. A vicious *pop* and then the Dag exploded in a shower of gore and kinetic force.

The explosion shook the street but did no real damage, luckily contained within the glimmering pink sheen of one of Olivvia's stasis bubbles. The commanding director had emerged from the portal behind Kyn, and stood with both hands up haltingly. Every Dag within visual range was ensnared, frozen.

Shar let the portal snap shut behind her, the wavering gateway seeming to close into her center. Ashe, Runa, and Dev'Lyn were nowhere to be seen, sped off to evacuate, or counterattack.

The deadly popping was replicated again, and again as frozen Dags exploded in crimson gore within the confines of their stasis shells.

"Get them away from the buildings!" Kyn ordered subvocally. Tuned to each other's frequency, the weave amps allowed direct communication over distance as if by the thought.

More popping explosions, farther away, followed by the tearing roar of collapsing infrastructure. Two streets down Kyn saw one side of a domed library fold in on itself. Blue flames licked the collapsing frame as terrace gardens crumbled to the porous-paved streets below.

Another Dag hit the lane in front of Kyn, dropped from a hovering air-transpo. Kyn snap kicked them hard in the solar plexis, sending the suicide bomber tumbling backwards through a portal Shar had torn open for the purpose. Kyn caught a glimpse of a moonlit quarry before the hole snapped shut again.

Citizens were streaming out of the surrounding buildings now, running towards designated short-range evac pads that would teleport them up the mountain.

"Stop!" Ashe's flanging voice commanded, freezing a cluster of Dags who were stumbling determinedly towards the fleeing citizens. The ex-Envoy had emerged from the housing complex wreathed in churning pink weave, a swath of citizens in tow.

The Dags objective was clear, and their frozen stillness began to crack, their compulsion to follow orders warring the influencers iron will. Legs trembled and gloved fingers twitched, as they struggled against Ashe's control, slaves to the self-destructive command of their chemical programming.

Not to be easily out done, Ashe's sheath of weave energy blazed, and they lifted their arms over their head, unleashing a rippling shock wave of neon pink that cascaded across the ground, slamming into the Dags, and throwing the approaching bombers backwards and away in the same moment that they exploded in a crimson cascade of angry *pops*.

Red droplets, warm and wet, sprinkled Kyn's face, carried on the gentle coastal breeze.

Shar had opened multiple portals and the response agents were throwing Dags through before she snapped them shut again. Still more fell.

Kyn struck a Dag in the kidneys with a quick rabbit jab before flipping them over his back to throw them through a fist sized portal. Then he ran, picking a direction at random. More Dags rained from the sky, and despite their power, the response agents and escaped Envoys were outnumbered. Explosions rocked the town center every few ticks, and buildings crumbled. Pained screams joined the chaos.

Kyn veered a corner and aimed a high kick at the first Dag he saw, cracking the helpless soldier across the helmet, and sending them veering away from a fleeing crowd of citizens. The pace of blue pulses in the Dag's chest told him how little time he had to get distance and, unable to risk the fleeing citizens by letting himself be decommissioned, he threw himself backwards, narrowly avoiding the close-range blast as the Dag exploded. The kinetic blast slammed into him mid-flip and he was thrown violently into a collapsed wall, cracking his skull on the loose bricks of re-carbon, and dislocating his knee. The crowd of citizens ran, escaping down side streets, seemingly unharmed.

An auto-transpo drifted by above, blocking out the stars, more dark shapes falling from it. A block over, Kyn saw three Dags launched into the air, propelled by shimmering wafts of Dev'Lyn's weave energy. The Dag's exploded mid-air, taking out clutches of their falling peers.

"Dealing with the drop ship." Runa growled in Kyn's ear; gravelly voice carried over the weave connection.

He pulled himself from the rubble, snapping his knee back into place as he stood. His head swam, and one entire side of his head itched maddeningly. He could feel skull fragments sliding over each other to click back into place.

"Runa don't..." Olivvia cautioned, too late.

Kyn looked up in time to see a blurring flash of hot-pink launch upwards, charging one of the dark silhouettes that blotted out the stars. The night was lit in brilliant flare of pink fire as Runa hit the dropship, detonating her weave field on impact to shred the whale-sized transpo in a corona of force. Flaming hunks of debris rained down.

At the same moment, a temple door across the laneway burst open and a cluster of young acolytes emerged, right in the path of a plummeting driveshaft.

Kyn was running even as weave energy filled the air. Dev'Lyn was grabbing falling debris and leading it gently to the ground as Olivvia seized other plummeting chunks in stasis, stopping jagged masses of flaming shrapnel mid-air.

Shar was tearing open portals beneath what she could, disappearing plummeting wreckage to places only she knew. But there was too much, falling too fast. The terrified children were frozen in the doorway, the jagged driveshaft lancing a flaming path towards them.

Kyn screamed, flaring in warning.

He barreled into the nearest child - a mousey haired girl - and bound her up into his arms as he crashed into the group, forcing the entire cluster of youth back through the temple doors.

The flaming driveshaft hit the ground where the girl had been moments before, splintering on impact, and lances of pain screeched across Kyn's spine as exploded metal shards thudded into his back, grating his vertebrae. He growled and stumbled. He could feel the children's panicked fear through the morphic field. He stumbled deeper into the temple.

Safe for the moment in the sanctuary of the temple, Kyn released the girl from his chest.

"Pull them out." He ordered the closest child, flaring with a cold, commanding efficiency. It calmed the panicked heat of the children, reassuring them. He crouched as they clustered around him, trusting his mask set to the simple blue + of rescue.

A wide-eyed boy, a slim few cycles away from his first decade, moved behind Kyn and gripped a protruding metal shard. He could feel the boy's fingers tremble against the metal, before, with a determined grunt, the child yanked the sliver free. A clank of metal to sandstone was followed by a second.

"Move. Closest evac" Kyn ordered the children, healing itch already moving up his spine.

The temple was simple, a harmonious blend of natural and synthetic forms, and the young acolytes, shamans, clerics, and seers in training, led Kyn down a short hall, through a circular greenhouse of woven willow and glass, then out a vaulted door to the outside. The children were calm now, feeding each other reassurance through the weave while simultaneously amplifying their collective watchful readiness.

Kyn clocked the area. The temple garden backed onto the rear of other domestic green spaces, branching alleyways of tended gardens behind resident complexes. The stars were returning, the dark shapes of the air-transpos slinking back out to sea, empty. Malicious pops still echoed from the streets. Burning structures lit the night.

The mouse-haired girl pointed down a branching alley, indicating the way to the closest evac.

Kyn took point, wary of any potential Dags stumbling from the shadows, and hustled the children protectively behind himself as he padded silently through the garden. Around a night flowering bush that smelled of honey and ice, and they were back on the street, the evac a diagonal shot past a stretch of market stalls.

A bear masked response agent appeared at Kyn's elbow, sliding immaterially from the brightly painted wall of an evacuated residence. A flashed hand signal instructed four of the children to link arms with each other, then, grabbing the closest, the agent phased through the wall of a market stall and ran for the evac, the linked children becoming immaterial to slide through the solid barrier behind him with ease.

Two children were left with Kyn, the mousey haired young girl and the boy who'd pulled metal from his back. He flashed them a quick hand signal, telling them to stay low and close, before following after bear mask, crossing the street, and keeping tight to the stalls as he rushed the evac pad.

He was really getting sick of not having any cool weave powers of his own.

Bear mask was getting their final two children onto the pad when the corner of the building beside them exploded outward with a violent spray of blasted timber and re-carbon, blindsiding the agent. The children were blinked away with a swirling snap of orchid-pink just in time, a tick before their savior, and the evac pad, were buried under blasted debris.

Kyn had the span of a single heartbeat to register what had happened before another Dag was on them, stumbling unnoticed from a darkened alley. The Dag was two paces from Kyn and the children, and moved as if desperate not to, a stumbling shamble like they were fighting the direction of their own feet. The grenade fused in their chest flashed maniacally.

The mouse-haired girl screeched in terror.

Kyn drew the children behind him, aiming to shield them from the imminent blast with his own body. The blue in the Dag's chest was one steady light. No time.

Bracing his boots into the flagstone, Kyn shoved the Dag away, a last-ditch bid to get space. Determined to stay standing as long as he could, he raised an arm protectively in front of his face just as the Dag's gene-hacked blue eyes widened beneath their visor and their chest exploded outward with a vengeful *pop*.

Kyn was aware of the moment the kinetic blast triggered. The rapid expansion of ferocious energy from a single point. A condensed moment building on itself, suddenly too powerful to be contained within the Dags fragile chest. An irrepressible force that rapidly expanded outward, tearing apart everything in its path. He saw the moment, could feel the expanding kinetic potential at the edges of his weave field, and met it, slamming all of himself against the incoming destructive force.

Ferocious-pink weave snapped solid in front of him, a rippling disk of translucent shock-pink energy expanding outward from the blade of his blocking arm in a shimmering, curved shield. Kinetic force slammed the weave shield, and Kyn could feel the destructive energy strengthening the protective barrier, even as he absorbed and transformed it, distilling it back to its original moment of pure potential. The blast's recycled potential built in Kyn like a scream, a ball of fury behind his navel that filled him until it threatened to spill over, burning him from the inside as it begged for release.

Unable to hold it any longer, Kyn threw the shield from himself with a howling battle cry, releasing the transformed energy. The shield broke apart as it left him, transmuting into a flock of silver-pink daggers that tore through the air to slam into yet another approaching Dag that had veered out of the darkness. The flock of iridescent daggers hit the Dag with such force that the Unity soldier was thrown backwards to slam into a wall. They slunk to the street, unconscious Kyn knew with certainty, the alarm blue at their chest gone dark.

There was no healing itch, no burn, or stabbing pain of injury. The children shook against Kyn's legs, and he was acutely aware of their fear turning to relief. A delighted grin pulled at his lips, threatening to break his angular face.

"Let's go." He ordered, hustling the pair from behind him. The children looked at him stunned, momentarily frozen by their brush with death. The mousey haired girl's chaos dirtied face was streaked with tears of relief. The boy's lips were pressed in a hard line of determination. Kyn winked at them. "Don't worry." He reassured; his pink-slashed gray eyes glittered playfully. "I'll get you out of here."

< = >

"What's your story?" Kyn demanded. "Why do you hate the Unity so much?"

Benn's projection hung his head. "I was a Dag." He explained from the comm circle set in the moss floor of Trinity's forest amphitheater. He looked haggard; the Informant's usually composed demeaner cracked. "Low rank. Patrol unit."

Ashe, Runa, Olivvia, Dev'Lyn and Shar sat on raised stones in the curved front row, watching as Kyn squared off with the projection. The AI watched from her folded position on the delicate silver dais. Her iridescent and too human faceplate was blankly serene, unreadable.

The last of the exploding Dags had been put down with the help of Kyn's new weave ability. Now they were seeking answers.

"Lower wards born," Benn continued. "Orphaned by seven. Ate the Unity line of honor and self-determinism, saw a way up and out. Just like every new scrip." He seemed younger, scared. "Went Nexx, had the best terms of service at the time. Swank new housing block, far dream from my squat." Edges of that desperate lowers kid creeped into his normally disciplined speech. "Then there was the pills, the programming."

The chemical cocktail. Two pills, loyalty tags, a hormonal steroid, and a narcotic neural stamp. Made the Dag's stronger and more durable than average, and completely unable to disobey orders - or even discuss them.

"Did wall duty a few cycles." The Informant looked wistful. "Then servo guard. Pills didn't really bother me, made me feel good. Go along to get along. Didn't notice anything. Had no reason to go against orders, to question." His perfectly manicured fingers tooled at the cuff of his fitted suit. "Then came my first culling." His dull blue eyes turned haunted, lost in memory. "Knew the deal, had survived the other side more than enough times, but..." He paused, his dark skin flushed with shame. "I thought maybe I could be the one who didn't shoot. Just march along. But no, the moment we had the percentile, I couldn't stop. Every twenty-ninth body put down. Mechanical." His chin dipped, and he was silent for a long moment. Something rustled in the trees above.

"I understood the collar then. I was being torn apart by guilt and unable to discuss it with anyone, even my squad mates. The people

I worked, slept, and ate with, physically incapable of talking about it. Every one of us. Crying ourselves to sleep and dead-eyed silent in our days. The best we could manage was a cortex approved, 'go along to get along.' Dead inside." A pause. "Tried to stash the pills, detox, but it wasn't long before the shakes, and then I was a mindless creature, desperate to shove them down my throat again. Tried to pitch myself headfirst off the wall but couldn't even manage that. Feet would turn away. Hands would forget the razor."

Kyn crossed his arms over his chest, saying nothing, his gray /pink eyes clear and intent. He listened without judgement, nor pity.

"Another culling, then another, and I grew colder," Benn continued. "Let it harden me, stopped letting the guilt keep me up at night." He sighed, lifting his gaze. "Got transferred from servo guard to Nexx SPIRE internal, then in another handful of years I'm personal guard to Iao."

Iao, Nexx Sentry, Sensat Tech and Virtual Intelligence.

"Iao decided to take an expedition beyond the wall. I don't know why. Was never told. A single rough terrain transpo, loose guard of personal Dags, and a Nexx Envoy, Fehl."

Kyn turned an inquisitive look to Ashe. He didn't recognize the name, and a negative headshake told him that they didn't either, gleaning him on Fehl's probable fate.

"We followed the road you began on to come here," Benn explained. "Though I didn't know where it led at the time. There were rumors, as there always are in the lowers, that people sometimes fled the city - rumors of a road - but I knew nothing beyond that."

Kyn's eyes flitted to Trinity. The AI was listening with a machine stillness. Her absence of breath haunting in the living, breathing forest.

"The Xion Envoy attacked on the second night." Benn blurted, rushing now, determined to be done with his story. "There was a fight. A short one. I lost my hands, cut off at the elbow. Fehl was killed. Iao was killed."

Kyn clicked his tongue. He knew Iao. Had seen the Sentry at the summit prior to fleeing the city. Iao was not dead. Not anymore anyway.

"Evac came. I was saved, but deemed a failure, given down cycled prosthetics and sent to a work colony in the resource zone, mining a trash deposit on the north edge. Three days later I saw Iao on the feed. Started walking the next morning, right out of the work camp. Low guard, programming didn't stop me." Benn shrugged. "Found the road when I hit the tether of my leash. Walked it as far as I could before the deep pain hit, the mindless need. But I didn't have any pills on me, and I'd gone so far, I just collapsed when it got bad enough. Woke up here." He nodded towards the AI. "Trinity found me. Deprogrammed me."

"You don't have an amp." Runa interjected, her expression dark. Kyn could feel how uncomfortably close the ex-Dag's tale mirrored her own.

"No," Benn agreed. "It wasn't needed to get me back to stable condition. But I was offered." The corner of his mouth twitched with the edge of a sad smile. "And I declined. I chose to return. To fight, help others escape."

"New face then?" Kyn pressed. His eyes flicked to the block pattern of onyx-black at the AI's wrist. He remembered the cuff's subtle, discreet weight. "Bit of a trick getting yourself up to Handler in Noav if you're the supposed to be dead guard of a re-living Sentry from a rival SPIRE."

Benn nodded, but the AI responded, stirring from her stillness. "Subtle cosmetic changes to deflect recognition." Her silver disk eyes blinked slowly as she looked to Kyn. "Augment upgrades for defense. New ident package, personal history, detailed service record. All fabricated. Insertion into desired prerequisite position with clearance for near future upgrade."

"You prettied him up, jacked his hands into cannons, and hacked him into a job that would make him a straight shot to Handler with a few well-timed promotions?" Kyn arched an eyebrow.

"The collective position of the citizens is not to move on Unity controlled territory. Previous consensus has seen interference as no better than the colonial war crimes of past generations." Trinity smiled, a slim, tricky thing. "The citizens have no such qualms about fully preparing those who choose to return to the walled city with personal safety resources, as well as assisting in their smooth re-entry."

"You can't impose change. But you can give them the tools to effect change themselves." Ashe's violet eyes were hot with understanding. They had seen what Kyn had in the weave space, seen what the Unity was. "We have to go back." They stated firmly.

Runa nodded. "After tonight I don't know how we can't."

Benn had gone silent, waiting. Kyn looked long and hard at his projection before turning to Trinity. "You sure he had nothing to with the attack?" He asked the rainbow-hued AI. More to state the accusation openly then anything. The AI blinked slowly and nodded her smooth head.

"What are you going to do Kyn?" Benn pressed.

Kyn clicked his teeth and looked to Ashe and Runa.

They said nothing, there was no need, he could feel the solidity of their certainty.

He turned back to the AI.

"Will you stop us from going back?" He tapped the amp at the base of his skull.

Trinity shook her head. "No. But it will make blending with your old society near impossible. Do you have a plan of action?"

An impish grin tugged at Kyn's lips. The seeds of an idea had taken root in his imagination the day he'd first met the AI.

"You said something about space stations?" He inquired.

Consensus

Kyn was back on the rocky beach, beneath the blasted, rainbow-streaked sky.

The towering tangles of driftwood stumps were still there, dotting the beach around him. Their ocean-buffed trunks stood at least twice as tall as Kyn, and crisscrossed the rocky shore, stretching infinitely in either direction to fade into the skirts of distant mountains - the tossed bones of primordial behemoths. The rocks beneath his boots sang, an unceasing pulse, the eternal chorus of stone. Waves lapped the rocky shore in a soothing, endless rhythm. He could hear voices on the wind as the tide pulled back; the distant, echoing whispers of countless minds.

He approached the nearest tipped stump, propped over on its own towering tangle of petrified roots. He knew this place now. Invisible forces pressed on him, and he could name and differentiate each, could focus on just the waves of attractive gravity that pulled between objects, or the dynamic swirl of the magnetism he walked through.

He circled the stump.

He could feel the infinite stories that pulsed beneath the smooth wood, but his hand stayed from the roots. Much of the driftwood came from trees that had been uprooted, ancient giants who'd tumbled into the ocean from distant eroding shores, while others, like the one he now stood before, had been chopped, trunk severed from the uprooted stump, cut short, amputated thumbs trailing sprouted masses of tendril nerves.

Kyn focused, listening through the disparate layers of the beach. He could feel the stories, the people and experiences emanating from the wood, like a pull under his skin. Parts of himself calling to like parts. There were other stories there too, beneath the wood, stories that were others, echoed through time. He could recognize the reflected pieces of Dev'Lyn and Alec in those places. Runa and Ashe in others. Stories he didn't recognize, beautiful and bright on the edges of his attention, unique things he knew were better meant for others. Stories that sang with friendship, determination, kindness, and indomitable will across the spiral of time. He could feel the density of the smooth wood. The density of the stories within, pressing against and interweaving with each other. Feeding and strengthening the barnacles, patchy mosses and crawling yellow-white lichens that grew on its fallen trunk. Feeding the fresh life.

There were other stories there too. Those that grabbed from the bottom, grasping tendrils that drained; devouring, rotting things that his skin pulled away from. Discordant notes that grated each other, leeching brilliance and light from those nearby. Things that screamed of narcissism and cruelty, the off-key chittering of arrogance and selfishness.

Kyn could feel these things under the driftwood, from the dark underside where the ancient corpse rested against the stones.

He hiked one boot against the massive trunk and pushed, kicking to roll the great stump over. It was a feat that should've taken Runa's advanced strength, but was easy here, a mere action of choice. The stump rolled, grating in the loose stones and sand to show its belly to the sky, exposing the rot beneath.

"They understand." Trinity acknowledged from the space beside him, there as if she'd always been. The dark haired woman with the eyes of infinite pink stars. A still point within the constant flow of the place.

Kyn listened to the voices on the wind. The countless connected minds singing to him, considering, and weighing his proposed action. Forming a consensus.

He looked up at the colour-streaked sky and fell, plummeting through the perpetual aurora of blasted pinks.

Falling Action

Alec kissed Kyn, full and passionate, crushing the slighter man's lips beneath his own.

"Knew it wouldn't take you long." The hacker breathed eventually, releasing Kyn.

Kyn patted his palm against the taller man's hard stomach and wafted warm wisps of affection between his fingers. The hacker shivered.

"That's new," Alec smiled. His muted green eyes were bright with understanding, reading the meaning imbued beneath the tingle. He pressed the smaller man's hand beneath his and leaned in, kissing him again.

Alec's lips tasted like electricity and spiced breakfast noodles.

Elsynn coughed. "Break it up, this ain't a jackjoint."

Alec pulled away, laughing. "Give me a break, we're doin' a suicide run on the Unity. Gotta get my happies while I can." One hand lingered on Kyn's neck, and the hacker's long fingers stroked the short-cropped hair at the back of his skull. Alec looked into Kyn's pink-slashed eyes. "Like the new look." He complimented.

Kyn winked and squeezed the hardness of Alec's flat stomach affectionately before turning to Elysnn. They were under her shuttered and darkened shop. The old woman was irate, still rattled by the sudden appearance of the glowing pink portal that had peeled open in the middle of her subterranean blast shelter. She glared balefully at Kyn.

"We appreciate your hospitality." He teased, repaying her glower with an toothy grin.

Shar had opened a portal in the middle of the shelter's cramped living area, and once through, while Kyn was occupied greeting Alec, Dev'Lyn, Shar, and Ashe had divided themselves among the rack of bunks welded into the thick walls.

Olivvia had claimed the one folding chair next to a sticky card table.

Elysnn regarded the strangers with open distrust. The gears of her prosthetic clicked and whirred as polymer fingers gripped and re-gripped the ornate handle of her wrought iron cane. Benn was at the heavy hatch where a narrow ladder led up into the shuttered shop above. Hours away from scheduled open, the noodle shop was closed and deserted, but the heavy aroma of simmering stock still wafted through the hatch, the scent of prep vats simmering in the narrow kitchen.

"Your kids got the packets?" The Handler asked the gruff proprietor.

Elysnn nodded.

"Aye, my lot will get people off the streets, no trick," she agreed. Her annoyance at having a clutch of fugitives and known terrorists materialize in her own bunker hadn't stopped her from enthusiastically permitting her young charges to volunteer for Kyn's plan. "Ain't no one who's inclined gunna turn down a chance to stab the Unity in the eye."

"You're not worried about these cultists finding out?" Shar signed. Many aspects of life in the walled city confused the outsiders, but Shar had been particularly struck by the concept of the cultists, repulsed by the fanatical Sentry worshipers' willingness to turn on their fellows.

"Counting on it actually," Ashe returned. "Only way it'll spread fast enough."

Kyn nodded. "After we leave here, we aren't going stealth. The Sentry will mobilize everything they have against us." He looked to Dev'Lyn and his sister, slashed gray eyes found cracked green. "You sure you're both good for this? No ones' going to fault you if you want a last tick out."

Dev'Lyn grinned his lopsided grin. "And let you have all the fun?" He teased. "No way. There are somethings you need a front seat for."

"This is important." Shar signed in agreement. "We are with you."

Olivvia nodded her silent assent from the folding chair.

Kyn flared with a sense of gratitude towards the three response agents, a wavering aura that undulated across his chest. He looked to Ashe. They wore cloth leg wraps in neon purples and royal blues, tucked into heeled boots, and a matte black tactile corset. Their indigo hair was loose. He could feel their eagerness and anxiety across the weave. The cold center of their preparedness that mirrored his own. Gently, he pressed the edges of his own field against theirs, and felt them return the gesture, a shared moment of silent understanding between them.

The pistons of Elysnn's arm hissed and clicked impatiently.

"We doin' this or what?" Runa asked, her gruff voice in Kyn's ear. He could hear the faint pound of punk rock behind her words.

"Moving." Kyn dug another long-range comm stone from the folds of his own leg wraps and pressed it into Alec's palm. "Toys from the machine." He told the hacker, tapping the identically smooth, bean-shaped stone in his ear – the current source of Runa's voice - then tapped his throat. "Subvocal. No need to talk. Just think clearly." Trinity had supplied the stones - augment boosters that would strengthen their weave connection, optimized for communication over longer distances. They were also a simple way to link in the non-amped. Alec tabbed the stone into his ear, and Olivvia, Shar, and Dev'Lyn activated their light masks. Flowered skulls and yellow emoticons glowed in the dim space.

The group climbed the ladder one by one to the deserted shop above. Last through, Elsynn clamped the hatch shut and moved behind the high serving counter. A faint *beep* and the slatted metal barrier shuttered over the shop's windows began to roll up into the ceiling with a whirring rattle.

A waiting Dag patrol stared in from the other side of the polyplex front, assault grade k-cannons raised.

"Word has spread." Ashe muttered to no one in particular. They made for the swinging door, striding gracefully between sticky topped tables.

"Shouldn't that be you?" Kyn nudged Benn. Rose had risen from behind Alec and the bot was floating along after Ashe. "Tell 'em to stand down? You got us in hand?"

"Cancelled." Benn answered. "0400h"

The dim mix of under-ward UV panels, and the weak bands of sunlight that signaled morning in the lowers, was leaking through the front polyplex, and around the shop the beginnings of the morning commute had trickled into the narrow streets and cross-ways overhead.

Ashe was through the door. The crowds were giving the Dags a wide berth, and passersby eyed the emerging Ashe with fearful curiosity.

Benn's denim blue eyes unfocused and his flawless fingers drummed through f-Link commands. Kyn could hear the muffled shouts of the Dag commander, yelling for Ashe to submit and surrender.

The screen above the counter changed, blanking to a warning-orange **EVACAUATE** scroll at the same moment Ashe raised their arms, sending out a rippling shock wave of weave that threw the surrounding Dags off their feet, slamming them backwards in a cascade of rolling pink.

The warning text scroll was now accompanied by a ward map overview. Pink neon outlined the area surrounding Noav SPIRE across all ward levels, and more text scroll prompted civilians to flee to a minimum safe radius of twenty-five klicks from the megastructure.

Battered and unconscious Dags littered the pavement outside the shop while early morning commuters stared in frozen amazement at Ashe.

"Evacuate." The glowering ex-Envoy ordered the stunned onlookers, their voice flanging with influential power. They turned back for the noodle shop's door, Rose following close at their shoulder.

Outside the shop, every visual feed had been hijacked. Evacuation warnings alternated with footage of Ashe weave-slamming the Dags across every shop window, vertical surface, screen, and output device capable of visual display.

Shar was opening a portal in the center of a plastic booth when Ashe swung the shop door back open, striding calmly through.

"You're like a big dog." Dev'Lyn quipped to Alec, clapping the lanky hacker companionably on the shoulder.

Alec had been staring at the expanding portal between Shar's hands, agape with foolish glee. Cracked baby blue tiling could be seen on the other side of the wavering tear. Elsynn retreated to her kitchen without a word, leaning heavily on her wrought iron cane and muttering profanely to herself.

"Dog?" Alec's head swiveled to look quizzically at Kyn.

"You'll love them." Ashe assured with a kindly smile. They stepped through the widened portal without pause.

Shar was somehow both in the center of the quivering pink energy ring, forcing it open, and, through some twist of perception, on both sides of the portal at once. Kyn could see tiled pillars on the other side now, and the overhead signage of a skytram station, hijacked to display the bright orange evacuation message. Confused and terrified commuters stared from the other side of the opening portal, frozen, ignoring the overhead warnings to stare in awe at the display.

"Evacuate." Ashe ordered them calmly as their boot heel hit tile. "Help others evacuate."

The flanging power of their voice seized the crowd, forcing the collected civilians from their amazed stupor, and they turned as one, obediently filing towards the nearest exits.

Alec ducked through the portal next, following Rose as the drone flitted after Ashe, a wide, excited grin plastered across his sharp boned face. Kyn followed, with Dev'Lyn on his heels. Olivvia came next, then Benn, and finally Shar, dragging the portal closed around herself as a skytram hummed into the station.

< = >

The skytram tilted and Kyn reached out, grabbing Alec by the back of his hooded vest to keep the hacker from sliding off the edge of the smooth roof. He smoothly rode the tip of the vehicle through the bend of his knees, his core screaming as he countered Alec's pinwheeling. The vehicle leveled out around a turn and the acid-haired punk swung back from the edge, panting.

"Whoooooo!" Alec screamed, eyes wide with exhilarated terror. "Again! No, not again! Never again."

"Stay low." Kyn instructed, bending his own legs demonstratively. They were riding the roof of the cross-ward AXY commuter express. Benn was crouched low at the rear of the carriage, the sleek aluminum roof gripped with one hand for balance, his perfectly manicured fingers biting dents in the metal. Dev'Lyn sat meditatively opposite, calmly surfing the tilt and roll of the tram. The vehicle beneath them made a hard bank left, and Alec stumbled again, careening for the opposite edge. A gentle waft of weave pushed the hacker back, saving him from smearing his face across a passing building, and plopped him firmly down on his butt.

"Stay low!" Dev'Lyn called from the front of the carriage.

Hacked by Benn to ignore override attempts, the tram hurtled through its next programmed stop, blowing past the Dag troops that had collected on the platform, and slamming through the weak ad-hoc barrier of trash disposal units that had been hastily rolled onto the tracks in a rushed attempt to disrupt the commuter vehicle.

"Whooooo!" Alec screamed again.

Urban tangle pressed in, and cross-platform byways whipped by overhead as they sped through the wards.

The difference of being back within the city wall was jarring to Kyn. Here there was no constant breath of trees. No simple sentience of animal life. No life other than the constant press of the overcrowded human population, scrambling for space. He found the lack of diverse natural life distressing. In their mountain refuge, Kyn had experienced for the first time how his internal balance and mental well-being was intrinsically linked to the world around him, his environment. How the breath of the trees calmed his pounding heart when his thoughts turned to dark memories. How the moisture of the air and the song of the rock soothed him when he woke in the night. He saw it in the others too. The simple joy in how the people of the community sourced their food, tending and nurturing the earth. How a walk in the moss thick forests would temper Ashe's burning resentments, or a brisk dip in a glacial mountain stream would slow the erratic bees of Dev'Lyn's thoughts. There was none of that in the city. Just the magnetic hum of steel and the dull silence of plastic, bouncing the echoes of people's pain between them.

Kyn could see the crystalline walls of Noav SPIRE approaching, looming through the seams of the tightly packed urban tangle. They were getting closer.

The opaque polyplex exterior of Noav SPIRE glinted jewel like through the surrounding stacks, the reflective surface bouncing stolen sun back into the shadows of the winding under corridors, granting dim light to the densely packed ward stacks strung between megastructures.

Every pro-prop holo and advo space along the route had been hijacked, and the orange evacuation warning flashed everywhere. Safe distance maps blared from almost every building, replacing looming glorifications to the Unity, and blanking over SPIRE advertisements. People were fleeing on the byways, and Kyn caught a wavering flash of pink weave energy as the tram flashed by one crowded ward crossway. Either Shar with Ashe teleporting groups to a safe distance, or some of Elsynn's kids, doing the same armed with Trinity supplied emergency evac pads.

"Incoming!" Benn warned from his place at the rear of the carriage.

The tram had dipped between opposing racks of mid-ward data hubs and Kyn snapped his head around just in time to see a cluster of jagged metal stars drop from the section of welded ward ceiling directly above to impale themselves into the roof of the tram. Spindly legs sprouted from each star, wagging awkwardly in the air before they clamped to the metal and yanked their jagged bodies free.

"Ziev crawlers." Kyn identified clocking eight.

He and Alec were surrounded, separated from Benn and Dev'Lyn by the attack drones on either side. An angry red eye opened in the center of each of the bots facing Alec, and Kyn threw an arm up protectively, summoning a weave shield that blossomed from his forearm, guarding the hacker. "Short 'em." He tossed to Alec.

Lasers slammed into his shield.

Potential energy built in Kyn's core as the shield absorbed the incoming attack, aching to be released. Electric energy crackled around him, and he growled as a laser lanced his shoulder from behind. Alec had managed to down some of the surrounding drones but not all, and a line of burning energy had narrowly missed the hacker to drill through the rear of Kyn's shoulder with a hiss and a waft of burned flesh.

Three attack drones, sheathed in glimmering weave, flew past to slam into a passing building. A blunt shot from Benn's hand exploded two more, their twisted remains pulled away in the tram's slip stream.

Kyn discharged his shield, slamming the final two drones with weave knives. Their jagged metal bodies flew backwards to disappear over the edge of the speeding tram. A healing itch had already replaced the burning in his shoulder.

The tracks ahead veered left. The next turn would take them close to the SPIRE.

A fist-sized tear of pink appeared in the air between Kyn and Benn, just as the tram hurtled around the corner, and Ashe and Shar slid through the portal with a bending twist of perception. The opaque wall of the SPIRE loomed on one side of the tram.

"I prefer when you open them wider." Ashe complained. They were flushed a nausea green around the jowls and swayed unsteadily for a moment in the buffeting speed winds.

Benn aimed a hand-cannon at the approaching wall of polyplex at the same moment that Shar grabbed onto Alec and tore open a fresh portal. Kyn grabbed Alec's free hand and gave it a quick, affectionate squeeze.

"See you through the looking glass." He reassured before Shar pulled the hacker away in an eye-aching bend of physics.

Benn fired his shot, blasting a jagged hole in the plastic barrier with a shower of glittering polyplex slivers

"Indestructible my ass," Kyn quipped, comms saving his words from being dragged away by the slip stream. Three beats of his heart and the tram would be within easy jumping distance.

"Runa!" He called over the comm as he moved with the others, taking a running leap for the fast-approaching hole. "We're here. Give us a beat!" They hung together as one over the open ward gap, briefly suspended

"Got it." Runa's gravelly voice returned in Kyn's ear before gravity inevitably took over and he was tumbling through the shattered hole. "Hurry up I'm bored."

Kyn hit the ground to roll across black tile just as the first rattling pulses and darkly uplifting beats of twentieth century indie-electro duo Diminutive Defense filled the comm channel.

His highly-tuned situational awareness had already clocked the heavy Dag presence mobilized against them, and he used the tumbling movement to position himself within striking range of the nearest visored soldier. A snapping front kick as he unfurled from the tile dropped the Dag, and a knuckle jab to a vulnerable nerve cluster in their neck kept them down.

They were on one of Noav SPIRE's mid-ward levels. An open concept maze of cubicles stretching from tilting opaque wall to tilting opaque wall. A bank of hyperLifts looped the wide central column, and security flow checkpoints granted ward level access at several points around the edges, granting access to exterior walkways.

All doors were firmly shut.

Civilians - mid-ward data jockey types and drab SPIRE corporate suits - choked the halls, restricted from evacuating despite the hacked screens and f-Link SPAM attacks warning them to run, sealed in as fodder.

Kyn threw up a guarding forearm, conjuring a weave shield just in time to absorb a volley of kinetic fire lobbed at him by an approaching Dag cluster. He'd launched himself across the floor to the cover a panicked data jockey who would've stumbled into the line of undiscriminating fire.

"Get to an exit." He ordered the drab suited civilian, shoving the terrified man behind him. He could feel the swelling build of transformed energy growing in his core.

The civilian's eyes were unfocused, erratic, scanning their f-Link.

Kyn knew what they were seeing, knew that Alec was somewhere hacking the feed, filling every device connected to the city's servers with images of the outside world. Ever-visible data streams were filling with proof of a world beyond the city's walls. Satellite footage of a glittering 3Seoul, next to bustling street views of Nuevo-Berlin. A moon lamp crowded night market in London. Aerial kite footage of the villages that dotted the coast to the north.

"It's true." Kyn reassured the dazed cubicle drone. The pressure in his core was threatening to break. His shield wouldn't hold much longer. The Dags were equipped with rapid-shot capacity assault k-cannons, and the curve of his neon pink barrier wavered erratically with each new impact. "Get to an exit." He ordered throwing the weave disk away from himself the moment he sensed a pause in the volley. Transformed energy tore from him as the shield became slivers of weave, each finding its target in a reloading Dag.

The civilian stood frozen, transfixed by their feed, confused, and terrified.

"Evacuate." Ashe's thrumming voice ordered, filling the cavernous office floor. They threw a cascading shock wave into a security check point. The rolling waves of hot-pink tore open the doors, clearing a path to the exterior. "Help others evacuate."

"What they said." Kyn parroted, shoving the civilian behind the safe cover of a plastic cubicle barrier. Focused under Ashe's influence they skirted the perimeter, keeping to the cover of the office barricades as they headed for the newly opened exit. Kyn kicked sideways, knocking the k-cannon from another approaching Dag who was swinging the weapon around. A rush of weave push from Dev'Lyn slammed the soldier through an empty cubicle, knocking them unconscious in a mess of rigid plastic barricades.

The quartet fought their way towards the central column. Benn opening new exits in the outer walls with blasting rounds from his hand-cannons and returning fire against his former comrades, while Ashe alternated between weave slamming Dags and ordering civilians to flee. Kyn countered oncoming fire, agilely protecting fleeing cubicle drones while gleefully knocking Dag after Dag unconscious. Dev'Lyn easily protected their flanks, juggling security forces by yanking Dags from behind cover and slamming them through cubicles when they tried to move on civilians.

Ashe reached the central column first and traced a square across the access panel with a blunt, indigo-tipped nail as the others clustered in.

Kyn checked his hair in a polished door.

The lifts had been powered down, restricting travel between floors, but a few taps of Ashe's blue acrylics bypassed the lockdown protocols, and the bank blinked to life.

The lift directly in front of Kyn slid open to reveal a smiling Lux, the Nexx Envoy Kyn had stood facing during the Unity summit. Trimly handsome with short-cropped blonde hair, the Envoy's smile was dazzling white.

"Have you just been waiting in there?" Kyn tried to mock the blonde Envoy - but no words came out. His lips forgot to obey his brain - all he could focus on was the brilliant white of Lux's uncannily symmetrical smile. Hypnotized by the mathematically perfect evenness of their spacing, held in thrall by the slight tip of the canine.

A noxious odor, thick and peppery, burned his nose and eyes. Benn coughed, gagging. All the lift doors had slid open and a burnt mustard-coloured gas was pouring out of every open tube.

Janxx. Sino Envoy.

Ashe quickly withdrew from the rabidly spewing gas, hissing in pain. The mid-ward level of the SPIRE was expansive, but the gas already choked their immediate area, and was spreading fast.

Kyn could feel the toxic fume burning his exposed flesh, slowly eating at him, but he could do nothing but marvel at the even whiteness of Lux's pearly white teeth.

"Kyn!" Dev'Lyn's warning voice was in his ear. He ignored it. The perfectness of Lux's dazzling white smile soothed him. The Nexx Envoy raised a blunt-nosed k-cannon and sighted the hand-held between Kyn's eyes, level with his dramatic slash of freckles.

Kyn could see the ignition mechanism glowing at the end of the barrel.

"Kyn!"

Weave energy slammed into him the moment Lux pulled the trigger.

Kyn was thrown sideways as the point-blank kinetic round singed the lobe from one of his ears. He hit the black tile with a snapping crack of his skull. The gas burned his eyes, turning everything to a crimson blur. He squeezed what was left of his eyelids shut, focusing on the sounds around him.

"Lux, shoot Janxx in the knee." Ashe's voice snapped across the gaseous air. Kyn could feel their anger through the reverb of their heeled boots against the tiled floor.

"Lux, no, that freak's contro –" Janxx words were cut off by a single k-cannon discharge. She screamed.

Kyn scurried on all fours, still within the crippled Envoy's cloud of influence, and the gas sizzled at his exposed skin, burning the flesh of his arms and face, each breath corroding his lungs. He could sense the jangled confusion of the Envoys' muted weave fields, and moved towards them, following the sadness of their anger, the violence of their hopelessness.

One of Ashe's shock waves slammed through the haze, rattling tile.

The weave energy did nothing to dissipate the gas, but it threw the injured Janxx backwards. There was a heavy sound as the toxic Envoy hit the central column, then Kyn felt their weave still, unconscious.

"Surrender Lux." Ashe demanded, their voice a dominating whip snap. The noxious orange-yellow haze was thinning even as Kyn's vision cleared, the agonizing itch of his regrowing cornea fading. Lux knelt on the black tile, his head bowed, mouth a firmly sealed line, the snub-nosed k-cannon held limp on his thighs. Ashe stood over him.

"I could make you eat that." They threatened. The flawless midnight of their exposed face and neck was marred with angry red burns. Merciful wrath blazed from between their sharp shoulder blades in hazy waves of cherry pink. "It will do you well to remember that." They crouched on their heels; fingers grazing Lux's still cheek. "Evacuate" They ordered, voice quivering with commanding power. "Help evacuate others." Ashe stood and made their way to Kyn.

"Thanks." He told them earnestly, pulling himself from the tile. Janxx was a dark lump crumbled against the bank of lifts.

Dev'Lyn was beside him. "Really can't resist a pretty face can you." He teased, gripping Kyn's bicep.

Kyn could feel the other man's eyes clocking his healing from behind the glowing emoticon mask. He smiled.

"My weaknesses are really not that hard to figure out."

The deadly gases had dissipated, and unconscious Dags littered the office floors. The civilians had fled.

Benn rejoined the group. Stepping over the unconscious Janxx, the dismissed Handler drew a square in the hyperLift security panel and tapped through another override. All the open tubes except one whooshed closed.

Kyn returned Dev'Lyn's affectionate bicep grip.

"This is your stop." He told the other man, squeezing the substantial bulge of his arm. He let a wash of appreciation seep from his fingers. "Get Shar here for pickup."

Dev'Lyn's fingers found the flat stone at his neck and his light mask winked out. Cracked green eyes bore into Kyn. He was reading all the unsaid things Kyn was pressing into him through the weave. The nebulous seed of hope he'd ignited in the rebellious ex-Envoy.

"You got me if you need me." Dev'Lyn returned, flashing his crooked smile once more.

"Nah." Kyn shook his head stepping back. "Won't work like that." He re-closed the gap between them to peck a kiss on Dev'Lyn's full lips. Nimble fingers found the stone at the man's throat, and he tabbed the mask back into place.

"Go. Evacuate." He ordered, echoing Ashe. "Help the civilians. Get as far away from the SPIRE as you can."

A fist-sized hole tore open in the air beside them as if on cue and Shar slid through with an eye-aching twist. Alec's drone, Sophia, was close behind.

The spherical drone zipped to Kyn immediately, hovering close to his shoulder. Shar flashed him a confirmational sign before dragging her hesitantly reluctant brother back through another freshly torn hole in space.

Kyn boarded the tube, the dutiful Sophia at his shoulder.

Following behind Ashe, Benn slid open a digital window in the lift's input panel and hurriedly tapped through an override. The panel flashed wildly as unseen SPIRE techs fought him, attempting to slap the intrusion down, but the Informant easily won out after a few ticks and the tube lurched to life, rapidly descending for the Operations sub-level

"This is the part where it's really a trap right?" Kyn chirped the ex-Handler. The lift was a narrow polyplex tube, and he and Ashe had maneuvered their backs to the curved rear wall. Benn was between them and the polished door, his back to the pair. Sophia hovered at Kyn's shoulder. The lift moved fast, and it wouldn't be long before they reached their destination.

"Is it still a trap if you know it's coming?" Benn returned, speaking to the door. The perfectly sculpted fingers of his left hand twitched and tapped at his side.

Runa's queued soundtrack still thrummed through the comms, a primal, background beat that surged to the rhythm of the combat adrenaline pulsing through Kyn's body. He turned sidelong to Ashe.

"Better make it quick and brutal then." He invited.

Ashe nodded, violet eyes fierce, their mouth set in a determined line. Kyn could feel the drag of the lift's deceleration through his boots. They were arriving.

"Wouldn't expect anything less," Benn commented affably, eyes still fixed firmly on the door. The lift slid to an abrupt stop.

Ashe raised their arms with a sweeping underhand motion as the polished door slid up into the ceiling, and a cascading shock wave of ultra-pink slammed into Benn's back with the gesture, throwing him from the lift.

Malvyc had been waiting on the other side of the door, and the bald Envoy smoothly dodged the incoming double agent before, he, too, was also overtaken by the crashing waves of iridescent force and thrown backwards with the disgraced Handler. The two tumbled limply across the reinforced concrete to rest, battered, and unconscious at Alexi's precariously heeled feet.

The gold-blonde Sentry waited at the central-ops table, surrounded by the circular hedge of servers, her heart shaped face the definition of disinterested boredom beneath her now brutally short white-gold coif. She was clad in a couture mock-up of military garb, pencil-thin skirt and sharp-shouldered coat in black-blues and royal purples. The Sentry's eyes were unfocused, turned to her feed stream, and her gold-tipped fingers tapped rapidly. She showed no sign of acknowledging Kyn or Ashe as the pair strode off the elevator.

Malvyc stirred at the Sentry's feet. The bald Envoy was tough, the shock wave had hit a glancing blow, it's force potential dispersed over the longer range, and he wouldn't be down long.

"Clever streaming the whole thing." Alexi deigned finally, still not bothering to turn her attention from her feed. She was unarmed, and Kyn felt no trace of fear from her morphic field. He felt nothing from her, just a blank coldness.

"Kudos on the soundtrack. Little on the nose for me, but I can see how it fits the larger theme." Her attention finally focused on Kyn, who had stopped paces from the Sentry, just out of each other's arms reach. Ashe stood beside him, and Sophia hovered faithfully at his shoulder. Alec's drones had been live-streaming their mutiny run on the SPIRE, blasting the feed stream with footage of their raid in tandem with the constant evacuation message. Sophia currently had them live across the walled city.

Kyn didn't respond, staying coyly silent. Alexi planned to talk; so, he let her.

"Feel better?" The Sentry obliged rhetorically, playing to the feed. "Now that you've thrown your little rebellion?"

Malvyc shifted on the floor, struggling to consciousness. Ashe crossed swiftly and stilled him again with a heeled boot to the temple. Benn was still out cold.

Alexi arched a thin eyebrow but made no comment. "I figured you as too clever to fall for the Dividers' lies. Thought we trained you better." She sighed, heavy with a worried pity for his naivety.

"You've bought that abomination's story. Fell for its false facts and fake history."

Kyn rolled his eyes, but otherwise stayed silent. Ashe remained stoically vigilant over the slumped Malvyc, his breathing low and shallow at their feet. Ashe's face betrayed nothing, but Kyn could sense the invisible power of their restrain through the weave, could feel how much they wanted to put Alexi in a similar state and worse, felt it as if the urge was his own.

Partially it was.

"You see how it's a con right?" Alexi lectured, fine pointed nails drilling at the base of her neck. "A bid for control. You've handed over your self-determinism to that thing." She tapped the control deck and a constellation of iridescent holo-screens blossomed from its surface.

The golden rooftops of Nii Dehli at sunset flashed by in one floating square. The neon streets of Manila at night on another. Different feeds, all blaring some evidence of the outside world, all streaming live across the walled city.

"Have you confirmed any of this? Seen it with your own eyes? Has it let you? Or has it kept you confined to that dinky little village until now?" She stepped over the crumpled Benn and around the curve of the table. All the residents of the walled city would be glued to their feeds, and she was sowing the seeds of doubt in what they saw. Her most blindly faithful would've already picked up on the coded instructions of her tones and word choices and would already be flocking to parrot her talking points across the forums and social market platforms. Alexi regarded Kyn coldly, a tinge of annoyance obvious in the slight purse of her gold dusted lips, a momentary crack in the ineffable veneer. "I can see you're not interested in talking." She pouted, pivoting tactics now it was obvious she wouldn't bait him into a maze of words. "I'll cut to the chase. Why I asked

Benn to bring you here." She still easily ignore the crumbled ex-Handler behind her and tapped one viciously tipped nail against the table. The bouquet of feeds vanished in a churn of pixels, resetting to a single image.

A young boy, barely out of his first decade, his hair a spray of unruly red curls. A black Envoy's mask covered the lower half of his face, and Alena hovered at his shoulder, her brother behind her.

Kyn's gut clenched.

Alena was clutching the boy's shoulder with one diamond-laced hand. They were in the Pinnacle Garden, and the mid-day sun overhead set the Sentry's jeweled hand to glitter brilliantly even as it cast shadows across the boy's face, his features beneath the burst of fiery red curls hidden in darkness. Alyn was even more his usual blank pillar of muscular blondeness, a background framing prop to Alexi's invitation.

"He is very promising," Alexi appraised. "Uniquely talented. His Ascension revealed a truly remarkable gift."

Self-loathing surged within Kyn. He'd known this was coming, known the Sentry would replace them, but he'd tucked it to the back of his mind, pretended to forget. He was careful not to let his gaze flick to Ashe, but he knew through their weave the image struck them the same.

"Take me." Kyn demanded, his slashed gray eyes burning. Ashe moved to Benn and proceeded to roughly shake the ex-Handler conscious, a darkly satisfied smirk cracking their stoic expression momentarily when Alexi shuffled tensely to keep herself out of the willowy influencer's reach. Benn groaned after a moment of bodily shaking, then slowly set to dragging himself from the floor.

"You hit like a transpo heavy." He complimented Ashe, voice dazed. He got wobbly legs under himself to stand. "I thought we were taking her out?" He asked, bewildered, and indicating Alexi who watched him dispassionately. A moments glance at the holo beside the Sentry quickly corrected his confusion, and he nodded solemnly. "I feared as much. There were rumors. I'd hoped we'd make it before that happened."

Kyn exhaled, short and sharp through his nose. He had no more use for Benn's layers of half-truths. "Get him handled." He ordered the sometimes Informant, nodding his chin towards Malvyc's still unconscious form. "Then evacuate anyone else left down here."

Benn obeyed without comment, fussily adjusting his suit before he gripped Malvyc by the heels and began to drag the bald Envoy away.

Kyn watched them go, Malvyc's bald head bouncing across the smooth concrete, before they disappeared, swallowed into the depths of the sub-level. He turned back to Ashe.

"Going to find Sandri?" He asked, knowing the answer. Alexi stood awkwardly between them, but neither paid her any heed.

Ashe nodded, their mouth set and determined.

Kyn had expected as much and saw no need to deter them. Ashe's choices were their own, that was the whole point. "See you on the other side?" He acknowledged. Ashe nodded again. Kyn looked back to Alexi, finally re-acknowledging the Sentry. "Alright then." He bowed with a harlequin flourish, motioning for her to lead. Ashe disappeared, swollowed by the shadows of a server tower. "Shall we finish this?"

Kyn and Alexi boarded the lift.

"My blood for my SPIRE. My body for my Sentry," Alexi mocked as they hurtled upward.

Kyn laughed, a sharp bark, painfully loud in the confined space. Sophia still hovered at his shoulder, it's optic trained on Alexi.

"Truer words." He confirmed. Then. "Check your feed. All the gory details on your creepy body swap program are hitting the stream now, complete with visual aids. Everyone within the wall now knows, or will very soon know, how fucked up that little chant of yours truly is."

"It's your chant." Alexi shot back, venomous. Her fingers tapped and her blue eyes glazed as she hurriedly confirmed his words.

"Nope." Kyn shook his head. "Never was. Just something you used to make me say." He smiled, showing teeth. There were tinges of worry around the edges of the Sentry's resonance.

"The people need our steady leadership." The gold-blonde Sentry justified. She spoke to Kyn but her words were meant for the transmitting drone. "We do not continue ourselves for ego, but to serve the last free people."

Kyn rolled his eyes.

"They've subjugated you." Alexi pressed. "You've been brainwashed. Look at what they did to your eyes."

"When I was a child, you injected me with a nanite virus that killed me." Kyn returned, deadpan.

"We Ascended you."

"You murdered a bunch of kids."

Alexi regarded Kyn coldly. "They were nonentities, as were you. Until we Ascended you."

Kyn said nothing as the lift decelerated, sliding to a stop, and the mirror polished door slid upwards, opening to the outer atrium of the Pinnacle Garden.

"After you." He bid with another, mockingly effected, bow.

They crossed the atrium, the Sentry a few paces ahead, well out of Kyn's reach, her absurdly thin heels clacking discordantly on the flat stones of the garden path.

Sophia drifted loyally at Kyn's shoulder.

"Fuck this place is obnoxious." He sneered, passing one of the mirror-still pools. The calm water cast flash-gold in the sunlight, and the air was perfumed with the scent of eternally blossoming topiaries. He could feel the sadness of the bio-hacked plant life, and he pitied its lost confusion. Like so many things in this place, life in the garden was twisted, out of sync with itself.

They followed the stone path, winding between meticulously tended squares of white sand and reflective pools of golden water, to come to the garden's wide, central platform.

Three figures stood in front of a round marble table of dazzling white, just as they had in the holo; the young boy with curly flame-red hair, his face hidden by shadow and black Envoy mask. Alena behind him, and Alyn behind her. The other two Sentries' garb mirrored their approaching sibling's, variants of couture military chic that enhanced the triplets' air of commanding power and total authority. Kyn's stomach lurched at the sight of Alyn, and he clenched his fists as they approached, briefly struggling to suppress the flare of violent rage that surged from within him. Weave flickered over his knuckles.

Alena's ice blue eyes bore into Kyn, cold and composed as ever.

Kyn stopped a handful of paces from the trio as Alexi moved to join her siblings, slotting herself in beside Alyn to flank their sister. The red headed boy's eyes above the Envoy mask were void black.

"I have a message." Kyn announced, projecting his voice so it filled the garden. He then crouched lightly on his heels, level with the masked boy across the distance. Lower he added. "It's gunna be okay. I'm going to get you out of here." His face split in a gentle smile. He could feel watchful wariness behind the child's black eyes, a confusion and fear that Kyn would've known even without his amp. He'd been this boy once. All of the Envoys had.

"The traitor returns." Alena acknowledged.

"In a fashion," Kyn deflected airily. He rose from his crouch. He had no interest in verbally sparing with the Sentry, events were in motion, and he was content to let them unfold with minimal comment. The assuring smile he'd flashed the child turned to a trickster's dumb grin. "I won't be staying long." He told the triplets. "Like I said, got a message to deliver. Be on my way once that's done."

"And what message is that?" Alena pressed tersely. "And why should we want to listen to the lies of a traitor?"

"Oh, it's not for you." Kyn corrected the Sentry. "It's for them." He pointed to Sophia. The drone was still streaming everything it recorded live across the feed network.

"The people of this city are too smart, too faithful to the Unity that sustains them, to believe the words of a glitch traitor." Alena insisted, playing to the drone. She gripped the boy harder, ice-blue tips visibly biting into his shoulder. "Show the people the Unity's protection." She hissed to the child, pitching her voice for Sophia to catch. "Bring pride to your SPIRE. Send a message to these invaders." Her words grew steadily louder. "These Dividers. Show them that the Unity will not be threatened. That the Sentry protect the freedom of this city as they have since the Fall. Show them what happens to those that betray the Unity."

The boy shook with fear beneath her grasp, though his spine stayed astoundingly straight, keeping his composure. Kyn knew the war within him, what was being asked. He knew how the child was desperate to disobey but didn't understand how, torn by indoctrinated loyalty. Devotion imposed by a lifetime of violence.

The boy's eyes, so dark as to be black, suddenly glowed an electric purple as they found Kyn's; twining swirls of brilliant neon violet that churned within his dark iris, visible even from Kyn's distance.

"It's gunna be okay." He urged, holding up a reassuring hand. The boy's eyes glowed brighter. "You don't have to do this. You don't have to do what she says."

He felt the boy's gift seize him, an undeniable ache, deep within the center of his bones.

"It's gunna be okay." He urged again, willing his eyes to prove the truth of his words. "It's gunna be okay."

The ache turned to an inferno, a deep smolder that ate at the edges of everything. *Molecular decay* the weave screamed through its interplay with the strong and weak force. The boy was crumbling the links that held his cells together, accelerating their radioactive decay, undoing him on an atomic level.

"Fuck." Kyn gasped, slumping to his knees. "This is a new one."

The boy's gift was corroding him from within. Breaking him apart. He felt hollow, his bones disintegrating from the marrow out, the fiber of his muscles decaying on fragile bone.

"It's okay." He pleaded with the child.

His vision was a blur of agony. His skin had begun to crack, peeling away in flakes as if burnt. He groaned, folding into himself, beyond screaming. The pain was an insane thing.

He was aware of his organs liquefying.

Through it all, his regeneration pushed back. The persistent healing itch racing the radioactive decay. Bright, shrieking life surged into the frayed edges of his crumbling self, blossoming new cells and rapidly replicating his flaked away flesh and bone, only to be instantly seized upon again by the boy's power and re-torn apart in howling agony.

"It's gunna to be okay." He reassured, choking around unwinding vocal cords.

The garden was a kaleidoscope of spectrum to his ravaged and re-growing eyes. Bursting flowers of brilliant light and colour eternally fell to void black only to burst again in dazzling brightness. He could feel the boy's internal screams through the weave, feel the purple agony of his resolve. Kyn's skin had long since burned away, and somewhere a part of him fell into the mouth of a giant goldfish that had once been a balloon.

His mind was unraveling.

It's gunna be okay. He reassured the red-headed boy. The pain was gone now, so was colour and sound. Only the electric purple of the boy's eyes remained.

I do this all the time.

The purple took him.

"It's like, that single moment of kinetic possibility when an action is going to be one thing or another," Kyn explained. "A punch, a pull, a cut, every single one of those actions has it's equal and oppositional reaction. A block, a push, a deflection. Basic physics. I just kinda meet that moment, the decision point of the action, that potential, and change it. Absorb its harmful intention and transform it, decide to make it something else." He smiled ruefully, unsure if he was making sense. He rarely spoke about himself, and he found the exercise of explaining his internal world uncomfortably exposing. He turned his burning face away from Dev'Lyn and focused on the sleek otters playing in the crashing surf. The pair had spent the day on a beach at the far side of the great island, Dev'Lyn helping Kyn hone his new skill conjuring weave shields by lobbing stones at him to deflect.

"This plan of yours. It's a bit crazy 'eh?" Dev'Lyn pressed. They had taken a break to sit in the sand. Out ahead of them, the surf crashed around a massive boulder, a towering tree-topped island cut from a single stone, narrower at the base than its overgrown crest. It seemed to balance impossibly in the sand. "Don't get me wrong." The response agent clarified. His torso was bare, and his chest and shoulders blazed gold in the setting sun. "I'm down. I think it's past time we did something tangible about that situation. And the consensus agreed, shows how many thought the same. Still, wild mad scheme you got."

Kyn looked out at the improbably balanced island. Yorri was there, at the periphery of his vision, standing at the seam of the ocean. The pulsing surge of the tide licked his bare toes. Dev'Lyn didn't see him and Kyn didn't turn to look. They had never been there. He watched the surf, absorbed by its rhythm, and thought of the Unity, the Sentry, his life in the walled city. He thought of the cramped vertical oppression of the wards, and the barbarism of the cullings. The violent absurdity of it all.

"It's gotta be crazy." He finally retorted, voice firm. The coastal breeze was cool on his skin. He thought of the easy simplicity he'd found in the world beyond the wall. How there was a world to find. "Crazy's the only thing that'll work." He smiled. He could feel it, the coming change. It was a humming deep in his gut, pulling at his center of gravity.

"So much about that place is wrong." He stated. "Needlessly wrong." He thought of the years of brutality, the training, the experimentation, the killing. He thought of all the missions he'd been sent on; all in service of some pointless, ego-driven, need his former masters had to assert their superiority over others.

Kyn rubbed his arm where an f-Link had once been tattooed on a since re-grown limb. He thought of the young boy, alone in a white room, waiting to prove his worth. He thought of all the other children who had been just like him, of all the people the Unity had robbed of a life their own.

"The Sentry need to suffer for everything they've done." He spat, a rage rising in him. He had survived them so many ways, died so many more. Now he would do more than survive them. "I will destroy them." He insisted. He could feel the change, churning within the core of himself. He thought again of the young boy he'd once been, alone in that white room, too defiant to die.

Dev'Lyn wound his fingers through Kyn's in the sand, and then they were Alec's. The setting sun cast the ocean and sky ablaze in every imaginable hue of pink.

"Show they can be beat." Alec encouraged, his voice everywhere on the moist breeze. Kyn turned to the hacker, but he was gone, as were Dev'Lyn and Yorri. He was alone on the beach, except for the pair of otters scampering in the surf, their sleek bodies turned silver in *the setting sun. The rage had returned, just beneath the surface, submerged under the sound of the crashing waves. The change was on the edge of everything. It was on the air, and in the sand, in the sound of the tide and the steady pound of his heartbeat. The air crackled with it, and he could feel it thrumming under his skin, itching to burst through the seams of him.*

"Kyn!" Runa's voice was gravel in his ear. "We gunna do this or what?"

The world changed around him, through him. At once he was both as he was, on the beach, staring at a smoldering pink sunset, and, at the same time, he was also his younger self again, sitting alone in the white room. Waiting. The impossibly balanced island cast a long, knife-slim shadow across the gray-silver sand even as dancing learning holos cast gossamer butterflies of light across sterile walls. The undeniable pulse of change thrummed through him, radiating from the core of his being, pressing at the edges of his skin with an ecstatic agony that seeped from him in beams of rainbow light.

"Kyn!"

The island's shadow was a knife, keen edged, that cut through him with the familiar agony of a lifetime of violence, splitting skin so more effervescent light leaked out. It danced across the walls of his room and spilled, twinkling like stars, across the sand. Every cell of him screamed with potential.

Then he was falling through the fish balloon, hurtling towards a ground that was rushing up to meet him. Chains bit his wrists, and gravity cracked bone. High velocity rounds burned through him, and acid melted skin. He fell through a lifetime of dying as iridescent light spilled through his eternally breaking skin. The shimmering rainbow light touched the pain of each wound, and transformed it, turning it back to its pure potential. Endless moments of possibility surged within him until he blazed with their power.

"Enough!" Kyn cried, exploding in a radiant blast of weave that lifted his boots from the stone path. A corona of multi-hued pink surged from him, lifting him in the air and slamming the clustered Sentry with a thundering wall of pink force that shattered the crystalline SPIRE ceiling. The triplets were thrown backwards to slam forcibly against the broad marble table, where they crumbled to the floor, battered and unconscious.

The fire-haired boy - purposefully saved from the blast - stared at Kyn with wide-eyed terror and awe. His eyes were dark again, the threads of electric purple vanished.

"I told you it was gunna be okay." Kyn beamed. His boots touched back down, and he landed in a soft crouch. His smile widened and he felt the flesh of his cheek rapidly shift back together with the motion. His regeneration was working overtime, supercharged when he'd released the kinetic rebound of the boy's attack, and he was already nearly fully healed. Residual weave energy wreathed him, wafting over him in iridescent waves. He went to the boy, boots crunching over shards of polyplex, and before the child Envoy could do anything else, he knelt down and wrapped the youth in a reassuring hug.

"I'm okay." He reassured as the boy broke down against him, weeping in shocked relief. "I'm okay."

Kyn held the boy as he wept, the child heaving against his collar bone. He could feel the terror draining from the youth, until finally the shocked weeping settled, and an indoctrinated distrust rose up within him to take its place. The boy started to tense, years of psychological and physical abuse crashing against conditioning that told him to attack, defend his Sentry. Kyn held the child strong, wafting sympathetic and reassuring weave in response, willing the child to understand that he truly meant no harm, that he was there to help - much like Dev'Lyn had once done for him. In the end, the boy's relief at not having killed Kyn, and a long-denied yearning to be free of the Sentry, won out, and the boy relented, sagging against him in a kind of defeat.

A moment of awkward and stilted back patting and Kyn released the boy. He held the red headed child at arm's length as Sophia - also saved from the blast - circled them energetically.

"What's your name?" Kyn asked the child.

"Mox." The boy answered. His black eyes, wide with awe above his mask, reflected the shimmer of weave energy that wafted from Kyn.

Kyn motioned for the boy to roll down the mask and a small hand complied. There was a razor thin scar, freshly scabbed and still raw in places, drawn along the left curve of the child's jawbone. A recent wound only a few days healed

"That's a good name Mox," Kyn complimented, smiling broadly. Mox started to turn his head, reflexively thinking to look for the fallen Sentry. Kyn squeezed his shoulder, keeping the boy's attention.

"Don't worry about them." He reassured. "I'll take care of it. I've got a friend who's going to get you out of here, okay?" Mox nodded, his face a mix of trust and relieved disbelieve. Kyn patted the boy's shoulder once more and stood. "Shar," he subvocalized. "Got a pickup."

Three beats and Shar appeared, tearing open a portal around herself. A sunny meadow winked beyond her.

Mox stared in delighted wonder.

The teleporter nodded for the amazed child to step through the portal before tipping Kyn a two fingered salute from the ridge of her cheek bone. Kyn raised a hand in reply. He could see Mox turning in disbelief in the field of clover before Shar pulled the spacial tear closed.

Alone, Kyn slowly made his way over to the unconscious Sentry. Arbitrarily starting in alphabetical order, he grasped Alena by the heels of her synth-leather pumps and started to drag her, head bouncing from path stone to path stone, towards the lifts. Sophia drifted dutifully behind.

< = >

He woke the Sentry with a blast of ice-cold water from the valve set in the wall by the door. They gasped to consciousness, sputtering in shock.

Kyn turned off the valve, arresting the torrent of water. The Sentry coughed and sputtered. Crossing his arms over his lean chest Kyn propped himself casually against one glowing wall. He'd cranked the rooms lights, and the walls and floor screamed blinding white.

The Sentry trio hung by their wrists in the center of the white room, dripping and gasping.

"So, this where you lecture us on your plan to dominate the faithful of our city?" Alexi finally demanded, teeth chattering. Sophia hovered level with the drenched Sentry's shade-stik streaked face.

"You are child killing, body stealing, genocidal psychopaths with crippling narcissism." Kyn reminded her. He fluttered his eyelids with exasperated exhaustion. "I don't have much to say to you at all."

The Sentry hung in stunned silence, unequipped to deal with disregard.

"So, it's a public execution then?" Alyn barked from the back of the cluster, mustering self-easing bravado.

Kyn ignored the outburst and moved to draw open a well-remembered command panel in one white wall. He tapped in a few concise commands and three person-sized holos unfolded around the Sentry.

"What is this?" Alena stuttered, her usually commanding voice edged with fear.

Each holo showed the planet as seen from low orbit. The sweeping blue-green curve of the horizon, rimmed by a void-black ribbon of star-studded space. A wild haired Runa stood at the edge of this cold strip of space, poised on the threshold of a silver door that hung above the planet.

"Space station." Kyn edified for the triplets.

Runa spread her arms wide and tilted forward on her toes, suspended easily over the endless expanse of stars. The cresting sun flared brilliant yellow in the band of her protective goggles.

Kyn tapped a few more commands into the drawn panel and summoned three more holo screens that unfurled between the others, completing the circle. The holos showed the exterior of Nova SPIRE from multiple angles, as seen from the mid and upper wards by more drone footage. The crystalline megastructure blazed gold in the sunlight while the rest of the city stood dark in its shadow.

"See, here's the thing about you lot." Kyn explained. In the holo Runa tilted at an impossible angle before pushing away from the silver door to float, suspended above the ever-spinning planet. "Somewhere along the way you've convinced yourself you're just better than everyone else, more deserving somehow."

An aura of hot pink wreathed Runa as she began to fall, pulled towards the earth. A dark humor tugged Kyn's mouth into a knife-edged grin as the expressions on Alena and Alexis' faces turn to understanding terror. Alyn inhaled sharply from the back of the cluster.

"We are the Unity that sustains this city." Alena hissed, her coldly beautiful face twisted in fearful rage.

"Yah, but see, you don't actually do anything." Kyn drawled, casually calm. "You ordered me to do things." He pointed at himself. "You ordered Runa to do things." He ticked off a finger. "Ashe, Benn." More fingers. "Sandri, the Dags, servos." Balled into a fist. "You ordered us to steal, blow up buildings, blackmail, kill." He took a few steps from the wall and knelt down on his heels in front of the Sentry, staying beyond the circle of holos. "I never wanted to kill anybody." He hung his head. "I liked the training, the physical talent of it, the skill." He admitted. "Found if I lost myself in perfecting the technique of it, I could lose myself, forget what I was doing, somehow separate myself from it." A baldly honest sadness had crept into his voice, and he'd done little to counter it.

In the holo Runa was plummeting at an obscene speed through the stratosphere, locked onto target, her body wreathed in a blazing corona of weave and held in a streamlined dive.

Kyn smiled bleakly and unfurled himself from his crouch. "Point is, you lot have convinced yourself of your superiority despite all evidence against it, and your egos are so fragile you kill anybody who counters that narrative or threatens your power structure."

"And what's your answer to that?" Alexi jeered venomously. "Kill us? You will martyr us! There are legions who are faithful to their true protectors."

"Why not?" Kyn rounded on her, angry now. The rage, always so close to the surface, snapping to the front. Runa was a glowing pink meteor above the SPIRE. "You stole peoples' bodies because you were too afraid to die." He spat in disgust. "I think you've lived long enough." Runa hit the shattered tip of the SPIRE in a brilliant flash of pink and gold. The room shook violently and the holos winked out.

The Sentry screamed in pain and terror as the megastructure's foundation trembled, and they swung wildly from their anchoring. The chains squealed angrily.

Kyn stood calm, at ease. Thrown into backup power, the room was pitched into the dim strobe of a single overhead emergency light. The room shook again. Tiles cracked and ceiling panels crashed to the floor. Cement dust rained down as the room shook with a roar of splintering foundation.

The Sentry whimpered in true, caged, terror as they swung violently from their binding, begging incoherently for a mercy they were beyond, their pleading lost in the rumble of collapsing sub-levels.

Kyn waited patiently through the thunderous roaring, easily keeping his balance on the bucking floor, his face slick with sweat from the immense heat that now pressed down on them from above. White walls cracked, and the ceiling buckled as the room was plunged into total darkness. The screams of the Sentry stopped abruptly, and the roar of imploding rubble stilled.

Phosphorescent flickers of silver-pink danced at the edge of the crushing darkness, illuminating Kyn's raised hand. Weave energy danced over his skin like fairy fire to press outwards in a glittering dome, shielding him from the ultra-tons of ruined debris that pressed down from above, threatening to crush him. Sophia's optic light blinked green in the dim glow.

"I don't need to kill you." Kyn explained to the triplet Sentry coward at his feet, his voice strained under the surge of transformative energy that churned in him, bursting to spill over. "I just needed to show that you can be beat."

Unable to hold it any longer, he threw his head back with a victorious scream and thrust upwards, releasing the transformed energy. His gossamer shield shattered with a powerful flare of brilliant pink force, disintegrating the crushing tons of debris pressing down from above and blasting through to clear blue sky beyond.

Kyn shook himself, hooting in delight. Residual weave energy flickered over his skin. He looked around. He stood at the center of a wreckage strewn crater several kliks wide, the surrounding debris of his childhood cell blasted away. Twisted metal beams and collapsed ward platforms dotted the crater; all that was left of Noav SPIRE, now a ragged circle torn in the wards.

Everything was covered in a fine rainbow silt. Polyplex ground to a fine sandy grain.

The chained Sentry huddled at Kyn's feet blinked and looked around in confused shock, unwilling, or unable, to move from their coward position.

"Oi, dickgulper!" Runa's rough voice carried easily in the silence of the aftermath. The adolescent was stomping through the rubble towards him, a stupidly joyous grin plastered across her face. "How was that?"

"I think they got the message." Kyn applauded, beaming back at her. He stepped over and away from the Sentry. Sophia followed, green light blinking excitedly.

In the distance, the crater sloped steeply upwards for the equivalent of several stories, and he could see thousands of tiny, person-shaped silhouettes rimming the outer edge.

Shar was opening a portal in the near distance, large enough now that Kyn could see flashes of Dev'Lyn and Alec through the flickering ring. Runa veered towards them, casually kicking debris out of her way as she went.

Kyn looked down at the coward Sentry. They were struggling in the plastic silt, failing miserably to untangle themselves from each other. He smiled wolfishly, his slashed gray-pink eyes glinting in the brilliant sun.

"None of this was ever for you, by the way. Not really." He told the Sentry in way of clarification, tone bright. Sophia flashed green. The silhouettes on the horizon had doubled. Tripled. "I just needed to tear down your symbol. Show that you could be beat."

Alec waved.

Confident his message had been received, Kyn turned and started to saunter gaily towards the waiting portal.

THE END

About the Author

When he's not seeking the advice of the Garden Gnome Council or getting hijacked for snuggles by his home's ruling stray, **Laurence Ramsay** [he/him] can be found wandering the rain-drenched forests of Canada's stunning west coast or jumping across rooftops and scaling urban infrastructure with his sexy live-in manfriend.

KYN is Laurence's debut novel.

ALEC AND DEV'LYN WILL RETURN IN..

CPSIA information can be obtained
at www.ICGtesting.com
Printed in the USA
LVHW011203170322
713617LV00011B/1191